REMEMBER MY NAME

SAM BLAKE

CORVUS

First published in Great Britain in 2022 by Corvus,
an imprint of Atlantic Books Ltd.

This paperback edition published in 2022.

10 9 8 7 6 5 4 3 2 1

A CIP catalogue record for this book is available from the British
Library.

Paperback ISBN: 978 1 83895 297 6
E-book ISBN: 978 1 83895 296 9

Corvus
An imprint of Atlantic Books Ltd
Ormond House
26–27 Boswell Street
London
WC1N 3JZ

www.corvus-books.co.uk

Printed and bound by Clays Ltd, Elcograf S.p.A.

For Rex
This one was waiting for you.

Chapter 1

*I*F SHE'D TURNED *her phone off, instead of listening in, perhaps nobody would have died.*

Later, this was the thought that leaped around in Cressida Howard's head, consuming everything else like wildfire, spreading as it found and engulfed every lie, each one tinder-dry.

She would – eventually – accept that this wasn't about her. It was all about him. His choices. His decisions.

And her. That woman.

But right now, she didn't have the benefit of hindsight.

'I'm going out.'

Cressida looked up sharply at the sound of her seventeen-year-old daughter's voice, her mind still reeling from what she'd heard. Emily-Jane didn't wait for a response as she passed the partially open living room door, her heels loud on the polished maple of the hall floor.

'When will you be back?'

On autopilot, Cressida raised her voice as she heard the front door open, the sound of the sea breaking on the rocks beyond the house spiralling in on a gust of wind almost drowning Emily-Jane's equally automatic reply.

'Don't know, won't be late.'

1

'Where … Em?' Cressida started to ask, but the dull thud of the front door closing cut off her words abruptly. A moment later she heard the engine of Emily-Jane's Mini roaring into life and the sound of the wheels spinning on the gravel as she turned her beloved cream car in the drive and went through the gates.

Staring blankly at her phone, Cressida slowly realised that her only child was leaving the house at 9 p.m. on a dark October evening – a school night, *and* it was only Monday – and she had no idea of where she was going. Had Emily-Jane mentioned that she was meeting friends tonight? Cressida felt as if she was trapped in some sort of vacuum, an airlock between what had been and what came next, every movement, every thought, laboured. And her husband's words were moving around her brain like a slow-motion movie of a giant moth flapping around a flame.

'*I won't be home. Got to work late … I'll stay at the 1796. Talk tomorrow, I have to go …*'

She'd hardly had a chance to reply. Had had her finger hovering over the *end call* button when she'd heard a clatter at the other end, as if he was putting the phone down. And then the sound of a door opening and a woman's voice, her accent Italian or Spanish. There had been a rattle, as if a glass containing ice had been put down next to the phone. And then her husband's voice again – low and throaty.

'Good evening, Nina.'

The pause had been too long, then a sigh … of pleasure? It had been a long time since she'd heard him sound like that.

'*Nina …*'

He'd almost sounded annoyed.

She'd hit the *end call* button then, her blood rushing to her face, pounding in her ears as she fought for breath, her chest constricting as her heart rate increased.

And then Emily-Jane's voice had blended into the maelstrom of confusion in her head, and a pain, acute like a stiletto, had pierced her chest.

As if it could sense her mood, a gust of wind and rain hit the curved Victorian bay window like spit shot. Cressida leaped up to close the curtains, rattling the heavy cream brocade along the brass rail with as much force as she could, shutting out the night and the storm that had been brewing all day, the sound of the curtain rings shattering the stillness of the room.

Her arms still raised above her head, she hung on to the draw rods, her brown eyes closed tightly, focusing on steadying her breathing.

Shock began to build into rage. She took a deep breath and slowly tucked her shoulder-length blond hair behind her ears. Turning to look into the room, at the white marble fireplace with its ornate gold mirror reflecting the light from the chandelier, the huge cream sofas, the glass-topped artisan coffee table where her white wine stood untouched, Cressida crossed her arms tightly.

She wasn't taking it this time.

What had Nina been doing to him to make him sound like that?

She'd ignored her suspicions before, all the times before, the times when he'd been inexplicably delayed, when he'd vanished 'back to the office' at the weekend for an 'important meeting'. She'd kept herself busy, focusing on their beautiful house, on Emily-Jane, on the school runs and juggling hockey meets and cross-country with work – the speech therapy sessions she gave that were so vital to her clients. On being the perfect mother, the woman who could do it all.

Then her colleague had proposed setting up their own speech therapy clinic, Phoenix Associates, and she'd become totally absorbed in moving out of the public medical system into private practice, in starting something of her own. Things were easing off now that Emily-Jane drove herself to school, that they had a team of therapists dealing with everyone from tiny children to elderly stroke patients. She only worked three days a week now, had time to swim in Laurence's ridiculous Disney nightmare of a pool, to get to the gym, to entertain his business associates ...

Cressida bit her lip, folding her arms even more tightly, gripping the baby-soft wool of her oversized cream sweater. She'd been busy, had been happy to get on with her own life while Laurence consolidated his family hotel business. He'd been devastated by his twin brother's death ten years ago, changed by it. Ferryman had been Pierce's brainchild, and the reason they'd been in Silicon Valley in the first place. They'd been on their way to a funding meeting when a driver, already drunk at 11 a.m., had jumped the lights at an intersection, hitting them side-on, at speed.

After Pierce's death, he'd become more focused, more ruthless, and he'd thrown himself into work, continuing their plans to move the Howard Group hotel bookings to a high-tech lifestyle platform that would (he'd said), as they brought their partners on board, become the go-to for everyone, whether they wanted to buy flowers or book a flight.

Despite his horrific injuries, Pierce had survived for three days, giving his wife Sinéad time to get to the hospital. He'd come around long enough for them to say their goodbyes. It had been a nightmare for all of them, but Cressida had always felt

4

that a part of Laurence had died with Pierce. He'd come back a different person. She'd understood. She'd made allowances, but he'd become more and more distant.

He'd been so quiet when he'd first come home, disappearing for impossibly long walks along the seafront. She'd wondered then if he was meeting someone, but those walks had given him time to think, he'd said. He'd said he wanted to keep going – he needed to keep going. Pierce's ideas would make them millionaires. Dublin was becoming the tech capital of Europe and now was the time to build. There would be long hours and he'd have to travel a lot, he'd said. He'd keep building what they'd started together, and it would grow exponentially, he'd said. He'd said a lot of things.

And now he'd said a name.

Nina.

Cressida took a long slow breath and, heading across the room, reached for her wine, sipping it, savouring the delicate fruity flavour. She lifted the glass to the light, looking at the teardrops caught on its crystal sides, and took another sip.

First she needed to find out who this Nina was. And then she would work out what to do about her.

Chapter 2

BRIONI O'BRIEN TURNED the page of her book, the movement making her heavy fuchsia-pink fringe fall into her eyes. It was more of a forelock at this stage, and the length reminded her that she needed to get it cut before she returned to work next Monday. But that was a whole week away.

She adjusted the throw on her knees, stretched out on the worn sofa and sighed, enjoying the gentle creaking of the wooden house in the onshore breeze, thankful that she and her sister Marissa had put in underfloor heating when they'd refurbished. Outside she could hear waves breaking on the sweep of smooth sandy beach below the house. Normally gentle and rhythmic, they had been steadily increasing during the afternoon as a storm built. One of the things she loved about Wexford, about this place – as well as its splendid isolation on the edge of the sand dunes – was how, when you were in it, you felt like part of the landscape, an integral part of the universe. Never more so than when the weather closed in.

Brioni yawned. It was only ten o'clock but she'd been for a swim and then for a walk this afternoon, down the beach to the headland, back up along the scrubby fields and home. There had been a bite in the wind that had left her cheeks numb, but she'd bought fish and chips on her way past the pub at the very end of the lane. Unwrapping the paper, she'd sat down in the shelter of the doorstep, savouring their heat and salty tang. As she'd looked out to sea, her rainbow-striped woolly hat pulled down over her ears, the squat single-storey house had protected her from the worst of the wind.

She was tired now but it was good tired, a physical exhaustion that was different from the mental fatigue she got from working on screens all day, looking at rows and rows of code. She'd thought her undergrad years had been gruelling, but it was nothing to the hours she was putting in juggling working at Riverview and doing her MSc. They were sponsoring her tuition, and they paid their software developers handsomely, provided free meals, workout rooms, sleep pods, even, but their staff were expected to put the hours in.

Brioni had never been so grateful to get to Wexford as she had been this weekend. She had an assignment due in next week, but now she needed time to recharge. She rubbed the back of her head, normally smooth shaven in a double undercut, but all she could feel was bristles. It didn't matter; she didn't plan to see anyone except the locals until next weekend, and they were so mesmerised by the pink hair, her piercings and the vague American accent she'd picked up, that they'd hardly notice a bit of regrowth.

Brioni picked up the mug she'd put down on the rough wooden coffee table beside her, about to take a sip of her raspberry tea, when her mobile began to ring from underneath the throw.

Pulling it out, she smiled at the name on the display – Marissa.

'Hi, big sis, how's things?'

'Good … just a sec.'

Brioni heard her sister close a door and move further into the house. She could picture it, the cosy pine kitchen littered with brightly coloured children's toys. They seemed to be on every surface, the home in West London that Marissa now shared with DCI Mike Wesley a total contrast to her own house in Highgate, with its designer folding patio doors and the clinical white decor. That house was an investment now, a place from her past that was haunted by memories of her husband Steve. A place none of them wanted to revisit.

'Did you get the heating going OK?'

Brioni heard the sofa creak as Marissa sat down with a sigh. She was obviously tired, but these days Brioni could hear the happiness in her voice, like the soothing middle notes on a piano. Whether she was ferrying teenagers to school or Daisy to nursery, she ran their blended home like a summer camp where there was always something to eat and something to do, the radio was always on in the kitchen and someone was laughing. Brioni smiled; it was such a contrast to the time before Mike, it sometimes made her well up. Marissa's life had been constricted by secrets.

She cleared her throat before she answered.

'I did, not a bother. I've decided to stay the whole week. I've been swimming every morning so far and walking every day. It's so quiet down here out of season, you can almost hear the hares chewing the grass.'

Marissa laughed. 'And we were so desperate to leave.'

'I know. Be careful what you wish for. You should try and get back more often, Daisy loves it.'

'I know. But the whole air-travel-with-a-toddler-and-all-their-kit thing is a bit of a struggle if we're going to get rained on for weeks. At least there's masses to do here when the weather's bad. She barely sits still for two minutes, I don't think I could manage it unless I could persuade Mike to take a week off, too, and he loves the heat.'

'Good point. Is he busy at the moment?'

'He's always busy. As he says, crime is a growth industry. But listen, I called because I was wondering if you could do me a favour? Well, it's for a friend actually, in Dublin.'

'Tell me more.' Brioni shifted on the sofa, tucking her feet underneath herself. She could hear a hesitation in Mar's voice which meant that this wasn't a simple ask. 'Tell me – who, what, when …'

'It's a bit of a long story, but there's this woman I met at a fundraiser at the London Irish Centre. Her husband's in hotels, they have a couple in London as well as their flagship hotels in Dublin – the 1796 in the city centre and the Reynolds Regency House in Ballsbridge. They sponsored the raffle at the London Irish event, I think. Anyway, we got talking. She's lovely, her name's Cressida Howard. You can look her up, her husband is Laurence Howard.'

Brioni picked up her laptop from beside the sofa and opened it, her fingers flying over the keyboard as she searched for Marissa's friend.

'The 1796 is right near my office, very fancy. It costs a fortune …'

'That's it. Right beside Grand Canal Dock. But the hotels are only part of his portfolio.' She paused. 'He's the founder and CEO of Ferryman. Their corporate headquarters are right next door.'

'Oof. Big. The Amazon for lifestyle.'

'I know. I didn't realise when I met her, we were just chatting. You know when you connect with someone? She must have googled me because she sent me this gorgeous card after the event, just saying she'd read about … well, everything, and if I ever needed anything, to call.'

'That was lovely.'

'I know, most people run the other way when they find out how Steve died, but … Anyway.' Marissa cleared her throat. 'We've been in touch ever since on and off, and she's just called me. She was really upset. She needs some help.'

'Fire away. What can I do?'

'She thinks … well, she knows her husband's having an affair, and she wants to get as much information about his movements and this woman he's seeing as she can. I told her about you when we met and she remembered. She suspects it's not the first affair but she's never had proof before, and now she needs to know everything so she can divorce him. Ferryman is worth millions and she says he's the type that would fight her for every penny.'

'More, actually.'

Brioni scanned the web page in front of her – an article about an investigation into the Ferryman empire. The company she worked for was a tech giant, but Ferryman was even bigger.

'Precisely. So he can get the best lawyers and the minute he knows she's on to him, he'll cover his tracks.'

'Why doesn't she hire someone? There are great investigators out there.'

'You know Dublin, it's too small. Something will leak. She doesn't trust anyone at this stage.'

'She wants me to do some digging and see what's going on?'

'Would you? You can find out anything online and you won't leave any tracks. Cressida's worried if she even looks at this woman's Facebook page she might accidentally like something and then she'll know she was looking. And ...' Marissa paused. 'I just keep thinking if I'd talked to someone sooner, looked for help, well, things might have been different.'

'Mar, don't. None of what happened with Steve was your fault. Some men think they control everything, that they don't have to follow the same rules as everyone else.'

Brioni could hear Marissa sighing at the other end.

'I know. Which is why I want to help Cressida. It's a big thing to reach out, and I'm worried there's far more she's not telling me. I know ...'

Marissa broke off about to say more, but Brioni could hear the emotion in her voice welling up like a wave.

'Don't worry, of course I'll help. One man taught a lesson is one more for the sisterhood.' Brioni kept her voice light but she was far from joking. She'd had her own bad experiences, like every woman, and she wasn't the sort of person who could stand back and let someone struggle when she could do something about it. It wasn't in her DNA. 'Does she know anything about who he's seeing?'

Marissa paused and Brioni heard her sigh again, but this time it was tense.

'She's called Nina.'

Brioni felt her eyebrows rising as Marissa explained.

'Yikes. That wasn't very nice.'

Brioni rubbed the tattoo on the inside of her wrist, a single black line looped on itself and uncurling into a straight line. A *unalome*, the Buddhist symbol of harmony coming out of chaos. She'd had it done in Thailand, just days before she'd been mugged. There were times when Brioni felt as if she attracted chaos, but she was sure helping out Marissa's friend couldn't be too complicated. And it sounded intriguing.

'I told her you'd have a go. She'd love to meet you. She lives in Dalkey but said she can meet you in Dublin if it's easier – it might be more discreet. She said she'll cover all your expenses, whatever you need. She wants to pay you.'

'No need for that. I don't know if I can get what she needs yet. And you know me, I can't resist a challenge.'

Brioni's mind had already started ticking, thinking about how she'd tackle this one. The whole point of being here in Wexford was to get away from the city, from work, from the pile of laundry in her tiny apartment, but Dublin was only a two-hour drive, and she could be back tomorrow evening. As well as the heating, the other thing they'd installed when they'd remodelled the beach house was super-fast Wi-Fi, so she didn't need to be in the city to do her research.

'Is she around tomorrow? Mid-afternoon? I need a haircut anyway.'

Chapter 3

IT WAS STARTING to rain in Dublin city centre as Cressida left the car park and skipped across the road to the alley that led through to Dawson Street. Chill drops stung as they hit her face. Winter was definitely on its way; she hated the cold but today's meeting wouldn't wait. Her stomach churned as she wound her red cashmere scarf tighter around her neck and pulled up the collar of her coat. She'd arranged to meet Brioni in a cafe called The Bestseller on Dawson Street, part of the elegant Georgian shopping quarter in the centre of the city. The cafe was old-fashioned-looking, with a red and white stripy canopy over the broad pavement, second-hand books and mismatched vintage china displayed in the bowed Victorian shop window. Possibly the last place on earth that Laurence would ever visit.

A rich aroma of coffee hit her the moment she opened the door. Brioni wasn't hard to spot. Even from the entrance, Cressida could see her bright pink hair glowing at the back of the cafe. She'd chosen a discreet table for two on the raised level beyond the counter, the dark polished wooden stairs and rail posts echoing the mahogany bookshelves that lined the walls.

Concentrating hard on her laptop, Brioni apparently didn't hear Cressida's approach, despite the sound of the high heels of her boots on the wooden floor. But she looked up when she heard her name, her smile broad.

She looked younger than Cressida had expected, in her early twenties, but as Brioni stood, her hand extended, Cressida could see the likeness to her sister. Marissa had said that there was a big age gap between them – almost eight years? Cressida wasn't sure, but whatever it was, they both obviously had very good genes.

'How did you know it was me?' Brioni's grin was mischievous, a diamond stud in her nose catching the light as she smiled.

Cressida laughed, immediately relaxed by her confidence.

'Your sister gave me a clue.'

'I'll never be able to join the secret service. Sit down. The coffee's amazing.'

Unwinding her scarf, Cressida slipped her bag onto the floor beside the table and sat down on the chair opposite Brioni. Nestled in the corner, Brioni had chosen a table where they could see the door. Pulling up the sleeves of her navy turtle neck sweater, Cressida leaned into the edge of the table so Brioni could hear her without her raising her voice.

'Thank you for this. I appreciate it.'

'No need to thank me until I've got the info you need. Mar gave me a bit of an outline.'

Cressida rolled her eyes, then leaned down to her bag to pull out her leather planner. Just as she was opening it, the waitress arrived. They ordered quickly and Cressida glanced up to make sure she had her back to them before she flipped the planner open.

'I wrote everything I could think of down for you. His date of birth, mother's maiden name – Marissa said you'd need Laurence's email addresses – I've included his Gmail, too. I don't think he's changed his passwords in years, his computer has a thumbprint recognition thing so he thinks no one can get into it.'

Brioni raised her eyebrows in surprise at Laurence's naivety and Cressida nearly smiled. Brioni didn't have to say anything; it was almost as if she was channelling Emily-Jane's thoughts on her father's lax attitude to online security.

'He hires people in for all the tech stuff. He honestly thinks he's untouchable, and because of all of Ferryman's firewalls or whatever you call them, he thinks no one could hack him.'

Nodding slowly, Brioni looked at the pieces of notepaper that Cressida handed her. Laurence Howard's birthday was at the end of January; he was coming up to the big four-oh. Perhaps this was all about some sort of mid-life crisis.

'These are great. Very thorough. So, you want more on who this woman is, and where they were the other night?'

'I think I'm ultimately going to have to hire someone to follow him, to take pictures, but I need more information to be able to do that. And it's so hard to find someone to trust. When they find out who he is, they'll know he's going to pay to stop anything getting out and charge me the earth.' Cressida pursed her lips. 'I daren't take the risk of alerting him until I've got as much information as possible. I know him. If he finds out, he'll make it look as if I'm hysterical.'

Across the table, Brioni screwed up her nose thoughtfully.

'Don't worry. Let's see what I can find. I can get inside his laptop and use his webcam so you might not need to have him followed at all. But if you do, we'll think of something.'

Cressida smiled at the sincerity in Brioni's voice, her eyes stinging with tears. Marissa had been right about her sister's willingness to help, Brioni hadn't even hesitated – and she'd refused to be paid for her time. But Marissa's own previous experiences with deceitful men had to be a major factor. And she'd mentioned Brioni had had some bad experiences of her own, had set up a support network through the Students' Union at her university in London. Momentarily lost for words, Cressida took a deep breath, trying to hold on to her emotions. She was about to speak when the waitress arrived with their coffees.

'Thank you, we'll be fine now.' Cressida smiled to her gratefully, trying not to look as if she was dismissing her. As the waitress left, Brioni's words sank in.

'How can you get into his webcam?'

Brioni's mouth twitched into a smile. 'Spyware.'

'But he has top-level virus protection. His whole company depends on internet security, it's a global retailer.'

Brioni's eyes flashed with a hint of mischief.

'Virus protection is only good against known threats. There are lots of ways to get in with something completely new it won't recognise. I write programs, all sorts of programs, and I spend a lot of my time breaking into big systems to find their weaknesses. It's part of my job.' She took a sip of her coffee. 'I'll work it out. But once I'm in, I'll have control of his system. I'll be able to look at all his email, and see what he's doing – watch Zoom calls or Skype – and as long as his camera isn't covered, I can see what's happening in the room.'

'Good God, really? That could be illuminating.'

Brioni grimaced. 'And I can screenshot it at my end.' She paused, picking up her spoon to stir sugar into her coffee. 'Has this happened before?'

Cressida sighed. 'Maybe, but I was never very sure before. Suspicious, yes, but he can be very attentive, was always at school plays, never forgets my birthday.' She took a steadying breath. 'I'm thirty-six and we've been married half of my life.' She could feel herself welling up again. 'He's away a lot. Trips to America and Europe to meet with brands and retailers. He set up the company with his twin brother almost straight out of college, so he's been working incredibly long hours for a long time. And it paid off.'

'It's a brilliant idea – the no-brainers always are. All your lifestyle choices in one place? You can't go wrong.'

Cressida took a sip of her coffee and nodded. 'He brought in friends when they started – guys he and Pierce were at boarding school with who had set up their own companies or, like him, were developing family businesses. Philip French's company specialises in flights and holidays; hotels – that's Laurence obviously. Eoin O'Reilly was a chef and when he met Aisling they developed a whole range of homewares and interiors products. And Richie Murphy grew his father's tailoring business, bringing high-end fashion to the mass market but keeping the bespoke feel. When Laurence and Pierce came up with the idea for Ferryman, having them on the board meant they had a huge market share before they'd even launched the site. It's truly global now. He's incredibly young to have this level of success, but sometimes the circumstances are just right.'

'Even I use it.' Brioni sipped her coffee.

'I think everyone does.'

'And have you any idea who this woman is? Nina?'

Cressida shrugged. 'I've never heard the name before. I really don't know who she might be.'

'Don't worry. I'll find out everything I can. It's Tuesday today, I should have something for you by Thursday, I'd guess.'

'That fast?'

'Well, it depends how easy it is to get in, but I've got the week off, so I've got lots of time.'

'Thank you so much.' Cressida bit her lip. 'If I hadn't heard her voice, I don't think I'd care so much. But that pushed me right over the edge.'

Chapter 4

KATE SPICER ADJUSTED her navy silk blouse, leaving the top button undone, making sure there was just enough cleavage showing before pulling her make-up bag and hairbrush out of her handbag. The en suite shower room adjacent to Laurence's office was spacious, but whoever had designed it had put in a basin with no surround. While it looked fantastic and complemented the black marble walls, it was deeply impractical.

She felt sure it was a man.

The whole Ferryman building felt very male-designed. Thankfully she'd insisted on a female designer for the spa rooms at the ultramodern 1796 and its period sister hotels on the south side of Dublin, in Cork and in London. Laurence had let her put in whatever she wanted.

There were some definite advantages to this relationship. And she never took it for granted.

Reaching for a hairband, Kate smiled to herself as she pulled her long blond hair back and tipped her foundation on to her brush. It had been a long day and she had a full evening ahead – another launch, another beauty brand. She'd dithered over the invitation, but as Laurence was always saying, it did them good to have her appearing in the social pages alongside TV stars and models. She just needed to freshen up before she left. She began to work the foundation into her skin.

Outside in the main office, Kate could hear Laurence laughing on the phone. It was almost lunchtime in LA, so he'd stayed late to take the call, which suited her perfectly. He liked to get the salon and spa figures weekly, and the longer they could spend going over them uninterrupted, the better.

He laughed again suddenly and she tuned in to what he was saying.

'Shouldn't be a problem, I can always bring the board around to my way of thinking. Especially for the right incentive. Not that *they* need to know the details.'

He laughed again as she put the lid on her foundation. He'd imbued the word *incentive* with an emphasis that screamed big numbers and secrecy. *Now what was that about?* Over the years Laurence had always been so generous, making sure she never wanted for anything, buying her jewellery and clothes. Kate knew she said it at least five times a day, but anything that was good for Laurence was good for her.

Outside in the office he laughed again.

'Of course, I'll get Nina to send you samples of the deep dive data we have. She understands all that stuff. Confidentially, of course, I don't need to say that. She'll encrypt it all.' He paused. 'Yes, I'm sure it can all be cross-referenced. She'll be able to talk to your people about that. I know we don't use it as much as we could, we'd need a team of data scientists to develop programs to do it, but I'm sure your team will be able to get what they need. With the right guys on the job you can mine the hell out of it. You'll be able to see what John Smith in Kansas is having for breakfast, what sort of porn he likes, where he goes on holiday and what brand he feeds his dog.'

There was a pause as he listened.

'Yes, that's right, the on-site advertising isn't an issue, your product dovetails beautifully. It's a no-brainer, and there's plenty of room in the market for another comms provider, but you don't need me to tell you that.'

In the bathroom, Kate quickly applied her blusher and looked for her mascara. She could tell from his voice that the conversation was winding up. She could also tell that he was very happy about whatever they were talking about.

Reapplying her eye make-up, she speeded up. She could hear him arranging a meeting in LA now. He ended the call as she reached for her lipstick, but then she heard him on the phone again.

'Nina? Yes, come up, will you? Have you got that data?' He paused, then laughed. 'Seriously? Excellent. That's exactly what I was looking for.'

Kate pushed the lid back on her lipstick and, glancing in the Hollywood-lit mirror, rubbed her lips together.

Now, who was Nina?

She must be working late to still be in the building at this time of night. Perhaps she was working on something specifically for Laurence? Kate quickly smoothed her hair, momentarily puzzled. She hadn't heard the name before, but then there were hundreds of people working in this building now, and the Howard Group of hotels was just one sector of the businesses that Laurence controlled.

As Kate pushed open the door to the bathroom and switched off the light, Laurence swung around in his chair to face her. His tightly cut hair was starting to grey at the temples – stress probably – but his blue eyes were bright, their colour emphasised by the sky blue of his shirt. Sometimes if she looked quickly, her heart would jolt – they hadn't been identical, but it was as if Pierce was still here. His sleeves were rolled up; Laurence had slung his jacket over the leather sofa opposite his expansive desk when they'd arrived earlier. He leaned back in the chair to look at her as she came in to perch on the edge of the desk.

'Is that smile for me or the deal you've just done?'

His face twitched. 'Were you listening?'

She shook her head, her smile amused. 'No, but I can tell from the look on your face you're up to something, and loving it.'

'Aren't I always up to something?'

She leaned forward to straighten his tie. 'What plot are you hatching now?'

He smiled enigmatically. 'Let's just say there's a player in the mobile phone market whose interest in expanding into Europe has been reignited. I told you Richie Murphy introduced us a few months ago – he spends a lot of time in the States.'

'SpeakEasy? Again?' She looked at him questioningly as he sat back, not answering, but she could see from his expression that she was right. 'But I thought you also told me the board vetoed hooking up with them?'

'They did, even Richie when it came to it, the bastard, but he's never been able to make an independent decision in his life, follows the others like a bloody sheep.' He paused, his tone smug. 'Let's just say, a few things have fallen into place since then, and their offer has become a lot more attractive.'

Kate raised her eyebrows. Something big must have changed. He'd been furious when the other three directors of Ferryman had thrown out his suggestion of a partnership. Between SpeakEasy's coercive high-pressure sales techniques and data privacy issues, they felt any association with the American phone giant could compromise the Ferryman brand. She had kept her mouth shut but she'd had her doubts about them, too. SpeakEasy had gained their market share in the US through some extremely questionable practices and political support from the right wing.

Kate opened her mouth to speak, but a knock on the door sent her off the desk and over to the sofa to pick up her jacket. She threw him a smile as she slung it over her arm and went to open the door. A woman with dark glossy hair which reached halfway down her back was outside. Turned away from the door, she had a mobile phone to her ear and seemed to be speaking in Spanish.

Kate turned and gave Laurence a wide-eyed look. He raised his eyebrows.

'Have a good evening, don't do anything I wouldn't do.'

She rolled her eyes at him. The woman still had her back to her. Kate raised her voice.

'Laurence is ready for you now. Come through.'

Kate inspected the woman closely as she turned, obviously surprised to see her. She wasn't very tall, was wearing five-inch black patent heels, but she was stunning, her cheekbones sharp, her olive skin set off by a bright pink silk blouse and black pencil skirt. Kate took a step back and held the door open to let her in, raising her eyebrows over the woman's shoulder at Laurence as she slipped out of the door.

Chapter 5

'**M**OTHER, DID YOU hear me? Are you listening?'
Emily-Jane pulled her head out of the walk-in fridge
with the door still open and looked over her shoulder at Cressida,
the light falling from it creating a halo around her poker-straight
blond hair. Her forehead was creased in a frown, her brown eyes
narrowed accusingly.

Cressida looked up, her mind momentarily blank.

'Sorry, love, what did you say?'

Sitting at the kitchen island, a glass of wine in front of her,
Cressida been mindlessly scrolling through her phone. She wasn't
sure what she was looking for – some sort of connection with the
outside world, a happy bump that would make her smile; something,
anything, that would lift her spirits. Whatever it was, the rational
part of her knew she wouldn't find the solutions she needed locked
in a small electronic device. But it didn't stop the dreamer in her
hoping. Cressida blinked as Emily-Jane glared at her meaningfully.

'Em, I'm not a mind-reader, what's the problem?'

Cressida was sure, whatever the fridge crisis was, it just wasn't
on the same scale as the one she was facing.

'There's no sushi.' Emily-Jane inclined the end of the sentence
as if an explanation was needed.

No sushi. The world was ending. Had Emily-Jane just said that? Really?

Cressida screwed up her face, trying to find a reasonable response that didn't involve swearing or giving Emily-Jane a lecture about food poverty. Instead her mind fought to focus, too many thoughts trying to jostle for position at the same time. When she was seventeen she'd never heard of sushi. If she was hungry between meals it was toast or cereal – or at a push, if they had some ham, a sandwich. Her name betrayed her parents' aspirations for grandeur, but she'd been brought up a long way from a palatial Georgian seafront five-bed in Dalkey village. Was she doing the best for Emily-Jane? Her mum's stock response to any question was 'We can't afford it', and she'd never wanted her daughter to have her wings clipped in the same way that she'd felt hers had been – money always placing a limitation on whatever she wanted to do. On everything.

But had that been the right thing to do?

Cressida had made sure not to spoil her. At least she thought she had. Emily-Jane was very grounded, wasn't she? She didn't drink, she had lovely friends. Cressida sighed.

'Add it to the list and I'll get some next time I'm ordering the shopping. I must have forgotten it.'

'But I *live* on sushi—'

Cressida cut her off with a glare. She couldn't deal with teenage histrionics now. She couldn't deal with anything, actually. Since she'd met Brioni at lunchtime, she'd been replaying conversations with Laurence in her head, looking for the cracks. All the late nights at the office, all the business trips. All the nights he'd stayed in town saying he had breakfast meetings. Sure that Laurence would never risk the daughter he doted on, his beautiful house,

25

their lifestyle, she'd *stupidly* believed all his excuses. But he was a born risk-taker. That's what Ferryman had been all about. It had been a massive risk, but it had paid off.

How was she only realising that now?

She'd turned a blind eye to her niggling suspicions before, but this time was different. Hearing Nina's name, hearing him speak to her, was like a seismic shift. Cressida felt as if she was poised on the edge of a precipice and what she did next would dictate whether she was able to balance or would plunge her down to a raging torrent below.

'Are you listening, Mother?' Emily-Jane closed the fridge door forcibly and flicked her hair over her shoulder. 'Honestly, you spend more time on your phone than you do talking to me.'

'I'm sorry, I was thinking.'

'You're always thinking. You're worse than Dad. Not that he's ever even here.'

'I'm working, Em, when I'm thinking.'

'But you're always working.'

'And so's your father – that's how we can afford to live somewhere nice and have a villa in Italy so close to your Aunt Sinéad, *and* how we were able to get you a car when you passed your driving test. If we didn't work, things would be very different.'

Emily scowled. 'I know, but Dad's got a team of a thousand people to help and he still works all the time. Apparently.'

Cressida didn't catch the end of the sentence, her thoughts focused on Emily-Jane's point. Laurence did have an army of staff, in both companies, the Howard Group and Ferryman.

Emily-Jane didn't notice her lack of response, continuing, 'What time will he be home tonight?'

'Who – your father? I'm not sure. Text him and ask.'

Emily picked up an apple from the fruit bowl and took a bite. She winced.

'That's really bitter. Yuck, where did you get these from?' Without waiting for Cressida to answer, she continued, 'I need his laptop. I started my *Great Gatsby* essay on it on Sunday.'

Cressida looked at her despairingly.

'Didn't you email it to yourself? Why didn't you use your own computer?'

'Because I can't move my iMac and I wanted to work down here.'

'But you know you're not supposed to use his laptop, he'll go nuts. How did you even get into it?'

'I used the password. He's hopeless, it's the same as the alarm code. *Ridiculous*.' She didn't quite say 'duh' but it was written all over her face. 'It's better I get the essay done, isn't it? I keep asking for a laptop—'

'Em, you've got an iMac and an iPad, and the latest phone, how can you possibly need a laptop as well? You should have used mine—'

'The external keyboard for my iPad isn't connecting properly and *you* were at the clinic. Necessity is the mother of invention.'

'When's it due in?'

Emily-Jane pouted, caught out.

'Tomorrow.'

'You'll have to text him to email it to you. Urgently. Honestly, Em. And you know he'll go mad when he finds out you were fiddling with it. I hope you didn't go into any of his files.'

Emily's response was accompanied by the withering 'as if' look she'd perfected in the past year.

'If you'd actually been at home at the weekend like everyone else's mother, I wouldn't have had to use it, would I?'

With that, she headed out of the kitchen door, pulling it decisively behind her.

Cressida ran her hand over her face. Was it her fault? She did spend a lot of time working from home, checking her email, keeping everything moving. But she loved her job. Was that wrong? She enjoyed working, enjoyed feeling needed, that she could make a difference.

Was that what the whole problem was here? That it was her, Cressida Maria Howard, that was the issue? Emily-Jane was independent now, she didn't need her mum as much as she had done when she was little. Had she become redundant in Laurence's life, too? The house was finished, the company was booming. Had she brought this on – this affair? Was she not attentive enough, or interesting enough? Perhaps it was her fault. Had she spent too much time building the clinic, getting the house right, looking after Emily-Jane, and neglected her relationship with Laurence? Was that why he was with this Nina woman?

Cressida drew in a slow breath, trying to calm her mind. The shock was making her irrational. Being busy was part of her psyche. It gave her something to talk about, to focus on; it was part of her. She ran her hand into her hair. If she was honest with herself, the thing that was really worrying her here was what Brioni might find out. Did she really want to know? They said knowledge was power, but it was also pain; was she ready for that? Ever since she'd heard Nina's voice there had been a dull ache inside her chest, a deep sadness.

And fear.

But she knew that she couldn't live with herself if she didn't act now, knew she would never be able to look at Laurence properly again, or listen to the lies that came out of his mouth without hearing their voices in her head. And she couldn't live like that.

It was time.

Things were going to change.

Chapter 6

Looking out of the window that ran the length of the living room to the windswept grasses undulating in the stiff onshore breeze, Brioni picked up her tea. She was sitting at the sun-bleached table that someone had pushed up against the window in about 1975. Even after the renovations it had returned to its familiar spot, sitting like an old friend waiting for plates to arrive laden with food and to leave scraped clean. It had never moved. Her dad used to come here to read the papers, spreading them out across the entire table as he sipped his coffee, trying to banish the reek of alcohol long enough for him to get down to the pub to start all over again.

But now it was her space.

Sitting here with her laptop in front of her, Brioni could see the beach sweeping away into the distance below, the waves rolling up the shore. The sky was glistening today, a rich blue that was mirrored in the water that swirled around the driftwood and piles of seaweed thrown up by Monday night's storm.

Taking a sip from her mug, Brioni switched her attention to the job in hand. After talking to Cressida yesterday she'd come back to base and worked out a plan, spending the evening researching the key players in Ferryman, creating files with photographs of the directors and senior staff members. She had yet to find anyone called Nina, but perhaps it was short for something else, or she wasn't on the payroll as permanent staff. Brioni was pretty sure that once she got into Laurence's laptop, she'd be able to find out who she was.

Looking at the screen again and opening her email, Brioni scanned the incoming messages and a gentle smile grew on her face. Laurence had already opened the email containing the link that she'd sent earlier this morning before her swim. It really shouldn't be this easy, but then this was what she did. She was paid a lot of money to find the weaknesses in systems and infiltrate them. Not normally with this particular worm, though. This was a piece of code that she'd been working on in her spare time since she'd left college. Getting it right had taken hours and endless patience. This would be its first outing into cyberspace, an excellent opportunity to test its strengths and weaknesses.

Brioni was a perfect example of a Scorpio, resourceful, and passionate, but she was also extremely stubborn and she didn't believe anything until she had all the facts. Right now she didn't have any of the information she needed, but she was about to get it.

Brioni could feel her heart rate rising as she opened another window and activated the camera on the computer she'd infiltrated. She just hoped Laurence hadn't decided to open this particular email on someone else's computer – on Cressida's laptop, or his daughter's. Getting him to click a supposedly innocuous link a second time would be something of a miracle.

After chatting to Cressida, Brioni had decided on a message from a specialist car dealer, inviting Laurence to a private viewing of a range of one-of-a-kind dream machines. The accompanying photograph had several stunning models demonstrating how the doors opened, with the implication that they would be there on the night. As an afterthought she'd added that it was a men only event. The 'I'm interested' link went to a 404 page on a website she'd mocked up. The moment he clicked through to it, her worm began its journey.

And it seemed to be working well.

The lid of his laptop was open, giving her a good view of the rear of what she guessed was his office – he'd obviously left it on his desk. Cressida had checked his diary and he had a regular Wednesday morning meeting with the heads of his Dublin hotels and a lunch afterwards, so the timing was perfect. There was no one sitting in the high-backed leather desk chair that was turned slightly away from the desk, as if someone had got out of it in a hurry. Behind it she could see a floor-to-ceiling window overlooking Grand Canal Dock, the distinctive red poles that formed the crazy giant sculpture outside the theatre blurred, but clear enough to recognise through the glass. There wasn't much else to see in the office, but more importantly, if the laptop had been left on the desk, there was no one to see what might be happening on the screen.

Sitting forward on the edge of her chair, her mouth drying, Brioni waited a few minutes just to be sure that there was no one in the room. She turned the volume up to its maximum, but she couldn't hear anyone. She strained to listen, focusing completely on the screen in front of her, trying to block out the sounds of the house, of the sea.

Someone could come in at any minute and see the cursor dancing around the screen as if it was possessed. Laurence might not be very careful with his password, but Brioni was quite sure he'd recognise the signs that his laptop had been hacked if he could see her moving things around.

Cressida had drawn her a map of the office and emailed her some photos they'd taken when Ferryman had first moved into the building. His room was on the top floor overlooking the canal basin. Brioni glanced over at the drawing. His expansive desk was at right angles to the door; in front of it were twin leather sofas and a glass coffee table. To his right as he sat at the desk was the door to the en suite shower room. (Why did he need a shower room in his office? Brioni hadn't wanted to ask.) To the left of the desk, tucked away in the corner, was an exercise bike. His secretary had a connecting office immediately outside Laurence's own, so she could screen any visitors before they entered.

Very cosy. But that meant that his secretary, who looked like a tiny, motherly woman in her late fifties in the photos Brioni had found, could come in at any moment and put something down on his desk.

Brioni just hoped she'd be able to hear the door opening.

Suddenly aware that her heartbeat was echoing in her ears, Brioni bit her lip and moved her mouse so that her movement was mirrored on his screen. Everything worked. She had full control.

Email first.

Opening the folder, Brioni scanned the messages on the screen. There was nothing from anyone called Nina.

She needed more time to go through the emails individually. Once Laurence's laptop was switched on, she could access it, but this would be a whole lot easier if Cressida could ensure Laurence was distracted.

Brioni moved the cursor to the email search bar and typed in 'Nina'. An email address immediately popped up with a

Ferryman address belonging to a Nina Rodríguez. Nina was quite an unusual name; with the balance of probability, this one had to be a strong contender for the woman Cressida had heard Laurence talking to. Brioni copied the address and, flicking to an open window on her own laptop, pasted it on to a sticky note. She hit *enter* and a string of emails to Nina appeared.

How much time did she have? Brioni needed to maintain access for as long as possible so she could get a clear idea of Laurence's day, his interactions, to make sure there wasn't anything else going on that might impact Cressida's case.

At the top of the page was an unopened email. She couldn't afford to look at that until he had. Her fingers flying over the keyboard, she opened the first email that Laurence had already opened. It was innocuous enough, not addressed personally, though, as if they were familiar with each other. Brioni rolled her eyes at the thought.

`I have all the info you asked for. N x`

Did employees usually sign off like that? Brioni didn't, but then she wasn't your average employee and her CEO sat on an exercise ball when he wasn't at his standing desk.

Brioni glanced at the time and date of the email. It had been sent on Monday, at lunchtime. He'd replied:

`Perfect. Talking to the client this evening`
`if you can stay late, we can catch up`
`afterwards.`

Catch up? Brioni would bet they were catching up.
It sounded as if 'info' was the last thing they would be sharing.
Perhaps this was the rendezvous Cressida had overheard in

Laurence's office? Brioni opened his Google location history, checking back to Monday evening. In a few more clicks she could see he had been in his office until 9 p.m., when he'd gone next door to the 1796 hotel, taking one of his devices with him – his phone, most likely. Cressida had said he preferred to use that when he was out rather than bring the laptop with him – he tended to only bring that home at weekends. So that part had been true. Full marks.

Conscious that she had limited time, Brioni looked at the clock on the screen. There was a good chance he'd be coming back from his meeting soon, before he went out to lunch, and she wanted to check a few more things.

Then she could start finding out who this Nina was.

Chapter 7

'SORRY I'M LATE, usual nonsense. Have you ordered?'

Kate Spicer looked up from her phone as Laurence finally appeared at the table she'd booked for them at their favourite restaurant. It was French, with lots of dark wood and low lighting. Cleverly built high partitions between the tables encased each one in a booth of sorts. It was very discreet. But then, the French were experts at discretion.

'Don't worry. I told you twelve, but I've only just got here.'

Slipping into his seat, one hand on his navy silk tie to stop it falling forwards onto the dark green and gold placemat positioned perfectly on a starched white linen tablecloth, Laurence frowned, his face half amused.

'It's 12.30, were you expecting me to wait for you?'

Kate looked at him reproachfully. 'You're consistently half an hour late for everything, Laurence, you have been your whole life. I booked the table for 12.30 so you're right on time. And we'll be out of here before it gets too busy.'

He scowled at her playfully and straightened the heavy silver cutlery before putting his phone face down on the tablecloth.

'You know me too well.'

Kate smirked at him and reached out to squeeze his hand.

'I've got a client coming in at two for a facial, so I need to be out of here by 1.30.'

He tutted impatiently. 'I really don't know why you're still seeing clients. Don't you have enough to do running the spas?'

Kate looked at him reproachfully. 'I enjoy it. I love my job, I don't just want to be a manager – or on the board, for that matter. Not everyone's got ambition at their core.' She almost snorted at the thought. 'Paper pushing and HR's not me and you know it. I'm very happy running the spas. I like things done my way, my girls are the best in the country because I trained them, and they're loyal. They love the culture I've created. But I trained in beauty so I could work with people, make their lives better.' She glanced over to see if the waiter was heading their way. 'You love what you do, continually expanding. I love what I do. Keeping in touch with clients' needs, and the latest products and techniques makes me *good* at what I do. That's why my team is the best, and our clients keep coming back.' She looked at him pointedly.

Laurence sighed. 'True. But I don't understand it, and you're at the beck and call of your clients. I sometimes feel as if I never actually finish a conversation with you. One day we'll be able to have a lovely leisurely lunch without one of us having to race off.'

Kate smoothed a strand of hair behind her ear and looked across at him, her eyebrows raised.

'It's normally you that's rushing. Perhaps you need to whisk me away to Paris and we can tie up all the loose ends?' She was only half joking.

'I can really see that happening, can't you?' There was a hard edge to his voice as he shrugged. 'And who'd look after Mitzi? She'd go mad without you.'

37

She shook her head despairingly. *As if her dog was the issue here*. But he was right about never finishing a conversation. That seemed to be a symptom of modern life, or perhaps they just had too much to say to each other in the very limited time that was ever available. They'd always brought out the best in each other, ideas sparking whenever they met. His calculated logical thinking complemented her constant flow of new ideas. He continued, interrupting her thoughts.

'I'm going to have to dash again today, I'm afraid.'

'Well, that makes a change. A meeting?'

Laurence shook his head. 'SpeakEasy's interest in Ferryman has got me thinking about the mobile phone market. I'm doing some exploring.'

'You sound just like Pierce, that's exactly what he always used to say. He'd organise meetings just to chat and get ideas. Finding out about what other people were doing helped him develop all sorts of projects.'

'And aren't we all glad about that?' Laurence shook out his napkin as the waiter appeared at his shoulder, his order pad in his hand. 'Cressida always says my brother was the real genius. Sometimes I think she got on better with him than she does with me.'

'Don't be silly, you're like two halves of the same apple.'

Kate acknowledged the waiter with a smile.

Laurence cleared his throat. 'What are you having?'

Kate didn't need to look at the menu.

'My usual, the Caesar salad with chicken, and we'll have a jug of water with lime, please.'

Laurence glanced up at the waiter. 'Steak for me. Rare. No potatoes.'

The waiter started to ask about wine, but Laurence dismissed him with a shake of his head. Kate let out a sharp sigh.

'Be nice to him, he's new. He'll get used to you.'

'They should send someone who knows us, we're in here often enough. How was that launch the other night?'

'The usual. Lots of young thin models with fake tan. They make me feel old.'

'You're gorgeous, Kate, you know that. You look amazing and your confidence lights a room. You've got more brains than those girls put together, remember that.'

'You'd charm the birds from the trees, you Howards.'

'I wish. All I want to charm at the moment is this SpeakEasy contract. I had everyone agreed, and then that damn story broke about their data sharing and everyone on the board changed their minds.' Laurence looked glum.

'The board do have a point, you know. They aren't just objecting to spite you. Selling personal data is big business. It doesn't exactly suggest that a company values its customers. Letting a shark like that into the Ferryman pool could be catastrophic – online credibility and customer trust is crucial. But you know that. Why am I telling you?'

Laurence shrugged. 'It's not that big a deal. Our phones are listening to us all the time. Look at all the instances where we've been discussing … I don't know, goldfish or something utterly random, and something related pops up in your Instagram feed or as an email ad.' She started to interrupt, but he didn't let her. 'Everyone's harvesting data all the time. Our smart homes, Alexa, not just our phones. It's what you do with it and how you use it that counts. Google's smart advertising has proven how effective targeted ads are. With the sort of information we hold, we can be even more specific – that's gold for advertisers and our corporate partners. This deal is potentially worth billions. And what SpeakEasy have are the data scientists who can deep dive and connect the dots.'

She glared at him impatiently in response. 'Get your own data scientists. You don't need SpeakEasy's, and you certainly don't want to be letting them near your customer files.'

She could tell from his face that he wasn't listening. He'd moved on in his head to the global success that an alliance could bring; she could see it in his eyes.

'Kate, you know it'll really cement our position, and comms is where it's at. We can develop all sorts of initiatives if this one comes together.'

He sounded annoyed that she was challenging him. But it didn't worry her – this was how they worked best. Sometimes she had to put the brakes on, just like she had when his brother had been alive. Kate sighed to herself. The problem was that Laurence Howard was one of life's winners, and they both knew that you didn't get anywhere in life if you sat behind your desk and waited for people to bang on your door. You had to create your own opportunities.

'God – you can't bear to lose, can you? Sometimes there are other routes to success, you know.'

'I know. That's what Pierce was good at – thinking outside the box.' Laurence paused, fighting to keep a grin off his face. 'I've got a plan actually. I've been thinking outside the box, too.' He frowned. 'I was talking to one of the team and something she said resonated. I reckon I have all the information I need to make Phil, Eoin and Richie see my way of thinking. Once I have their support, it doesn't matter what the rest of the board think. I just need to get hold of some details. As she's always saying, *everyone* has secrets.'

'That's for sure.' Kate looked at him, her face creased with concern. Something about the way he said it gave her a chill. 'But those three guys are your friends, yours and Pierce's. You've known them since school – they helped build Ferryman. It would have been all uphill if it had just been the two of you. You owe them a lot.'

'I know, and they've been richly rewarded for their faith in our idea. You have to put friendship to one side if you want to really build a business. You can't afford to get sentimental.'

'I think we'll have to agree to disagree there. Just be careful. You don't want whatever it is you're planning to come back on you.'

Laurence looked at her in that way that always made her heart melt.

'Don't you worry, Kate Spicer. I know what I'm doing. Just like you do. Now tell me what plans you've got to make me a fortune out of those salons. You've an interest in this company, too, don't forget. What's that phrase about all ships rising on the right tide?'

Kate rolled her eyes despairingly just as the waiter arrived with their order. Laurence had always had a reckless streak, could be so blinded by what he thought was a brilliant idea that he forgot to stress-test it, to think about the dark side. That's how they'd been in Silicon Valley in the first place, heading to a meeting that he'd been convinced would be a turning point.

Instead, the turning point had come with Pierce's death. Kate felt a dull ache in her heart. It was a long time ago now, but that accident had changed the paths of all their lives.

Chapter 8

THE DRIVE DOWN to Wexford was much quicker than Cressida had expected, her Range Rover Sport eating up the miles on the N11. Brioni had been right to suggest they meet down here, well away from waggling ears – there was always a danger that a phone call could be overheard, or worse, recorded.

It was a long drive, but it was worth it. As she crossed the county border from Dublin into Wicklow, the road slicing between the two Sugar Loaf mountains, their peaks silhouetted against the sky, the traffic became lighter. Fields opened up on both sides of the road and Cressida caught glimpses of the autumn sunshine glinting off the sea to her left. It was as if the sky had been washed clean by the rain, the type of day that lifted your spirits whatever was going on in the rest of your life. Despite the anxiety she could feel hanging over her, manifesting in what felt like a dark hole in her stomach, looking at the sunlit countryside, Cressida felt a glimmer of hope.

She turned the radio up a notch. Ever since her meeting with Brioni she'd felt less alone in this mess, and much less powerless. Waves of sadness still hit her, but she knew it wouldn't be long before she converted the hurt to rage. It was the way her mind worked. And she'd always found anger to be a very productive emotion, one that drove her forwards.

She'd been driven to better herself all her life. A chance remark from a girl in school had upset her so badly that she'd thrown herself into study for a scholarship exam just to prove the bully wrong. That had got her into a top-notch school – and it was true what they said about the old boy network and how the right connections could get you anywhere. Perhaps her mum had had some sort of sixth sense giving her a posh name. It had always attracted the wrong sort of energy in her state junior school, but she fitted right in at a private one.

It had been through a friend in school that she'd met Laurence, at a party, although it had been Pierce she'd met first. They'd given her a glimpse of a world of privilege that she could only have dreamed about when she was a child. Their father owned one of the biggest hotel chains in Ireland and had already begun expanding, with flagship premises in London and New York. The family holidayed in Marbella, owned yachts and racehorses.

It had been anger at what she'd thought was her own bad luck that had driven her on when she'd found out she was pregnant at seventeen. She'd felt derailed, had so many plans that she'd thought would have to be put to one side. But it had all worked out OK – at the beginning, at least.

She knew not everyone was lucky enough to marry into a family where money wasn't a problem, but she'd needed that anger to keep focused, to drive her to stay in college and get to university. She'd wanted to bring up Emily-Jane herself, but she still had ambitions, had had a constant battle with Laurence's mother, who thought her place was running his house, that leaving Emily-Jane in the university crèche was neglect. Thankfully their daughter was bright and had thrived on contact all her life, and Cressida had got her degree while Laurence built his business.

Had they started to drift apart then? Or later, when Pierce had died and Laurence had taken the company forward on his own? Now, looking back, Cressida wasn't sure they'd ever been truly together; they both doted on Emily-Jane, but a fast marriage so young hadn't been what either of them had planned.

The past didn't justify Laurence cheating, though, in any shape or form. Not then, and not now. She'd been dating other people when they first met, had even had a one-night stand with Pierce shortly before she'd met Laurence. But from the moment they'd become an item, she'd been loyal to him. For all the good it had done her.

Passing into County Wexford, Cressida spotted the sign for Ballycastle and flipped on her indicator, pulling off the motorway on to a narrow road that suddenly became a lot smaller as it wound through the countryside towards the sea. Brioni had said she needed to look out for the pub and take the next left, and not to be worried when the road turned into a bumpy track. There was no sign for her house, but it was the only turning off the track. Once Cressida had crossed the cattle grid between the stone gateposts – overgrown with brambles and practically part of the landscape – she'd see the house in a couple of minutes.

When Brioni had said 'track', Cressida hadn't thought she meant it quite so literally. Sitting forward in her seat, peering over the steering wheel as she bumped along the unmetalled lane, the hedges high on both sides, she felt a surge of relief as she reached the top of the hill to see the single-storey wooden house, long and low, nestled into the thick gorse.

Brioni must have been watching for her. She had the front door open before Cressida had got out of the car. Cressida reached across the front seat for her handbag and the paper bag that had been wedged in safely all the way here. She'd ordered a Thai takeaway from the restaurant on the curve of the hill in Dalkey village and had collected it on her way past. If she had to face the reality of Laurence's deception, she was going to do it in comfort and enjoy a good lunch.

'What have you got there?'

'Green chicken curry, noodles, all sorts. I thought you might have difficulty getting deliveries here and we deserve a treat.'

Brioni's eyes lit up. 'Wonderful. Did Marissa tell you Thai was my favourite?'

'I remembered she'd said you'd been travelling and had loved Thailand.'

Brioni stepped back to let her inside the long low house.

'I could eat Thai food every day for the rest of my life.'

As Cressida stepped on to the porch Brioni held up her hand, revealing a tattoo on the inside of her wrist. Cressida smiled, recognising the Buddhist symbol. They'd been to Thailand several times when Emily-Jane was younger, getting out from the hotel with a guide who had shown them how beautiful the country was.

Following Brioni, Cressida stepped straight into a huge living room lit from enormous windows along two sides. Decorated in shades of cream, the wooden floor was polished, huge paintings of the sea dominating the inside walls. A vintage sofa sat under the far window, a driftwood coffee table in front of it. To her right, a weathered pine table was piled with textbooks, Brioni's laptop open in the middle.

'Wow, this is a beautiful room.'

'Thanks. It's very simple but we love it.'

'It almost feels as if you're outside.'

Cressida handed Brioni the takeaway bag and went over to the window above the sofa that looked directly on to the ocean. There was something wild and untamed about the view from here that was missing from her own house – the garden in Dalkey ran down to a private mooring and the sea, but the coastline was rocky. Here the dunes seemed to slide down into a magnificent pale yellow sandy beach, which swept around in an arc as far as she could see. And there wasn't a soul on it.

'It feels so isolated and safe, as if you're right on the edge of the world.'

Brioni smiled. 'Let me put the kettle on and we can eat and talk.'

*

'So it worked?' Cressida reached for the jug of water Brioni had put on the table with the bowls of food, shaking her head incredulously. 'Marissa said you were brilliant online, but it seems so easy.'

Brioni laughed. 'It's like Olympic skiing, the trick is to make it *look* easy. I've been working on this code since my second-year undergrad. I took some semesters at MIT as part of my course in London, and hooked up with some brilliant coders – we're all still in touch. This is a new generation. There are lots of worms out there that will do similar things, but this one is unique, there's no protection against it – yet. You can spend years working on something and then only be able to use it twice. Once its presence is spotted, people like me are tasked with finding ways to block it.'

'What would you use it for, though?'

Brioni's look was enigmatic. 'Let's say it depends on the threat. This is military-grade. It still needs a bit of refining but ... well, the less you know ...'

Cressida nodded. The less she knew was right. Brioni continued. 'You were spot-on about the car dealer's email – he clicked as soon as he opened it.'

'As is becoming clear, he can't resist the lure of a pretty face.'

Brioni cleared her throat. 'I've been having a look around his laptop, but I need more time to have a good look at his files. He's got quite a few that are password-protected, which is interesting. I can get into them no problem, but I didn't have time before he got back from his meeting this morning.' Brioni paused. 'I did find out he was in the office when he called you on Monday night, and that a Nina Rodríguez works for Ferryman. She seems to be on the data side, but she doesn't have an exact job description.'

'Did you find a photo?'

Brioni turned her laptop so Cressida could see the screen more clearly.

'Why did I ask? She looks like Angelina Jolie. She'd be hard to miss in a crowd.'

Brioni grimaced. 'Her page on LinkedIn isn't nearly finished. It looks as if she set it up before she came here and doesn't use it. But from what I've gathered, she's Colombian, has been in Ireland for four years, speaks several languages, and has a master's in data science.'

'Bright as well as beautiful?' Cressida ran her fingers into her hair. 'She looks about twenty.'

'Thirty-two. She's very discreet, though, no other social media, no pictures of her online apart from this professional one – and this one ...' Brioni put her finger on the trackpad. 'But she's only in the background here.'

It was a photo of Laurence at an event, an attractive blonde with long hair standing beside him, a glass of champagne in her hand. She was laughing at something he was saying. Among the crowd of onlookers they could just make out Nina.

'That's the launch of the new beauty range they created for the 1796 spa. It's only stocked in Howard Group hotels, and in a couple of exclusive department stores in London and New York. I only stayed for about half an hour. It was mainly Ferryman staff and a bunch of ridiculous model and TV types with fake boobs and teeth so white you needed sunglasses. They use some PR company that plants famous faces at parties so the society media pick up the event.' Cressida paused. 'Laurence was in his element. That's the spa manager he's talking to. I can't remember her name, but she came up with the idea for the brand.'

'Attractive woman.' Brioni checked her notes. 'Her name's Kate Spicer.'

Cressida pursed her lips. The picture must have been taken after she'd left. There was something about the way Laurence was looking at her, about the expression on the Spicer woman's face, that suggested they knew each other a bit too well. And from the expression on Brioni's face, she was seeing it, too. Cressida knew Kate Spicer had worked with Pierce and Laurence from the start, but their paths had never really crossed. Had she missed another business relationship that had crossed a line?

'I'm starting to think that model looks must be some sort of a prerequisite for working with Ferryman. That and a D-cup.' Cressida scowled, trying to push thoughts about Kate Spicer out of her mind. She really had enough to worry about. 'So, tell me more about this Nina.'

'I don't have a whole lot of information right now, but I should be able to get into the company personnel files from Laurence's laptop. She doesn't seem to be on the electoral register and she doesn't have a car registered in her name, she's a bit of an enigma. But if I can get her PPN I can see where else she's worked.'

Cressida nodded slowly. 'So what's next?'

'I'll keep going through the emails, find out what she's working on in Ferryman, see if I can find out about her personally. This worm isn't designed to infiltrate a whole network yet, just the one destination, and I don't want to send it out again to her terminal or laptop just in case the Ferryman security systems spot a second breach. I think I can get a lot from Laurence. Ideally I want to find out when they'll next be meeting in real life, and I'll see if I can get some photos.'

'Won't they spot you?'

Brioni raised her eyebrows mysteriously.

'I thought I'd invest in a wig. If I wear a skirt I'll look totally different. They won't even notice me.'

A grin twitched on Cressida's face. She'd prepared herself for the worst, but she was finally going to find out what was going on. Brioni O'Brien really was a match for Laurence. He was going to have a lot of trouble wriggling out of this, and Cressida was going to enjoy every minute of watching him squirm.

Chapter 9

I<small>T WAS DARK</small> when Brioni sat down to check her laptop. After a long afternoon walk on the beach, Cressida had left for Dalkey, texting her on the way home to say Laurence had been in touch to say that he was staying late at the office. Again.

He says he'll be home by 8.

Brioni had checked with Google Maps and reckoned he'd need to leave his office in the Ferryman building by 7.30 at the latest to be home by then.

Cressida had booked the little Italian in the village for 8.30 p.m., giving Brioni a clear few hours to go through his documents.

Brioni glanced out of the living room window and took a sip of her raspberry tea as she waited for the screen to load. The sky was inky, phosphorescence making the tips of the waves breaking on the beach sparkle in what little moonlight there was.

Focusing on her laptop, Brioni adjusted the microphone at Laurence's end so she could hear if a cleaner – or anyone else for that matter – came into the office.

And then nearly jumped out of her skin at the sound of a heavily accented female voice.

'I have everything. More than everything, in fact.'

Was that Nina? In Laurence's office? Holy crap. He was supposed to be heading home.

Cressida was waiting for him. Brioni could see precisely why she was running out of patience.

Brioni sat frozen, not daring to move the mouse in case someone was looking at the screen. The camera was activated and there was no one sitting at the desk – she'd thought she was in the clear.

Brioni suddenly realised that she was holding her breath. Which was ridiculous, as nobody could hear her. She let it out and cursed that the desk was facing the wrong way. If the laptop was facing into the room, she'd be able to see what was going on, and to record it. As they'd discussed on the beach, what Cressida needed now was insurmountable evidence of Laurence's indiscretions – something her lawyers could present to him.

Peering at her screen, she listened hard. The office had gone quiet, then there was a sound like a glass being put down. And something moved. It took her a moment to realise it, but the huge windows behind the desk were reflecting the room. With the darkness outside, now she focused on it, she could see everything inside the office perfectly. The antique-looking lamp just beyond his open laptop threw out a soft glow, pooling on a photograph in a silver frame beside it, but there was plenty of light in the room, bouncing off the window glass, creating a mirror.

And she could see movement. The reflection of the desk itself blocked some of the picture, but she watched a slim woman with long dark hair sitting on the end of a sofa. The woman reached forward for a champagne flute. Now Brioni was seeing it, the image was so clear she felt as if she could almost see the bubbles in the tall slim glass. The woman's nails, the same coral as the fitted dress she was wearing, were bright against her sallow skin.

Brioni searched the reflection. She couldn't see Laurence – perhaps he was sitting on the other end of the sofa, out of view behind the desk? Moments later she heard his voice.

Brioni reached over for her phone so she could record the conversation. She didn't want to risk touching the mouse again in case it delayed the system going back to sleep and they noticed the light from the screen reflected in the window. Brioni bit her lip, praying it went to sleep quickly, leaving her watching the tableau in the office without anyone present being any the wiser.

A man's voice. It had to be Laurence Howard.

'Tell me exactly what you found.'

Brioni saw the woman smile over the edge of the glass.

'Are you sure your office is not bugged? These Americans do not play clean, you know.'

He chuckled in response. 'Nobody gets in here without my knowing, not even the cleaner. Dora looks after that herself.'

'Your secretary does not like me.'

'I wouldn't worry about that. I like you, that's what matters.'

There was a pause as she leaned forward, her voice husky.

'But do you like me enough, Laurence?'

Brioni frowned. The woman's tone was tense, and full of what Brioni was sure was thinly disguised anger.

Laurence didn't seem to have picked up on it, though, as he replied, 'Nina, you know the answer to that ...' His voice held a warning.

'I know. And I know that after all the work I have done for you, the risks I have taken, you need to show your appreciation.'

'Don't I show it enough already?' He sounded as if he was only just holding on to his patience. 'That bracelet you're wearing is a limited edition from No. 42. Those stones aren't paste, you know.'

A diamond bracelet from New York's most exclusive jewellers – nice.

Brioni was sure that would go down well with Cressida. When Marissa had sent her the diamond nose stud she was wearing in its No. 42 box, Brioni had been blown away. Nina, however, didn't seem so impressed. As Brioni watched, Nina played with the bracelet around her thin wrist. She was obviously thinking.

'This information you want is valuable. You have asked me to gather data on your fellow board members – your friends – in order to …' She paused. '… *persuade* them to allow this partnership with SpeakEasy. For these American – how should I put it …? Crooks? – getting a foothold in Europe, in association with Ferryman, is worth billions.'

She inclined the end of the sentence, looking for his comment. His reply was brief, testy.

'And—'

'And I am not stupid, Laurence, far from it, in fact.'

'That's not very friendly. I thought we had an understanding.'

'You have an understanding. I thought we did, too, but I seem to have been wrong. I *do*, however, have a lifestyle to maintain and rent to pay.'

Brioni's eyebrows shot up. Her tone was clipped, the emphasis on the last three words even greater with her accent. She really was pure business. She obviously knew Laurence very well, and knew she was in total control of this situation. Whatever information she had must be dynamite. Brioni could sense the tension in the office ramping up as if she was standing there herself.

Laurence didn't answer, or perhaps he was about to, but sitting into the sofa, one arm along the back of it, her glass in her other hand, Nina allowed a beat to pass before she continued.

'I think a significant payment into an offshore account would be a very good sign of your appreciation, no? Perhaps a million euros?'

Chapter 10

'IT'S GOOD TO see you, Minnie Mouse. When are you going to send me another one of those fine pictures?'

His voice was gravelly, as if he was trying too hard to be sexy. Or he'd had too much to drink. Probably the latter, actually. His face was flushed, the lights in the room reflecting off his bald patch, the comb-over not sufficient to hide it. Today he was wearing a soft yellow open-necked shirt with a collar, like something you'd see someone wear on the golf course. The sun was streaming in from the right of the shot. He was using his phone, his camera in close so she couldn't see anything in the background that might give her an idea of where he was.

Which was a pity.

Previously he'd dropped the phone as things had got more heated, and she'd got a look at his office. Once, he'd been in his car, the phone resting on the dashboard, thick green pine trees all around the vehicle, as if he'd gone into the woods to talk to her.

The only good thing about all of this was that his need was getting more frequent. And every meeting was another step closer to her goal.

Emily-Jane leaned forward so her cleavage was clearly on camera, the pale pink frill on the edge of her silk nightdress reflecting the pink and white fairy lights strung around her bed. She'd pulled her hair up into high bunches, and twirled her fingers around the end as she thought of the answer, trying to look more like the fourteen-year-old her profile suggested. Slowly she unwound her finger and laid it purposefully on her full lips, glossed deep pink. She heard his sharp intake of breath as she moved, the satin straining against her nipples.

'Is there anyone else there?' His voice was getting raspy. He liked it when they were on their own; it made him feel as if he had her all to himself.

As if they were safe.

Emily-Jane raised her eyebrows and pouted, wriggling on the bed as if she was getting comfortable, adding to the show.

'Mum's meeting Dad for dinner when he's finished work. They'll be ages. It's just you and me.'

'You're so beautiful. Show me more.'

'I can't, you know that, I'm not allowed.'

'You're such a tease.'

He said it as if he loved her being coy. She could hear his breathing quicken. His eyes were so focused on her breasts that he hadn't noticed she'd hit the *record* button.

'Did you like the picture of my red polka-dot bikini? It's a bit small. I was worried about diving in, in case I popped out of the top.'

She massaged the fullness of her breast through the pink silk and looked at him from under her eyelashes.

'I loved it. I've got it here beside me. I love you all wet.'

She knelt in front of the screen, the spaghetti straps on the silk negligée straining against her shoulders. In the viewing window, she could see the shape of her breasts was emphasised by the shadows. It had taken her a while to get the lighting right, but

56

with the pink glow of her bedside lamp and the fairy lights behind her, the bed looked like a stage set.

'Do you like my hair?'

'You know I love your hair like that. I want to run my hand through it and pull it tight and hear you moaning.'

'Do you? Tell me what you want me to do.' Running her hand down the front of her nightdress, she slipped her fingers under the hem. 'Will I touch myself like you said? Right here.' She moved her hand as if she was rubbing herself. Putting her head back, she moaned, saying breathily, 'What would you like to do?'

'Fucking tear off that nightie and satisfy Mr Wonka.'

Emily-Jane giggled like an intoxicated schoolgirl and continued to rub, her breasts moving with her hips. She licked her lips slowly.

'How's Mr Wonka doing now?'

'Oh my God. Oh. My. God. Mr Wonka's very …' He paused, panting. 'Very happy.'

Thank God it was fast.

Taking her hand out from under her nightdress, she leaned forward so her face and chest filled the screen.

'Was I a good girl?'

'Oh yes, Minnie, you're always a *very* good girl.'

He was sweating now, his face bright red.

She smiled. It had taken her a while, but she'd built his trust enough for him to show part of his face on screen. He was still careful, but at moments like this when his guard was down, she could get a good clear picture.

'Are you happy?'

'I'll send you some more pocket money. You mustn't buy too many sweets, though. I like you plump but we don't want you to get fat.'

Emily-Jane raised her eyebrows and looked at him archly.

'Gotta go!'

She flicked off the webcam and closed the window.

Sweets?

She'd be buying a gun if this plan didn't come together soon. But money created a digital trail – every transaction logged. He thought he'd been clever asking her to set up a new account with the online bank, but every interaction secured the connection.

Chapter 11

WAITING TO SEE how Laurence would react to Nina's question, Brioni's eyes were glued to her screen and the reflection of the office in the giant windows behind his desk. She wished she could see Laurence's face. Nina was playing him at his own game. Which must have come as a bit of a shock. But then Laurence struck Brioni as the type of man who underestimated women, particularly extremely bright women like Nina Rodríguez. But perhaps he'd been too focused on her other talents and had forgotten how she'd ended up working for Ferryman in the first place.

As if to confirm Brioni's suspicions, his voice held a touch of sarcasm as he replied.

'Nina, I'm paying you well enough for this job. How long did it take you? An hour?'

Brioni watched as Nina took a sip of her champagne and looked at him from under long dark lashes.

'Maybe only an hour, but many years of experience working with different systems in different companies. I make sure that my actions cannot be linked to me, that I do not leave a trace.'

It sounded as if she meant more than just breaking into systems, but she continued before Brioni could think about it more.

'I cannot just call up customer files and check accounts. I have to disguise every move, or someone will spot me.'

'Tell me what you've found out. I need to know the data is worth the investment.' Businesslike, his tone was hard-edged. Laurence Howard clearly didn't like being outflanked.

'Why would I give you this information that will earn you many millions when you will not look after me?'

'I'll look after you, Nina, you know I will. Now tell me what you found.'

He'd switched to speaking to her as if she was a child – persuasive, convincing. Brioni couldn't help smiling.

'The money?'

'I'll look into it …'

'I'm not sure we can wait. The next board meeting is the middle of next week. I think a transfer to an anonymous account would need to be initiated now.'

'Nina, this is ridiculous. You're behaving like a child. Just give me the information and I'll think of a way to show my appreciation. I don't think I've been lacking in that department before.'

Brioni almost winced at his crassness. She was quite sure that if Nina hadn't been in a delicate negotiating situation here – or perhaps hostage situation was a more accurate description, although Laurence didn't seem to quite realise it – she would have got up and slapped his face. Brioni bit her lip. Even in the glass she could see Nina tense. Her voice was strong and clear when she spoke, her eyes flashing.

'I do not think it would be good for you – for anyone – to find out what you are doing, Laurence, I really do not …'

Her voice was laced with vitriol. Whatever ground Laurence Howard had held in this discussion, he'd lost it.

'What do you mean? Cressida trusts me implicitly, there's—'

'I was not talking about your wife –' Nina said the last word with utter distaste – 'but I am sure she wouldn't be impressed. I meant the board, and SpeakEasy, your bus-i-ness associates.' She drew out the word out like a hiss.

Brioni heard Laurence take a deep breath and let it out slowly.

'I don't know how you could doubt me. The money's yours. Now I need to see that information—'

She cut across him. 'First, the transfer—'

'Nina, don't make me lose my temper. You aren't the only data expert in the company, you know ...'

'Really? And you think any of the others would involve themselves in industrial espionage? In blackmail? Or do you have a close relationship with one of them, too?' Sitting forward slightly in the seat, she spat the words at him.

Brioni checked her phone; it was still recording. She propped it up on its side so the camera was recording the screen, too. She had no idea if the reflection in the window could be enhanced to see what was going on more clearly, but she was pretty sure it was enough to prove that the audio recording hadn't been faked. It was very clear that Laurence didn't play fair, in love or business – Brioni was quite sure he'd try to discredit any evidence Cressida had against him.

She heard a rustling sound and the click of what could have been a pen nib being propelled. A moment later Nina leaned across the sofa and as her hand came back into view, Brioni could see she had a piece of white paper between her forefinger and middle finger. Leaning forward to put her glass down, the sound sharp in the stillness of the office, she flipped the paper over and looked at it, nodding. Looking up, she smiled at him, her teeth bright against her lipstick, movie star perfect.

'How quaint – an IOU. You will initiate the transfer tonight?'

'Of course.'

She smiled again. 'Very well then. I think what I have discovered, you will find extremely interesting. As I say, everyone has secrets, Laurence. It is my speciality.'

She bent forward and pulled a small gold handbag on to her knee, flipping the buckle open. She extracted something that Brioni guessed was a USB stick and passed it to him.

'I looked at the Ferryman accounts of your three partners – at their orders, delivery addresses, the bookings they have made for services, travel and accommodation through Ferryman and their partner companies, the names on tickets.' She paused. 'Eoin O'Reilly appears to have ordered a substantial amount of leather harnesses. Some with spikes.' She said it with such disdain that Brioni smiled. 'Perhaps his wife knows all about this, as much of it is for women, but he has also bought ladies' shoes in a size 12. I feel this may be too big for his very tiny wife, whose clothes are all a size 10. It appears from her account that she is a 36B and the equipment is all somewhat larger. They have both been several times to a hotel in Wales that has something of a reputation for, shall we say, parties, so I feel that this is a shared pursuit, but obviously not something that is reflected in his wholesome homeware brands.'

Laurence laughed out loud. 'The dirty bastard. And the others?'

'Mister Philip French has a fondness for gardening. Among other things, he has ordered several *Salvia divinorum* plants, which don't particularly stand out in a large delivery of other shrubs, but are in fact a controlled species with leaves that have opioid properties. In the words of one online forum, they "make weed feel like Canderel". Should anyone look closely at his greenhouse, I believe he could have some explaining to do which would not look good in court, particularly as the extensive renovation of his home office and its glasshouse was billed as a company expense. As was the refurbishment of his villa in Marbella.'

'So we're paying, are we? I'd like to hear the explanation for that. And Richie? What's he got hidden in his closet, apart from interesting American business contacts?'

'Your colleague Richard has a definite appetite for X-rated content. This is downloaded via his account. That is not unusual, but the nature of the videos he chooses would suggest he has a liking for girls who are a little young. There are also some interesting designer clothing and make-up purchases on his account that would suggest that he has a teenage daughter.'

'He's single, he doesn't have any kids.'

'Precisely my point. There is obviously more – those are the highlights. I have the addresses of everyone that each of them has sent flowers to in the last six months, also lingerie and jewellery – gifts of all sorts, in fact. It is quite illuminating.'

She seemed to draw out the last few words, and Brioni leaned in closer to the screen. It was obvious when you thought about it, that Ferryman with its broad product base would hold damning evidence if it was drawn together by the wrong person. Brioni wondered if this had been Nina's idea or Laurence's. But she had a feeling she knew the answer to that. Nina was as sharp as a shark's tooth.

'It sounds as if there's enough there to get us started.' Laurence chuckled. 'It's so interesting to find out the inner lives of your business associates. I'm sure they can be persuaded to support a partnership with SpeakEasy now.'

The leather on the sofa creaked as he stood up, and for the first time Brioni saw him properly over the top of the desk. He was in shirtsleeves, his collar undone. He put his hands into his trouser pockets and stared into the window glass. Brioni drew in a sharp breath. Thank God the laptop screen was asleep – he couldn't fail to notice its reflection from that angle. He appeared to be thinking.

Nina flicked her hair over her shoulder.

'Everything is on the stick. Orders, delivery notes, all screenshotted in case someone should try and get in and change them.'

Brioni watched as he nodded slowly, still looking at the glass, his face creased, his eyes narrowed.

'I need you to email them in the morning, from an address that looks like press, saying that you've discovered some interesting details. Give them a flavour of what you've got, but not everything. They'll be too shocked to report anything but we want to be careful. We let the information sink in and then I'll get in touch around lunchtime and say I've received the same information. I'll invite them in for a chat individually on Friday morning. That'll give them time to stew on the ramifications overnight tomorrow, and then I'll tell them I can make it go away and ask for their support at the meeting.'

In the reflection in the glass, Brioni watched Nina sit forward on the sofa.

'As soon as I receive confirmation that the transfer has been actioned, I will email them.'

As if he'd snapped out of whatever deep thought he was entertaining, Laurence turned to her abruptly.

'It takes time to get things like that organised, accounts set up. Don't you trust me?'

'It is electronic, Laurence, it takes minutes. The account details are on the stick.' She inclined the end of the sentence as if it was a done deal and stood up, reaching for her bag and smoothing the skirt of her dress. 'We will meet tomorrow evening to christen the deal.' She paused and her eyes narrowed. Brioni started at the complete change in her body language. She was poised like an eagle about to swoop; her face was suddenly hard, the shadows from the soft lighting making her high cheekbones razor-sharp. Brioni could almost feel the temperature ramping up in the room. 'Unless, of course, you will be visiting Kate Spicer tomorrow evening? I see the black Chanel dress you ordered was a size 12. Is she not a bit heavy for you, my darling?'

'What?'

Laurence did a double take; his eyes flashed wide with shock, but he recovered quickly, keeping his hands in his pockets, his body language deliberately relaxed.

'You think I checked everyone else's accounts and didn't check yours? That would have been silly, no? I am sure she loved the necklace from No. 42, the one that matches my bracelet. Is that not where you bought your wife's birthday present from? The two necklaces seem to be remarkably similar.'

Brioni held her breath, waiting for his response. The anger in Nina's tone was arcing like electricity, and it was about 1000 volts.

'That's none of your business.'

Brioni winced. He was shaking his head, casually brushing her off.

How was he not seeing how mad she was?

There was a long pause. Brioni felt as if she was watching a nuclear reaction: Laurence the unsuspecting neutron heading towards Nina's uranium atom, unaware of the huge amount of heat, energy and radiation that was about to be unleashed.

'Really? I do not like being two-timed, Laurence, it is not something I will tolerate for one minute.'

Her emphasis on the last two words sounded vicious. Finally he seemed to hear her.

'That sounds like a threat – I very much hope it isn't.'

Before she could answer, Laurence's phone began to ring.

'I think that is your wife's ringtone? Do you want to answer it? Or perhaps I should?'

Nina's tone was light now, scathing. As if she'd gone past the rage to that calm place where the real danger lay.

He hadn't taken her seriously – bad move.

Brioni glanced at the clock on her screen. It was 8.30. Cressida would be in the restaurant waiting for him, probably assuming he'd got caught in traffic. Watching their conversation unfold, Brioni felt as if she'd been sitting here for a lot longer than thirty minutes.

'Nina.'

Laurence's tone was deep, laced with anger as he turned around and Brioni saw him reach over to the sofa. A moment later he was holding his jacket, one hand in the inside pocket, apparently searching for his phone. He put it to his ear as Nina pirouetted around the arm of the sofa, walking behind it towards the door, a slow smile on her face. As Laurence began to speak, Brioni heard the sound of the office door slamming shut.

'Sorry, love, I got held up. I'm leaving in ten minutes, order me the octopus and get them to put some champagne on ice.'

He flipped his wrist to look at an impressive watch, the metal bracelet catching the light and bouncing off the window glass. 'I'll be there by 9.15 latest, the traffic will be clear by now.' He stopped to listen to her. 'Yes, I promise. It's worth it, really, I wouldn't be this late if it wasn't important … Yes … See you shortly.'

Brioni was sure Cressida was impressed with that.

Laurence hung up and looked at this phone for a moment, then began to scroll through, looking for a number. He put the phone to his ear again, looking blindly at something on the carpet. A moment later the call was answered.

'Dirk, it's Laurence … Yes, everything is falling into place. There will be no problem with the board. I'll be talking to them individually on Friday morning to confirm. The only slight hitch is that Nina Rodríguez has worked out why I wanted the data, and let's say she's being a bit too clever than is good for her. But I'll sort it out.'

He nodded slowly in response to whoever was on the other end. Brioni needed to double-check, but she was pretty sure that the CEO of SpeakEasy in California was someone called Dirk Ackroyd. With a name like that, there weren't too many other people it could be.

'It's quite a narrow window.' Laurence smiled. 'Of course I trust you, Dirk, this relationship is all about trust. She's expecting some information from me in the morning. I'll send that over first thing and make sure she's put the wheels in motion. I'm going to meet her tomorrow evening. She'll have done all I need her to do by then.'

He paused again, nodding. What on earth was he planning?

'That would be no harm. I don't need any details. I'll be

reinforcing the message in no uncertain terms myself tomorrow. She's a bright girl, she knows what's good for her.'

He hung up, putting the corner of the phone to his mouth and tapping it on his teeth, obviously considering the conversation. Looking at the phone, he dialled again.

'Nina? Confirmation of that transfer will be with you first thing. It'll come from an account in the Cayman Islands. I want that information communicated by ten. Why don't you take a couple of days off, then? Keep clear just in case any questions are raised?'

Brioni heard him pause as she answered.

'Grand,' Laurence replied. 'I'll see you tomorrow evening at the Reynolds, in the Kai Lung bar? I'll be there at seven.'

Chapter 12

BRIONI LISTENED SEVERAL times to the recording on her phone of Laurence's meeting with Nina. The only piece of information she didn't have was how much SpeakEasy were paying Laurence to blackmail his friends. As Nina had implied, it had to be a substantial amount.

He was playing a very dangerous game at every level. If his fellow board members got together and realised that he was attacking them individually, would they have the combined voting power to oust him from the board? Obviously, in order to *know* that Laurence was blackmailing more than one of them, they'd have to admit to one another that they had things to hide, which was exactly what Laurence Howard was banking on them *not* doing.

But what had he meant about Nina being a problem? Sacking her from Ferryman would be the simplest way to get her out of his life, but Brioni was pretty sure that the realisation that Nina was way ahead of him had only hit Laurence after this conversation – which didn't say much for his ability to judge people. Underestimating the women in his life seemed to be a fairly consistent failing on Laurence's part. Brioni still couldn't believe that he hadn't seen the jealousy in Nina's eyes when she'd mentioned Kate Spicer. What did they say about a woman scorned? In Nina's book that clearly applied to mistresses, too.

Brioni didn't think she'd ever seen anyone quite so angry.

And he seemed to have totally forgotten that he was married, and that Cressida might have an opinion on his activities as well. Perhaps Cressida should suggest that Laurence have her name tattooed on his arm so he could remember it – his wedding ring certainly didn't seem to be doing the trick.

Brioni checked the time on her screen. It was after nine. Laurence had left the office a few minutes earlier than he'd suggested and should be arriving in Dalkey around now, so she wouldn't be able to update Cressida fully yet; she'd have to wait until the morning. The whole objective of this evening and their going out to dinner was for Brioni to look through Laurence's files and find out more about his activities, but his meeting with Nina had been quite illuminating on its own.

To help Cressida in the divorce court, though, Brioni knew she needed much stronger evidence of Nina's relationship with Laurence. It had been implied but not expressly stated, and a good lawyer would shoot holes in what she had now, no matter how furious Nina had appeared to be. What Brioni did have recorded didn't exactly paint Laurence in glory, and made him look about as trustworthy as a hurricane, but she knew it wasn't enough.

Brioni tapped her nails on the tabletop as she thought. She really needed to get photos or video of them being affectionate to back up what she had here. Then a relationship would be hard to refute. He'd mentioned buying Nina jewellery, but that didn't amount to the admission of an affair.

And Nina wasn't the only woman Laurence had bought jewellery for, apparently. Nina *really* hadn't been impressed about his relationship with Kate Spicer. Brioni had almost been able to feel the sparks coming off her. Laurence had a lot of making up to do to if he wanted to keep Nina on side.

Opening a new window, Brioni googled Kate's name. Her suspicions that she'd already heard it once today were confirmed. She was the blonde in the photo Brioni had found when she was looking for a photograph of Nina – the hotel spa manager. It sounded as if he was having a relationship with her, too. When she'd looked at the shot the first time, Brioni had thought they'd looked very friendly.

And these were the women they knew about – how many more had there been? Brioni felt her heart ache for Cressida. Her sister Marissa had found herself in a very difficult relationship and that really hadn't ended well. There was nothing easy about a marriage break-up, whatever the cause.

It sounded as if this deal with SpeakEasy was going to be decided at the next board meeting. It was likely to enhance Ferryman's stock value and Laurence's personal wealth quite considerably, in addition to any payment he'd be receiving for making it happen. Brioni very much doubted he was doing this for free – SpeakEasy had to be offering him a personal incentive for getting the dirt on the people Cressida had said were his friends.

Whatever cash was on offer, half of it was technically Cressida's if it could be tracked down – just like half of Laurence's shares in Ferryman were hers. They'd got married before the company had been launched, at a time when prenups – and divorce – were virtually unheard of in Ireland.

Brioni reached for her now-cold raspberry tea, wondering how Laurence would conceal a big cash payout. He'd mentioned the Cayman Islands and had sounded very familiar with offshore accounts. Brioni was quite sure that the Irish Revenue represented more of a threat to Laurence's wealth than even his wife. Perhaps Cressida would know if he had offshore reserves? Brioni made a mental note to ask her.

If Laurence felt Nina had double-crossed him, and Nina had discovered there was another woman in the picture, this could all get very messy. But while emotions were running high, it was also the ideal time to gather incriminating evidence.

Tomorrow evening in the Kai Lung cocktail bar at the Reynolds would be perfect timing; it might give Cressida everything she needed.

The Reynolds Regency House was one of Brioni's favourite haunts, ideally located on the south side of the city with a huge underground car park and several bars. She regularly met her old school friend Alex there, often as his emergency text support when he needed rescuing from a clingy date. The Kai Lung cocktail bar was gloriously opulent, like the rest of the Georgian building, a complete contrast to the architect-designed 1796 in Grand Canal Dock. Whenever she walked into the Reynolds, she marvelled at how magnificent the original town house must have been, with its high ceilings and sweeping staircase. There was something very elegant about it – with all the marble and gilt, grand period fireplaces and massive chandeliers. And the cocktail bar itself looked like an intimate private club, decorated in an oriental style typical of the period. The choice of bars was the main reason why Alex had all his dates there – that and the fact that the staff seemed to change almost daily and never remembered him, so there was no danger of an embarrassing situation when he met someone new. She didn't quite know how he'd managed it, but every single girl he'd met on Tinder since he'd joined six months ago had been a total disaster.

Focusing on the problem at hand, Brioni reran Laurence's conversation through her head. What had Laurence meant when he was talking to that American about Nina knowing too much? Brioni felt a darkness unfurling inside her like the petals of a black rose. If Nina was a threat to a deal this big, would they try and frighten her to keep her quiet? Brioni wasn't sure, but she hadn't liked Laurence's tone one little bit.

Suddenly this all felt as if it was moving very quickly. And Brioni was going to make sure she was there to see what happened next.

Chapter 13

K ATE SPICER YAWNED and looked into the empty coffee cup sitting beside her on her desk. She'd been trying to concentrate on paying invoices, but despite two cups of espresso, she was finding it hard to concentrate. If she had another cup now, she could end up wired but still shattered, which wouldn't help anyone. She yawned again, stretching, pushing the strands of hair that had strayed loose off her face. She'd pinned up her hair to keep it out of the way, and undid the clip now, shaking it out before rolling it around itself and clipping it up again. It felt better, but it was as if the first yawn had set off a series that she couldn't control. Kate rubbed her face with both hands, trying to smooth away the cloud of fatigue that hung around her. She needed to pull herself together.

Laurence had called at 2 a.m. to ask her if he could get a massage at six. She'd been in a deep sleep, his ringtone reaching her in the depths of a dream. He'd hung up when it had gone to voicemail and then tried again a second later. Pushing aside the cream satin duvet, much to Mitzi's disgust, she'd thought for a moment something terrible must have happened, that there had been an accident or something. Groggy, she'd reached for the phone, charging beside her. She always kept it next to her bed in case he texted. He rarely did, but she wanted to make sure she was there if he did.

Often when he dropped in, she just let him talk, making sure that he had his favourite whiskey to hand, some smoky jazz on the stereo. She didn't have children to worry about, only Mitzi, who was easy enough to please as long as she got her walk every evening and the gourmet treats Kate ordered from London. She made sure Laurence had everything he needed to make a visit to her apartment the oasis in his day. So when the sound of the phone had reached into the deepest recesses of her sleep, she'd been ready to answer it, even if she hadn't been fully awake.

He'd been brief – he had a heavy schedule the next day apparently and he wanted to start it properly. She could tell he was stressed – he wasn't really asking, more telling her that's what he needed, without any question that she might have an issue with starting her day so early.

And he'd been insistent on coming to the treatment rooms rather than calling over to her apartment. He wanted an essential oils massage to get him alert and focused and ready for the day. He didn't have the time or the headspace for coffee or conversation.

She'd tossed and turned, trying to get back to sleep, eventually dozing off around 3.30, but she'd had to be up at five o'clock to get ready and get over to the hotel.

Kate yawned again, looking blankly at the invoices on her glass-topped desk. They were spread across the staff roster. She closed her eyes. She loved her job but the admin wasn't her favourite part. Across the two hotels in Dublin and the Godolphin in Cork, she had twenty-six girls and even with a manager in each location, making sure each spa had a full complement of staff every week could be a challenge. The signature of each hotel was completely different, and they attracted different clientele, which meant different treatment menus in each location. Here in the hipster 1796, the guests were younger and extremely high net worth, and had expectations to match.

Kate flexed her hands behind her neck and stretched both her arms towards the ceiling. Disturbed sleep was the worst kind. It was just as well she'd been in early, though – he'd appeared at the door of the spa before six o'clock, his foot tapping as he'd waited for her to open up.

She'd smiled as she'd headed down the copper-walled corridor towards him, her heels echoing on the raw wooden boards in silence that was normally filled with classic sixties hits. The spa had been designed to resemble a submarine, echoing the industrial nautical themes upstairs, inspired by the surrounding docklands. It felt a little surreal being here this early, and more surreal with him here – she usually looked after him at home, the portable massage table she'd bought when she was training still coming in useful to treat friends.

He'd obviously not had much sleep either – she could tell from the creases in his face – but he was wearing a new cornflower-blue shirt and hand-stitched navy suit that was a perfect fit. He was obviously going to go straight to the office afterwards.

Kate glanced at the time on her phone. It was 8.45 now – the rest of the girls would be here in a minute, to get ready for their clients. The first booking wasn't until eleven o'clock but they had to be available to hotel guests and the 1796 was full. The whole trade had taken an absolute beating last year, with see-saw lockdowns, and everyone was doing their bit to make sure turnover was maximised while they had the opportunity. All her girls had been furloughed but they'd stayed loyal, returning part-time to the landmark hotel as lockdown restrictions had eased. It was a nightmare Kate never wanted to repeat. She rolled back her chair and glanced at the time. She'd thought about going home when Laurence left at seven o'clock, but he'd been so keyed up that it had affected her, and she knew she'd never be able to get to sleep again. Plus, she had her weekly Thursday staff meeting at ten this morning, and there seemed little point in traipsing backwards and forwards. Mitzi would think she was coming home for the day, and Kate knew she'd cry non-stop when she left.

Part of her was a tiny bit annoyed that Laurence felt that it was completely fine to wake her up in the middle of the night and expect her to go in to work at such an early hour, but when he'd arrived, he'd been so distracted, the muscles in his back and neck knotted so tightly, it had taken her ages to loosen them. She'd infused the room with spearmint and sweet orange and used a peppermint scrub and massage oil, the candles she'd lit reflecting off the dimpled steel-clad walls adding to the relaxing, subterranean feel. And he'd definitely left in a better mood than when he arrived, kissing her quickly as he slipped out of the spa, the cleaner arriving just as he left.

He'd said he had meetings all day today, was talking to SpeakEasy again, apparently. She could imagine those negotiation would be delicate.

Kate's thoughts were interrupted by the sound of voices outside – her girls had arrived to start the day, their bubbly laughter immediately lifting her mood. She heard the staffroom door bang – they'd be a few minutes putting away their bags and making sure their make-up was perfect. She pushed her chair away from the desk and went out to reception. Alvera was already behind the glass and chrome desk, crouching down to turn on the music, the sounds of whales and water filling the air. She looked up as Kate appeared, giving her a broad grin.

'You're in early.'

Kate rolled her eyes. 'I had paperwork to catch up on. I thought I'd get loads done but I'm starting to regret it now. You'll have to keep an eye on me later and make sure I don't drift off.'

Alvera laughed, lowering her voice conspiratorially. 'That's exactly what Sadie said, but she wasn't doing paperwork last night.' She raised her eyebrows meaningfully. 'But look what came for you. The delivery girl caught me just as I was coming in.' Alvera reached into an alcove under the desk and picked up a huge bright pink box wrapped with black grosgrain ribbon. 'It looks verrry expensive.'

Kate laughed; when Alvera rolled her r's, she made everything sound more exotic. Kate picked up the box. It had a gold and white sticker on the corner with the name of an exclusive city centre florist in the middle. With or without the rolling r's, it *was* very expensive. The magenta wrapping and box was as distinctive as No. 42's lavender jewellery boxes.

'I'll just open these in the office. Remind the girls the meeting's at ten.'

Alvera nodded as Kate turned towards her office door, hiding the tears pricking at the corners of her eyes. Perhaps she was feeling so emotional because she was exhausted, or perhaps it was the coffee, but her heart felt as if it was swelling. *Gorgeous Laurence*. She'd expected a text some time this morning, but flowers were a lovely touch. He'd been so preoccupied that she thought he hadn't noticed her tiredness, but he obviously had, and this was his way of saying thank you. At moments like this she let her guard down, and the tenderness she felt for him surged inside her. After all the years, they'd grown so close, and now he filled her waking thoughts – there were days when she didn't hear from him and she felt wretched, and then there were moments like this that made everything worthwhile.

Pushing her office door firmly closed, Kate put the heavy box on the desk and pulled off the ribbon. He probably hadn't included a card, but just in case he might have sent a message, she wanted to open it before anyone else saw it. Carefully unwrapping the cleverly folded paper, Kate pulled it back. Inside, the pillar-shaped box was the same colour as the wrapping, edged in black and gold. The lid was deep, sealed with gold discs halfway down each side. Pulling out a pair of scissors from her pen pot, Kate scored the discs and gently shook the lid free, marvelling at the arrangement as the scent hit her. As she'd expected, the interior was jet black, showing off a stunning hand-tied bunch of exotic blooms, bright orange parrot flowers and orchids, several cream lilies nestled between. Leaning in, she inhaled deeply. The fragrance was heavenly.

Kate felt her head buzzing as the room began to swim. Disorientated, she could feel a tightening in her throat, nausea rising as her whole body felt heavy, lethargic, as if she was wrapped in a heavy black cloak. Turning away from the flowers, she stumbled, trying to reach for the edge of the desk. Everything seemed to slow down and she was suddenly crashing to the painted concrete floor, cracking her head on the corner of the desk on the way down. Blood trickled down the side of her face as her eyes closed.

Chapter 14

A s CRESSIDA WAITED for the gates to open so that she could pull into her drive, she was relieved to see that Emily-Jane's car had gone. She checked the time on her dash. It was just after nine, so at least her daughter would be on time for school this morning. It was only a five-minute drive, and she insisted on taking the Mini, but she wasn't a morning person. Although Cressida had set Alexa to start playing Emily-Jane's current favourite tracks at the same time as her curtains opened, giving her plenty of time to wake up, she'd half-expected to get home from the gym to find her still in bed. She'd still been up listening to music when they'd got home from the restaurant last night, not at all impressed when Cressida had reminded her about getting up for school.

Laurence had woken up at some ungodly hour this morning. After sailing into the restaurant late and being thoroughly curt all evening, he'd gone straight to his study last night and hadn't come to bed until about three. Cressida reckoned he'd had about two and a half hours' sleep.

Normally she might have had some sympathy with his business issues, his tension, but not now. As he'd got up, she'd been lying with her back to him. She'd kept her eyes closed, pretending to be asleep.

She'd turned over as she'd heard him pad downstairs, praying his agitation wasn't caused by her recent activities. Part of her was terrified he'd somehow found out that Brioni had hacked into his computer. But, as Cressida had rationalised with herself, she knew him well enough: if he'd got wind that she knew anything about Nina, he would have been a lot more focused on her than he had been last night. He would have been questioning her – he could be very subtle, niggling around the edges – to see if he could find out what she knew. And he would *never* have been late for dinner.

On the occasions when she'd been suspicious before, she'd only had to ask a few leading questions, and his behaviour had changed pretty dramatically. Once he'd even suggested a week in Italy, which Cressida was sure would have pleased whoever he was seeing, assuming that was the case, particularly as they'd ended up buying a villa close to the hotel they were staying in.

Sinéad, his sister-in-law, had invited them to stay with her, but Cressida had always found it uncomfortable. Whenever they met it was almost as if his brother Pierce was still in the room, a ghostly presence bringing with it unspoken tension. For Cressida at least. The villa had been the perfect solution to their visits. They both loved Italy; Sinéad had never wanted children but doted on Emily-Jane, just as Pierce had – but there were only so many times you could refuse someone's hospitality.

That trip, Cressida had made sure she'd put lots of pictures on Facebook for the benefit of anyone who might be following Laurence's activity.

Pulling up on the gravel outside the house, Cressida grabbed her gym bag and the *Irish Independent* off the passenger seat and slammed the door behind her, heading into the house. She'd had a great workout, and then had decided she should treat herself to a swim and a sauna. For the first time since she'd heard Nina's voice she was starting to feel more relaxed, less keyed up, more like she was in control of her life. *Perhaps that should be 'back' in control.*

Now it was definitely time for coffee.

Whatever had been wrong with Laurence last night, she was pretty sure it had to be something happening at work – something big. He'd been preoccupied for ages – ever since, in fact, Cressida had read out that article in the *Irish Times* about the squabble over the granting of mobile phone licences. There'd been war over some American company that had been refused a licence in the UK wanting to get into the Irish market instead. She'd guessed the geographical proximity of Ireland to the UK had to be a factor, and no doubt Ireland's position in the EU would be a bonus.

Cressida couldn't remember the details, but the drama in the UK stank of patrimony and brown envelopes stuffed with cash. What she could remember was Laurence's reaction to it, which had been both unexpected and explosive enough to mark itself in her mind. He'd definitely become more tense around then. Which apparently had also, according to Brioni, coincided with this Nina creature starting work for Ferryman. When SpeakEasy had come up in conversation over dinner a few days later – Emily-Jane had been thinking about changing her mobile operator – he'd been so utterly dismissive of his daughter's concerns about data mining and privacy they'd barely spoken for weeks afterwards.

Leaving her gym bag at the bottom of the stairs, Cressida was hit with the scent of beeswax polish as she crossed the airy hallway with its mezzanine and glazed roof. Even at this time of year, it was filled with soft light, and the kitchen was the same, with its huge open-plan sunroom and views over the sea. It was beautiful today, the water reflecting an azure blue October sky so clear that it made her feel as if she was in the Med. But it was a lot colder than Italy, and she didn't doubt that the sea was freezing, the white-topped waves darkening as the water got deeper in the channel between the end of the garden and Dalkey Island.

Throwing the newspaper onto the marble-topped counter, Cressida put a capsule into Laurence's state-of-the-art coffee machine – the only thing, apart from the ridiculously oversized TV, that she'd let him decide on when they'd designed this room. She'd chosen the stone herself, a creamy grey that matched the off-white cabinets and cream walls, and reflected even more light into the room. The huge scrubbed pine table, sofas and central island made it feel homey and comfortable, and despite all the white, it was cosy in here even on the greyest day.

Slipping a mug under the spout, Cressida put her hand on the back of her neck and rotated her head.

Her workout really had done her the world of good. And she did her best thinking in the gym. She cleared her head there, giving her the space to focus on one problem at a time, to look for solutions.

And she was all about solutions right now.

She glanced at the clock on the oven. Brioni had texted last night to say she'd call this morning to give her an update. With a bit of luck, she might have more of an idea of what was going on with this Nina woman. Not that Cressida needed a diagram to work that one out.

Cressida bit her lip, waiting for her coffee mug to fill. Part of her was desperate to know what Brioni had found out, and part of her was terrified that everything she suspected was true.

There was still a tiny part of her hoping that they'd got it all wrong, and that the Nina she'd heard Laurence with wasn't Nina Rodríguez, the Angelina lookalike computer wizard, at all, but maybe someone else entirely.

Would that make his betrayal easier to bear? Cressida didn't even know any more.

The coffee machine gurled and filled the room with a delicious aroma, bringing Cressida back to it. She pressed another button and watched as her mug filled with frothy milk.

Realistically she'd gone beyond being hurt. Hearing him say Nina's name had been a literal 'game-changer', as Emily-Jane would have put it. Cressida felt as if she had suddenly shifted gear.

Laurence had always been married to his job and prioritised his business over her and Emily-Jane. They got what was left of his time – if they were lucky. And she'd accepted that, and thought she was being unreasonable in looking for more. But now it seemed she hadn't just been sharing him with Ferryman, but with his staff, too, and she was mad as hell.

He'd been the one who'd pursued her at the start, when they'd first got together, and it had been wonderful for a few years, but there was no question now that they'd grown apart. People changed as they got older, developed new interests, and while she'd kept up with all of his, supporting him through each challenge, he'd left her to build her career and then the clinic, barely asking her how it was going. There were times when she wondered if he even knew who her business partners were.

His indifference and lack of interest implied that what she was doing wasn't important, that he thought it didn't matter. It might never bring in the millions that Ferryman did, but it was part of her and it *was* important, to Cressida *and* to the clients they saw.

What she did made a difference to people's lives, a real difference.

She couldn't say the same of Ferryman. Putting small traders out of business and encouraging debt with 'easy' payment terms had never been elements she'd been happy with.

And now she'd found out about these women, it really was the last straw, the icing on the cake … every cliché she could think of that described the mid-life crisis of a successful middle-aged businessman. He'd bought the sports car and now he had a bit on the side, too.

But she wasn't a cliché. She'd worked all her life for what she wanted; she'd made sacrifices for Laurence and his dream. Her mind ran to all the nights she'd sat up on her own when Emily-Jane was little, waiting for him to come home; to the days when she'd taken Emily-Jane to the zoo on her own, or met with friends to go to the beach. He'd never been there. He splashed out on fancy holidays all right, but he'd never really been present in their lives.

Well, all of that ended now.

But before the situation got any worse, she needed to make sure her position was totally secure financially. There was no way she was losing this house, or the villa in Sorrento. She needed as much proof as possible of Laurence's dalliance – she didn't even want to think of this Nina as 'the other woman' – and then she'd make absolutely sure that she got what she was due.

Chapter 15

'KEEP YOUR PHONE under the table or Dorky will see it.'

Emily-Jane opened her eyes wide and gestured wildly to her friend Chloe, who was sitting opposite her in the school canteen. Chloe hid it as Ms Dorking, the PE teacher, walked between the long refectory tables and went up to join the queue for her mid-morning coffee.

Chloe rolled her eyes, outlined as always in heavy black winged liner, and swooshed her glossy brown hair over her shoulder.

'Pass it under the table quickly so we can see.'

Beside Emily-Jane, Georgia leaned forward, keeping her voice to a loud whisper. She wrinkled her nose, her many freckles crinkling. Today she had her long curly red hair in a high ponytail, the wild ends tucked into the back of her navy V-necked school jumper. Her hair was almost down to her waist, and tying it up was the only way to keep it under control. Emily-Jane loved it, as much as Georgia coveted her railroad-straight baby blond hair.

'Quick, she's looking the other way. Let me see.'

Chloe passed the phone to Emily-Jane under the table and, keeping it down low between them, kept watch while they inspected Chloe's latest Tinder match.

'He's gorge, Clo, but that looks like a studio shot, do you think he's actually real?'

'It says he's in UCD, second year economics. I'm going to get my brother to check.'

'Without telling him why, I hope.' Georgia opened her eyes wide.

'Duh – of course.'

Emily-Jane shook her head. 'It's so easy to be anyone online. I mean, you can literally put up any photo and call yourself anything. You need to be careful.'

'You mean like a catfish? But you have to be really stupid to fall for them. I mean, a bit of checking and you'd know really fast.'

Georgia started to peel the orange on her plate and glanced across at Chloe's chocolate cake.

'You'd think so. Most people are total dopes, granted, but the good ones set up other profiles to reinforce the main one. So a quick check makes it look like they're the real deal. I mean, some people don't even know about reverse image searching – it takes seconds to find out if they've used a fake profile picture.'

Emily-Jane frowned as she spoke.

If Tiffany, the American girl she'd met online, had had half an ounce of common sense, she'd never have got herself into the mess she was in now.

She still found it amazing how you could become such good friends with someone you'd never met in person. She hadn't expected that, even though Chloe and Georgia had whole networks of friends they'd met through Tumblr, chatting endlessly after lights out.

Tiffany had been in New York when they'd first connected, had swallowed a story about a 'model scout' – Emily-Jane mentally did the rabbit ears thing with her fingers whenever she thought about it – finding her photos online. Beautiful, silly, naive Tiffany. She'd told Emily-Jane how she'd gone, on her own, against her strict parents' permission, over five hundred miles from Fayetteville, North Carolina, to New York City – for a 'casting'. When they'd first started chatting, Tiff was living the dream, bowled over by the glamour and the parties, until it dawned on her that all the other girls were around sixteen, too – some even younger – and that none of the fashion photos that were supposedly taken at the shoots they were sent to ever landed in the press. And that *maybe* the attention they were getting from the men at the agency parties – much older well-known businessmen – wasn't about furthering their careers at all, but was all about sex. The women minding them had created the illusion that this was the way the business worked, that this was the way sophisticated city girls – top models – got their breaks. And then one night, something horrible had happened that Emily-Jane didn't even want to think about, and Tiffany's bubble had burst.

Ever since, Emily-Jane had wondered if their meeting up had been some sort of serendipity. She'd been checking out something her dad had said, and had stumbled across a seemingly innocuous snap of a party online, and it had started her thinking. Particularly about the age of the stunning blonde girl standing between the two older men in the photo. One of whom she recognised.

Tiffany was safe now, but still refused to tell anyone except Emily-Jane the truth, and she was too frightened to reveal the address of the houses and apartments where the other girls were 'staying'.

The whole thing had added to Emily-Jane's resolve.

'Have you tried that, Clo? Reverse image search this dude and see if he's appeared anywhere else?' Munching on an orange segment, talking with her mouth full, Georgia interrupted Emily-Jane's thoughts. 'I bet he's a Calvin Klein model and someone's photoshopped him into Dublin.'

'Well, they must be damn good at photoshopping, that's all I can say.' Chloe rolled her eyes again. 'I'll do it after lunch. I never thought of that. Let's see if this honey is who he says he is.'

Her mind still troubled, Emily-Jane reached out to steal a chocolate chip from Chloe's plate. Their mid-morning break was only fifteen minutes, but Chloe always managed to get through enough cake to feed about three people.

'Did he swipe right on you?'

Waving Emily's hand away, Chloe grinned cheekily.

'He certainly did.'

'But which picture did you use? Does he know you're only seventeen? He must be almost twenty if he's in UCD.' Emily-Jane glanced over to the lunch queue as she spoke, keeping an eye on Miss Dorking's progress.

Chloe cut off a chunk of cake with her fork and popped it in her mouth.

'I might have adjusted the information a teeny bit.'

Emily-Jane frowned. 'Clo, I keep telling you, you're playing with fire, please don't do anything silly.'

Chloe scowled at her across the table. 'You care too much, Em-J, it's been your problem since forever. Really just try to stop worrying about everyone else and look at yourself for a change. What about you and Mr fucking Chocolate Factory?'

Emily-Jane sighed and focused on picking a piece of lint off the sleeve of her sweater.

'That's different. You know it is. I'm on a mission.'

'And I'm not? Doesn't sound much different to me.' Chloe looked at her archly, but before Emily-Jane could reply, Chloe's face changed.

'Oh crap, here's Dorky. Slip the phone into my bag, Georgi, it's under the bench. If she sees it she'll confiscate it.'

'Again,' Georgia chimed in from across the table.

Ms Dorking passed them, her full concentration on the tray she was carrying, a cup of tea balancing precariously in one corner.

'All clear.' Chloe's eyes glowed with mischief. 'I'm going to message him later. Will you two come into town with me on Saturday? If I meet him by the Stephen's Green Centre we'll be able to see if he's the real thing from miles away.'

Emily-Jane rolled her eyes, laughing at her friend.

'He's probably about five two, you know. There has to be some hitch here or why would he be on Tinder?'

Chloe pursed her lips, obviously annoyed.

'Maybe he just wants to have a bit of fun, like I do? Why else do people hook up on the internet? Duh.'

Chapter 16

WAITING FOR THE phone to ring, Cressida was finding it very hard to concentrate. She'd spent the few hours since she'd returned from the gym organising her diary with the office manager and checking patient notes. She thankfully didn't have many appointments this week, and had moved them all up or reallocated them to other staff so she could have a few days clear. Without too much jiggling she could free up the next week, too. Which might not be a bad idea. There was no way she could give her clients her all at the moment; it was better to go back when she could focus fully.

Getting up to make herself another coffee, Cressida glanced at the clock for the hundredth time, then turned to the kitchen island and pulled out her stool, flipping open the paper to scan the headlines. But her mind wouldn't stay still; she really wasn't seeing anything, her nerves were as taut as piano strings.

Last night, as Cressida had sat at home waiting for Laurence, eventually texting him to say she'd meet him in the restaurant, she'd been terrified that if he was still in the office, delayed by some call or something, he'd see Brioni trying to get into his computer.

If he *was* still in the office, he was bound to be at his desk.

Cressida closed her eyes, thinking about it. She'd felt physically sick as the waiter had shown her to their table in the restaurant, had been convinced Laurence was late because he'd found out everything, that he knew that she knew, that he would be fuming by the time he arrived.

And then he'd stalked in, so obviously in a temper that she'd almost died inside.

Thank *God* she hadn't said anything.

He'd knocked back a glass of red wine and muttered something about not being able to trust his staff. She'd only half-heard him, had been sure he was starting to say he couldn't trust her, but then she'd realised he was talking about something else completely.

Even sitting in her kitchen now, she felt her stomach flip at the memory.

He'd ranted under his breath about deals being endangered and how hard he'd worked to build Ferryman and how it had been his idea and how his partners were basically the three stooges and wouldn't be anything without him. She'd hardly been able to hear him over the Gypsy Kings, or whatever the music was that was playing. They'd been at their usual table right at the back of the dining room upstairs, just a few young couples at the other tables. He preferred it up there, was always conscious of people overhearing their conversation. Dalkey was so tiny that everyone knew everyone else. He'd stopped talking whenever the waiter had approached, but she hadn't needed to do more than occasionally nod and say 'I know, that's terrible' every now and again all evening. Which had been something of a relief.

Whatever it was that was bothering him was obviously big, and had kept him awake half the night. She hadn't seen him like this since the start of the Covid lockdown. He'd been up all night then, his accountants and business partners on conference calls that had gone on for what felt like months.

They'd weathered it, pivoting where they could. The hotels had started selling takeaway food, and Ferryman's traffic had exploded. Fast thinking had taken them through the worst of it and brought them out the other side with new lines and an expanded marketplace.

And it had kept Laurence busy.

Thank God they had a big house – months of being stuck inside together had tested them all, especially in the winter.

Watching him across the table last night, Cressida had been sure that whatever was going on now was as big as that. Laurence only got this agitated when there was money involved. And *if* there was money involved, that meant whatever it was concerned her, too.

Only half concentrating, Cressida took a sip of her coffee and suddenly realised that the doorbell had rung. Her head was so full, she'd barely heard it. She frowned. She wasn't expecting anyone. And she hadn't heard the gate buzzer. Perhaps the gates hadn't closed after her when she came in?

Anything was possible with the amount going on inside her head right now. She'd need to get them looked at, if that was the case. Laurence's supposed state-of-the-art smart-house system had been doing strange things recently, with curtains opening unexpectedly and the fridge telling her shopping list, ridiculously, last night, that they needed guavas. She didn't even know where you'd start looking for those in Ireland.

Putting her coffee down, Cressida swung off the stool and went out of the kitchen to the solid oak front door. Looking through the spyhole, she could see that the gates were firmly closed. So how had the doorbell rung? Another glitch?

Puzzled she put the chain on and eased open the front door. There was no one there. Weird. About to close the door, Cressida glanced down and saw a huge pink box on the doorstep, luxurious black grosgrain ribbon and a gold sticker telling her exactly which florist it was from.

Knocking off the latch, she bent down to pick it up. Was this supposed to be some sort of apology from Laurence? For what? Being late and foul-tempered last night, or waking her up this morning? Cressida wasn't sure. She picked up the box and carried it into the kitchen, slipping it on to the island. One thing she *was* sure about was that he was going to have to try a bit harder, if this was his idea of an apology.

Looking at the box, she rapped her nails on the island's marble top.

It was *literally* years since Laurence had sent her flowers. Perhaps he deserved some marks for trying, but really, using a florist that was part of your own company wasn't very impressive, was it? Cressida's temper flared inside her as she shook her head slowly. After the events of the last few days, flowers were more of an insult than a peace offering. They could stay in the box until he came home. Anger began to curl around her thoughts, licking and spitting like hungry flames, but before she could dwell more on the delivery, Cressida heard her phone ring. She glanced over and saw Brioni's name on the screen.

At last. Now this was a call she really wanted to take.

Chapter 17

As Brioni ended her call to Cressida, she could still feel her pain, white hot, through the virtual phone line. Brioni ran her hands over her face. The silence at the other end, as Cressida had taken it all in, had been the worst. Brioni had had to be frank with her. She knew she was on the right path, and Cressida had asked her to find out the truth, no matter how unsavoury that might be. And it was pretty bad.

This morning as Brioni had opened her curtains, the sky had rewarded her with the most incredible cerulean blue. If it hadn't been so cold, it could have been summer, fluffy white clouds scudding across the horizon, the sea calm and Ballycastle beach washed clean. It was moments like that which restored her soul. And she'd needed the boost. She'd been tossing and turning all night, rerunning everything she'd heard in her head, mentally replaying the conversation she'd recorded between Laurence and Nina. Dreading the conversation she'd just had.

Last night, as soon as Brioni was sure Laurence had left the office, she'd gone through his emails and files. She'd started with his trash – if he was careful he would be deleting sensitive emails as he went, but like many people, it hadn't occurred to him to delete the contents of his trash bucket.

It was always the most interesting place to start.

There had been several messages to and from Nina, although from their tone and content it was quite clear that Laurence was being very careful what he said. There were also several from dirk.ackroyd@speakeasy.com – most of them related to arranging virtual meetings, which was very interesting in itself. The pattern and frequency of engagement suggested that they were discussing something that needed a lot of negotiation. Sitting at the table in the living room, her eyes trained on the screen, it had only taken her a moment to google Dirk Ackroyd. There was a slew of search results, masses of recent press surrounding the UK refusing to grant SpeakEasy a licence, more on privacy issues, and several focusing on his relationship with various British government ministers. It was very clear the British press didn't like the idea of American companies gathering data, particularly as SpeakEasy appeared to be regulated by some very loose and spurious laws in its home state of Texas.

It had been getting later and later, but Brioni didn't know how many opportunities she'd get to delve into Laurence's email so she wanted to be thorough. Scrolling down through the deleted folder, she could see that there were also several emails from Kate Spicer, the spa manager – one from an account at the 1796 hotel and the rest from her Gmail.

But Kate wasn't nearly so careful. There was nothing overtly sexual, but it was very clear that they were good friends and that Laurence called around to her apartment regularly. Confirming what Nina had implied last night, it was looking a lot as if she wasn't the only woman that Laurence had on the go.

Brioni had printed off everything as she went so that she didn't leave a digital trail, and had gone on to look through his most recently opened files, finding herself trawling through accounts statements at 2 a.m., at which point she'd decided it was time for bed.

One thing was absolutely certain – there would not only be a lot of cash, but also considerable assets on the table when Cressida's lawyers got started. Brioni knew this wasn't just about money, or divorce, any more – Cressida was hurting and wanted to get even with him. Dragging his reputation through the mud might not be very dignified, but it would give her a lot of satisfaction.

'*I can't believe he'd do that. Not just with her, but to his friends?*' Cressida's voice reverberated through Brioni's mind; it had cracked a little as she'd spoken, the strain evident, even on the phone. Brioni could imagine her face. '*We're going to need photographs of him with this Nina woman, aren't we?*'

She was right. Brioni was quite sure Laurence would try and talk his way out of the emails, claim they'd been faked, or that these women were obsessed with him and it was all one-way. He was, as she'd quickly established from her brief insight into his online activity, as slick as oil on water.

It hadn't taken Brioni long to outline her plan to Cressida. If she could go to the Reynolds Regency House at the same time as Laurence and Nina, she might get exactly what Cressida needed. And at this stage Brioni wanted Laurence Howard to get what he was due almost as badly as Cressida did. It was his arrogance that truly irked her – the fact that somehow, in his head, it was perfectly acceptable to behave like this, to break every moral code in the book.

It was after lunch by the time Brioni had finished researching the key players she'd found in Laurence's inbox, and was ready to head to Dublin, her file growing as she compiled page after page. To build a case, Cressida's lawyers would need names and dates of possible transgressions. And she needed profile pictures of Laurence's team so she'd know who he spoke to if he bumped into anyone at the hotel.

She'd had a good think about how she could blend into the background in the cocktail bar at the Reynolds Regency House, but no amount of preparation would stop the nerves dancing in her stomach.

Despite it being the middle of the day, it was a Thursday and the main Dublin road was busy as she drove into the city. Her plan was to buy a wig and pop to her apartment for a change of clothes, so that she could get to the Reynolds early.

She'd passed the wig shop a thousand times driving between the house in Wexford and her apartment in the city centre. It was on a section of the road where the traffic always slowed, and she didn't know how many times she'd looked in the window.

As she approached it, she realised there was a parking space right outside. Serendipity indeed – although her mud-splattered Citroën looked pretty terrible next to the sleek, regularly washed sports cars and BMWs. She hadn't realised how mucky it had got on the lane down to the house – she'd have to get it washed when she got a minute. But that was the least of her problems right now.

The door to the shop had one of those old-fashioned bells over it that tinkled as she pushed it open, summoning a girl of around her own age from the rear of the shop. Brioni wasn't too sure if she was wearing a wig, but her hair was down to her waist, a natural-looking blond.

As it turned out, the shop made bespoke wigs, but explaining that she had a vital meeting and her boss had made it very clear that pink hair shaved up both sides wasn't an option, the girl had found her a dark real-hair wig cut in a sharp bob that they'd used for display, and another one to try in platinum blonde. It had only taken Brioni a moment to decide that they would both be perfect. The assistant had put the dark one on for her, showing her how to hide her own hair and making sure that it was secure.

'That's fabulous. It really suits you. What's your natural colouring?'

The girl had stepped aside to let Brioni look in the full-length mirror opposite the reception desk. The sleek style was slightly at odds with her skinny jeans, leather jacket and nose stud, but it showed off her high cheekbones.

Brioni had laughed. 'A sort of dirty mouse?'

'I love your pink, but this definitely looks much more corporate.'

Brioni had looked at the girl over her shoulder in the mirror.

'It certainly does. I'll nip home and get changed and *nobody* will recognise me.'

Taking another look at herself in the mirror, Brioni had taken a quick selfie and sent it to Cressida and then Marissa, smiling to herself. This disguise wasn't so much about Laurence not knowing who she was – they had no connection at all – but she needed to blend in, just in case she had to follow him again. If she kept popping up, he'd have to be a right dope not to notice her with her normal look.

And changing her hair made a huge difference. Heading to her apartment close to Grand Canal Dock, her mind occupied with the next part of her plan, Brioni almost gave herself a fright getting into the lift, forgetting for a moment that the dark-haired person in the mirror was her.

She'd only been gone a few days but as she swung open her front door, the mat was deep with mail, her *New Scientist* magazine and a pile of circulars almost stopping the door from opening. The place felt strangely empty without music on and the coffee machine bubbling away, both issues she rectified as soon as she walked into the galley kitchen.

She loved this apartment – there was no way she could afford to buy in the city centre and finding anywhere half-decent was a major challenge, but she'd been blessed that she'd arrived home from London mid-Covid last year, when people were leaving the city in droves and the prospect of being locked down again in a high-rise clearly didn't appeal to many. The auctioneer had been half-afraid to show her the apartment in the recently completed complex, had arranged for her to collect the key from the concierge and take a look around herself. As she'd opened the living room door, the sun had been streaming through the floor-to-ceiling windows and she'd been smitten. There wouldn't be many days with the Irish weather that she'd be able to use the balcony, but she loved the way it wrapped itself around the corner of the building to the bedroom. The living space was tiny but exactly what she needed; it was only a ten-minute walk from work and fully furnished. *And* the Wi-Fi was insanely fast.

In her bedroom, Brioni opened her mirrored wardrobe and dug around until she found the little black dress Marissa had bought her in the sales. High-necked and fitted, it had demure capped sleeves and stopped just on her knee. It was, as Marissa had insisted, the perfect interview dress. Hauling out the hanger and throwing it onto her wonderful super-king bed, Brioni started to search the bottom of the wardrobe. She might live in her DMs but she loved shoes, and kept them all neatly stacked in their original boxes. She had a pair of black patent heels that she had picked up on clearance in Macy's that would be perfect. Her bag was more of a problem, but after a bit more rooting she found a neat fake black satin Prada rucksack she'd bought in Chinatown on her last trip to New York.

She was going to blend in so well she'd be invisible.

Chapter 18

'DORA, HOW ARE you?'

The phone to her ear, Cressida walked across the kitchen and leaned against the table so she could look out of the French windows. The blue skies of the morning had gone and the wind had come up, the waves white-tipped. She glanced at the barometer-clock on the pillar between the concertina windows. The tide was turning.

'I'm grand, Cressida. But if you're looking for Mr Howard, I'm afraid he's in meetings all afternoon.'

Dora's Belfast accent was still thick despite all the years she'd spent in Dublin. She was almost sixty now, looked after Laurence like his mother, and was, as he said himself, the perfect guard dog outside his office. She'd worked for his father before him, and as the Howard Group had grown, she'd taken on more responsibility, could almost run it better than Laurence at this stage. Cressida smiled to herself at her use of 'Mr' Howard. That's what Dora had called his father. She managed to say it in a way that indicated whoever she was talking to should have due respect for her boss.

'No, it's you I was looking for. I hope he isn't working you too hard. I know he's a devil for long hours.'

'He is, but he always makes me leave at five. He's a pet really. He always says there's nothing happens after five o'clock that can't be dealt with in the morning. In this business you could be going all night. But then the hotels are working 24–7, as they say.'

'But the staff have rosters so they only put in their eight hours. We both know how often you work through your lunch.' Cressida smiled, knowing it would come through in her voice. 'You run that place, Dora, I don't know what he'd do without you.'

She could tell from Dora's tone that her flattery had landed.

'Not at all. I just do my bit. Mr Howard's the worst for the long hours. He's always telling everyone else to delegate but he's here so late sometimes.'

'I know, and you know better than anyone what he's like. He's lucky he's got you.'

Cressida let Dora run on for a few minutes, making appropriate noises as the older woman ruffled her own feathers and preened a little, then chuckled as she confided an incident with some American guest at the 1796. Eventually she realised Cressida hadn't just rung for a chat.

'So how can I help you?'

'Well, I wanted your advice really, talking about long hours and dedication. Laurence has mentioned a few of his staff have really been pulling it out of the hat recently.' She paused, knowing using one of Laurence's favourite phrases would further butter Dora up. His stock phrases, most of them echoing his father, drove her mad, but she'd seen the dreamy look Dora got when he repeated them, as if he'd learned his lines well and needed a pat on the head. 'I was thinking it might be nice for him to show his appreciation – something small, you know. I know it's not usually done, but there are two in particular who seem to crop up in conversation a lot and I always think showing your employees your appreciation makes such a difference, don't you?'

'Well, I'm not sure, it wouldn't be something we'd normally do. What is Mr Howard thinking? I'm surprised he didn't say anything this morning.'

'Oh, he's not thinking about it yet. It's an idea of mine, but I wanted to test the waters, so to speak, with you first. You know the place so well. And then if you thought it was a good idea, I can see what he thinks.'

'Oh. Oh, I see.'

It was very clear from her tone that she didn't. Which was hardly surprising really, given that Cressida was making this up as she went along. Sitting on the edge of the kitchen table, Cressida laid it on a bit thicker.

'Obviously, if you think it's a terrible idea, then we don't even need to mention it to Laurence. That's why I wanted to run it past you. You know the staff better than I do and sometimes singling people out can be counter-productive.'

'Who are we talking about?'

'Well …' Cressida lowered her voice conspiratorially. 'There's a girl called Nina Rodríguez who has been so helpful. I know she's been working late compiling some sort of data for him … Do you know her?'

Cressida could almost hear Dora thinking.

'I do, she's up here a lot actually. I have to say I did wonder what she was working on.'

'She's Spanish, isn't she?'

Cressida could hear tapping from the other end as Dora's nails ran across her keyboard, looking her up.

'No, Colombian, she's only been with Ferryman about six

months. Her visa is almost up, actually, I'd better look into that. She's got a master's in data science, works for Ferryman on the business side. She's in what I always call the numbers part of the company, rather than the people side. They can be a bit strange in that department. She's very attractive, though.' It was as if Dora had forgotten that she was speaking to Cressida and had drifted off into reading Nina's file. 'Says here she speaks several languages and worked at a string of companies before us. Always in data. She doesn't seem to have stayed very long anywhere but perhaps the roles were project-based.'

'Really? She must be very good at what she does.'

'Funny you should say that, that's exactly what Mr Howard always says about her.'

Cressida gritted her teeth, resisting the urge to fling open the doors in front of her and throw the phone into the sea. She took a deep breath.

'Does she live in town? I was thinking a nice restaurant voucher, or perhaps a voucher for the beauty salon in the 1796 might be appropriate. Laurence wouldn't think of anything like that, being a man, which is why I thought I'd start with you.'

'I'm not sure a beauty voucher would work just now – the spa manager was taken ill earlier today. It was *quite* a drama. The general manager of the 1796 is looking after it, though.'

'Oh goodness, what on earth happened?'

'She collapsed, they found her on the floor of her office at about ten this morning. She was supposed to be running a staff meeting and when one of the girls went into her office to look for her, there she was turning blue on the floor. Of course that caused hysterics, some of those young ones are very silly. But my goodness, we've never had anything like that happen before, not to staff anyway. Guests are always keeling over, but that's because half of them are indulging, shall we say, in practices they aren't used to.'

Cressida would have laughed if she hadn't been so surprised at Dora's salacious tone. Then she realised who Dora was talking about – the blonde they'd seen in the only photo Brioni had been able to find of Nina. She'd been drinking champagne and laughing with Laurence.

'That sounds terrible. And worse, I've forgotten her name, I've only met her once or twice.'

'The spa manager? Kate Spicer. She's been here since Mr Howard took over, but there are a lot of people working for Howard's now, over a thousand across all the hotels and Ferryman, too, you can't remember them all. Mr Howard always speaks very highly of her, he almost gave her a blank chequebook for the spas when we did the last refit. That was right before Covid, of course, they no sooner had the grand opening and the whole place closed down.' She said it as if Kate was somehow personally responsible for the coronavirus and its impact on the company.

'But is she all right now? I mean, collapsing sounds quite serious.'

'The ambulance came and took her off to St. Vincent's, I haven't had an update yet. They brought in some extra staff to cover, so thankfully there was no need to cancel any of the guests' appointments, but really … I do wish staff wouldn't come in if they feel unwell, it creates more problems rather than less, and we all know that's how things spread …'

'Indeed. Well, it sounds as if you've had enough drama for one day. Let's not worry about my idea just yet, no need to mention it to Laurence. I don't like to bother him when he's got a lot on his plate. He seems to be very busy at the moment.'

'He certainly is, I've never known anyone work as hard as him, really, he's incredible.'

Cressida could think of many words to describe Laurence, and incredible certainly wasn't among them. Thanking Dora, she rang off.

So, Nina's employment visa was about to expire. Well, perhaps that was a good thing. And Kate Spicer was in hospital.

Interesting.

She knew she should feel more sympathetic, but if what Nina had said last night, and if what Brioni had found in Laurence's emails was true, and he was 'double dipping', as Emily-Jane's friends so crudely put it, then perhaps it was some sort of karmic rebalance going on.

Cressida tapped the phone on her teeth as she thought. She needed to google visa regulations, but she was pretty sure they were very tight. And if someone could find a reason for it not to be renewed, Nina would have to go right back to Colombia, which, in Cressida's opinion, wasn't nearly far enough.

Chapter 19

B RIONI'S PLAN TO be invisible would have definitely started better if she hadn't walked into the glittering reception hall of the Reynolds Regency House and immediately spotted her school friend Alex lurking beside the internal lifts. She hadn't been *in* school with him exactly; he'd been head of the Model United Nations debating team for the exclusive boys' school, Campbell College, and she'd been head of the team from the not even vaguely exclusive St Mary Immaculate Girls' School.

Back then, even though they'd done their best to destroy each other on the debating floor, he'd remained dignified and shaken hands with her every time his team lost to hers. Which had been rather regularly. It had only been more recently when she'd come to Dublin to work that she'd bumped into him again, right here in the Reynolds in fact, and they'd caught up. He'd just broken up with his long-term girlfriend, and even then his Tinder hook-ups had had her crying with laughter. She'd bet he had a date planned tonight, and part of her kicked herself for not checking. He spent more time in this hotel than she did.

As their eyes met across the marble-floored foyer, a flash of recognition passed between them, and she had all the confirmation she needed that that was exactly what he was doing. He raised his eyebrows and pointed to his head, sending her an OK signal that he liked her wig, and resumed scrolling through his phone as if he didn't know her, looking, as much as you could in a Burberry coat and college scarf, as shifty as hell. She smiled to herself – they'd talked about it a lot, how so many girls were insecure about their boyfriends having close female friends. She wasn't about to cramp his style by going over to chat to him when his date might appear at any moment. If this one turned out to be a keeper, Brioni knew she would meet her in due course.

She just hoped this date worked out OK – she wouldn't be able to rescue him tonight.

Conscious of her heels clicking on the white marble, Brioni swung to her left and into the bar itself. She glanced over her shoulder at Alex as she went inside. He was half concealed by a huge bamboo plant and still looking at his phone.

The bar itself was dimly lit, the red and black chinoiserie styling with its black leather tub chairs and ebonised tables painted with gilt Chinese scenes, like stepping back in time. Elegant wall lamps, glowing soft gold, threw the corners into shadow. Taking a quick look around, Brioni spotted a table on the far side, well away from the entrance, a location that was both dark and had an excellent view of most of the room. She was early. Laurence and Nina wouldn't be here for another half an hour, and she wanted to get settled so that she looked as if she was part of the place. She knew Alex would be heading into the Orangery, the conservatory-style bar that overlooked the hotel's landscaped gardens. Given how she was dressed, he'd assume she was meeting a date, too, so would steer clear, knowing they'd text later.

As she sat down, a waiter materialised beside her with the cocktail menu and Brioni realised she hadn't eaten since her muesli and yoghurt this morning. Ordering a virgin mojito, she pulled her phone out from her backpack, flicking on to widescreen in selfie mode so she could check the light levels. She'd chosen this model for its superb camera and, switching to the main one, settled back with it in her hand, pretending she was scrolling. As she moved it around the room, she was pretty sure she'd be able to pick up a clear shot. If Laurence and Nina sat too far away she'd have to move, but she had a good view of about three quarters of the bar from here.

It was a shame she couldn't see Alex lurking behind the plant – she'd like to see who he was meeting. Tonight he looked nervous, as if he was working very hard to play it cool, so perhaps this date was a bit more special than some of the others. Brioni's mouth twitched; she'd have to get the scoop on his evening later. It was funny how people changed. She was pretty sure he'd hated her in school, given that she was the main obstacle between him and chalking up another success on his CV. She'd always felt his eyes following her across the room from the moment she arrived, not daring to look back and challenge him and make the situation any worse. But then when they'd met again, they'd connected as if they'd been friends forever.

Brioni's mocktail arrived, accompanied by a very welcome bowl of nuts and olives, only seconds before Laurence Howard walked in. One hand in the trouser pocket of his navy suit, he had his phone to his ear, nodding and frowning at the same time. All thoughts of Alex gone, Brioni focused on Laurence fully. Behind him a couple had walked in, making straight for a table opposite Brioni on the other side of the room. Clearly not wanting to sit close to them, Laurence scanned the remaining tables and moved towards Brioni's side of the bar, sitting near to the entrance, about four tables down from her. Hiding behind her phone, she took a still of him and, checking the time on the screen, took a sip of her drink.

Nina was late.

Picking up the tall leather-backed menu with its gold foil logo, Brioni set it in front of herself as an additional barrier and fiddled with her phone. She had a clear view of Laurence's table and with a bit of luck, she might even be able to hear their conversation from here. The ambient music was jazz, very low, barely there in fact. Brioni extracted a Bluetooth microphone from her bag and as Laurence looked away from her towards the entrance, she leaned forward and sent it spinning along the gully where the seat met the high back of the banquette. It was tiny, black, and virtually invisible on the leather. If anyone came to sit there, it would look as if someone had dropped it, but it should be close enough to where he was sitting to pick up his conversation. Which meant she could record it.

Brioni popped her earbuds in, and as she sat up and took another sip of her drink, she heard the tattoo of heels on marble and Nina swept into the bar. She was wearing a heavy wool coat belted at her waist, her hair loose. There was something harried and anxious about her whole demeanour as she hurried towards him.

Laurence stood up as he saw her, pulling out the chair at the table beside him. Brioni clicked her camera on to *record*.

'How was your day?'

He sat down and Brioni smiled to herself; she could hear him perfectly from here via the microphone. As she watched, pretending to read something on her phone, Nina glared at him and, ignoring the proffered chair, leaned forward with both hands on the table.

'I've had better. What have you done? Who is following me?' Her voice was low but sufficiently filled with venom that Brioni caught every word. 'I left my apartment this morning to drop in my dry-cleaning and I swear I could feel someone watching. Then I see a woman. She is everywhere, Laurence – at my salon, at the gas station. Now I park below and there she is again … Who is following me? She moves as if she's military …'

He looked genuinely surprised.

'I—'

'This is not the sort of woman who wants to wish me a good day. I have seen this look, she is professional.'

'That's ridiculous, you're overreacting. Who on earth could be following you?'

'You tell me. How did she know I'd be in my apartment today?'

Nina glanced over her shoulder anxiously, her hair falling forward as she leaned towards him over the table. Intrigued, Brioni checked the camera was still recording.

'Why am I being followed, Laurence? Are you trying to frighten me?' She snorted as she said it, looking at him with utter disgust.

'That's ridiculous, you—'

'I'm not going home, Laurence, and I'll make sure I'm not alone. You can tell her that right now. I'm not stupid. You *really* don't want to try and get clever. Bad things happen to people who upset me.'

Tossing her hair over her shoulder, Nina pulled her handbag into her elbow and turned abruptly, leaving him sitting there open-mouthed.

'Come back …'

He half-rose, shaking his head as if she was being hysterical, but she had gone. He sat down and pulled out his phone, obviously waiting for her to come back.

She didn't.

Brioni clicked her video off.

What was that about?

Chapter 20

'**M**OTHER, WHAT *IS* the matter with you tonight?'

Emily-Jane glared at her mother across the kitchen island. Cressida looked up quickly. Her daughter was still wearing her school uniform, the collar of her honey-coloured shirt crooked under the regulation V-neck sweater, her hair in a ponytail.

'I'm sorry, I've got a lot on my mind.' Cressida looked at her properly. 'Did you wear that much make-up to school? Was that why you were late back?'

Emily-Jane shrugged non-committally and Cressida knew for sure she'd had another detention. It hardly seemed worth it when you could have been doing just about anything else, something considerably more constructive, for the sake of black winged eyeliner.

'Have you only just noticed? You've looked at your phone about a hundred times since I came down. Did you even know I was here? And you say I spend too long online.'

'Of course I knew you were there.'

Cressida sighed; if Emily-Jane had noticed her looking at her phone, she must be much too obvious.

Cressida rubbed her face with both hands, trying to massage away the feelings of anxiety and anger that she was sure were written there. With every minute that ticked past this afternoon, Cressida had found herself getting more agitated, the thoughts starting to spiral until they turned in on themselves and she felt quite sick. But she needed to learn to hide her emotions a lot better, or Emily-Jane would let something slip to Laurence, and all of this sneaking about could end up being for nothing.

Laurence was meeting Nina at the Reynolds Regency House cocktail bar this evening, to celebrate their 'deal', and Cressida couldn't help wondering if the celebration would end after cocktails, or if they would be just the start.

'So what's for dinner, Mother? I'm dying here.'

Emily-Jane's voice interrupted her thoughts and Cressida snapped back to the kitchen. Emily-Jane was looking at her incredulously, her hands open in a 'I'm still waiting' gesture as if she'd asked the same question about four times. Cressida sighed.

'Have you finished your homework?'

'Yes, Mother.'

'Have you had that essay back yet? The *Great Gatsby* one?'

'Tomorrow. Miss Thomas had a quick look when I handed it in, she was delighted with it.'

Cressida tried to keep the doubtful look off her face. When Laurence had finally emailed the draft Emily-Jane had written at the weekend, time had been getting short and she'd ended up working on it past midnight on Tuesday night. Cressida rather doubted that it was likely to be her best work. But Emily-Jane did work hard, and she was rarely late with homework.

'Takeaway? I'm sorry – I've got an issue with a client, my head's not very clear.'

'Takeaway? Calories, Mother, and it's only Thursday. Honestly, all you do is work, you wouldn't even notice I was here half the time.'

Cressida looked at Emily-Jane in disbelief. She might only be five feet six but when she was in the room, she made her presence felt. She got that from her father – a sort of inbuilt confidence that she was the centre of the universe. Cressida felt her heart soften for a moment. Despite the occasional teenage moments, Emily-Jane was very definitely the centre of her universe, that was for sure.

'Em, you know that's nonsense. Sometimes I just need five minutes to myself.'

'I've been here for ten minutes, Mother, at least.'

Emily-Jane glared at her and pulled out a stool to perch on, at the end of the island. Her phone, never far away, was already in her hand.

'Right, what'll we have so? How about Japanese? We haven't had that for ages, and they'll deliver so you can have a glass of wine.'

'Gee, thanks.'

'Your usual?'

Grinning, Emily-Jane deftly placed the order.

'Gold card?'

Cressida nodded, about to ask Emily-Jane how much she'd spent but then thinking better of it. She wasn't even hungry, but she could put the rest in the fridge for Laurence when he came in later.

Assuming he came home, of course, and didn't find a reason to stay at the Reynolds.

The words made her stomach react as they went through her head. She could still hear his voice on the phone, like an echo, taunting her.

Brioni had said this morning that she didn't want to tell Cressida everything she'd found out over the phone, that it would be better if she could come down to Wexford and they could talk about it properly. But Cressida had insisted.

She'd been on her own in the house, had been feeling good after the gym, despite the arrival of the ridiculous flowers that she'd stashed in the laundry room without even opening them. She'd thought she was as ready as she could ever be to hear what was going on.

But she'd been wrong.

It had been worse than she'd expected.

As she'd sat in the kitchen listening to Brioni sum up Laurence's meeting with Nina in his office, and then what she'd found in his emails, the sheer pain in her heart had meant she only heard half of what Brioni was telling her.

And then Brioni had said that the spa manager – this Kate Spicer – appeared to be 'in the mix' too; that she had no proof of anything going on, but that Laurence had been buying gifts for her. Cressida had suddenly had a vision of tangled bed sheets going around in a washing machine. *Mix* seemed to be the right word.

Perhaps she should have waited to talk to Brioni in private, but she'd needed to know. The moment she'd put the phone down she'd started googling Kate Spicer. She found her quickly – on Facebook with a fluffy little white dog, one of those ridiculous ones with a bow in its fringe and tiny legs. And whenever Kate appeared at an event, Laurence seemed be somewhere in the photographs, too. Cressida had gone on to Instagram – Kate's account was private, but the 1796 spa had its own feed with dreamy photos of subterranean luxury, candles and perfect nails, and shots of the various members of the team. Part of her wished she'd never looked. Kate was beautiful, and whatever products she used, she looked younger than the thirty-five years the press credited her with.

But for now they needed to focus on Nina.

Cressida knew the first thing a divorce lawyer would ask for was evidence – she needed some photos or video of Laurence and Nina that showed their relationship was more than professional.

Cressida bit her lip; she really hoped Brioni could get something this evening. She'd laughed at the selfie that Brioni had sent. The sexy bob made her look very French, and totally different from normal – and it was vital, if she needed to follow him again, that Laurence didn't notice her enough to recognise her.

Now, waiting for some sort of message from Brioni on the progress of the evening, Cressida's stomach was doing somersaults. At 6.30 Brioni had texted 'In the Reynolds', but she'd heard nothing since, and as the minutes ticked on towards seven o'clock, she'd felt herself getting sicker and sicker.

She'd also, this afternoon, been dissecting what Brioni had told her about Nina's data gathering. What on earth was Laurence playing at? Why did he need to know the secrets of the guys who had helped him set up Ferryman? The only reason she could think of was that he was planning to use the information to blackmail them somehow. But what could possibly make that level of a betrayal worthwhile? He'd known them for so long – he'd been to school with them, had a photo of them all in the school rugby team on the mantelpiece, for goodness' sake.

'Right, I can see you're really listening. I'll come down when the food gets here, will I?'

Cressida suddenly realised Emily-Jane was talking to her again, her tone laced with sarcasm. Her head whirling, she must have completely tuned out.

'Yes, of course, I'm sorry, love, I've got a lot on my mind. I'll call you as soon as it comes.'

A lot on her mind.

That was an understatement.

What Brioni was hoping to discover tonight could be the irrefutable evidence she needed.

Chapter 21

BRIONI REALLY HADN'T planned to spend her whole Thursday evening in the Kai Lung bar, but she wanted to find out why Laurence was still sitting there after Nina's abrupt departure, and, more importantly, she didn't want to cross the bar in front of him. It was very clear from the few women who had walked in while he'd been sitting there, that he looked at them all, a little too closely for Brioni's comfort.

She had no idea where Nina had vanished to, but she had definitely been furious about whatever she thought was going on. Why would Laurence have had her followed? Did he think she was planning to double-cross him with the data she'd retrieved? Brioni thought back to what she'd heard last night. Nina really hadn't been impressed with him sending Kate Spicer gifts, and now Brioni had seen inside his email she could see why. Nina had said something about him needing to be more careful with his passwords, too. Had she hacked his email as well when she'd seen the pattern of gifts being sent from his Ferryman account to Kate Spicer's address? If Nina was already on the inside, given her obvious talents, it would be easy enough for her to do exactly what Brioni had done, and connect with Laurence's laptop.

Laurence's email password was his house alarm code, just repeated. Cressida had rolled her eyes when she'd told Brioni. So much for Laurence Howard being a tech genius. He obviously thought he had his laptop secured, and Brioni would bet he used the same code for his Ferryman account as well.

He was the type of guy who had the arrogance to assume his security was perfect.

Brioni was quite sure that when Nina was retrieving the data about his shopping habits from his Ferryman account, she'd taken a note of his password and tried it in some other places. Brioni looked back at her phone screen, pretending to be absorbed in it as her thoughts unfurled. There was every chance that Nina had been able to see all the information Brioni had found – but she'd probably had more time to look around. It wouldn't just be his emails that she'd have looked at – his location history was quite revealing, too. Playing with fire was a well-worn cliché, but Brioni couldn't think of a more apt way to describe Laurence recruiting Nina to spy for him. Had he been so shocked at how much Nina had found out about him, that he was trying to frighten her?

Brioni shifted in her seat. It was almost nine; her bum was going numb and she needed the loo, but the entrance to the Ladies was on the other side of the bar. The manager of the Reynolds hotel had appeared after Nina had vanished, immediately greeting Laurence like a long-lost friend. He'd sat down for what looked like a quick chat and almost two hours later he was still here.

After the small talk, the manager – Brioni couldn't remember his name, but she recognised him from the page she had on him in her file – had started talking about restaurant covers and some conference that they were pitching for, and the price of the floral displays.

At this stage she really didn't care. It was late now. At least she'd eaten – she'd had to really. Seeing Laurence starting on a second round of drinks and settling in to his conversation, she'd decided to order herself. And she'd discovered there was an electric socket right below her, so she'd been able to plug in her phone. But now she'd read the day's news, checked all her social media accounts, and texted Alex to see how his date was going – he hadn't replied, so that had to be a good sign. She'd also texted Cressida to say she didn't really have anything to report, and discovered that the man who had walked in with a very much younger woman half an hour ago and announced he was on his way into the casino, was a well-known Dublin criminal. She'd vaguely recognised him, had caught the waiter calling him Mr McQuaid, and after a quick search had found out that he was in fact Red McQuaid, the head of a Northside family whose main interests seemed to be armed robbery, drug sales and bumping off members of their rival gangs. Nice.

Perhaps Nina hadn't been far wrong that someone was following her.

Finally, Laurence got up to leave.

Brioni watched him out of the corner of her eye, relief surging through her, and signalled to the waiter to bring her the bill. Thankfully he was quick, and as Laurence hovered around the entrance to the bar checking his phone, she punched in her credit card PIN. She just hoped he moved fast now so she could go straight from here into the Ladies. She shimmied forward in her seat, ready to move, and watched in horror as he turned around and came into the bar. She picked up the menu and held it in front of her face as he disappeared down the opposite side of the bar.

Not wanting to risk him turning around and reappearing, Brioni moved fast. Grabbing her bag, she squeezed out from behind the table and picked up her coat. Scooping up the Bluetooth device from further along the seat, she walked, as swiftly as she decently could without running, towards the foyer. She probably should have got up sooner, but even in the wig and dress, she didn't want to give Laurence any reason to notice her.

Hurrying into the Ladies, as soon as the door was closed she hurtled down the short corridor, through the next door and straight into the first open stall she spotted.

Sitting down, she sighed with relief, her dignity returning.

There was no way she could do this surveillance thing for a living. How did the police survive when they were on a stake-out? You never saw them desperate for the loo in cop shows.

The ladies' powder room was as decadent as the rest of the hotel, and Brioni spent a few moments washing her hands with their heavenly scented designer liquid soap and reapplying her lipstick in the mirror. A strange woman with dark hair looked back at her, the diamond in the side of her nose catching the overhead lights.

Putting her lipstick away, she checked the time on her phone again. She needed to be sure Laurence had left ahead of her, or her numb behind and bursting bladder would have been for nothing. As it was she hadn't managed to obtain the type of video or photographs of his meeting with Nina that she'd intended. All in all, her evening hadn't been a huge success.

Giving herself another minute, Brioni checked she didn't have any lipstick on her teeth and headed out of the bathroom. She was tempted to sneak into the Orangery and see if she could see Alex's latest date, but she really didn't want to risk running into

Laurence Howard. At the door to the lobby she paused to slip her coat on, then, taking a deep breath, confidently opened the door and made for the lift beside the main entrance, her head down just in case Laurence was standing there talking to someone.

Had she been looking where she was going, it wouldn't have been such a shock when someone grabbed her arm from behind. Swinging around, she came face to face with Alex. His face was alabaster and although he had his coat on, it was unbuttoned, his scarf askew and his shirt not quite tucked into his jeans.

What on earth?

'Jesus, Bri. I've got to get out of here.' He looked wide-eyed, as if he was in shock.

'What's …?'

'Not here. Have you got your car?'

She pulled her car keys out of her coat pocket and he steered her towards the lift. Hastily glancing into the entrance of the Kai Lung bar, she couldn't see Laurence, but she'd be a lot less conspicuous with Alex in tow, even in his slightly dishevelled state.

What on earth had he been doing?

The moment the lift doors opened Alex stepped inside, hammering the door-close as she hit her own button. She'd parked right beside the lift on the third level underground. The doors slid closed and, half-collapsing, he fell back on to the mirrored wall and thrust his hands deep into his pockets, his eyes closed tightly. Brioni looked at him, puzzled, but she knew better than to start questioning him now. He'd had some dating disasters before, but this looked catastrophic.

A few minutes later she had waved her credit card over the parking machine and he was sitting in the passenger seat of her little Citroën. Finally able to relax now, safe in the knowledge that Laurence would have parked on the forecourt outside the hotel, she put the key in the ignition and turned to Alex. He was leaning his head against the headrest, staring at something he didn't appear to be focusing on.

'What on earth's wrong, Alex? Tell me – you look as if you've seen a ghost.'

When he turned to look at her, she could see he had tears in his eyes.

'There was this woman. She's dead, Bri. I was with her and now she's dead.'

Chapter 22

CRESSIDA CHECKED HER phone to see if Brioni had sent another text. From the few brief ones she'd received this evening, she'd gathered that Nina had arrived and left in a temper and Brioni had got stuck in a corner for ages while Laurence had a meeting of some sort. Frustratingly, since then, there was nothing new. Cressida took a sip of her wine.

When the takeaway had arrived she'd made a supreme effort to chat to Emily-Jane, but it had been a waste of time. Whatever umbrage she had taken earlier about Cressida not paying attention to her had been forgotten in the drama of one of her friends breaking up with their on/off boyfriend. Emily-Jane's message notifications had been so distracting that Cressida had insisted she put her phone on silent, at least while they ate. As soon as they'd finished, Emily-Jane had disappeared upstairs to the privacy of her room, to supposedly finish her homework.

Needing some space to think, Cressida had decamped to the living room. She'd brought the bottle of wine with her and put on a lamp, sitting on the sofa in the half-dark with the curtains open so she could see when Laurence's car arrived.

She put her head against the sofa cushion and closed her eyes, thinking over what Brioni had told her.

Part of her was relieved that Laurence hadn't disappeared with Nina, either to her apartment or upstairs in the hotel. That same part was delighted that they'd had a row about something, but annoyed that, yet again, he'd got the upper hand and Brioni hadn't managed to get the photos or video she needed. She felt bad asking her to follow him again – Brioni had a proper job in real life, as well as trying to study, and didn't have the time to stalk company executives. Plus there was the danger that if she followed him again, Laurence would spot her.

He didn't often miss an attractive woman.

Opening her eyes, Cressida leaned forward and poured herself another glass of wine, just as her phone began to ring. Putting the bottle down with a crack on the glass coffee table, she snatched it up.

But it wasn't Brioni.

It was Laurence.

For a moment she thought about not answering. She really wasn't in the mood to talk to him. But part of her was very interested in whether he'd tell her he'd spent the evening at the Reynolds. She let it ring again and then hit the *answer* button.

'Cress, it's me. I'm in the car.'

'Are you on the way home?'

She tried to keep her voice light and cheerful. It wasn't easy. But she knew if she didn't keep herself under control, she might let rip at him and then all their planning would be wasted.

'I was. I was just leaving and I got a call from the manager at the 1796. One of the staff was taken sick there earlier today.'

It only took a moment for Cressida to connect the dots. He had to be talking about Kate Spicer. She could feel anger rising inside her.

'So …?' She tried to sound puzzled. 'Doesn't that happen all the time somewhere? There are a thousand staff, aren't there?'

'Yes, but this is a bit more complicated. I'm just on my way in to speak to Frank. He's meeting me at the hospital.'

Cressida sat forward on the sofa, her conversation with Dora this afternoon running through her mind. What was the manager of the 1796 doing at the hospital?

'Why's he there at this time of night? Do they think it's some sort of notifiable disease?'

She heard a pipping noise on the line, as if another call was coming in. She spoke quickly before he hung up to take the other call, the impatience, she knew, clear in her voice.

'Laurence, it's late. You pay him a stonking great salary to deal with this sort of thing, don't you?'

Laurence sounded weary as he replied. 'Yes, but the guards have just got involved.'

In the background she could hear a siren. The Reynolds Regency House where he'd met Nina was only ten minutes from St Vincent's hospital, on his direct route home – it sounded as if he was very close.

'What's happened? Is it drugs?'

Laurence cleared his throat. 'It's the spa manager, she's not that sort of person. The doctors who took her in think she's been poisoned. She was completely fine when she arrived at work – they think it must have occurred in the hotel.'

Cressida narrowed her eyes.

'What do you mean, poisoned? You mean she's eaten something from the restaurant?'

'They don't know what it is. It's taken them all day to do the tests, they've only just got the results now – that's why Frank called me. I don't know why the hell he waited so long. It's definitely not food, though.'

Leaning forward on the sofa, Cressida tried to concentrate on what he was saying as he continued.

'They think she might have inhaled it, which means it could be linked to the air conditioning. I've really no clear idea at this stage. I'll know more when I get to the hospital. But we need to keep it out of the papers, it could be catastrophic for business.'

Cressida reached for her glass, taking a moment to absorb what he was saying. Kate Spicer had been poisoned? Perhaps she was seeing someone else's husband as well and they'd got to her before Cressida could? The thought shot like a flame through her head before she could haul it back.

Perhaps this was the universe rebalancing Kate Spicer's behaviour with the hurt that it had caused.

Cressida was normally the first person to feel empathy, which was why she got such good results with her speech therapy clients – she was calm and patient – but as far as Kate Spicer was concerned, she was all out of any sort of sympathy.

Taking a sip, she rested the foot of the glass on her knee.

'Surely the press is going to spot you going into the hospital and they'll turn it into something, even if it's got nothing to do with the hotel?' Cressida couldn't keep the annoyance out of her voice. 'Perhaps she's been doing coke and it was badly cut or something? Can't you sort it out on the phone with him? I think that would be much more sensible. If he's there, he can deal with the police.'

'I'm going in the back. I'll be careful.'

Cressida was tempted to say that he hadn't been nearly careful enough, but she bit it back, keeping her tone non-judgemental.

'How long do you think you'll be?'

'Not long. I just need to suss what's going on and then I'll be home. An hour maybe?'

Just long enough for him to see Kate Spicer.

Cressida could feel herself scowling.

'There's takeaway in the fridge for when you get here. Em's got an early start so don't make too much noise.'

'I won't. I'll see you later. I'll be as quick as I can.'

'Great.' Cressida paused. 'Why are you so late leaving anyway? I was talking to Dora earlier, she didn't mention a meeting.'

'Why were you talking to Dora?'

His tone was sharp. *Did he think she'd been checking up on him?* A smile curled at the corners of her mouth.

'I wanted to check on holiday dates. We ended up chatting about nothing, and then Em came in so I never actually asked her. If you could sync your calendar with mine it would make planning so much simpler.'

Lacing her tone with just the right amount of irritation, she knew mentioning his diary would mean he'd never bring up her call with Dora. Syncing their diaries was an ongoing issue, one his secretary had suggested repeatedly. Cressida brought it up whenever they had a clash, which was pretty regularly, and she now understood why he didn't want her to see where he was at any given moment. Or supposed to be.

'Can we talk about it when I get home?'

'Of course, there's no hurry. Go and sort out this mess first.'

Cressida hung up and, taking a large sip of her wine, put her phone down on the coffee table, her anger leaping inside her like wildfire. Mess was the right word.

Ever since they'd met, he'd constantly commented on her almost OCD approach to organisation, complaining when she sorted out the clothes he left all over the bedroom floor or the Sunday papers that he'd spread across the kitchen table.

He created the mess. She tidied it up.

And now he'd made a mess of their marriage.

She just needed to work out how she was going to sort this one out.

Chapter 23

'ALEX, WHAT ARE you talking about? Who's dead?'

Still in the car park, her hand on the ignition key, Brioni twisted in the driver's seat and looked at her friend, trying to keep her face calm. He didn't need someone yelling at him now.

He closed his eyes and put his head in his hands.

'The woman.'

Suddenly he choked up, sobbing and trying to catch his breath at the same time.

'Calm down, Alex, it'll be fine, I promise. I'll sort it out.'

Brioni reached over to squeeze his arm. Whatever was going on, she needed to get him somewhere where they could talk properly. How could the girl he'd been meeting be dead? How did he even know she was dead?

Putting the car into drive, she whizzed up the levels in the car park to the exit, her tyres squealing as she took each corner. On the other side of the barrier, it was pitch dark, her headlights illuminating gossamer rain that seemed to be falling in sheets.

At this time of night, they were only ten minutes from her apartment.

What on earth had happened? Had he taken something and hallucinated?

She glanced anxiously across at him as she took the road into town, braking at the lights to go over the canal, but they changed to green and she pulled through them. A few minutes later she was outside the car park entrance to her building. She triggered the remote on her dash, and the roller shutters slowly began to slide open. She looked across again at Alex.

She was getting a horrible feeling in the pit of her stomach. He really wasn't making this up.

'Won't be long, Alex. Are you absolutely sure she was dead? Are you sure she doesn't need an ambulance?'

Why hadn't she asked that in the car park? Why hadn't she gone to check the situation herself? Leaving the hotel in such a hurry suddenly seemed like the worst idea she'd ever had. Questions ricocheted around Brioni's head as she drove down the slope into the underground parking area below her building.

Beside her Alex choked back tears.

'There's nothing a doctor can do, Bri. Someone shot her in the head and … and … Oh Christ, I think I'm going to be sick.'

'We're almost there, hold on.'

Brioni pulled into her parking space, jumped out, ran around to his door and pulled it open. He was staring at the dash in some sort of paralysis, as if he was waiting to vomit.

'Come on, Alex, get out and you can come up to mine. Have you been drinking? Maybe some coffee will help?'

He turned to look up at her as if she was mad.

'But her head, the blood … Christ, my dad's going to kill me.'

Brioni jumped backwards as he leaned out of the car and heaved onto the tarmac. He vomited again.

'Come on, let me help you. The lift's this way.'

Grabbing his arm, she levered him out of the car, realising that he hadn't put on his seatbelt when he'd got in. Thank God they hadn't had an accident.

This evening was just getting better and better.

Upstairs in her apartment, Brioni showed him into the living room, unwinding his scarf and pulling off his coat before he sat down on her cream sofa. He looked dazed. Not too sure what to do with his vomit-stained coat, she took it into the bathroom and threw it into the bath. She could hose it down in the shower later to remove the stain on its tail.

Steadying herself on the door frame, Brioni closed her eyes tightly and took a deep breath. She needed to slow her brain down and take one step at a time – she needed to talk to Alex and find out what the hell was going on.

Heading into the kitchen, she switched on the coffee machine. Searching through her cupboards, she found a mixing bowl, taking it through to put down beside Alex in case he needed to vomit again. He had his head in his hands, was looking as if he needed something a lot stronger than straight coffee. She went over to her bar cart, looking for the brandy miniatures Marissa had laughingly given her at Christmas in case she ever had guests who wanted more than herbal tea. Glancing at him anxiously, she picked up the little bottles.

'Won't be a sec.'

Back in the kitchen she poured one of them into his coffee. Then decided to add a bit from another bottle. He looked as if he needed more than one measure. Brioni didn't drink, but as the scent of the brandy reached her, she began to see the attraction.

In the living room, sitting down beside him on the sofa, she handed him the mug.

'I need you to take a deep breath. Start at the beginning and tell me everything. You had a date, right?'

He took a sip, wincing as the brandy hit his tongue, and nodded.

'We've been chatting on Tinder for ages. She seemed really nice, so I suggested a drink at the Reynolds.' He drew a breath. 'I waited ages for her, we were supposed to meet at 6.30, but I thought maybe she'd got the time wrong and thought it was 7.30. She didn't text – that's what made me think she was just late or something. Maybe her battery died.' The words were tumbling out. 'But she must have blown me out.'

'Slow up, I want to get the full picture.'

Taking another sip of his coffee, he glanced at Brioni.

'So I'm standing there minding my own business, trying to decide whether to wait any longer, and this drop-dead gorgeous woman comes running in the front door as if she's on fire. She had long dark hair, and I thought for a minute she was this girl I was supposed to be meeting. I stepped forward and started to say hello and she sort of stopped and patted my arm and then kept on going into the bar. I realised once I was looking at her it wasn't her at all – this woman was older, maybe thirty. She looked really furious about something. I felt such a fecking eejit, but I don't think she noticed – whatever had annoyed her was more of an issue.'

'Was she wearing a thick grey coat with a belt, by any chance?'

He nodded. 'As if it was made of a blanket or something. Did you see her?'

Brioni grimaced. *Nina, it had to be.*

'Go on.'

'I checked my phone again to see if my date had messaged, but she hadn't, so I'm about to go when the woman comes out of the bar, and she stops again beside me. It's as if she's going to say something, and then she smiles at me and she goes over to reception. She must have checked in because they gave her a key card. And the next thing she comes over to me and puts her arm through mine and holds the key card up.'

'Did she say anything?' Brioni tried to keep the amazement out of her voice.

What had Nina been playing at, picking up a total stranger in the lobby of a hotel? He was a very good-looking total stranger, but …

Brioni frowned, trying to make sense of it. *She'd said something to Laurence about not being alone.* If the woman following her had come in and seen her, did she think she was safer with Alex in tow? Or perhaps it was as simple as Nina being on the rebound and making a point to Laurence.

Brioni realised Alex had started speaking again.

'She didn't say a thing. She didn't even tell me what her name was. She just started kissing me in the lift and honestly I didn't think to ask.'

He took another sip of his coffee. His colour was starting to come back, slowly.

'What happened next?'

For a long moment Alex stared at the huge square painting of the sea that Brioni had hung on the wall opposite the sofa. It was an oil, a storm, the grey of the waves and sky almost merging, birds tossed on the wind into the clouds above, tiny dots of colour that suggested boats far out from the shore. She'd loved it since the moment she'd seen it in the gallery in Wexford town.

He bit his lip, his face clouded as if he was reliving the whole evening in his head. A moment later he began speaking again.

'She'd booked a suite, it was gorgeous. Well, I didn't see much of it, but there was a living room and the bedroom, and this incredible bathroom off the bedroom. We … I … Well, we did some lines and then we ended up in bed pretty quickly.' He ran his hand into his fringe and pulled at it. 'She was amazing.' He sighed. 'And then, afterwards we talked for a bit. She said she worked in tech and hadn't been in Dublin long – she'd been working in London. She said she was lonely and she didn't normally do that sort of thing, but she hadn't wanted to be on her own right then.'

He closed his eyes as if he could see her leaning on the pillows, her dark hair tangled around her.

'So then she calls room service and orders champagne. She was laughing. And I go into the shower. The bathroom has this really intense surround sound system, so I've got *The Planets* suite on full blast and I'm having a bit of a soak. The shower was amazing. Well, the whole thing was amazing. I don't know how long I was in there, I was a bit stunned really. I was trying to work out what to say to her. Then, when I'd finished, I came out and I was talking away and I realised she wasn't answering. I turn around and the champagne's there on the floor and she's lying on her face on the bed, as if she'd just got back in, and my God, Bri, there was blood everywhere. Like everywhere, all over the bed.' He closed his eyes tightly and gripped the mug. 'The sheet was over her, up to her shoulder, and someone had blown off the back of her head. All I could see was her hair, and … Christ, the blood.'

Brioni put out her hand and rubbed his arm.

'Too late for an ambulance then?'

'That's for fucking sure.'

'What did you do?'

'I sort of froze. I had no idea what to do, I couldn't look at her. So I got dressed like really fast, thank God most of my clothes were in the living room. Then I thought should I call the cops ... but, Bri, I just didn't know what to do. All I could think about was that I'd just had sex with this woman and my DNA was all over her and there was coke all over the table, and there she was dead. A scandal like that would ruin my dad's business, would ruin me, I mean, after he'd disinherited me. Who else had been in the room?' He took a breath, trying to calm down.

Brioni gave him a double take. 'The guy who brought the champagne, maybe? Perhaps he didn't just have glasses and an ice bucket with him?'

Alex looked at her, his eyes wide. 'Shit, I never thought of that.' He ran his hand into his fringe and pulled at it. 'I couldn't think straight, maybe it was the coke. I don't know, I'd had a couple of vodkas before I even got there.' He closed his eyes as if he was recalling it. 'I just sort of panicked. I called room service back, and I put on this voice and I said there had been a bit of an accident and they might need to send someone up. I hung up before they could ask any questions. Then I wiped down the phone and ran back into the bathroom. I mean ... I wiped the taps and the door handle with a towel and then ...' He paused. 'Then I left.' He glanced sideways at her. 'You're right about the champagne. That must have been it. But now I've left the scene of a murder. And there's going to be CCTV and DNA all over the place. What the fuck am I going to do?'

Brioni put her hand on his knee.

'Look, you called room service to tell them. You were in shock. Someone will go up there and find her and they'll call the police.

You're going to have to talk to them – I think you can explain that leaving the room was down to shock, and the CCTV in the hall will show her picking you up. And the lift ... And then you coming out of the room. You're looking pretty shook.'

He put his free hand in his fringe.

'What am I going to do?'

Brioni took a deep breath. You heard so many cases of people being wrongly convicted, she could see why he was so frightened.

'Her clothes are still in the room? Her bag?'

He closed his eyes tightly for a moment, trying to remember.

'Yes, her bag was on the sofa in the lounge, under my shirt. It had her phone in it, it was sticking out the top. It'll have ID so they'll know who she was?'

'Exactly, the guards will be able to sort it out. Maybe she was being followed ...' Brioni stopped herself, suddenly realising the truth in what she was saying. She continued hastily. 'Perhaps she had a violent husband or someone who was following her.'

At least the CCTV in the bar would show Nina's conversation with Laurence.

The guards would check out all Nina's movements from the moment she arrived in the hotel – they'd see her arguing with Laurence and then he'd have to explain what he was doing and he'd be able to identify her. *And she'd told him she was being followed.* Surely the woman following her would be on the CCTV, too, if she'd come into the hotel? Laurence had an alibi, had been sitting just a few tables along from Brioni talking to the hotel's general manager all evening. He hadn't moved. Brioni closed her eyes, trying to sort it all out in her head.

Alex hadn't said it in so many words, but he could be – in fact, probably *would* be – arrested for leaving the scene of a crime.

Without really thinking, she pulled off her wig and ruffled up her hair.

She turned to Alex, about to speak, but as she opened her mouth she realised he was looking at her, frowning.

'Bri, why were *you* in the Reynolds tonight? What's with the wig?'

Chapter 24

A S CRESSIDA PULLED into the lane winding up to the seafront house, she could see Brioni hadn't arrived yet. When she'd texted last night, Brioni had said she was staying in her Dublin apartment but would be driving down to Wexford this morning. Cressida checked the time on her dashboard. It was almost 11.30. They'd arranged to meet at midday, but Cressida hadn't been able to wait at home in Dalkey any longer. After the gym, she'd paced the kitchen trying to kill time, getting more and more anxious.

She'd been lying in bed listening for Laurence's car on the drive when a text had come through. Needless to say, his 'hour' had turned into three. She'd been sure the text was from him, but then when she'd turned over and reached for her phone on the bedside table, she'd seen Brioni's name and her stomach had flipped.

Something's come up. Bit complicated.
Meet you in Ballycastle at 12?

What could have come up? Did Brioni know Kate Spicer was in intensive care?

Laurence had come in shortly afterwards, had been gruff and unresponsive, so Cressida had dragged the duvet over her shoulder and turned over and tried to sleep.

Pulling up the last steep sandy incline to stop outside Brioni's single-storey wooden house, Cressida turned off her windscreen wipers and looked out over the dunes. It was damp and misty today, the line between the grey of the sky and the deeper slate grey of the sea virtually invisible, as if someone had taken a giant eraser and smudged the horizon. A keen wind was whipping off the water, buffeting her jeep. She could see why Brioni came here. There was something wild and untamed about the place. The road she'd arrived on, after the farm gate and cattle grid, had turned into a rutted lane that wove between gorse bushes to swing around the front of the house. To Cressida's right, the hill the house was built on fell away into an overgrown hollow peppered with gorse, the long grasses flattened by the gusts of wind, like mermaid's hair wreathing with the tide. There was another house opposite on top of the next rise, but it looked empty.

Cressida had been busy turning everything over in her head as she'd driven down, but now she turned the radio on and leaned her elbow on the car door, her hand in her hair. The lack of sleep was starting to catch up with her.

The news came on.

'Gardaí are investigating an incident at the 1796 hotel in central Dublin, where a member of staff was taken ill yesterday. In what looks like a suspected poisoning attempt, they are treating the attack on the hotel's spa manager, Kate Spicer, as attempted murder.'

Suddenly Cressida felt very awake. She turned the radio up as the presenter continued:

'General Manager Frank Mahony declined to comment, saying that the incident is being handled by the gardaí and that it appears

142

to be a personal attack on Ms Spicer. The hotel is fully open today, but several British and American guests have expressed concerns that with the Dublin Internet Privacy Summit scheduled for later this month, and with revelations in the US and the UK about voter influence, this could be, unlikely as it sounds on Irish soil, a repeat of something like the Salisbury poisonings in which Sergei and Yulia Skripal were attacked.'

The reporter sounded breathless trying to fit all the drama into her thirty-second report. But it was no wonder that Laurence had been delayed so long. Not that he'd hinted at any of this last night – and this morning he'd left early without speaking to her, thinking she was asleep.

What on earth was going on?

As Cressida changed station to see if she could find a more detailed report, she heard a car pulling up behind her. It was Brioni's little black Citroën. Cressida flipped the radio off and pushed open her door, immediately hit by a blast of icy wind that almost took her breath away. She kept her head down until she got to the rear of the car. Brioni was already making for the front door, indicating that Cressida should follow her. It was too windy to even try to speak outside, the cold air sharp with salt that Cressida could feel on her lips as she made for the shelter of the porch.

'Sorry – were you waiting long?'

Brioni ushered her inside, closing the door against the wind as Cressida walked into the living room, putting her bag down on the wooden table.

'No, I was listening to the news ...' As Cressida turned to explain, she could see Brioni looked exhausted. 'Good God, are you all right? You look shattered.'

Brioni smiled weakly. 'I am a bit.'

'Did you hear …? No, wait. Will I put the kettle on? I brought lunch. You look as if you need to eat. Then we can talk.'

Brioni gestured towards the door to the kitchen at the back of the living room.

'Be my guest. I'm sorry, I didn't get much sleep. Coffee would be amazing.'

Cressida looked at her hard. She didn't know Brioni well, but she knew that she was fit – she'd mentioned sea swimming and running on the beach, and that she was used to working long hours. A late night didn't impact someone her age in the same way it would someone older.

Something must have happened.

Brioni looked pale and drawn, and as she slowly pulled off her woollen hat and slipped off her coat, it was very clear that she was worried about something. Cressida could almost see it hanging in a cloud around her.

This *had* to be to do with Kate Spicer.

What did Brioni know?

'Sit. Give me five minutes and then you can tell me what's been going on. We've got lots of time.'

Brioni headed for the sofa, throwing her coat over the back of it.

'Thanks.' She sat down, rubbing her face with her hands. 'You're not going to believe it.'

Cressida almost said *try me*, but instead pointed at the cushions.

'Relax, I'll get the coffee.'

Cressida made herself a coffee, too, leaving the fresh focaccia bread and cold meats she'd brought on the counter in the galley kitchen. In the living room, passing Brioni a frothy latte, she sat down on the other end of the sofa.

'So tell me.'

'OK.' Brioni took a sip of her coffee and let out a big sigh. 'So this really doesn't make any sense.' She paused. 'Has Laurence said anything to you about the guards being called out to the Reynolds hotel?'

'This is to do with Kate, isn't it? She's based in the 1796, though, not the Reynolds.'

Brioni looked at her sharply, her face puzzled.

'Kate?'

Cressida leaned forward, nodding. 'The guards are involved.'

Brioni screwed up her face, looking confused.

'The guards, maybe yes – Kate, no. Unless you've got something to tell me?'

Confused herself now, Cressida raised her eyebrows.

'You go first.'

'So Laurence hasn't said anything?'

'Only about Kate. Is there something else?'

Brioni's eyes opened wide. 'There sure is.' She took another sip of her coffee. 'Last night, after Nina left Laurence, she went out into the hall of the Reynolds where a friend of mine was waiting. He'd just been stood up and he was about to leave.' Brioni ran her hand into her fringe, pushing it out of her face. 'Let's just say she came on to him really strongly and they ended up in a suite upstairs.'

Her coffee forgotten, Cressida looked at her, speechless.

'Are you serious? She just picked him up?'

'Essentially, yes.'

'Did Laurence know? Did he see them?'

Brioni shook her head. 'Unless Nina texted him to tell him – which I really don't think she had time to do, from what Alex told me.'

'Wow. So that put an end to any plans Laurence might have had for the evening. I can't say I'm not happy about that. But I don't understand – what do the guards have to do with this?'

Brioni screwed up her face and took a deep breath.

'So – this is the short version – apparently things got quite heated quite quickly, and afterwards Alex hopped into the shower. She called room service for some champagne, but when he got out of the bathroom ...' Brioni rubbed her face with her hand. 'Room service had been, all right, but someone had shot Nina in the back of the head. She was lying there in the bed, dead.'

'What?'

Cressida's reaction was explosive, causing her coffee to slop onto the floor. She hardly noticed. Utterly stunned, she looked at Brioni.

Brioni sighed. 'I had a lot of questions, too. Alex said he didn't hear anything because he had the music in the bathroom turned right up – and they must have used a silencer. It wasn't exactly something he was expecting.'

Cressida found herself shaking her head. 'Who is this guy? I mean, could he have done it? Or maybe it was someone looking for him?'

Brioni shrugged. 'Alex's as straight as they come, he's studying law. He's been interning at his dad's firm forever, but he does corporate, not criminal. He wouldn't know one end of a gun from another, never mind what a silencer is. He was so shocked when I met him, I'm sure he was telling the truth.'

Cressida looked at her, trying to absorb was she was saying. Violent crimes didn't happen to people like them, they just didn't.

'There wasn't anything on the news about it. Are you *sure*?'

Glancing across at her, Brioni nodded.

'Absolutely, Alex has no reason to lie. He doesn't even know who Nina is.' Brioni sighed. 'I really don't know what happened. Nina definitely said to Laurence she thought she was being followed, I heard her. It sounds as if she must have opened the door to room service and got more than she bargained for.' She paused. 'The madness of all of this is that it doesn't end there.'

'There's more?'

Brioni nodded slowly. 'Alex didn't know what to do, so he rang room service and said there'd been an accident. Then he legged it and I met him in the hallway. I had no idea what was going on at that stage, so I brought him to my apartment and ... well, then he explained.' Brioni sighed. 'I don't know if she told you, but my sister Marissa's partner is a detective in London – so I rang him. I didn't know what else to do. Alex had left the scene of a murder and I'd helped him, and it was easily midnight at that stage.' She paused again. 'Mike took all the details and called someone he knows in Harcourt Square for us, they checked with Donnybrook, which is the closest station to the hotel, I think. He said to wait until they called us. There was no question that Alex would have to make a statement –' Brioni took another sip of her coffee – 'but Mike said he'd see what the situation was.

'At four o'clock he rang back, and this is where it gets really weird. He said the guards had called to the hotel but had come up with nothing. Alex didn't know what floor the room was on, let alone the number, but it was definitely a suite. Apparently the staff had checked all the suites. There were none that had been booked in Nina's name and none that had ordered champagne around 9 p.m., or at any stage last night. And, more importantly, none with a dead woman in it.'

'But the CCTV? It must have shown them going up to the room?'

'There was nothing on the hotel CCTV at all. Alex said he watched her go over and collect the key card, before she came back and whisked him into the lift. But the guards watched the footage and there's no sign of them together at all. Mike said you can see Nina come in, she's on the video in the bar talking to Laurence and then she leaves, but she's not picked up again in the hall. And neither is Alex. The staff say they must have gone out of range of the cameras, straight to the car park; maybe the camera in the car park is dodgy or something.'

Cressida looked at her, astounded. 'But they didn't? Someone must have messed with the security tape.'

'There wasn't even footage of them in the lift, apparently.'

'Are you sure you believe him, this friend of yours?'

Brioni sighed. 'Yep. I really don't think he made it up.'

Chapter 25

SITTING ON THE sofa beside Cressida, Brioni took another sip of her coffee. It was almost cold.

Cressida was obviously having problems processing the news of Nina's murder, too.

'So someone tampered with the hotel security tapes, with the guest check-in *and* removed a body – all in the time it took for you to get home, get the story out of your friend, and for the guards to get to the hotel?'

'From what Alex said there was quite a lot of blood, too, but …' Brioni cleared her throat, not too sure how much detail Cressida really wanted – she'd had a lot of time to think about this. '… I'd imagine they shot her at very close range, so the blood spatter might have been limited to the bed. There would have been a lot more …' Brioni paused again, choosing her words. '… mess, if they'd shot her from a distance or she'd been standing up.' She grimaced. 'That's the bit I find really strange. She must have got out of bed and put on a robe or something to answer the door. But Alex said she was lying face down on the bed with the sheet over her when he came out of the bathroom.'

'Perhaps she didn't get up to answer the door at all. Room service would have had a pass key.' Cressida paused. 'I mean, someone at the hotel must have been involved to get rid of all the evidence, so what's to say they weren't involved from the beginning? She thought Laurence had had her followed, so perhaps that person was gearing up for something happening, but had to adapt when she booked into the room?' Cressida let out a sharp breath. 'I can't see how Laurence wouldn't know about this. I mean, from what you said you heard the other night, Nina was blackmailing him. And he controls everything that happens in the hotels.'

Cressida put her cup down on the floor beside her feet and ran her hands into her hair, cradling her head as if it was hurting.

'He was late last night. He said he was going to the hospital, but it's only half an hour from our house at that time of night, less even. You texted at about 9.30 and he didn't ring me until almost ten to say he'd just been informed about Kate Spicer collapsing. He was really cross, it sounded as if they'd only called him when they'd realised she'd been poisoned, and the guards had got involved. So there's about twenty minutes when we don't know what he was doing. And several hours more when he could have left the hospital, before he came home.'

Brioni nodded slowly, considering Cressida's implication. Laurence may not have been involved in the murder, but he could certainly have been involved in the clean-up. Then her brain caught up.

'Did you say Kate Spicer had been poisoned?'

Cressida glanced sideways at Brioni. She let out a sigh.

'She's in hospital. That's what I thought you were talking about when you mentioned the guards. It was just on the radio. The hotel is playing it down, but it happened at the 1796.'

Brioni looked at her, aghast. 'Are you serious? First Nina and now Kate Spicer?'

'Or maybe the other way around, given the timing, but yes.' Cressida left it hanging there. 'And it wasn't me, before you say anything. Much as I've thought about murdering both of them since you overheard that conversation.' She paused. 'What *exactly* did Nina say about Kate the other night?'

'Do you want to listen to the recording?'

Cressida shook her head quickly. 'No, I really don't.'

Brioni turned towards her, pulling her feet up on to the sofa. She should have kicked off her DMs but she didn't have the energy to unlace them. Thank God the coffee was slowly getting her brain moving.

'Nina found out he'd bought her gifts – a Chanel dress and jewellery from No. 42 in New York.'

Cressida rolled her eyes. 'He's so imaginative. Me too.'

'She was looking up the other directors' accounts. It's mind-boggling really, what some companies know about you and your spending habits. I'm sure half of them don't use the data the way they could, but she very obviously did.'

'Do you think it could have been Laurence? I know he didn't get to where he was today by being a pushover, but murdering people who get in your way is a bit extreme.' Cressida paled as she said it, her voice barely more than a whisper.

Brioni put her cup down on the table. When Marissa had asked her to help Cressida out, she really hadn't expected to get caught up in anything like this. The two women Laurence Howard appeared to be having extramarital relations with had *both* been attacked yesterday. A tiny voice in the back of her head was asking whether Cressida was really as innocent as she made out.

His wife had to rate pretty highly in terms of a prime suspect.

But perhaps Laurence had as much reason to get rid of the two of them as Cressida did.

Cressida was staring across the room, her eyes fixed on the unlit stove opposite them.

'I mean, he couldn't have had them killed, could he? I know he's on the verge of some huge deal but ... I mean, nothing's worth somebody's life, is it?'

Brioni could see exactly the way that Cressida's mind was going – if she challenged Laurence Howard in the divorce court, could she be next?

'You'd hope not.' Brioni swung her legs out from under her. The coffee was finally doing its job and she was feeling almost human. 'But don't forget, if it helps, he didn't actually kill anyone himself. I could see him the whole time Nina was upstairs, and he didn't move.' Brioni bit her lip, thinking, then said half to herself, 'It was almost as if he was establishing his alibi. I mean, talking to the manager of the hotel on camera puts them both in the clear, doesn't it?'

'But it doesn't mean they didn't get someone else to do it.'

Brioni pursed her lips thoughtfully, her mind running over the events of the previous evening. Cressida looked up at her.

'What do we do now? Talk to the police?'

As she was speaking, Cressida's phone began to ring from inside her bag. Fumbling with the navy leather flap, she found it, glancing at Brioni again.

'It's Emily-Jane, I'd better take it. She must be on her lunch break.'

Feeling chilled, Brioni crossed the living room to open the stove and riddle the ash, ready to light it, as Cressida took the call.

'Slow down, Em. Just say that again. Why are you at home?'

She paused while Emily-Jane answered.

'Do you still feel ropy now? Maybe it was the takeaway? Calm down, Em, I'm not following. What's happened?'

Detecting a note of concern in Cressida's voice, Brioni glanced behind her. She'd moved forward on the sofa. Cressida looked up, her eyes worried as they met Brioni's.

'I see. Look, I'm sure it's something that's just got blown up by the tabloids. Call the guards if you're worried and don't open the gates. I'll see if I can get hold of your father and find out what's going on.'

Brioni raised her eyebrows in question as Cressida continued.

'I know, I know, darling. It'll all be fine. Close all the curtains and don't answer the phone. You'll know if it's me, I'll text. And if your friends call, just say you don't know anything about it. No, I know you don't, but you know what the press are like. Yes, yes, I'll be back later. You're completely safe in the house, it's your father they want to speak to. Look, I'll call the guards and get the photographers moved. They must be blocking the road or something. I promise. I'll call you as soon as I know anything.'

Brioni looked at her, the poker in one hand.

'What's wrong? Has someone found out about Nina?'

Chapter 26

I N HIS OFFICE, Laurence Howard pushed the *call* button and spoke to Dora.

'Can you let the board know I'll be through in ten minutes?'

He didn't wait for her to answer. The detective sitting opposite him had flipped open his notebook. The other one was standing just outside his peripheral vision, looking out of the picture window behind his desk. Laurence heard him rattling the change in his pocket.

'Great view you've got here.'

'Thanks. Yes, always something happening out there.'

The detective sitting in front of him looked up at him hard.

'That's for sure.'

Laurence didn't want to give the other one the satisfaction of turning around, or trying to explain that he'd been talking about the weather.

But they weren't far off in terms of things happening. Jesus Christ, it was one thing after another. What the hell had he done to be hit with this much bad luck? And he was worried sick about Kate. Every time he thought of her lying in that hospital bed he was hit with a wave of emotion that took him right back to Pierce after the accident ... Holding his brother's hand in a hospital room in LA as his life slipped away.

He could feel his palms starting to sweat.

'So, gentlemen, what do we do about this ransom demand?'

'Can you run through with me exactly what the story is to date?'

'I have explained all this—'

'I know, but it never hurts to go over things again.'

Laurence glanced at the clock on his desk. Everyone would be gathering in the boardroom now. Keeping them waiting was going to make them even more anxious. The Ferryman stock price was tumbling and Dirk Ackroyd from SpeakEasy had already been on the phone.

'I got an email about an hour ago, as did apparently half the country's media, stating that the Ferryman database had been hacked. It was sent bang on midday. The hackers claim they have customer details: addresses, shopping habits and obviously customer credit card details. Apparently they've also found a way into our credit systems, too. The email I received was sent by a group calling themselves Nemesis.'

The guard at the window turned to look at Laurence. In his fifties, balding, he was wearing a navy suit that really needed to go to the cleaners and brown shoes. 'What did this crowd say they were going to do with this data?'

'Publish it. I'm not sure where. The Dark Web maybe, like that lot who hacked Ashley Madison.' The detective raised an eyebrow as Laurence continued. 'That dating site in the UK, for people who wanted to have affairs. They'd obviously pissed someone off. Probably because they were charging a fortune for people to *remove* their profiles. That breach cost them over eleven million dollars in lawsuits. I'm not taking any risks with this one.'

Laurence glanced at the clock again. He'd been through all of this with some young guy in the garda cyber security team already, when he'd reported it. He'd been very impressive, sharp and quick. Laurence had had him on speaker in the office, with Ethan Feeney, Ferryman's head of cybersecurity, beside him. These two were a complete contrast, like Laurel and Hardy without the humour. From the moment they'd walked in, Laurence had got the distinct impression that they were here to check him out. As if he'd create a hoax of this magnitude for any reason on earth.

'Sharp practice never does you any good in this world, does it?' Laurence looked at the guard standing at the window as he spoke. The detective had his hands in his pockets and needed to get into the gym; the layers of flesh that had gathered above his shirt collar were florid. His face was impassive but the emphasis had been on 'sharp' as he continued. 'Remind me what the hackers want again – this Nemesis lot?'

'Twenty million dollars in bitcoin. It's untraceable.'

The detective nodded, his colleague silently taking notes on the other side of the desk. Laurence glanced across at him, part of him amazed that they still used those little black notebooks you saw in nineties cop shows. Part of him was waiting for one of them to ask what bitcoin was.

The detective by the window raised his eyebrows. 'And do you think this blackmail attempt could have anything to do with your employee who is currently in intensive care?'

Laurance picked up the gold fountain pen on his desk and played it through his fingers, trying to keep calm, conscious of time moving on. The board members who hadn't already been in the building had come straight to the office as soon as he'd called them, leaving meetings all over the city. They'd be steaming if he left them alone together to discuss the situation for too long.

'Kate? I very much doubt it. Two totally different sides of the business. I run Ferryman, but my original business is the hotels. Kate works on the hotel side.'

'Seems strange the two events occurred so close together.' The detective with the notebook looked up sharply. 'Bit of a coincidence, like.'

Coincidence was damn right.

There was just too much happening, too fast, for him to be able to think straight.

Laurence looked across the desk at him.

'Anything is possible, officer. It seems to me to be coincidental, too, but then I've never had anyone try and murder one of my employees before or to ruin my business by compromising our data. Can you tell me what the gardaí can do? I've got a board meeting starting imminently, and we need to make some decisions.'

The detective at the window scowled. 'Are you thinking of paying? We wouldn't recommend it.'

'It's one option in an otherwise rather barren field. We'll have to discuss it. I have to bring them up to date.'

The detective opposite him cleared his throat. 'There's nothing to stop them publishing it even if you pay, you know that. Honour among thieves is a myth.'

'I'm only too well aware of that. I've got my data team on it, and we're looking to bring in a team from the States to find a patch and determine exactly what this Nemesis gang were able to get access to, if anything. We also have to consider whether this is an elaborate hoax. We have incredibly sophisticated virus blocking systems.' Laurence paused. 'What I need your cybercrimes guys to do is track down the perpetrator.'

The detective beside the window rattled the change in his trouser pocket.

'They're on it as we speak. The original message has been bounced around the world and is looking as if it might have originated in Russia. They'll keep us posted. And we'll keep you posted.'

Laurence nodded curtly. 'Do you need anything else?'

'We'll see what the team can discover. See if we can't come up with some sort of trap for them. If they contact you again, suggest you give them cash in unmarked bills. At least we can follow that.'

Laurence looked at him, the incomprehension he was feeling obviously written on his face. The officer shrugged, smiling at what was obviously supposed to be some sort of joke.

'Worth a try. You never know, perhaps they like to feel their cash rather than looking at strings of code.' He glanced at his colleague sitting on the other side of the desk, who stood up.

'We'll be liaising with the team investigating the poisoning, too. Your co-operation would be appreciated.'

'You've got it, obviously, whatever you need.'

Chapter 27

HER PHONE STILL in her hand, Cressida looked across the room at Brioni and shook her head, her stomach churning.

'It's not Nina.' She closed her eyes for a moment. There was just too much happening at the moment for her to keep up. 'There's been some sort of data breach at Ferryman, millions of accounts have been compromised. Em said it's all over the news.'

Cressida took a ragged breath, trying to slow her heart rate. It had risen in step with Emily-Jane's growing panic as she'd said she was looking out of the upstairs window at the road below, describing the seething mass of photographers outside the gates. Cressida looked at the floor, trying to focus on the shiny boards, on the lines between them. Anything to stop Emily-Jane's voice from swirling inside her head. Right now she just wanted to jump in the car and get home and take Emily-Jane in her arms. But then they'd both be stuck in the house. She needed to keep calm so she could think. She'd be no help to Emily-Jane if she broke down now.

Why hadn't Laurence called to warn them?

Brioni's voice broke into her thoughts.

'Has she spoken to Laurence?'

Cressida shook her head silently. 'She can't get through to him. She was so upset. She said she wasn't feeling well so she came home from school, and now the house is besieged by the press. She'd just got in when someone started on the gate buzzer.' Cressida put her hand to her forehead. 'I need to talk to him.'

'She's safe inside, though? As long as she keeps out of sight, the press won't get anything.'

'Exactly, she's safer there than at school, so that's one good thing at least. Can you put the news on? Em said there was a TV van outside the house, too. Someone in school's given her number to one of the journalists and he keeps texting her.'

Brioni picked up a remote control, flicking on RTE's twenty-four-hour news channel, but it was showing the weather forecast.

'Emily-Jane should block him – the journalist.' The TV switched to the weather. 'Have a look online, thejournal.ie is always pretty fast. It's bound to have been on social media. But I don't get why the press are going bonkers. Data breaches happen a lot. Maybe they've linked it with what's happened to Kate?'

Cressida was already scrolling through her phone.

'It's something about customer accounts and credit cards.' Her face creased in a frown. 'I'll find out.'

Cressida hit her husband's number and waited for him to answer. It rang out to his voicemail.

'He's not answering, for God's sake. I'll have to try Dora and see if she knows.'

As she spoke, the weather report finished and the news came on, a red ticker crossing the bottom of the screen.

'Reports suggest millions of Ferryman customer accounts have been compromised ...'

Cressida sat forward on the sofa as the newsreader switched to a shot of the Ferryman offices, a ring of burly black-clad security men around the front of the glazed building, more press photographers hanging around outside.

'And now we're going to Ferryman headquarters at Grand Canal Dock. What does this mean for customers of the tech giant?'

The camera swung around to the reporter. Behind her, on the opposite side of the dock, the glass façade of the 1796 hotel rose against the sky.

'Well, Claire, it could be potentially catastrophic. We are waiting for a company statement now, but experts are telling customers to change their passwords immediately, and obviously banks have been alerted to look out for fraudulent card activity, but it's the scale of this problem and its international nature that is truly shocking.'

'Ferryman is one of those home-grown Irish success stories, and the spearhead of the tech quarter in Dublin. Do we know how many accounts are involved?'

'As you know, Claire, the media received a release this morning apparently sent by a cyberterrorist group calling itself Nemesis. It stated that customer accounts have been breached, not stating a figure, but given what we know of Ferryman, that could be thousands, or perhaps millions, and they have customers from all over the world. Until we get a company statement speculation is rife, and it's having a negative impact on the share value, as you can imagine.'

As Cressida and Brioni watched, the camera swung around again to a flurry of activity and flashes as two men in dark suits left the Ferryman building.

'They're guards, I'm sure of it.' Brioni had her eyes fixed on the screen. 'They've got that look about them.'

Before Cressida could comment, as if reading her mind, the reporter began speaking in the background.

'The garda cybercrimes unit have been briefed ...'

'Oh God, turn it off, I don't think I can watch any more.'

As Brioni flicked the TV off, Cressida bent down to pick up her bag.

'I need to go, I'm going to have to go to the office if I can't get hold of Laurence. This could ruin the company. He's kept the hotels separate, but online booking is key to their trade. And trust is crucial. This could be the end of Ferryman.'

She paused, looking at her phone. Still nothing from Laurence. She sent him a text.

> Call me, press besieging house. Em at
> home on own and scared. What's going
> on?

Cressida put her hand to her forehead as a thought suddenly struck her. She could feel herself paling as she looked across at Brioni, who was still standing with the remote in her hand.

'Nina worked on the data side. Her murder could be linked to this. My God, this is terrifying. I need to get to Emily-Jane. I'll call you as soon as I know what's happening.'

Chapter 28

THE TIDE WAS turning when Brioni got down to the beach. As she'd seen Cressida into her car earlier, she'd looked out to sea and had felt the waves calling her. The whole situation with Laurence and Ferryman felt as if it was imploding. She needed some headspace, to switch off so she could reboot. The past twenty-four hours had been insane.

The wind had dropped, leaving behind a layer of mist and soft rain that enveloped the beach and made the thought of a swim even more welcome.

When she needed thinking time in order to solve a problem, the sea had always been the place she would escape to. As a child she'd felt as if she was always waiting for something. For her dad to sober up, for Marissa to get home from school, for the kettle to boil.

Waiting to get away.

And every day she'd waited for the tide so she could immerse herself and feel the chill water wash over her, revitalising her.

Since she'd left home, she'd stopped waiting, making up for lost time by hurtling forward, first to Thailand, then to London and university, to Cambridge, Massachusetts for a semester, and then to Dublin.

Getting back here had grounded her again, like the moon going full circle. It was as if those years of living so intensely – of travelling, studying, partying, going to galleries and museums, and the theatre – had made up for the barren years of her childhood when her whole life had been going to school and trudging home across the fields from the bus stop. Waiting for the rain to stop.

She'd been hungry then, hungry for knowledge, hungry to get on with her life. Discovering the *New Scientist* in the stack of magazines in the library when she was fourteen had been like a door opening. A door that she'd shot through the moment she'd had the chance.

But the thing she'd missed most, all the time that she'd been away, was the feeling of the pull of the water, the total freedom that came with sea swimming. And now, spending all her waking hours hunched in front of a screen, the sheer release of the sea was like an elixir.

At the water's edge, the beach was deserted as far as she could see, the mist swirling in, getting thicker by the minute. The tide wouldn't be fully in again until later this evening, but they were between neap and the higher spring tides that came twice every lunar month, and even though the beach shelved slowly, she knew she wouldn't have to go too far out to find some depth.

Wading out into the shallows, her bare feet gripping the fine sand, as soon as the waves reached her waist, Brioni slipped forward on to her front, letting the salty froth wash over her head. Enveloped in freezing water, she immediately felt as if all the air had been sucked out of her. Surfacing, the need to focus on breathing slowly completely centred her mind, wiping it clean of all the events of the previous few days. As the cold caused a rush of adrenaline to hit her, excitement coursing through her in an instantaneous burst of endorphins and serotonin, she felt completely free, alive in the moment – the rush and gurgle of the water loud in her ears, her heart pounding.

She wore a wetsuit now that she wasn't swimming every day, but she could still feel the exhilaration of the icy water. Overcoming the cold was part of the mental reset that came with sea swimming – she knew the fear was all in her head, and once she got further out, she'd be weightless, at one with the ocean.

It was like a secret addiction, this need for complete release.

Watching their father drink himself into oblivion after their mother's death, both she and Marissa had recognised that they may have inherited that addictive gene, had consciously avoided anything that could suck them, too, away from reality. While they'd been here at least.

Meeting Mike had been the catalyst to Marissa realising that Steve, her ex-husband, had been an addiction. Offering the support she'd lacked at home, she'd been so happy when she'd first met Steve in America, but that support had quickly morphed into control, and when they'd moved from New York to London, things had got worse. Much worse. The outwardly successful businessman with the perfect home had been something quite different on the inside.

The similarities with Cressida were striking. Appearances could be deceptive.

Everyone has secrets. Nina's words popped into her head.

Slowly adjusting to the temperature, Brioni cut through the water, swimming parallel with the beach, pulling through the waves. Flipping on to her back, she looked up at the sky, at the steel-grey clouds above her, scudding inland as if they were being chased. They looked angry, foreboding, but she knew that they'd already dropped their load further out to sea, the horizon streaked as if someone had taken a dry paintbrush and marked in the rain.

At one with the elements, her mind began to open up. Nina certainly had secrets, as did Laurence Howard, but there were a lot of players in this game. What were Cressida's secrets? What else was going on here that she couldn't see?

Chapter 29

CRESSIDA REACHED THE N11 motorway and hit the cruise control. There was so much going on inside her head that the last thing she needed was a speeding ticket. She had wanted to spend an hour today with Brioni working out where they were, what they knew, and what they did next, but now there was this thing with the data. It had to be related to Nina somehow. Cressida felt her stomach flip. How could Nina be dead?

As if it wasn't bad enough that her husband was spreading himself around, now things had just gone mad. She still couldn't really believe it.

And if there were bodies disappearing, that meant more than one person was involved, which was more than terrifying.

When the private house that was now the Reynolds Regency House had been originally built, no one had wanted to see the staff. They were an invisible entity who made things happen, but who the family and their guests didn't want to engage with. It really wouldn't be hard to get a body out of a room and into the service corridors – although clearing up blood was a totally different thing, if the true crime dramas Emily-Jane was obsessed with were to be believed. She was always saying that it was impossible to remove completely, even by experienced teams who had to deal with all sorts of horrors as part of their daily routine.

But one thing was for sure – the publicity that would result from a woman being murdered in one of the hotel's most prestigious suites, a woman who worked on the data side of the Ferryman business that was now under attack, would make things even worse.

Nina had said she was being followed. Someone really meant business.

But how did Kate Spicer fit into all of this – could it really be a personal attack on Laurence, something this big? Surely if someone was that mad with him, they could hire a hit man and kill him much more simply and quickly, and be less likely to leave a trail? This felt just so malicious, as if someone wanted to make him suffer.

There was so much more Cressida wanted to know about how Nina had approached this friend of Brioni's, about what had really gone on upstairs. Did women do that? Pick up random men? It was so bizarre. But perhaps her fear at being followed had made her act like that? And precisely what had transpired when Alex left? Cressida could only guess at that.

The biggest questions in her mind now were how involved Laurence was in it all, and where exactly Nina's body had ended up. Perhaps killing Nina had been the first part of someone's plan, but it had backfired when her body had been whisked away, and this data thing was their next attempt to destroy him.

Emily-Jane had called as she got into the car; she'd sounded weak and utterly miserable and Cressida had told her to go to bed and to turn her phone off. Emily-Jane just couldn't cope with this level of stress. Whatever was going on at Ferryman, no matter how much he was distracted by business – or his women

– Laurence needed to come up with a plan to protect his family. And fast.

Leaving Wexford behind and heading through Wicklow on her way to the city, Cressida slowed as she approached the Glen of the Downs, the thick woodland on both sides of the road giving way to views of the Sugar Loaf Mountain. But she wasn't looking at the scenery. Her mind was too busy.

Cressida pressed the *call* button on her steering wheel and tried calling Laurence again. Voicemail.

Again.

She felt a burst of rage as she left another message. Pacing Brioni's living room, she'd called Dora to discover he'd gone into a board meeting.

But he should be out by now.

Why wasn't he answering? He had to see her name on the screen – he'd set a special ringtone for her, for God's sake. Emily-Jane hadn't said how many press photographers were outside the house but it sounded like a lot. How long would this go on for? Would they be able to leave once they got home? Cressida could see they could be holed up for a few days until the next bit of news came along and took Ferryman off the front page.

But if that next bit of news was about Nina – or Kate, for that matter – then this was only going to get worse.

How had Laurence brought this down on them? How could he not have warned them?

Cressida felt panic beginning to rise. This whole situation was whirling out of control and she was in the middle of it. Cressida never got involved in Laurence's business, never called to the office, but now the business had involved her. She needed to know exactly what was going on and what the impact would be on her and Emily-Jane. And she needed to know now, not when it suited him to tell her.

Ahead of her, the traffic lights turned red and Cressida slowed. As she'd got into the car, she'd texted Laurence to say she was on her way up to the office. When she got into town, she'd ring ahead and make sure the guy on security in the parking bay was ready to flip the door open for her, just in case the press were hanging about there as well. Hopefully any reporters would be around the front of the building and not at the rear car park entrance.

She was almost there, the Friday afternoon traffic heavy. She needed to find out how long they were likely to have the press hanging about outside the house. If it looked as if it was going to be more than a few days, she'd book flights to Italy to stay in the villa for a week. It wasn't great timing at the beginning of term, with Emily-Jane just starting the Leaving Cert, but whatever Laurence had done, they didn't need this sort of stress. And Cressida was quite sure the school would agree – they'd want the minimum of disruption. She could imagine Mother Superior's face at the thought of photographers trying to get shots of 'her girls' in the school grounds.

The paps could be absolute bastards when it came to getting pictures. And the press in this country loved knocking anyone who had done well – Laurence had been too successful, too young, for a lot of people. There were journalists who seemed to make it their sole focus to look for every possible crack in the Ferryman machinery in an effort to discredit the company. If this data breach was for real, they'd be in their element.

Cressida had never courted any sort of celebrity status associated with being married to one of the country's richest men; she didn't hang out with the in-crowd or accept a fraction of the invitations she got to awards dinners and charity balls. And she'd brought Emily-Jane up to understand that you needed to keep the media at a distance. Ever since she'd been photographed by a friend at a private party, and the picture had ended up in the tabloid social pages, Emily-Jane had learned to be careful. She'd been devastated at the time, had felt utterly betrayed by the girl who had taken it. She'd thought she was a good friend.

But now, whatever had happened at Ferryman, the media had come to them.

And they didn't even know about the real elephant in the room yet.

Cressida had hated Nina with a white-hot passion from the moment she'd heard her voice on the phone, and there was no way she was going to let her damage her life any more – alive or dead.

The lights changed and Cressida pulled slowly off, slipping through before they changed again.

It was early afternoon, why on earth were there so many people on the road? She tapped her fingers impatiently on the steering wheel.

Laurence would probably be furious with her for going to the office, but it could be hours before he was home, and she wanted to hear exactly what the situation was. From him.

And how Kate Spicer fitted into it all.

When she'd called earlier, Dora had said that the last she'd heard, Kate was stable and they hoped would be out of ICU in a day or so. She'd lowered her voice – as if anyone would have been listening.

'*They've no real idea what it is, one of the staff overheard one of the doctors say something about an aphrodisiac. Can you imagine taking something like that in work? Goodness only knows what might have been going on.'*

Cressida could. It had taken all her willpower not to break the phone in two.

'And there's all this talk of poisoning. I really don't know what to believe. I think the guards went to look in her medicine cabinet at home. Which was just as well, as it turns out she's got a little dog that had been crying pitifully all night, according to the neighbours. You'd have thought they might have investigated what was wrong. I mean, she could have been dead on the floor of her apartment. One of the other girls is looking after the poor little thing now.'

Cressida had made the appropriate sympathetic noises, the word *aphrodisiac* thumping in her head as if someone was punching her.

Pressing the button on the steering wheel, Cressida dialled Dora's line to let her know to alert security. Engaged. She left a message. She'd be there in ten minutes.

Chapter 30

WHEN LAURENCE FINALLY got out of his meeting – a meeting Dora had stressed was vital and couldn't be interrupted – Cressida had been sitting on the sofa in his office for the best part of two hours.

After scrolling through her phone looking at the headlines – now there were articles springing up about the founder directors of Ferryman; someone had even found the rugby team shot of them all from school – she'd decided social media was the last place she needed to be, and had started flicking through a pile of magazines she'd found under the coffee table. God only knew why Laurence had copies of *Vogue* in his office, but she'd found some business magazines that had looked interesting. She hadn't been able to concentrate on anything more than the editorial snippets.

When he'd finally arrived, his face had been a picture – Cressida could almost hear her mother's voice as her favourite phrase sprang straight into her head. He'd swung the door open and marched in, calling over his shoulder to Dora for coffee without listening to her telling him he had a visitor.

Cressida had looked at him archly. Her presence was obviously a surprise. Perhaps, more of a shock.

'Where the hell did you come from? Why are you here?'

It wasn't the reaction she had anticipated or wanted. Cressida looked at him hard; she could feel rage burning inside her as if someone had just switched on a blowtorch. Taking a mental deep breath, she spoke slowly, as if she was talking to a child.

'The house is besieged by journalists. Emily-Jane is there on her own – she came home from school feeling rotten, and now she's terrified. Ferryman is all over the news. And you ask me why I'm here?'

'For God's sake, Cress, I don't need you—'

'I'm sure you don't need me … but could you give me a clue as to what the hell is going on? When precisely were you planning to bring me into the loop? I need to know, Laurence. When something you do affects me and Em, I need to know.'

'I haven't done anything.'

Striding past her, he rounded the desk, sat down hard on his chair and, picking up a pen, tapped it on the leather blotter beside his laptop. She could tell from his face that he was trying to work out where to start.

He wasn't the only one.

'There's a bunch of hackers – Nemesis, they call themselves – claiming they've got into our systems. They're threatening to publish customer details, not just credit card details but purchase history as well.' He ran his hand over his face. 'Credit cards can be cancelled, but a lot of people don't want their employer or their spouse knowing what they get up to in their private life. It's a total fucking cat-as-trophe.'

He drew the word out.

Cressida looked at him, the irony not lost on her. He wasn't wrong.

174

'So what's being done?'

He scowled, his eyes on the pen. A moment later he came back to her.

'Our cybersecurity team are investigating to see if these bastards actually have the data, and to find out how they got in. We need help. The CEO of SpeakEasy was in touch offering his team, but the board aren't interested.' She could see the tension in his face as he drew in a breath through his teeth. 'They seem to think we can just delete the files if they appear on the Dark Web – honestly, they're utterly clueless. They can see the issue with the credit cards, but they don't seem to have copped that the credit card companies simply can't block this number of cards in a few minutes. We're talking thousands, probably tens of thousands. If they fall into the wrong hands, there will be massive fraud, it's going to cost everyone millions. And that's before we even get to the purchase history issue.'

'What are they asking for – the hackers?'

'Twenty million dollars in bitcoin.'

'That seems cheap, honestly, given the situation.'

He closed his eyes and shook his head slowly. 'We can't afford that – it's crazy money. And even if we paid there's no guarantee they'd stop there. Dirk Ackroyd from SpeakEasy suggested we put some code in somewhere to try and track it. I don't even know if that's possible, but he has a point. It's not as if we can shadow the money like we could if someone was delivering a suitcase full of cash, is it? If we want to stop them, we have to find them first.'

'What do the board want you to do?'

'Ride it out. They reckon it could be a bunch of tech nerds holding us to ransom. They have a point, too, we have incredibly secure systems. I mean, we employ professional hackers to try and infiltrate the systems, to look for weaknesses.'

Cressida could feel his anxiety from across the room, like static electricity, arcing over to her and making her own chest tighten. Getting angry wasn't going to help anyone here; she needed to keep calm.

'So how did they get in?'

'A worm's most likely – someone must have connected their personal computer or an infected USB key to our system. It's been done before in other companies – it's just been kept quiet, rarely makes the papers.' He sighed. 'I can't see how else it could have happened. The team will be searching for that as soon as they've checked there are no holes anywhere else.'

Cressida felt her world stop turning for a split second. Hadn't that been exactly what Brioni had used to get inside Laurence's computer? If they found it, could they trace it back to her? Cressida fought the urge to pull out her phone.

'How long will that take? To check everything, I mean.'

He shrugged. 'Twenty-four hours at least. Maybe longer.'

Cressida moved to look out of the window behind his desk, trying to breathe evenly. Her heart was hammering in her chest.

'What are you doing about the press? Will you be making a statement?'

'It's being prepared now. We need to downplay the whole thing, say everything's under control.'

'Can you say you don't believe the information they're claiming to have has been taken at all? Reassure people their information is safe?'

'I don't know, that could be a red rag. We don't want to goad them into releasing any information. On the outside we're playing it down. On the inside we've got a negotiation team from the garda cybercrimes unit working to buy us time and see if these guys make a mistake, while we try to fix the leak at the same time. The thing is, the amount of data we're talking about is huge. To have managed to access, download and store it takes time, and also huge servers. The guards think it's likely they've actually only got to a small part of the customer database – enough to make it look as if they've got everything, but in real terms they'd have to have government-sized servers to be able to handle it.'

'Well, that's something.' Cressida sat forward on the sofa, the soft Italian leather creaking slightly as she moved. 'So where does that leave Em and me?'

Chapter 31

IT ONLY TOOK Brioni a moment to fire up her laptop. She took a sip of her coffee and looked at the screen, entering her password, mulling over everything she'd heard on the news. She'd had it on constantly in the background since she'd got home from her swim. She glanced over her shoulder at the TV. Sky News had a pair of experts discussing other data breaches now. It must be a slow news day elsewhere. This was exactly the type of thing news stations loved – they could keep going off at tangents forever.

Brioni turned her attention to the laptop again and opened the file she'd compiled on Laurence Howard and his activities. Since Cressida had left, she'd been doing some deep thinking.

From everything she'd seen, it was very clear that Laurence Howard thought people – even men he'd grown up with, men who were his closest friends and who had helped build his business – were dispensable. Which made Brioni wonder where that left Cressida. But this had turned into so much more than trying to get evidence on a cheating husband. Whatever was going on at Ferryman was much bigger. And scarier.

Beside Brioni lay a ruled A4 legal pad, its yellow pages now covered with arrows and circles. She'd created a mind map of all the bizarre events that had occurred in the past forty-eight hours, and their intersections. On another page that she'd torn off and laid beside it, she'd created a timeline of the events of last night, detailing who was where and when.

Or, at least, where they said they'd been.

With Nina's murder, this had become about so much more than a divorce case. Brioni's involvement might have started there, but then everything had blown up, and being a natural problem solver she was hard-wired to keep battling with an issue, whatever it was, until she found the answer. She was pure Scorpio, and now, more than ever before, she wanted to know what the hell was going on. It felt as if she was in the middle of a giant crossword puzzle where you had some of the intersecting answers but you had to guess what the clues were.

She'd listed the names of everyone involved at the top of the page – from the manager of the Reynolds Regency House to Kate Spicer and her staff in the spa – their names conveniently detailed on the hotel website. Focusing on Ferryman, she'd added Nina and the names of everyone on the board.

The one person who connected them all was Laurence Howard.

This data breach seemed incredible after everything else that had already happened. And it made her think that Howard had upset someone very powerful, very badly, someone who had completely lost their patience. Brioni rubbed the back of her head.

Was it something to do with this SpeakEasy deal? She'd only found hints of it in his emails, nothing specific, but with SpeakEasy's failed attempt to move into the UK, it was only logical that they were looking hard at Europe and a base in Ireland would bypass the issues they were having. Ferryman's customer base had to be priceless to them. Which would suggest that whatever deal Howard was doing, he was going to be richly paid for it.

Had Laurence Howard's fellow board members realised that he was using Nina to get information to blackmail them? He'd had a series of meetings scheduled with them from early this morning, according to his diary – had those gone ahead? Brioni couldn't be sure – when the news of the hack had hit it must have derailed his day, but that had been at lunchtime. The media had all received the same information at midday, so in theory, those meetings had occurred before anyone had an inkling of what was to come, of the full-on storm that was about to hit them.

It was one big mess.

Listening back to Nina's conversation with Laurence from the other night, it was clear that she was a very focused lady. And it had taken Brioni a lot of digging to get information on Nina, which was strange in itself. Everyone – at least everyone normal – had an internet footprint, their personal details spread across the web. Even if they were spread thinly, they were there.

But not Nina Rodríguez.

Which made Brioni wonder why.

From what Brioni could piece together, Nina had grown up in a wealthy area of Bogotá, a city dominated by violent cartels, but she'd gone to a private school where she'd scored top grades, and then on to a master's degree and a series of jobs for companies on the tech side, each one bigger than the last.

And, according to Alex, even in his brief contact with her, he reckoned she had a very passionate, fiery temperament. She knew what she wanted and she knew how to get it.

But someone who had seen Nina as a threat had murdered her – so she couldn't be behind this Nemesis group and the cyberattack herself. Could she have told the board what Laurence was doing? Had they retaliated against him with some sort of hoax hacker story that would result in his resignation? Thoughts whirled as Brioni sipped her tea, looking out of the long window over the windswept dunes to the sea. It was still raining, the sea and the horizon meeting, the line blurred, but she hardly noticed.

If what she was thinking was anywhere close to the truth, the board could claim he'd mishandled everything and use Laurence's removal or 'resignation' to reassure the public, perhaps claiming it was all some sort of scam. With him gone, Ferryman would be stronger than ever. The share price would bounce back and everyone would be happy.

But where would that leave Cressida and Emily-Jane?

On balance, Brioni wasn't sure the other members of the board had the capability for some of the events of the last few days – individually, at any rate. She'd investigated their backgrounds and companies, and it looked to her very much as if it was Laurence Howard's vision that had brought them together and given them the success they now enjoyed. But a common enemy resulted in the most unlikely alliances. Would they risk everything to get rid of Laurence Howard?

Kate Spicer's poisoning; Nina's murder; the data hack: it all smacked of someone who either didn't give a damn about the law, or who considered themselves outside it. Someone who would stop at nothing to get what they wanted. It was entirely possible that everything was coincidental, but that would be very, very bad luck, statistically as unlikely as it got. Brioni couldn't believe that this wasn't all linked somehow; it must have been instigated by someone who stood to gain from it all.

And from what she'd heard of Laurence Howard's moral code, despite the fact he *appeared* to be the one who could lose out big time, he was the prime candidate. Had he double-crossed everyone and, knowing that Nina could compromise him, made some sort of spread bet against the share price dropping?

Her raspberry tea cooling, Brioni tapped her nails on the side of her mug and looked out into the dusk. The sky was slate-grey, the sea darker. Below her the beach curved away in a perfect pale arc, deserted, the seagulls the only sign of life.

Ideas bobbed around Brioni's head like buoys on the water. Perhaps there was someone watching Laurence. Was this all some sort of strategy to control him? But if it was, what did they want? Brioni wasn't sure. It felt as if this was more about money and power than a personal attack. If it was personal, wouldn't harming Laurence or his family be easier? The thought sent chills through her. Perhaps that was next.

With everything coming back to Ferryman, there was a lot of money at stake. The company was worth billions; its rapid expansion in 2020 had seen it secure a huge market share, putting many smaller retailers out of business, not just in Ireland but across the globe. If you were a high-end company and you weren't listed on Ferryman no one would find you, but you had to pay a significant percentage of your business to be there. With a valuation that made it a global player, there were billions of reasons why someone might want to frighten Laurence Howard. Someone who knew as much about him as Brioni did, who wanted to influence him to do something. Someone who wanted his job and his power as CEO.

Brioni looked at her list of names – everyone who stood to profit from Laurence's problems. Ferryman's rival companies were right at the top, along with this Dirk Ackroyd and SpeakEasy.

And there were several members of the Ferryman board who would benefit from Laurence's fall. The three board members who had helped build the company, and who had known Laurence the longest, were the very men whom he'd threatened to blackmail. If he was on the way down, any accusations he made against them would look like desperation. Brioni chewed the end of her pen. And they weren't stupid, these guys; they all ran companies that were successful in their own right.

The two or three journalists Cressida had mentioned in one of her texts, who seemed to make a habit of targeting Laurence personally, were also on the list.

At the end of it, Brioni had added Cressida.

Approaching everything she'd discovered methodically, the way she tackled any data issue, Brioni couldn't leave Cressida off the list. She might not benefit from Ferryman collapsing, but she had lots of reasons to make Laurence suffer, and she did, at the end of the day, have her own company and income. Brioni was sure their house was paid for, and she had the strongest possible reason to go after Laurence's mistresses.

It felt weird adding Cressida's name, but the only way to get answers was to look at every possibility.

Brioni looked at the page in front of her. It was quite a list.

She took a sip of her tea. Whatever was happening, one thing she was sure of, thanks to the data breach, was that the Ferryman systems would come under scrutiny and her worm could be spotted. It was extremely unlikely that it could be traced to her, but Brioni hadn't spent years developing it for someone to create a data patch against it on its first outing.

Her fingers flew over the keys. She'd written a self-destruct instruction into the code in case of this very eventuality.

Chapter 32

B Y THE TIME Cressida got home to Dalkey, the guards had managed to clear the road of press vehicles. She'd called them to tell them Emily-Jane was on her own as soon as she'd left Brioni's house in Wexford, before calling her daughter to say she was going to Laurence's office to find out exactly what was going on and then she'd be straight home.

Thank God she was home from school.

Emily-Jane was safer in the house than anywhere else, even if she was ignoring Cressida's texts to make a point.

Now, as Cressida drove past Blackrock garda station and on down through Monkstown, a bike cop fell in behind her, flashing to tell her he was there. As the local detective inspector had explained when it was first published, Laurence's constant presence on that ridiculous *Sunday Times Rich List* made them a target, and details of their cars and personal numbers were on a priority list at the local station. Which had its definite advantages at times like this.

As they neared Dalkey, he passed her to drive in front of her Range Rover, ensuring the remaining members of the press parted as she reached the gates and didn't try to follow her in. He sat on his bike positioned across the mouth of the gates, giving her a wave as they closed behind her. She hopped out of the car, her head down, and ran to the front door.

Cressida had expected Emily-Jane to be waiting for her, but as she swung the door closed behind her with a very firm clunk, the house was silent. Perhaps, for once in her life, her daughter had actually done what Cressida had told her and gone to bed. She usually hauled her duvet downstairs and set up a bed on the sofa when she was ill, apparently so she could watch TV. She had a TV in her room but from the living room she could see the drive, and who was passing on the road.

Slipping off her coat, Cressida hung it on the newel post at the end of the banisters and skipped up to Emily-Jane's bedroom. Sweeping to the first floor, the stairs joined a mezzanine corridor that overlooked the huge square hall – the bedrooms, study and bathrooms opening off it. Their bedrooms were at the back of the house overlooking the sea, with Laurence's study between them. The guest rooms were all at the front of the house, the blinds drawn to stop the neighbours on the other side of the road, some of whose houses were slightly elevated, from looking in. A balcony wrapped around the back, French windows opening on to it from all the bedrooms, which would have been lovely in the south of France, but they'd only managed to have coffee out there once since the renovations had been completed. The decking off the kitchen was far more practical – it didn't have quite the same view, but was a lot more sheltered. Living by the sea sounded amazing in principle, but it also meant that every single storm hit the house full on, with salt water often whipping the windows as well as rain.

Upstairs, Emily-Jane's door was ajar and Cressida pushed it open. The room was dark. The curtains were closed and her daughter was obviously fast asleep; Cressida could see the white of her arm thrown out over the pillows. Creeping in, Cressida flipped on the lamp from the panel beside the door.

The room smelled of vomit.

Emily-Jane's hair was plastered to her face, the ends spread across the pillow as if she'd been writhing in her sleep. Deathly pale, her breathing was shallow. Panic exploding in her chest, Cressida was beside the giant sleigh bed in a moment. She put her hand on Emily-Jane's forehead. She felt hot.

'Em, Em, can you hear me?'

Emily-Jane moved marginally but didn't open her eyes. She seemed barely conscious.

Something was wrong – very wrong.

Realising she'd left her phone in her coat pocket, Cressida flew out of the room and down the stairs, spinning around the post at the bottom and grabbing her coat. She had the doctor's number in her mobile and the reception was better in the kitchen.

Almost running past the island, fumbling for her phone, she pulled it out of her pocket and headed towards the French windows, searching for the number. She caught a flash of colour out of the corner of her eye on her way across the kitchen, but didn't register what it was. A moment later her call connected. Catching her breath, she kept her eyes focused on the end of the garden where it dropped to the jetty, trying to keep her voice steady and calm.

'Doctor Stevens? Yes, it's Cressida Howard. I'm sorry to call your mobile after hours but Emily-Jane's very ill. I don't know what's wrong, she's almost unconscious and her room smells of vomit.'

She paused while the doctor answered.

'Yes, she came home from school before lunch. She's been here all day on her own.' Cressida glanced at the time. It was almost 6.30. 'I know … the press … I don't know if she's taken something. Yes, yes, of course. Thank you.'

Harriet Stevens only lived a few minutes away. She'd get here quicker than an ambulance, and she'd know what to do. Cressida closed her eyes and put her hand to her forehead. Fear ripped at her insides – fear and anger.

This was Laurence's fault. He should have told them about the problems at Ferryman so Emily-Jane could have stayed away from the house, gone to a friend's home if she wasn't feeling well. Instead she'd been held hostage by photographers. She hated the thought of ending up in the papers again; had the stress made her ill?

Cressida turned around slowly, taking a breath, trying to slow her heart.

Harriet would be here in a minute.

As she focused on the kitchen, Cressida saw the flowers Laurence had sent on the kitchen counter. They were still in their magenta box, the black ribbon curling around it. Huge orange spiky things that looked like flames, and orchids, cream lilies. Emily-Jane must have found them in the laundry room where Cressida had dumped them, and brought them in here to find a vase.

Suddenly Cressida felt a wave of absolute fury. How *dare* Laurence do this to them? How dare he have all these other women? How dare he send her flowers and think that would make everything all right? His inattention, all those late nights at the office … *How dare he?*

Heading for the drawer in the island, Cressida pulled out a roll of black sacks and, peeling one off, shook it out.

The rubbish was the only place for these. She didn't care what they cost, or that they were from the smartest florist in Dublin.

Making a balloon of the bag, she looped it over the whole arrangement, scooping it up and pulling the ties tight. She didn't even want to touch them. Inside the laundry room, she went to the back door, unlocking it with one hand, the other dangling the sack as far away from her as she could. Outside, she heaved open the lid of the wheelie bin, dumping the black sack into it.

Just as she slammed the lid closed, she heard the gate buzzer. Harriet had been as good as her word. Heading into the main kitchen and the intercom, Cressida checked the video screen and pressed the release to open the gates, praying it was cold enough and late enough that the last straggling photographers had gone home.

A moment later the front door bell rang. Cressida had it open before the sound had even died away.

'Harriet, thank God you're here, I don't know what's wrong. She's deathly pale ...'

Harriet started unbuttoning her pillar-box red coat before she even stepped into the hall, her medical bag slung over her shoulder.

'Don't worry, that's what I'm here for. Show me the way.'

Chapter 33

THE STOVE LIT, Brioni stood looking out of the living room window, a cup of berry tea warming her hand. It was dark outside, the waxing moon hidden by the clouds. The mist that had thickened as the afternoon progressed had rolled inland, leaving her view of the sea clear. With the living room lights off, she could see flashes of light on the horizon from buoys anchored far out to sea, and what looked like the dark hulk of a tanker heading up the coast to Dublin port.

Brioni rolled her head, stretching her neck. She had a lecture online at 8 p.m., two hours on artificial intelligence given by a Russian professor whose accent was as heavy as the snow in Moscow and whose favourite word was 'business': 'We look at this business and it indicates multiple variables – this business.' She loved being connected to the hub of knowledge that was Empress College in the heart of London, while being able to breathe Wexford air.

As she took another sip of tea, she looked down at the tattoo on her wrist and traced its pattern, the loops and curls of the *unalome* symbol, representing chaos. She was sure that was exactly how Cressida felt tonight – everything she had known in ruins. Her life looked so perfect from the outside, but just below the surface, everything she held dear was being tossed around as if it had been hit by a tornado.

And then she'd got home to find Emily-Jane was seriously ill.

Cressida had texted from the hospital earlier, but had been understandably brief.

Up until now, a tiny part of her had wondered if perhaps Cressida had more to do with everything than she was letting on. But Brioni knew for sure she would never endanger Emily-Jane. If she'd been behind this hacking thing, she'd have known the press would descend and would have made sure she and Emily-Jane were out of the country, in the villa in Italy that she'd mentioned. It wasn't as if money was a problem.

So that meant it was someone else.

And in Brioni's mind, the other board members in Ferryman were the strongest suspects right now. They'd all known Laurence Howard a long time, and if he was prepared to blackmail them in return for a cash payout, who was to say they didn't feel the same way about him? You didn't get to the top in business by being nice to people.

Each of the three founder directors had piloted their family companies to great heights: Philip French in the holiday industry; Richard Murphy in fashion, taking a traditional men's wholesaler into fast fashion that had teenage girls queuing for the latest release; and Eoin O'Reilly in interiors. Ferryman was the icing for them – thick icing, it had to be said – but they were all independently successful and, she reckoned, could weather the fall in the Ferryman stock prices that this cyberattack would inevitably result in.

But equally, a fall in the stock value weakened the company and made it ripe for a takeover, whether that initiative came from the inside or outside.

Was that what this was all about? Had Laurence's behaviour and general unpleasantness finally persuaded them to get rid of him? There was a good reason that greed was one of the seven deadly sins, and what did they say about money being the root of all evil?

There was definitely evil in the air in the Ferryman office.

Brioni's phone pipped, interrupting her thoughts. Leaning over, she checked the screen. She'd been expecting Cressida, but it was Alex. Brioni smiled, putting her tea down to pick up the phone. His *Hey, how u doing?* sounded as if he needed to talk.

> Just about to start a lecture,
> how's you?

Still alive. Have convinced parentals
to stay at sea.

> Is that good?

Defo.
Flight from Peru 2k x 2 coming out
of my wages.
Lots of shouting.
Am an idiot obvs.
Cost of education. Place in firm.
Demotion to mail room imminent.

Brioni grinned, shaking her head. Alex didn't seem to be able to put all his thoughts into one text; instead they came separately like machine-gun fire with hardly a break for her to reply.

It wasn't your fault she got shot.

My fault in suite.
FYI left out bit about recreational
substances & taking clothes off.

How did you explain being in the
shower?

Accident with champagne.

And they believed you?

No.
Potentially disinherited.
At least from when they get back.

Brioni's thumbs flew over the keys of her phone.

When's that?

Another 2 weeks. Cruise is a month.
Have to call if I get arrested.
Dad textd number legal aid solicitor.

He's not going to get someone in
his company to rep you?

Depends on how much shame I
bring on family name.
Plenty so far.

There was a pause while Brioni worked out something to say that would give him some support. She hated that he was on his own trying to deal with this, not that she could fix any of it, but when her friends were in pain, it broke her heart. Her laptop pinged with a message saying the lecture was about to start.

> Come down here when you can.
> Lecture starting. Will mess when
> done.

> TY B xxx

Her heart jumped as his last message came in. Sitting down at the table, she pulled her laptop towards her, trying to focus on artificial intelligence and decoding Kuznetsova's accent. She glanced at her phone again, an image of Alex sitting alone in his apartment jumping into her head.

She might not be able to work out what was going on in this mess right now, but she was damned well going to find out. For Cressida and for Alex.

Chapter 34

'THAT'S WHAT I said, Laurence. I'm in St Vincent's hospital with Emily-Jane.'

Cressida paused, keeping her voice low. Standing in the corridor outside Emily-Jane's room, she ran her hand across the back of her neck. She was exhausted and hot and had zero patience left. She'd left three messages for Laurence during the course of the evening; it was past ten and he'd finally picked up.

Obviously he hadn't thought of returning the calls – she knew he was in the middle of a crisis, but she was his wife. And she was having her own crisis. She continued speaking before he could answer.

'They don't know what's wrong. They think she might have taken something, or it could have been a violent reaction to the takeaway we had. They're running tests. She's on a drip and they're worried about her heart rate – it's uneven, apparently.'

She drew a breath long enough for him to reply: 'I'll be there as soon as I can. I've got some stuff happening here—'

'I do know that. I've been here for hours, Laurence, I've been texting and calling you since I got here. I need you to organise Sally to clean up Emily-Jane's room and her bathroom and to air the room. She was sick everywhere. I don't know how long she's going to be here, but I'm not going to be back tonight. I can't face having to explain to Sally and getting into a load of speculation. You need to be at home to let her in in the morning and make sure she doesn't speak to the press.'

There was a pause at the other end.

He was obviously working through his options.

'OK, OK, I'll leave a note for Dora to organise it.'

Cressida rolled her eyes. She could have done that herself.

'Were there photographers there when you left for the hospital?' He continued before she could reply, 'Are the doctors sure Emily-Jane didn't take anything?'

Cressida felt her voice shake with anger and emotion as she answered.

What was he more worried about – that pictures of an ambulance leaving their house would be on tomorrow's front page, or that the press would report that his daughter had taken an overdose?

'The photographers had gone by the time the ambulance arrived. The doctors don't know if she took anything. They were asking if she was on heart medication. I don't know what it can be. Harriet and I had a good look and there weren't any pills or drugs or anything in her room, so unless she took something at school, I really don't know.'

Cressida turned to lean on the smooth cream wall of the hospital corridor, glad that it was deserted. She suddenly felt utterly exhausted.

'I've texted all her friends to ask. Chloe was with her all morning and says she was feeling a bit queasy. Then she saw the thing about Ferryman in the news on her phone and she said she felt unwell and she wanted to go home. Obviously the nuns thought she was well enough to drive. Sister Mary said she felt it was the shock – she said Em looked perfectly well, but she understood she wanted to be in her own home, not with three hundred girls all whispering about her.'

'Sister Mary should never have let her drive home.'

Cressida sighed loudly. 'Well, obviously she wouldn't have done if she felt there was something genuinely wrong with her physically. I spoke to her at lunchtime and she wasn't feeling well then, but she didn't say anything about it being this bad. I don't know … it could have been some sort of panic attack, being home alone with the press camped outside.'

'At least she's in the right place now. I—'

'Laurence, this is your daughter. Please don't be long.'

She ended the call and went down the corridor to the room Emily-Jane had been assigned. She'd come in via A&E, but they'd transferred her to St Vincent's private hospital now, where at least she had some privacy and space. As Cressida opened the door and went inside, Emily-Jane barely stirred, her face still alabaster, even against the white of the pillow. The machines she was hooked up to continued their reassuring beeping as Cressida paused for a moment, watching her.

Reaching down under the bed, Cressida pulled out the two bags she'd hastily packed while Harriet had waited with Emily-Jane for the ambulance.

When Emily-Jane was very little she'd fallen off the swing in the garden and Cressida had ended up in hospital with her, blood pouring from a wound to her scalp. With a suspected head injury she'd been kept in overnight, and Cressida had realised she'd left the house with absolutely nothing except the clothes she was standing up in. Laurence had been away, and she hadn't wanted to leave her daughter for even one minute to go down to the hospital shop and find a toothbrush.

It was a lesson well learned.

As Harriet had taken Emily-Jane's temperature and checked her heart rate, Cressida had whizzed around collecting nightclothes and her hairbrush, make-up and toothbrush, as well as clean underwear. Packing them into her hockey bag, she'd gone over to her own room to pack a similar bag. She'd had a feeling she might not get home for a while.

Now pulling Emily-Jane's Bea Bear out, Cressida tucked the almost threadbare soft toy in beside her daughter. She had had the bear since she was a baby; it still slept with her curled up under the duvet.

Resting the bag on the side of the bed, Cressida found Emily-Jane's chapstick and leaned over to rub it on her lips. They looked dry and cracked, probably from vomiting earlier, but also from the dry air in the hospital. It was boiling in the room and Cressida had draped her coat and sweater over the back of the chair.

Her phone pipped with a text. Brioni.

Any news?

Cressida smiled. Brioni seemed to be more concerned about Emily-Jane than her own father was. Cressida replied:

Nothing yet, results in the morning.
All stable.

She bit her lip. She hoped they had some results in the morning. She couldn't bear it if anything happened to Emily-Jane.

Chapter 35

'No, stay there, I'll come down to you. I'm on my way out.'

Laurence put his desk phone down and reached to turn off the green glass-shaded lamp illuminating his desk. Kate had given it to him. It always made him feel as if he was in a 1950s detective novel.

Today more so than ever.

With the office lamp off, the lights outside in Grand Canal Square lit the room with a ghostly glow. Across the water, the 1796 was ablaze as always, the ripples created in the canal basin by the incoming tide catching its light, swirling around the houseboats moored further down, their deck lights bright against the coal-black water.

Right now Laurence needed to find some light somewhere. The twists and turns of the last few days would have surprised even Raymond Chandler.

And now Emily-Jane … He closed his eyes for a second, taking a steadying breath. He needed to get down to the data analysis floor for their latest update, and then he could call into the hospital on the way home. Between the guards, the press, constant calls from Ferryman suppliers, the managers of the hotels having individual meltdowns about the hacking, and updates from Ethan and the tech team, he'd barely had time to think.

It was almost eleven o'clock; Cressida was still at the hospital with Emily-Jane – the same hospital Kate was in – and his fellow board members had gone home hours ago. Once the press statement had been released – the 'don't panic, we've got it all under control' bullshit – they'd gone to their respective homes, leaving him to 'sail the ship', as they'd put it – and, he was sure, to consider their respective conversations this morning.

He'd managed to drop the bombshells of his knowledge of their various vices in an *'I've learned today and we really need to be careful because of the press'* kind of way, that had made it sound as if he was genuinely concerned for their welfare and their position in the company. Then he'd slipped in the bit about SpeakEasy and needing their vote as they'd each left the office, their mouths drawn in tight lines of worry, the enormity of what could blow up in public, very real.

By eleven o'clock this morning he'd spoken to all of them, and they'd thought their biggest problems were personal.

*

'How the fuck did you find out?'

As the colour had drained from Eoin O'Reilly's face, he'd stood up and gone straight to the drinks cabinet concealed in the brushed chrome panelling behind the bathroom door, grabbing the first bottle that came to hand. Laurence had cringed inwardly as the twenty-five-year-old Powers Gold Label whiskey had been liberally splashed into the glass. Eoin had taken a large mouthful before slowly turning back to Laurence.

'It's not me, you know, it's Aisling. She's always been into all that kinky stuff. It can't get out, people know her.' He'd taken another gulp.

Laurence hadn't had to explain how he had the information; each of them had jumped to his own conclusions. He had to laugh at Eoin blaming his wife. He rather doubted her feet were size 12, given that she was only just five foot two. Eoin had let it all out then.

'It was that tart, wasn't it? I knew that party was a terrible idea, even with a mask people still recognise you.'

Laurence had controlled his eyebrows, fighting to keep his face serious as Eoin had spilled more details. When he'd heard enough, he'd interrupted him.

'We need to handle it carefully. It's like that deal I was talking about with SpeakEasy. There's nothing wrong with it at all, it's just the perception that needs to be managed.'

Eoin had nodded, his eyes locked on the deep blue carpet, apparently reliving the experiences of a private party during which he'd been chained to a wall.

'Can you do that? Can you make it go away?'

'I think so, leave it with me. I'll see what I can do.'

*

He'd said the same to Richie – whose interest in teenage girls wasn't only explosive, it was sickening. Laurence needed his vote now, but after Nina's revelations, he was having serious doubts about whether he wanted to work with him at all. He certainly wouldn't be inviting him to the house, or out sailing, or *anywhere* he could get within sniffing distance of Emily-Jane.

'Don't tell me you don't like a bit of porn, Laurence –' Richie had shrugged as if it was completely normal – 'and what am I supposed to do about the girls? They're models, they have their clothes off half the time. And the Chocolate Kisses clothing range is aimed at sixteens to eighteens. They get crushes, I mean … It's huge in the States, look at the revenue we generate.' Thrusting his hands in his pockets, he'd looked out of the office window over the docks, shaking his head. 'Nobody understands how stressful it can be running a company. Sometimes you just need to let off some steam. The parties are just a bit of fun. But I know … the press.'

Controlling his own temper with difficulty, Laurence had pointed out that the press would be the least of his problems if anything got out. He'd still been making excuses as he'd left.

*

They'd all been so worried about their own stupid arses, the news that had come only an hour later that Ferryman had been hacked had hardly registered until Laurence had spelled it out. Even then, when he'd called the emergency board meeting and they'd sat looking at him around the table, he could see from their faces that, despite his fears that they'd be baying for blood, they didn't have the emotional capacity to deal with a problem of this magnitude on top of everything else.

He'd made it very clear that morning, that if any of the information he'd heard leaked, they'd each be ruined. But he could tell they knew that before he said it – and from their responses, he'd quickly gathered that in every case, there was a lot more that he didn't know.

Everyone has secrets. Nina's voice came back to him like an echo.

Boy, she'd been *so* mad the last time he'd seen her, hissing about him having her followed. Since he'd got to know her, he'd learned that her temper flared at the slightest thing. He closed his eyes for a second, his mind travelling back in time. She was brilliant and incredibly sexy, but also quite nuts. The sex had been a mistake. He'd been drunk the first time, and she'd been devastating.

She was always devastating, that was the problem. She was like an addiction, super-intelligent – and dangerous, like a stick of dynamite.

She'd hinted at her past, at her family's involvement in crime and how she'd had to fight her way out, but he'd hardly known which bits were true and which bits, frankly, she'd made up. It had all sounded as if she'd been brought up in the middle of Beirut or somewhere. He knew Bogotá had a reputation, but some of the things she'd told him about her family and how normal it was to carry weapons had been an eye-opener.

It really didn't matter now. She'd got him the information he needed and after this morning, he'd had each one of his fellow board members in the perfect position to agree to a partnership with SpeakEasy, and to agree to allow him to bring in their data team to help with the hacking fiasco. Once this meteoric cybersecurity problem was solved, he'd be able to get them to agree formally to bring the mobile giant into the Ferryman family.

His hand still resting on the telephone receiver, Laurence focused on the darkened office. Thank God the day was nearly over. Reaching for his briefcase, he strode out of the office towards the lift. The data team would be working all night to get this invasion sorted, and probably for days to come.

*

Downstairs on the third floor, the corridor lights flicked on as Laurence exited the lift. He could see through the glass wall that the lights in the main meeting room were on. The team had decamped to there, bringing their terminals with them so that they could share their progress behind closed doors. He should have got down to them before now, but he'd hooked them up with the gardaí, and the SpeakEasy team had come online this afternoon. He was doing everything a CEO could, given the circumstances. He checked his watch. He needed to show his face and make the appropriate noises to keep them going through the night, and then get over to the hospital.

He pushed open the double doors on to the data floor and headed over to the meeting room, the only sound the whirring of electric fans. Ahead of him the doors were firmly closed, the blinds pulled down. When they'd converted this floor they'd made sure this room was fully soundproofed. It was the most sensitive part of the whole company, and he'd insisted on multiple levels of security clearance – the team that worked here were the best in the business and were paid accordingly. Which was what had attracted Nina to Ferryman in the first place.

Pushing the door open, he was greeted by the smell of coffee and pizza, boxes piled up on a side table beside the Nespresso machine. Ethan, the team leader, looked up from his laptop as Laurence came in. He was sitting opposite two other members of his team, both wearing heavy metal T-shirts, one with a crew cut, the other with a ponytail. Both of them had a medley of piercings. They looked more as if they should be hanging out on a street corner than in one of the world's most successful tech giants, but this was one area of the company where business dress wasn't required.

'Evening, guys. How's it going?'

Ethan looked up from his screen. 'It's going, but we haven't found anything yet.' He ran his hand over his buzz cut. He was about ten years older than the other two and his age was showing in his face. 'It's weird. We've built the database like a submarine, with airtight compartments between different sections, so the customer accounts and their purchasing history are linked to the payment data, obviously, but the information isn't all in one place. Whoever did this had to get access to several parts of the system to get what they're claiming they have.'

Laurence frowned. 'Any idea as to how they got in?'

Ethan shrugged, shaking his head. 'Not yet.' His eyes still fixed to the screen, his fingers flew over his keyboard.

Laurence nodded curtly. 'Anything you need, you've got it.'

Ethan looked up and, pausing his typing, reached for a bottle of Coke standing open on the desk beside him.

'Thanks, boss. We're doing all we can with a man down.'

About to leave, Laurence stopped.

'Who are you missing?'

Ethan scowled. 'Nina bloody Rodríguez. She was out yesterday, too. I've been texting and leaving messages all day. We need her on this one, she's so sharp. I guess she must be sick.' He paused, his face lined with the day's stress. 'She has to have heard it on the news at this stage. I'm surprised she didn't come in.' He ran his hand over his head again, frowning. 'I was going to send a taxi over to her place this afternoon but we got caught up. My head's been so fried, I haven't had a second. She must be dead in her bed not to have at least called in.'

Laurence took a breath. 'Keep calling her, she has to be somewhere. I'll be back in a few hours. You've got my mobile, call if anything happens.'

Letting the door close behind him, Laurence walked to the lift, his stomach churning.

Chapter 36

B RIONI LOOKED UP sharply from her laptop as the twin headlights of a low-slung sports car cut through the darkness in front of the house. The driver had the high beams on, illuminating the long grass and gorse that grew along the tops of the dunes, surrounding the house like a protective embrace. As the car pulled up and the driver cut the engine, the lights died.

She'd turned off the security lighting – it triggered every time a fox walked past and she was having enough trouble sleeping at the moment.

She sat still, her eyes fixed on her own reflection in the window, trying to see past it to the car, her heartbeat accelerating.

Who the hell?

She wasn't expecting anyone and this house definitely wasn't on anyone's route anywhere, unless they were planning a midnight swim. She'd turned on the lamp beside the sofa when her lecture had finished, and the stove was burning merrily, but even with the low level of lighting in the living room, she was conscious that she could be clearly seen from outside.

A moment later an interior light came on inside the vehicle and she relaxed. The driver got out, waving to her over the roof, a bottle bag that he'd picked up from the passenger seat in one hand.

Getting up, she went to open the front door.

'What on earth are you doing here, Alex, it's the middle of the night?' A blast of cold air whipped into the room, its icy fingers damp with sea mist. 'Come in quickly before you freeze. Why haven't you got a coat?'

'I drove. From my place. Sorry, it look a bit longer than I expected. New car, well, old new car, no satnav. I got a bit lost.'

Looking sheepish, Alex came in and jerked his head to indicate the car, as if this was a perfectly logical explanation for driving around in the chill of an autumn night in a Calvin Klein T-shirt and jeans. Bottles clanking, he held out the bag to her as if it was some sort of peace offering.

'I bought you some of that grape stuff. How did your lecture go?'

'Great, thanks.' She looked at him, unable to think of anything more intelligent to say. But he obviously felt just as awkward.

'You said to maybe come down? And … Well, it's Friday night. I thought you might be able to use some company.'

She'd suspected earlier that he needed to talk, and now she could see from his messed-up hair and listless expression that what he was actually saying was that he needed some company; he just didn't quite know how to put it. Hardly surprising, given his recent experiences. She felt a surge of guilt for not checking in on him properly.

'Yes, of course, silly. Come in.' Tired and pale, and ridiculously unprepared for the trip, he looked lonely and vulnerable. She felt an urge to hug him. He looked a lot as if he needed a hug. 'Come and sit down. I was just finishing my notes.'

'Oh, I'm not interrupting, I can …'

A look of concern crossed his face, and he turned as if to say he could come back another time. She almost laughed.

As if you could just pop by here from Dublin.

'You're grand, stop loitering and sit.'

He walked into the middle of the room, looking up at the white-painted wooden ceiling with its angled skylights. He wasn't even wearing socks.

'Nice place. I always wondered what your house was like.' He suddenly looked anxious. 'Not in a weird way. You just weren't like the other girls at your school.'

Brioni smiled reassuringly; she wasn't sure if that was a compliment or not, but she knew what he meant. She'd always felt different, like a whirlpool in a millpond, but she hadn't realised anyone else had noticed. Although she had been the only person with pink hair sitting her Leaving Cert.

'Do you mind me dropping in? I thought …' He sighed, but she cut in before he could finish.

'Alex, don't be daft. Of course not.'

She loved being on her own, but if there was anyone else in all the world with whom she felt completely comfortable, it was Alex. On top of being very nice to look at, even more so because he didn't seem to realise it, he was very bright. And he was funny. And more to the point, he was the only person she could talk to about all of this, and *she* was the only person he could talk to. And he must need to talk – if she had gone through what had happened to him the other night, she knew she'd have PTSD. Guilt hit her again. It had only been twenty-four hours ago, and she knew he hadn't slept at all last night.

'Let me get some glasses.'

'I should probably be drinking coffee, but one glass will be fine. I'll be sober as a judge by the time I get to the main road. You think you've arrived when you turn off, don't you, but the last bit along those lanes is miles. I think I took the wrong turn off the N11 and then went wrong about four times trying to find you.'

Brioni glanced out of the window at his car, the fire-engine red paintwork glinting in the light from the windows. It looked like a Mazda MX-5, an absolute classic.

'How long have you had that?'

'About fourteen hours. You know that thing when you get a bit down and ...?'

'Add to cart?'

He nodded guiltily. 'It was a bit of a big add, but hey, life's short. I work hard and I needed a lift.' He took a ragged breath. 'I *have* had my eye on it for a while, it wasn't a total snap decision.'

She indicated the sofa. 'Sit down. What's up?'

He gave her a withering look, as if she needed to ask.

'OK, I'll try that again. Anything new?'

Alex stalked over to the sofa and sat down, fiddling with his car keys.

'Well, like I said, I've persuaded my dad everything's OK for the moment, so he's not coming home yet, thank God.' He stopped. Brioni could see that his parents returning from their cruise wasn't the real issue here. But before she could say anything, he continued. 'The thing is, I know this sounds crazy, but I can't stop thinking about it. About the hotel.' He sighed and looked directly at her. 'Why didn't they shoot me?'

'Who d'you mean?'

'Whoever shot Nina. I was right there in the bathroom, the music was really loud, there's no way they could have thought it was empty.'

The bag in her hand, Brioni paused as she turned to go into the kitchen for the glasses.

'Maybe they didn't know you were there and thought she was getting ready to go in herself – that she was running the water to get the shower warm or something.'

'But my clothes were all over the floor in the living room. Whoever it was came in, killed her and left. Just like that.'

Brioni sat down next to him on the sofa, putting his bottle of wine down between her feet. She was wearing thick woolly socks under her regulation skin-tight jeans. Not the sexiest choice, but then she didn't have any make-up on either. Not that Alex was likely to have even noticed with the mood he was in.

What on earth was she thinking?

'Perhaps they were in a hurry. Perhaps they needed to get in and out fast.'

'But what if I'd have come out while they were in the room?'

Brioni let out a slow sigh. 'Then things could have been a bit different all right.'

'If I'd come out, she could still be alive.'

He put his head in his hands and rubbed his eyes. Without thinking, Brioni put her hand on his shoulder and gave it a rub.

'Honestly, I doubt it. I think it's more likely you'd be dead, too. You couldn't have stopped someone with a gun. They knew exactly what they were doing.'

'I just keep thinking—'

'Don't, Alex, really don't. I mean, there's just so much about this that doesn't make sense. You'll go mad trying to figure it out. It's not like a game of chess where all the pieces are on the board. I think there's a whole lot going on here we're not seeing.'

He turned to look at her, his fringe flopping into his brown eyes, wet with tears. Her hand was still on his shoulder. She pulled him into a hug.

Chapter 37

CRESSIDA BLINKED AS the door opened and the overhead lights came on in Emily-Jane's room.

'My goodness, have you been here all night? You'll be as stiff as a board.'

The nurse picked up Emily-Jane's chart from the end of her bed and pulled a pen from the top pocket of her scrubs, frowning at Cressida.

She *was* as stiff as a board – stiffer, actually. And the light was making her eyes hurt. Cressida blinked again. The nurse had her hair cropped close, and was wearing a striking shade of pink lipstick that contrasted with her dark skin and made her look like a cover model. Her smile was bright and cheerful and exactly what Cressida needed this morning. The medical staff had been amazing, every one of them.

'I must have fallen asleep.'

'Why don't you pop into the bathroom for a shower while I check on Emily-Jane. She won't run away, you know.'

Cressida pushed her hair behind her ears. A shower was exactly what she needed. A good long soak to wash the hospital off her skin.

'Will she be all right?'

It was the most ridiculous thing she could have said, but the nurse smiled at her warmly again, obviously appreciating that she was still groggy.

'She'll be grand. Use Emily-Jane's towels, I'll get fresh ones for her for later.'

Cressida stood up, her hands at the small of her back as she flexed. She leaned forward and smoothed Emily-Jane's fringe off her forehead. She felt dehydrated and a bit dazed. But once she'd had a shower she'd feel much better, she knew.

'I'll stay here until you're done. The doctor's coming in first thing to look at her results and you'll want to be fresh for that.'

Cressida reached for her bag. Her phone was lying on the bed beside where she'd been resting her head. She picked it up. Laurence had texted at midnight.

Sally sorted, at home, will let her in before
I go back to the office. Text when you get
an update.

Cressida sighed. At least he'd sorted out the cleaning.

*

Cressida had showered and changed, and Emily-Jane's breakfast had been delivered by the time the doctor arrived – McCarthy, she thought his name was. Emily-Jane had woken briefly, bewildered to find herself in hospital. Unable to face food, she'd had a few sips of orange juice and fallen asleep again.

Now the doctor stood at the end of the bed, looking at the magical clipboard that seemed to hold all the answers. In his thirties, his hair shaved, he didn't look old enough to be a doctor.

Replacing the clipboard at the end of the bed, he crossed his arms, frowning thoughtfully.

'We were able to stabilise her last night, and we've got the results back from toxicology.' He paused. 'It's a bit of a strange one. We've another patient here with similar bloods. It's looking as if they were both exposed to a potentially lethal toxin. There was evidence of digoxin concentrations, although we've established that neither of them was taking digoxin.'

Cressida looked at him blankly. 'Can you try that again in English?'

'Sorry. Digoxin is used to treat heart failure, usually alongside other medications. It's also used to treat certain types of irregular heartbeat – it's a drug administered in tablet form. In neither your daughter's case, nor the other case that has presented to us, has digoxin been prescribed, so we need to dig deeper. Cardiac glycoside poisoning – essentially what we're seeing here – can occur from ingestion of various plants and animal toxins, so that's what we're looking at now.' He paused. 'The most common, if common is the right phrase, source of this type of reaction is venom from the glands of the cane toad. It contains large quantities of cardiac glycosides.'

'The cane toad? Are they native to Ireland?'

Frowning, the doctor shook his head.

'This is what makes this so challenging. It's a very large marine toad, native to South and mainland Central America, but which has been introduced to various places like Northern Australia, but not here.' He paused. 'The venom is actually a Schedule 9 drug in Australia, alongside heroin or LSD, but it's used in the "herbal medicine" market, most often in aphrodisiacs.'

'How on earth could Emily-Jane have got hold of that? I mean, why would she?'

Cressida looked at the doctor for several seconds, stunned. An aphrodisiac? Why, who? It took a moment for the cogs to start turning again.

He paused. 'I think Emily-Jane is the only person who can tell us if she took some strange tablets – perhaps she already wasn't feeling well and made a mistake in the medicine cabinet.'

Cressida gave him a side eye as he mentioned the medicine cabinet. They didn't even have a medicine cabinet at home. They had a box of paracetamol and insect bite creams and the usual stuff in the bathroom cupboard, but they kept their own medicines separately. She had tablets she occasionally took for thrush. Laurence had a supply of 'uppers', as he called them, some supercharged caffeine supplement that he ordered online for when he had to go to the States and function in a totally different time zone on full power. He kept them in the drawer beside the bed.

Cressida's thought process stopped suddenly, as if she'd reached the edge of a cliff and was looking over at a swirling river thousands of feet below. What else did he have in that drawer? With all these women on the go, did Laurence use some sort of performance-enhancing drug? He was almost forty now – perhaps he felt like he needed it?

Holy God, if he had something in the house that had almost killed Emily-Jane, she wouldn't be responsible for her actions. But surely he couldn't have – and why would Emily-Jane take tablets from his bedside drawer, assuming that's where they'd been kept? Cressida shook the idea away.

'Did you say you had another patient with a similar problem? I don't understand …'

'It does seem very strange. She came in on Thursday morning after collapsing at work. It took us a bit longer to work out what the problem was, but there seems to be a striking similarity with the toxins we're seeing here. We have to notify the authorities in cases like these. I'd imagine you'll be getting a call from the guards – they might be able to shed some light on where it came from.'

He looked at Emily-Jane, obviously turning everything over in his mind.

Cressida frowned; 'collapsing at work' was bouncing around her head like an alarm.

'On Thursday? Her name isn't Kate Spicer, by any chance?'

Chapter 38

SATURDAY MORNINGS WERE always busy on Ballycastle beach and this morning there were more people about than usual, even with the October weather – dog walkers and parents with small children who had evidently woken early. Despite the chill, the sun was trying to struggle through the clouds as Brioni returned to the house after her walk, her cheeks pink and numbed by the brisk sea breeze. She'd walked to the end of the sand and back through the fields, trying to sort everything out in her head.

Alex had left at six this morning, having spent the night in the spare room. But something had changed. His hug as he'd left had been longer than she'd expected. And this morning the colours were brighter and the sound of birdsong was definitely louder as she crossed the fields.

Brioni's phone rang just as she was coming into the house. Her key in the front door, she fumbled to pull her phone out of her pocket, and seeing Cressida's name on the screen, pulled off her gloves with her teeth.

'Hello, how's Emily-Jane?'

Cressida's voice was low, slightly echoey as if she was in a stairwell or somewhere with a high ceiling. Brioni pushed open the front door with her shoulder, bringing a blast of cold air with her into the living room, leaning on it to shut it as Cressida explained how Emily-Jane was. And the hospital's discovery that both Emily-Jane and Kate Spicer had been poisoned by something commonly found in an aphrodisiac.

Leaning on the door, listening to her, Brioni closed her eyes, trying to work out how this new piece of information fitted into her growing crossword puzzle. Cressida sounded tired and confused. And cross. She'd been trying to get hold of Laurence since early in the morning, and he wasn't answering his phone again.

'Christ, Brioni, I'm going to kill him. He texted to say he was going to call into the hospital on his way home last night. The nurse said by the time he got here I was asleep, so he went home. And I'm sure he's in the office this morning, but he hasn't even dropped in to see how she is. I texted to tell him Em was sick, and then that she was starting to talk a bit now, but why the hell hasn't he texted back?'

'I'm so glad she's OK.'

Brioni meant it. It now seemed more than ever as if someone was closing in on Laurence Howard and attacking the people and things closest to him.

Did Cressida realise that?

Brioni didn't think so; she was too focused on Emily-Jane to realise that she could be next. Brioni didn't get a chance to say it as she continued.

'She's still very tired. They're monitoring her in case this stuff has done something to her heart.'

'She's in the best place. You really need to look after yourself, you know …'

Brioni came into the living room properly and threw her gloves and hat on the table as she spoke.

'I know, I'll rest when we get her home. There's no specific antidote but the doctor said he wouldn't be surprised if she suddenly bounced back. She's young and fit and he thinks she only got a mild dose. They think her stomach upset was something to do with our takeaway, she had some of the leftovers for breakfast apparently, would you believe it?' Cressida paused. 'Did you sort out that other thing?'

Brioni knew immediately what she was talking about – how worried she was about the worm and her access to Laurence's computers.

'I did indeed, nothing to worry about there. That was the first thing I did after you left. But, Cressida, whatever is going on here really seems to be escalating.'

'I know.' Cressida lowered her voice even more. 'I'm starting to think Laurence is the target here. If this Kate woman and Em were both poisoned with the same thing then there must be a connection. And Nina, well …'

'You really need to be careful, you know. Until we've a better idea of what might be happening.'

'I know. I will. But thank you, Brioni, really thank you for everything, I—'

Brioni interrupted her. 'I'm going to take a few extra days off next week, so I'm around if you need me. I'll probably stay down here until tomorrow night. I'll see.'

'I'll keep in touch.' In the background Brioni heard voices, as if someone had come into the stairwell. 'I'd better go.'

Brioni leaned against the kitchen table as Cressida ended the call.

Thank God Emily-Jane was going to be OK.

Turning, she looked at the notes she'd made, the yellow pages of the legal notepad spread across the table. The more she thought about it, the more SpeakEasy seemed to have the most to gain from Laurence's weakened position. Were they thinking of taking a bigger step and not just partnering with Ferryman, but taking them over? If the Ferryman shares dropped significantly that made them vulnerable.

Brioni slipped off her coat, slinging it around the back of a chair and went to put the kettle on, her mind humming. Nina's murder felt like something out of Hollywood. People got shot in Dublin regularly, but not people like Nina. And not in suites in luxury hotels.

Had this Dirk Ackroyd character feared that Nina knew too much about the deal he was trying to do with Laurence? If she was prepared to blackmail her boss, what might she know that could make life uncomfortable for SpeakEasy?

At the table, a cup of tea in her hand, Brioni looked at her phone. It had picked up a bunch of WhatsApp messages as it connected with the Wi-Fi when she came in.

Most of them were from Alex. She smiled as she read them. He could be very funny, even in these dire circumstances. The guards still hadn't found anything to substantiate his story, and he was starting to think he'd dreamed the whole thing.

But Brioni had seen him. She knew when someone was in shock, and he hadn't faked puking his guts up in the car park under her apartment. Something had definitely happened to Nina.

Brioni took a sip of her tea as her phone started to ring again, Alex's name appearing on the screen. Smiling as she answered, she didn't even get a chance to speak as he cut across her.

'Bri? Have you seen the news?'

'Nope, I've been for a walk, I'm just in the door.' At the other end he took a long deep breath, as if he was trying to keep calm. 'What? Tell me?'

'Jesus, Bri, a woman's body's been found in the Dublin Mountains.'

'Holy God.' Pulling out a high-backed wooden chair from the table, she sat down heavily.

'It has to be her. They're saying they need to identify her by dental records or DNA – the body had been badly injured.'

Getting shot in the back of the head was pretty badly injured.

He drew a breath and continued hurriedly. 'The news said her identity had been disguised – that wasn't the word they used, but her face …' She heard his voice waver, before hurrying on. '… and her fingerprints. There was deliberate damage to her hands.'

Nasty. Someone really didn't want anyone to find out that this was Nina Rodríguez.

'Are you absolutely sure it's her?'

'Bri, who else can it be?' He said it as if she was about five years old. 'They said she had sallow skin and they thought, dark hair – her head's been shaved or something, though, so they're speculating about that. And she was naked, Bri, no ID at all, of any sort.'

It couldn't be a coincidence. Brioni had always believed that everything was connected in this world. Like the correlation between the ratio of the age of the universe and the atomic unit of time, and the difference in strengths between gravity and the electric force for the electron and proton. Were they coincidences? It seemed unlikely. Just as it was unlikely that this body was anyone else but Nina.

'Did you call the guards?'

'Yes, as soon as I heard. They're going to try and get in touch with her, but I couldn't remember what you said her surname was.'

'Rodríguez, she works for Ferryman, but you told them that in your original statement.'

'Did I? Jesus.' He paused. 'I can't remember what I said, that part of the night is all just a blur now. When are you back in Dublin, Bri? I can't talk to anyone about this except you. What if it is her, and they think it was me?'

Chapter 39

'THANK YOU, NURSE, and thank you for looking after her so well.'

Cressida woke suddenly at the sound of Laurence's voice. She had been dozing on the side of Emily-Jane's bed, the heat in the room and her lack of sleep catching up with her. The door closed behind him with a gentle clunk and he came to the end of the bed, his face betraying his shock at all the machines his daughter was still wired up to. He opened his mouth to speak but in those few seconds Cressida had woken up fully, sleep swept away by rage, white-hot.

'Where the *hell* have you been? It's almost one, I've been trying to get you all morning.'

Cressida kept her voice low but couldn't keep the fire from it. Her elbows digging into the sheet, she glared at him.

'I didn't realise ... How is she?'

'You didn't realise she was so sick or you didn't realise you were needed here?'

He looked at her, his eyes wide, his mouth open but no words coming out. It was a common delaying tactic he used when he was losing an argument. Looking as if he was about to speak but not actually saying anything. Long ago Cressida had realised it was his way of defusing the tension, or trying to. But Cressida wasn't buying it today. She straightened up, reaching for Emily-Jane's hand. Emily-Jane began to stir and, seeing she was about to wake, Cressida worked hard to keep her voice steady.

'She's fine now. She was exposed to some weird poison. She didn't ingest it, thank God, so they didn't need to pump her stomach.'

'Dad, is that you?' Emily-Jane's eyes fluttered open; her voice was raspy.

Cressida stood up and reached for the glass on the bedside locker.

'Here, love, let me get you some water.'

'Thanks, I'm parched.' Taking a sip, Emily-Jane let her head fall back on the pillow, her brown eyes focusing on her father. 'Have you been here long? It's so warm in here, all I seem to be able to do is sleep.'

'It's good for you, darling.'

Laurence perched on the side of the bed across from Cressida, taking Emily-Jane's other hand. He was wearing a sports jacket and jeans, his checked shirt open at the neck. Too smart for the weekend – Cressida felt sure he was on his way into or back from the office. Given the hacking fiasco, she shouldn't be surprised, but somehow she felt doubly irked. It was as if he'd only dropped in to the hospital because it was en route to somewhere more important. She bit back the recriminations that were fighting their way to the surface of her mind.

'I'm sorry I couldn't come sooner,' Laurence went on. 'So much has been happening and you were asleep when I called in last night. There's a thing at work, Em, a data thing. It's a bit of a disaster.'

Cressida was about to point out that his daughter getting poisoned was a bit of a disaster, too, but Emily-Jane spoke first.

'What's happening now? The press ... they were outside the gate. They kept ringing, it was awful.'

'I know, darling, I'm so sorry they came to the house. We're handling it, but Ferryman has been hacked and the media are all over it.'

'Do you know who did it?'

'Not yet, we've got our data people working on it and some guys from a company in the States. They're working 24–7—'

'What company in America?'

'You're too tired for this now, pet, you don't need to worry—'

'Dad, what company? Tell me what's happening, please. I'm seventeen, you know, not five. Why do I have to keep telling you that? I'm in this, too.'

For someone so sick, her tone was surprisingly curt. Cressida could almost feel Emily-Jane rallying, her temper giving her new energy.

She was her mother's daughter.

Cressida hid a smile as she busied herself topping up Emily-Jane's glass.

Laurence sighed, apparently oblivious to her change in tone.

'I'm sorry, love, the guards are trying to negotiate, it's all a bit tense.'

'So the American company ...?'

Surprised at her ferocity, Cressida sat down beside her and rubbed the back of her hand as Laurence continued.

'It's the data team from SpeakEasy, they're—'

Emily-Jane interrupted him again, rolling her eyes. 'A mobile phone company. I do know, Dad. I also know their licence was turned down in the UK, where, let's face it, privilege and money talks, because of their lax privacy policies. They have to be really bad for the British government not to let them in.'

It was the longest speech she'd heard Emily-Jane make since she'd been brought in. But perhaps Cressida shouldn't have been surprised; this wasn't the first time SpeakEasy had come up in conversation between her and Laurence, and the last time they'd had a huge row, the air between them frosty for weeks.

'If they can help us get out of this mess, I'll worry about their privacy policies later. There's a lot of money at stake.'

'How much? Do the hackers want money or do you mean the share value?'

'Em …'

Cressida could tell Laurence was starting to tell her not to worry, but he changed his mind. The look on her face was steely as he continued.

'Both. The hackers want twenty million dollars.'

Her retort was fast. 'You should pay it.'

'We can't, Emily-Jane, we can't be seen to give in to terrorists or more will come behind them, and they aren't just going to give the data back. They'll come looking for more money with more threats. We need to plug the leak, find out how they got in, and let the guards negotiate. We have to stop it happening again.'

'You're letting SpeakEasy into your database?' She paused, shaking her head. 'That's not going to end well.'

'You don't have to worry about it, Em. I know the CEO. He's coming over next week actually, he's a good guy. Really.'

'You think so?'

He patted her hand again. 'Look, I'd better get moving. I'll make sure I'm home when they let you out. I've been so worried about you.'

'I was worried about me, too. I'm lucky someone else got spiked first, though – the woman who works at the 1796. Doesn't she run the spas, Dad? Kate Spicer?'

Emily-Jane had obviously heard more of her exchange with the doctors than Cressida had thought. She looked at Laurence to see if he would react to Kate's name, but he had his poker face on, his eyebrows knitted as if the only thing he was worried about was Emily-Jane.

'Yes, she's been with Howard's for years. I better drop in to see her, too, now you've reminded me.'

'I don't think she'll be expecting the CEO, do you, Dad? You'll give her a fright. No one wants to see anyone when they're sick and looking horrific, trust me.'

'Still, I want to talk to her doctors, see if they know how you both got sick.'

'You could talk to my doctors. I'm sure they'll tell you the same as hers. They're probably the same guys, actually. Maybe you should take Mum home for a rest? She came in with me in the ambulance, she's been here every minute.'

Cressida patted her hand again. 'Don't worry, darling, I brought spare clothes with me. I'll hang on here until they discharge you. You're so much perkier now, hopefully it won't be long and then you can rest in your own bed.'

'Are the press still there, at home?'

Cressida shook her head. 'I called the guards and they moved them on. They're doing regular patrols past the house, so hopefully they'll stay away.'

Her hair spread out across the pillow, Emily-Jane shuddered. 'I can't bear the thought of them looking in the windows.'

Laurence stood up. 'Don't worry, love, I'll sort it out. I promise. I'll look after everything.'

As the door closed behind him, Emily-Jane looked at Cressida.

'I don't know how you put up with him. He's never at home and when he is, he's on the phone.' She glared at her. 'I wouldn't leave putting out the bins to him.'

'He's just worried, love, we both are.'

Emily-Jane scowled, her stare penetrating. For a moment Cressida wondered if Emily-Jane knew more than she was letting on about Laurence and his 'business interests'. Perhaps she'd overheard him on the phone talking to someone? Part of her stomach fell; worry about Emily-Jane feeling insecure, about what sort of example they were setting as parents – all her failures were rolling around like marbles inside her.

Emily-Jane closed her eyes. 'I got an A in my *Gatsby* essay, thanks for asking.'

Chapter 40

BRIONI KEPT THE TV on in the living room as she packed the few bits she needed to take to Dublin, one ear on Sky News's revolving headlines. Ferryman had hit the world news now, it wasn't just the top story in Ireland.

Her kitbag open on her bed, she laid the blond and dark brown wigs she'd bought on top of the sweaters and spare T-shirts she'd already packed. She always left her hiking boots and a pair of jeans here in Wexford on the off chance she had a really bad day at work and needed to escape for the night. It hadn't happened yet – she loved her job – but an escape route was something she'd cherished since she was a child. You always needed a plan B.

It was just as well Brioni was an expert packer; she could hardly concentrate on what she needed to put into her bag. Her mind was in top gear working through everything she'd heard. Somehow a body being found in the Dublin Mountains made this whole mess all the more real. It wasn't that she didn't believe Alex, but an actual dead person brought everything crashing into technicolour and right now, what neither she nor, more importantly, Cressida had was a plan B.

Brioni had got involved with this whole drama to help Cressida get information on her philandering husband so that she could divorce him – that objective seemed to have faded with the events of the last few days. The way things were going, though, Laurence was heading for an enormous fall all of his own making. Although Brioni had a feeling he was one man who knew how to bounce back.

If anyone had a plan B around here, Brioni was pretty sure it was Laurence Howard.

The news had said that the gardaí needed to identify the body. That would take time.

Brioni was sure the guards would call to Nina's apartment, and to Ferryman, where they'd be able to talk to her colleagues. Had someone reported her missing? She didn't appear to have any family here, but surely she had friends or work colleagues who were wondering where she was.

Brioni paused with her packing, frowning for a moment. Had the guards taken Alex seriously? They'd been to the Reynolds Regency House, but when they'd found nothing, had they just filed his report – or binned it? It did seem quite incredible, even Brioni had to admit. She'd racked her brains trying to work out how they couldn't have found traces of blood *somewhere*; she'd seen enough TV to know the guards had a special light that showed up blood spatter even if it had been cleaned up. But if Alex was right about Nina being shot in the bed, then the headboard would have taken the worst of it, and let's face it, it was a hotel, they had lots of beds. When they'd moved the body, had they swapped the whole bed for one in storage? It was certainly one explanation.

Turning around, Brioni picked up her mobile. Her almost-brother-in-law DCI Mike Wesley might be able to find out what was happening. Although he was based in London, he'd made friends in the Dublin force over the years, working on various operations that had crossed the Irish Sea. Perhaps he'd be able to get an update.

Mike picked up almost as soon as she dialled.

'Bri, how are you doing? Any more dead people turned up?' He sounded as if he was eating.

Brioni cleared her throat. 'Can you talk for a minute?'

'I can indeed, at my desk, on my tod with a cup of tea and a Marks and Sparks prawn sandwich. It's all glamour when you get to the top.'

Brioni grinned. 'Stop messing. Listen, you know that thing I called you about?'

'The dead woman with her brains blown out who wasn't in the hotel room? Uh-huh.'

'She was, Mike. I don't know what happened, but I told you, Alex is training to be a lawyer, he doesn't do imagination. Anyway, a woman's body's been found in the mountains. It has to be Nina. From the news it sounds as if someone's tried to conceal her identity. The thing is, after the guards went and checked the hotel, I don't know if they would have kept Alex's report on file.'

'This is the guards we're talking about, Bri. Everything goes into the PULSE system now, it's like our HOLMES. If they've found a body with a gunshot to the back of the head, I guarantee they'll have made the connection with your friend Alex. They've probably brought him in for a chat already.'

Brioni winced. That was a good point. She hadn't heard from Alex since he'd called earlier, so perhaps he was down in the garda station right now. Perhaps he hadn't had a chance to text her an update. She felt a bit of an idiot.

It was just as well Mike was family and didn't mind her calling with stupid questions.

He interrupted her thoughts. 'Want me to find out what's happening?'

'Could you? Just see if they're checking if it's her.'

'If it is, someone's got some serious explaining to do as to why they moved the body.' He paused. 'And made such a mess of dumping it. I'll call you back.'

*

An hour later, just as she was leaving her packed bag beside the front door, Brioni's phone pipped with a text. She hadn't expected Mike to ring her so soon, but as she picked it up, she saw it was from Alex. It was as if he knew she'd been thinking about him.

> In the cop shop. Lots of questions. Send
> reinforcements if I'm not out by 6.

Mike had been right.

He was also right about them investigating Nina.

She'd hardly digested it when her phone rang.

'You there? I've only got a few minutes, we just got a shout.' Mike sounded as if he was squeezing in his call as he walked briskly down a corridor. 'They're looking very closely at this Nina. She hasn't been reported missing, but she hasn't been in work either, and her team are the ones dealing with some sort of massive cyberattack on Ferryman.' She heard a door swing shut as he continued. 'The murder enquiry team are liaising with the cybersecurity guys. Given that Nina worked for Ferryman, there could well be a connection with the hack. They're also looking for dental records at the moment. It's faster than DNA, but that'll be in process, too.'

He paused, the distant sound of someone saying something to him interrupting his flow.

'That's great, thanks.' He came back to her. 'They're also taking a look at this Howard guy that runs Ferryman. Apparently another member of his staff and his daughter were taken into hospital with some sort of poisoning. If you know anything, now would be a very good time to share it. I know the guy running the show in Dublin, he's a friendly face.'

'Thanks so much, Mike. I don't know if I have anything useful—'

'Let them be the judge of that.'

'Good point. Text me his name when you get a sec. Have they any idea on how the poisoning thing occurred?'

'Flowers, apparently. At least the first woman, the employee, was sent some flowers that had been sprinkled with a noxious substance. Gotta go. Call me if you're worried about anything, I hope you're not too involved in any of this, sounds like a shitshow to me.'

'I'm fine. I'll keep in touch. Thanks, Mike.'

Flowers? Someone had sent poisoned flowers to Kate Spicer? This was all getting weirder and weirder.

Chapter 41

IT WAS DARK by the time Cressida and Emily-Jane got home from the hospital, but Laurence's BMW was in the drive, and the house was lit up – although he'd had the sense to close all the curtains.

It took Cressida a few minutes to find the remote for the gates in her handbag, but thankfully the press had left. She almost sighed with relief as the taxi pulled through the gates. Emily-Jane looked across the back seat at her.

'It's good to be home.'

'I'd be happier if you'd stayed in hospital till tomorrow.'

'I know, but I'll be able to sleep here and I'm feeling so much better.'

Cressida leaned across and rubbed her arm. The colour had returned to her cheeks, thank God, and she was almost back to her normal self. The doctors hadn't been keen on letting her out so soon, but she was young and strong and by late afternoon she'd been chatting away to everyone who came in. It would take her a while to get up to full speed, but once they'd taken her off her drip, there wasn't much more they could do for her. It seemed silly to block a bed for another night.

'Dad's here.'

Cressida threw her a grin of acknowledgement. They'd discussed calling Laurence to pick them up, but had both decided that they didn't want to wait. He was bound to be busy with something that would delay him getting to the hospital, and there was a taxi rank right outside.

Swinging open the rear door of the car, Emily-Jane took a deep breath of sea air.

'Wow, that's good.'

'Come inside before you get a chill on top of everything else.'

Cressida paid the driver and walked quickly to the front door, her keys in one hand, their overnight bags in the other. The cab reversed, its wheels crunching on the gravel as Emily-Jane came to join her on the doorstep. She was wearing Cressida's long navy coat, the collar turned up and the belt tightly knotted at her waist. Her fine blond hair was piled on the top of her head in a messy knot. One of the main things propelling her home was her need to wash it.

Cressida swung the door open, greeted with a rush of warm air and the scent of beeswax polish. Sally the housekeeper had been, at least, and she would have done a lovely job on Emily-Jane's room, Cressida knew.

'We're back!' Heading into the empty hall, Cressida called ahead of her.

There was no sign of Laurence.

'I'm going to go up and have a shower and change into my jammies. Can we have pizza for tea? I'm starving.'

Cressida almost laughed. Emily-Jane had obviously stopped worrying about calories after twenty-four hours of hospital food, most of which she'd barely touched.

'I'll order in. Let me put the kettle on. Do you want to come down when you're ready, or go to bed now and I can bring your tea up?'

Emily-Jane slipped off the thick llama hair coat.

'I'll come down. I want to watch *The Voice* and just crash out.'

Cressida watched her as she headed up the stairs, and then dipped her head into the living room, looking for Laurence. The fire was lit, the guard in place, and the lamps were on, but there was no sign of him.

The kitchen was the same. Cressida dumped the two overnight bags in the laundry room and came into the kitchen to put on the kettle. Coffee grounds and a steel pod scattered around the machine indicated he'd been home.

Where could he be? Perhaps he was in the pool?

The pool area connected with the laundry via a room they used for storing towels and robes. Heading through, Cressida pushed open the outer door, and was immediately hit by the smell of chlorine. This part of the house was Laurence's baby, the pool itself and the glass-roofed extension that housed it a gift to himself when Ferryman had gone public. He'd even had a bar installed at this end, elegant stools arranged in front of it. Emily-Jane swam fairly often, and had pool parties in the summer with her friends when they could open the French doors to the deck and enjoy the sunshine, but Cressida preferred her gym.

About to call her husband's name, Cressida suddenly caught the sound of his voice carrying over the water. She took a step further inside, checking the bar to see if he was there. The room was huge, star-like lights under the water making it sparkle, the water a stunning blue, picking up the colour of the tiles Laurence had ordered from Italy.

Looking around, Cressida still couldn't see him, but guessed he must be somewhere around the entrance to the changing rooms at the opposite end. About to walk down beside the water, she suddenly heard him more clearly.

'You think you can blackmail me? Seriously?'

Cressida froze, holding the door open to keep the sound of it closing from alerting him to the fact that someone was there.

'I don't know what the fuck you think you're playing at, McQuaid, but if you've moved some woman's body it's sure as hell got nothing to do with me.'

Cressida held her breath.

'You what? Yes, Nina Rodríguez works for me – she works for Ferryman. What the fuck are you talking about? "Tony called you to solve a problem."' Laurence mimicked a child's voice. 'What does that mean?' He paused. 'It sounds as if I need to talk to Tony Strachan, doesn't it? I'm not paying you a penny. I don't know what the hell you're talking about. If you're so friendly with Tony, perhaps you need to talk to him?'

Cressida leaned against the tiled wall, listening hard. Tony Strachan was the manager of the Reynolds Regency House, but surely Laurence couldn't be talking to one of the McQuaids who were always in the papers? How on earth did Laurence know *them*? There was a long pause and she heard his voice again.

'Tony? Laurence Howard. Red McQuaid's just been on to me. What the fuck's been going on there? He says someone shot one of the Ferryman team and you asked him to get rid of the body.' There was a pause before he continued. 'No, no one's listening, why the fuck do you think I'm using this phone? It's a burner.' Another pause. 'You're damn right we don't need the bad publicity.'

Cressida heard footsteps, as if he was pacing on the wooden boards outside the changing room.

'I appreciate you having my best interests at heart in keeping me out of the loop, but McQuaid wants 10k now to keep quiet. He says you hired his clean-up team.'

Cressida felt her stomach turn over. Brioni had been right. Someone *had* moved Nina's body. She shivered involuntarily. And not just anyone – the McQuaids were rarely out of the news, and none of it was good. One of the key families involved in the gang warfare that seemed to simmer in Dublin, they had a fearsome reputation. Hadn't Brioni said she'd seen McQuaid at the Reynolds the night Laurence had been meeting Nina, and he'd been about to head into the casino? Perhaps he was a regular. The manager, Tony Strachan, obviously knew him well enough to call him in in an emergency.

Laurence's voice interrupted her thoughts.

'We need to talk, somewhere private. I'll get over as soon as I can.'

Utterly rattled, Cressida slipped through the laundry room and into the kitchen. Leaning on the closed door, her heart hammering, she could feel herself physically shaking.

What was Laurence involved in?

She started as the kitchen door opened, her heart skipping a beat. Seeing her, Laurence stopped short in the doorway, his face a picture of surprise. She didn't give him a chance to ask how long she'd been home; instead, she said in the brightest voice she could muster, 'Oh, there you are, we *literally* just got back. Em's upstairs. I'm ordering pizza.'

Chapter 42

IN HER DUBLIN city apartment, Brioni scrolled down her laptop screen and realised that she hadn't actually read any of the notes she'd made last night in the AI lecture. She rubbed her eyes and picked up her mug, discovering it was empty. She needed to focus or she was never going to get this assignment finished.

Part of her wished she'd called Alex earlier and invited him over, but after getting totally distracted by his visit last night, getting the bones of this assignment written before anything else major hit her had become urgent. It was crucial to her final mark, and one thing about Empress College was that they expected the very highest standards at all times. It didn't matter what your extenuating circumstances were – excuses didn't breed success.

She'd thought she'd have loads of time to get it finished. The drive up from Wexford had been easy this afternoon, the traffic always much lighter on a Saturday. She'd decided to order her shopping before she left the beach house, rather than schlepping around a supermarket on the way back, and had met the Tesco delivery man outside. So now she was home, the apartment was warm, and her fridge was full.

Everything should be perfect, but ever since she'd arrived Brioni had had a weird unsettled feeling that was interfering with her concentration. It was as if someone had thrown stones into a pool and the intersecting ripples were washing over her, disrupting her thoughts, breaking the surface of her world.

Was she missing something? Was there something obvious in all the crazy events of the last few days that explained things? She tapped her nails on the side of her empty mug and, needing to move, got up to make herself some more tea.

She didn't bother putting the lights on in the kitchen; the glow from the city came in through the window. In Wexford the night was truly dark, but here the sky seemed to always be filled with light. Flicking on the kettle, its glass body illuminated by an electric-blue bulb, she watched the bubbles rise to the surface as the water boiled.

Was this what was happening to Cressida? Was everything suddenly coming to the boil? Everything Laurence touched seemed to be red-hot right now, and everything kept coming back to him.

Last night in Wexford, as he'd finished off the wine he'd brought, she and Alex had ended up talking about Laurence Howard, about what an incredible concept Ferryman was, about how it could only grow. And Alex had mentioned a *Forbes* article he'd read about how many successful CEOs demonstrated psychopathic tendencies. They'd sat up talking so late that she'd only thought to google it when she got home from her walk this morning.

And she'd discovered that he was absolutely correct. It had been published a couple of years ago, in 2019, but it was all there in black and white.

According to the article, between 4 per cent and 12 per cent of men who ran significant companies displayed psychopathic traits.

The article had said they were 'also chameleons, able to disguise their ruthlessness and antisocial behaviour under the veneer of charm and eloquence'. Which pretty much summed up Laurence Howard. Every article she'd found about him had mentioned his charm, his ability, like a politician, to work a room and make every individual in it feel special.

But it was the mention of chaos that had really got her thinking.

An expert from MIT had been quoted: 'I would say that psychopaths, or people with psychopathic traits, thrive in chaos and know that others don't, so they will often create chaos at work for this reason.'

Brioni couldn't get the words out of her head.

The cyberattack on Ferryman was peak chaos – could it be something that Laurence had staged? It had struck her that her worm hadn't been spotted despite the company going into a full-on security alert, which could obviously have had a lot to do with her brilliant coding, the months she'd put into perfecting it. But what if there had been no cyberattack at all, and Laurence had created it from the inside, like a magician draws the audience's eye, to take the focus off Nina's disappearance?

Appearance and reality could be two very different things.

Cressida thought he was distracted because he was having an affair, which – to her – was as bad as it got, but what if the problem was far bigger than that? What if he was orchestrating some sort of merger with SpeakEasy, and had deliberately created the attack as a diversion to cover his tracks in Nina's murder? Then *he* could be the one to find the solution to the hacker crisis and, like the crusading knight, ride into his kingdom battle-scarred but victorious. What then?

Selecting a herbal teabag from the row of boxes at the back of her counter, Brioni popped it into her mug, deep in thought. At least Emily-Jane was out of hospital – thank God. Cressida had texted earlier to say that she was getting a cab home, and that Emily-Jane was exhausted but looking remarkably bright, given the scare she'd had.

So that was something.

And Alex had been grilled in the garda station, but was now in his apartment with a pizza and a bottle of wine. He'd texted her photos, which had, in all the grimness, made her smile.

But if Laurence was at the heart of all of this, did that mean that Cressida was in danger? If he thought she was on to him, what might he do?

Chapter 43

IN THE KITCHEN, Cressida steadied herself against the counter and closed her eyes. Laurence had to go to the Reynolds Regency House, to 'sort something out' apparently, so he'd gone upstairs to say hello to Emily-Jane, before he left.

She'd innocently asked if the 'something' meant there was any progress on the hacking, but he'd been so preoccupied he'd hardly heard her. Now she was feeling sick. Very sick.

She heard his feet on the stairs, then his face appeared at the kitchen door.

'Won't be long, I promise. Order a capricciosa for me and I'll have it when I get back.'

And with that he was gone.

The minute the front door closed, Cressida reached for her handbag, searching for her phone in the muddle of lipsticks and business cards. Like the rest of her life, it was beautiful on the outside and chaos on the inside. She'd put her and Emily-Jane's phones into her bag as they'd left the hospital – she found her daughter's first and pulled it out, glancing at the screen. She'd heard both their phones pinging with messages as she'd gone to look for Laurence, updating as they'd come into the house. Emily-Jane's battery was almost dead. Cressida paused, looking at the most recent message displayed on the screen from someone called Danny Boy:

Missing you. Can you come out to play?

Cressida looked at it, puzzled. What the hell was that about? Was one of her friends messing about? Who was Danny Boy? The tune of the folk song immediately started running through her head. That was all she needed tonight.

Cressida looked at it again. 'Come out to play'? Did that mean go out for the night, or to a party or something? Or …? Cressida didn't want to think about what else it could mean.

Drawing a deep breath, she closed her eyes. One problem at a time.

She searched her bag again, this time finding her own phone, trapped between the leaves of an old theatre programme.

She needed to call Brioni. She was the only person Cressida could talk to about all of this; they'd become inextricably connected by the events of the past few days.

Dialling Brioni's number, Cressida stuck her head out of the kitchen door. Emily-Jane was still safely upstairs. Just to be on the safe side, Cressida closed the door firmly and went into the laundry room, closing that door, too. She leaned on the counter, tapping her foot on the tiled floor as Brioni's phone rang at the other end.

'Brioni, is that you? Can you hear me?'

'Yes, give me two seconds to turn the radio down. What's up?'

'I can't talk for long. Laurence has gone up to the Reynolds to meet Tony Strachan, the manager there. That guy Red McQuaid called him earlier. *He* moved Nina's body.'

'What? Sorry, slow down there.'

'I heard him say it, Bri. Your friend Alex was right, she was shot. McQuaid had a clean-up team or something.' Cressida heard Brioni draw a breath at the other end.

'You'd think the McQuaids would be a bit more thorough. Have you heard the news?'

Cressida froze. 'What news? I've been at the hospital all day.'

'A woman's body has been found in the Dublin Mountains. It sounds as if McQuaid's clean-up team isn't as good as he thinks it is.'

'My God. He wants ten thousand from Laurence to keep quiet. This is mad, Brioni, it's just mad.'

Brioni went quiet for a moment, obviously digesting the news; Cressida could hear her breathing. Then she continued.

'It is, but it makes sense. I was talking to Mike in London before I came up to Dublin. Remember he said that according to the guards there was nothing on the hotel security tapes. But there had to be. Whoever tampered with those security recordings did it so well that there were no jumps in the time clock, so it didn't look as if they'd been edited.' She paused. 'I've been thinking about it. They must have used footage from another evening. Just copied it over and spliced it in. It's only a few minutes, isn't it? And the same with the recordings in the lift. But that would mean the hotel management had to be involved.'

'If McQuaid's a regular at the hotel, who knows what's been going on there. I just hope your friend Alex is safe. If they know he's been to the guards, could the McQuaids go after him? He's a witness.'

'Crap, you're right. I'd better call him. They must have seen him on the security tapes even if the guards didn't.'

Cressida heard Emily-Jane calling her from the kitchen.

'I have to go – talk later?'

'Yep, for sure.'

Cressida clicked off the phone, her hand shaking. Everything had suddenly got very real. Far too real. Someone had murdered Nina Rodríguez and Laurence was mixed up in it. She took a deep breath, trying to calm her heart, pounding in her chest. She heard Emily-Jane moving around the kitchen.

Cressida pushed open the laundry room door.

'I'm in here, darling, just sorting out your clothes. I haven't ordered yet, what do you fancy?'

Emily-Jane had showered, her pale hair hanging wet over her shoulders, and she'd changed into a fluffy pale pink onesie, Bea Bear under her arm. She already had the pizza company leaflet in one hand, her phone in the other, and was scanning the menu. It gave Cressida a precious few seconds to gather herself.

Emily-Jane frowned thoughtfully. 'I'm not sure … What are you having?'

Cressida wasn't sure she could even think about food right now.

'Doughballs? I'm not that hungry. You've got a ton of messages, I heard your phone updating. Who's been texting you?'

Emily-Jane glanced at the phone, barely looking at it.

'Georgia and Chloe, I expect. I'll message them back.'

'Who's "Danny Boy"?'

Cressida did the rabbit ears thing with her fingers that Emily-Jane was so fond of. Emily-Jane continued to study the pizza menu, unconcerned.

'Chloe's brother. Total muppet. He's always taking the piss.' She leaned forward, her elbows on the counter. 'I'm starving. Will we get a Hawaiian and chicken strippers as well?'

Inside, Cressida mentally sighed with relief. Emily-Jane was so sensible, she wouldn't do anything silly. At least that was one thing she didn't have to worry about. And never mind pizza, Cressida really needed a glass of wine right now.

Chapter 44

PACING HER APARTMENT after Cressida's call, Brioni realised she was too keyed up to wait for her to call back before taking action. She really wanted to know what Laurence was going to say to Tony Strachan – she couldn't see how he could be totally ignorant of the situation – and she certainly wasn't going to learn anything sitting in her living room. If he was true to form, there was every chance Laurence would meet Strachan in the Kai Lung bar. And if he did, Brioni wanted to be there, too.

Pulling her clothes out of her bag, Brioni found the blond wig before digging around her wardrobe to find an outfit that looked right for a Saturday night in a five-star hotel, but not as if she was on the game.

The car park was packed when she arrived thirty minutes later, and it took her a while to find a space. Coming up in the lift, Brioni held her phone in her hand as if she was texting friends, keeping her face down as the doors slid open. Even from the atrium, she could see that the cocktail bar was busy, soft jazz and laughter spilling out into the marble hallway. She should have expected it on a Saturday night.

Crossing the main atrium, Brioni walked into the bar, scanning it as if she was looking for someone.

She was, obviously. But not someone who was expecting her. And there he was. Just like the last time.

Laurence Howard could have used any private room in the hotel, but here in the bar, he was hiding in plain sight. Meeting Nina in such a public place, and staying here after she left, had given him a solid alibi for the time of her murder. And he was doing the same now; it would be very hard to accuse him of conspiring about anything tonight. The busy bar was a perfect location. The ambient noise was sufficient to ensure his conversation would be private, and the more people who saw him, the better.

Brioni walked towards the bar and, catching the eye of the barman, indicated she'd be at a table in the corner. Sitting down with her back to the wall, she hoped that her black eyeliner would counteract any attention she might get from the blond wig. In her leather jacket and black T-shirt she was going for hipster rather than blonde bombshell. The wig and black dress had been a bit too 'look at me' sexy when she'd tried everything on in her apartment. The whole point of this exercise was that she wouldn't be seen.

As he had the other night, Laurence was sitting at a round table within hailing distance of the door and the bar, and the staff were being understandably attentive. He was sitting facing the entrance, looking casual in a sports jacket and open-necked shirt. His choice of seat was calculated – he could see anyone coming in, without looking as if he was watching. But Brioni could see him perfectly from her corner as he chatted jovially to the bar staff. He was playing with his phone the whole time, though, turning it over on the table nervously, rolling it through his fingers from end to end. He looked tense.

A few minutes later the hotel manager arrived. After her last visit Brioni had looked him up. Tony Strachan had been the general manager of the Reynolds Regency House for two years. Prior to that, he'd been at another five-star city centre hotel. One reportedly owned by a shell company that routed back to the McQuaid family.

Strachan joined his boss at the table and signalled for a round of drinks. The two men chatted for a few minutes before Strachan leaned in to say something to Laurence Howard. Frustratingly, Brioni couldn't hear them. The bar was much busier than the last time she'd been here, the ambient noise drowning their conversation, and there was a couple sitting on the banquette exactly where she had positioned the Bluetooth microphone on her last visit. Brioni wished she could get a bit closer, to be in with a chance to hear what they were saying, but she really didn't want to draw attention to herself. Their body language was telling her a lot, though. It all looked a bit forced. Even from here she could see there was tension in the way Laurence was sitting.

Laurence nodded sagely in response to whatever Strachan had said. Thinking for a minute, he shuffled forward in his seat, sitting more upright as he asked Strachan something – had he said 'when?' Brioni wasn't brilliant at lip reading but she was sure that he had.

Strachan leaned in again and made a gesture with his hand as if he was shushing Laurence, patting the air as if he was telling him to calm down.

Brioni picked up the menu and pretended she was looking at it, staring at them hard over the top.

What was going on?

For the hotel security footage to be tampered with, Strachan had to know what had happened to Nina's body. From what

Cressida had overheard, it sounded as if Strachan had ordered its removal.

Had Strachan been worrying about his job? Brioni could imagine that the negative PR linked to a woman being shot in the back of the head in one of the Howard Group hotels, on top of the whole Ferryman cyberattack and Kate Spicer's hospitalisation, wouldn't be good for business. The papers could destroy consumer confidence and literally sink the chain. So many hotels had gone under in 2020, and Brioni knew many more were hanging on by a thread.

As Brioni watched, Howard suddenly stiffened, his eyes on the doorway. Following his gaze, she could see a group of people had gathered beside the potted palms, the fronds waving in the air conditioning. A moment later Red McQuaid walked through the middle of them, although *strutted* would be a more accurate description. He was a small man, slightly round, his face flushed in the warmth of the hotel – he looked more like an accountant than a gang boss. But perhaps clever accountancy was the reason he hadn't been picked up by the Criminal Assets Bureau.

Sitting back in her seat, Brioni watched as McQuaid greeted several people at other tables, then turned and, seeing Tony Strachan, managed a look of surprise and delight.

As McQuaid reached them, Strachan half-rose and introduced him to Laurence as if they'd never met before. Brioni wrinkled her nose. It looked as if he was a regular here, and he was a very wealthy businessman, with several 'legitimate' businesses – including a greyhound track, Brioni was pretty sure. Was it likely that he'd never met Laurence Howard before?

As she watched, Laurence invited McQuaid to join them. He was smiling but there was a tension in his jaw.

The three of them chatted for a few minutes, their heads together so Brioni couldn't see their mouths properly, but she could see Laurence leaning in, his hands on the table, fingers interlocked. He was trying hard to look relaxed, but from here, she could see his stance was rigid.

Were they talking about Nina? Given the conversation Cressida had overheard, it seemed remarkable timing that, of all the people in the world to walk into the bar, it was these three.

Brioni checked the clock on her phone, at the same time taking some discreet shots of the three men. If the security video was to misfire again and their meeting was erased, she was going to make sure she had it on record.

Now she *really* needed to talk to Cressida, to find out exactly what else she'd overheard during Laurence's phone conversation. From what she knew of the McQuaids, while body disposal might be fairly routine, somehow the delivery of the poisoned flowers that Mike had mentioned seemed a bit hit-and-miss for them. The McQuaids were usually much more direct.

And who would want to harm or scare Laurence Howard so badly that they'd attack his daughter?

Chapter 45

AS CRESSIDA OPENED the front door wide to the two detectives, a blast of chill air filled the hall. It was raining hard outside and raindrops glistened on their navy jackets like tiny jewels in the light from the chandelier in the hall.

A Detective Inspector Gallagher had called her to ask if they could drop in to talk to Emily-Jane. It was after ten, and Emily-Jane was exhausted, but whatever they needed to discuss was important, apparently – he'd said something about a statement. Cressida's stomach had clenched when she'd answered the phone and the inspector had introduced himself. For a moment the thought that Laurence had been arrested loomed in her mind. After the conversation she'd overheard in the pool room, he'd said he'd only be an hour, but obviously whatever was going on was taking much longer.

The discovery of a woman's body brought things to an entirely different level.

To Cressida, hacking was something that went on in cyberspace, somewhere not quite real. She appreciated that no one wanted their private information leaked, but – hopefully – it didn't result in violence and death. But whatever was going on with this McQuaid character was very real. Earlier, as she'd waited beside Emily-Jane's hospital bed, watching her sleep, Cressida had decided to try ringing Nina's office line. Part of her still hadn't fully believed Brioni's friend's story. If Nina answered, then Cressida would know for sure that he was mistaken.

Cressida had pretended to be a dry-cleaner checking up on a forgotten dress. She'd bitten her lip when whoever had answered the phone had said Nina hadn't been at work for a few days. He'd offered to take a message as she wasn't answering her mobile right now.

As she'd hung up, Cressida had felt a chill radiate from deep inside her, reaching every extremity.

It confirmed what she'd overheard.

And now the guards were here to talk to Emily-Jane.

If something Laurence had done had put Emily-Jane at risk, she'd damn well kill him herself.

The two men showed her their badges as she stepped into the hall to let them in.

'I'm Detective Inspector Frank Gallagher and this is Sergeant Jamie Fanning. We're both based at Harcourt Square now, but this used to be our old stomping ground when we were in Dun Laoghaire. We know your husband well. We'll be as quick as we can. We just need to ask Emily-Jane a few questions.'

Cressida smiled. The detective inspector did look familiar now he was in the light. At least that was something. She started to relax. She indicated the open door to the living room opposite.

'Come in, please. Emily-Jane's still up. Can I get you coffee?'

'Thanks, we'll be grand, though. We won't keep you long.'

As Cressida followed them into the living room, Emily-Jane swung her legs down from where she'd been curled up on the sofa and turned to look at them, her hair dry now with the heat from the fire. She'd definitely got a bit more colour in her cheeks.

Showing the two men to the sofa opposite, Cressida sat down beside Emily-Jane, her eyebrows raised expectantly. DI Gallagher got straight to the point.

'When your toxicology results came through, Emily-Jane, the doctors advised us there had been a similar case in Dublin. There's a public health directive in cases like this. The National Poisons Information Centre has to be notified, and the Director of Public Health. They let us know if they feel there could be a bigger problem. As the nature of the toxin in your case was so unusual, we're investigating how you and the other case became exposed to it. The other patient has been extremely ill – it looks as if the dose she received was much, much higher.'

Sitting beside Emily-Jane, Cressida leaned forward.

'Was that Kate Spicer, Inspector? She works for my husband.'

'We're not at liberty to give details of the other case, but I can say that we are investigating if the two of you have any connection, and it would appear you do.'

Cressida bit her lip. They must have realised the connection as soon as they spoke to Kate.

'She was taken ill before Emily-Jane. Do you know where this poison actually came from?'

'There are several possibilities. She collapsed in her office, so our officers have been taking a close look at it, and everything she did in the preceding hours. She had been using massage oils, but Mr Howard had no ill effects, and neither did the cleaner who tidied up when he left – we've analysed everything just to be sure.'

Cressida felt her stomach drop, but fought to keep an understanding look on her face. Laurence had been to see Kate Spicer on the morning she collapsed – *for a massage?* The detective inspector obviously assumed Laurence would have mentioned why he was leaving the house so early that morning, and perhaps using one of his own hotel spas made his visit appear completely above board. To anyone on the outside.

Trying to focus on the two men opposite her, Cressida could feel rage building inside her. Had it *just* been a massage?

She suddenly tuned into what the inspector was saying.

'We're currently looking at a bouquet of flowers that arrived immediately before she collapsed.' He paused and flipped open his notebook. 'From a company called—'

'Blooming Fabulous? A big pink box?' Cressida could feel her mouth setting in a line as hard as the edge to her voice.

'Mum?' Emily-Jane's eyes darted from the inspector to Cressida. 'You got a delivery of flowers. I found them when I came home on Friday. They were on top of the tumble dryer in the laundry room.'

The inspector sat forward on the sofa. 'Really, Mrs Howard? When did they arrive?'

Suddenly Cressida could feel her head spinning as if she was on an aircraft and they'd suddenly hit turbulence, the room closing in on her.

'Mrs Howard?' The detective repeated her name.

Blinking, Cressida pushed her hair behind her ear and cleared her throat.

'Yes, yes, they came on Thursday. From Laurence, I guessed. I ... I didn't have time to open them so I popped them out of the way. I totally forgot about them to be honest. Quite a lot has been happening in this house recently.'

The other guard, younger, good-looking, his sandy hair cropped short, leaned forward, his face serious.

'But you found them, Emily-Jane?'

Emily-Jane blushed as she replied nervously. 'Yes, I brought them into the kitchen and put them on the counter. That company always does gorgeous flowers, I wanted to see what they looked like.'

'So you found them, and you opened them?' Jamie Fanning prompted her gently.

Emily-Jane opened her eyes wide. 'Yes, they came in this big fancy box. I undid the ribbon and pulled the lid off and then my phone rang, so I left the lid and the flowers on the counter and went and talked to my friend upstairs.'

Fanning scribbled something in his notebook.

'What time was this?'

Emily-Jane shrugged. 'I hadn't been home long. I was feeling a bit queasy and I went into the kitchen to see if there were any of Dad's stomach tablets in the island drawer.' She glanced across at Cressida. 'Those antacid ones. I wanted to go to bed, so I went into the laundry to look for my fluffy pjs. It was about 12.30, I think.'

Gallagher nodded encouragingly. 'And when did you start feeling ill?'

'Like I said, I was already feeling really queasy. I was sick about half an hour later and then I don't really remember much after that.'

Cressida rubbed her arm. 'At first the doctor in St Vincent's thought she had a mild dose of food poisoning, but the other symptoms definitely weren't food poisoning.'

The inspector wrote something down. 'Yes, he mentioned that. Do you remember if you smelled the flowers?'

Emily-Jane sighed, 'I was just about to when Chloe rang. There were these orchids and lilies, and these big orange things. I got a waft of their scent, but I didn't actually, like, literally sniff them.'

He nodded again slowly. 'That was probably just as well. And what did you do with the flowers after that?'

Cressida looked straight at him. 'I put them in a black sack. They're in the wheelie bin.'

Emily-Jane turned to her, looking surprised.

'But they were lovely – why did you put them in the bin?'

'I came home and found you so sick, Em. I came down to call the doctor – she's a family friend, she lives just down the road – and I saw them on the counter.' She took a ragged breath. 'Laurence never sends me flowers. I've been pretty cross with him about the hours he's been keeping at the office, and I think I was a bit stressed. He wasn't here to deal with the journalists, and they'd upset Em, and she was so sick … I was just so cross with the whole thing, so I put them in a black sack and threw them out.'

'You obviously didn't inhale any of the scent?'

Cressida shook her head. She'd been so furious she was sure she'd been breathing fire rather than smelling anything.

'And were they addressed to you, Mrs Howard, rather than Emily-Jane, and sent by your husband?'

Fanning turned over the page in his notebook as Inspector Gallagher spoke. Cressida thought hard, trying to remember the flowers arriving.

'I don't think I saw a card. But I knew from the box that they had to have come via Ferryman, so I sort of guessed they were from him. It wouldn't be like Laurence to be very original with gifts. His secretary does most of his shopping.'

Em looked at her, surprised, about to speak when Gallagher cut across her.

'Have the bins been emptied?'

Cressida shook her head. 'They normally go out on Wednesday. They must still be there.'

He reached for his radio. 'We'll need to take them. Our forensic team will want to analyse them and compare them to the flowers sent to the other victim.'

Victim.

The word rang in Cressida's ears. Emily-Jane was a victim – of something Laurence had caused.

It was time to find out exactly what was going on.

Chapter 46

IN DUBLIN CITY centre, Brioni was talking to a different set of garda officers.

They were standing outside her apartment door when she stepped out of the lift. She'd left Laurence chatting to the hotel manager in the cocktail bar at Reynolds Regency House – Red McQuaid had apparently gone on into the hotel's casino. She couldn't hear what the two of them were saying, although it was obviously a tense conversation, so she'd decided to slip away. Her fingers had been itching to text Cressida but, aware that Emily-Jane might hear a message arriving and be curious, she'd resisted the temptation. Brioni knew she wouldn't sleep with everything going around in her head, but she'd just have to wait before she could fill Cressida in.

Brioni's mouth went dry the moment she spotted the two blue uniforms standing on the landing outside her apartment. As the lift doors closed silently behind her, she took a deep breath, smiling broadly.

'Hi there, are you looking for me?'

The two officers, one male, one female, turned to her.

'Brioni O'Brien?'

'That's me.'

The female guard looked her up and down.

'You've changed your hair?'

Smiling, she pulled the blond wig off to reveal her pink hair, saying breezily, 'Fancied a change. I've a brown one, too, but today was a blond day. Some days I'm just not in a pink mood. Can I get you coffee?'

They stood aside as she swung open the dark navy front door to her apartment, then followed her inside. She walked to the end of the corridor, conscious of the squeak of their thick rubber soles on the polished tiles. Pushing open the living room door, she switched on the lights.

'Come in and sit down. I've herbal tea, if you prefer?'

The living room ran from the front to the back of the apartment with huge windows at either end, but with three people in it, two of them in hats and thick padded jackets – with, Brioni was sure, stab vests underneath – it felt crowded.

The female guard shook her head at her offer of tea.

'Please sit down. How can I help.'

'You don't seem surprised to see us?' The female guard took off her peaked hat, revealing dark hair slicked back in a low ponytail.

Brioni shrugged. 'I suggested Alex went to the garda station the other night. He was so shocked when I met him at the Reynolds that I brought him here for a bit, and he told me the story. I'm guessing it must be about that?' Brioni sat down in the armchair opposite the sofa. 'I've never seen anyone as shocked, honestly. I didn't doubt what he told me for a minute.'

The female guard unzipped her jacket and sat down, followed by her male colleague, who now took off his hat as well.

'Why didn't you come to the station with him when he made his initial report?'

Brioni shrugged again. 'He said he'd be fine – he's doing law, he's used to dealing with the guards, and I hadn't seen anything. I mean, I saw him at the start of the evening waiting for his date, but I didn't have anything to add.' Brioni sighed, smoothing the silky ash blond tresses on her knee as if the wig was a small animal. 'Should I have done? Has something else happened?'

'You might have heard on the news today that a woman's body was found in the Dublin Mountains? The killer tried to conceal her identity, but she has a serious injury to the back of her head, caused, the pathologist believes, by a gunshot.'

Brioni nodded slowly. 'I heard a bit of it, but not about her injuries or identity being concealed. I didn't really connect it, honestly – it's so far away. I mean, how could she possibly have got there?'

The male guard leaned forward, pulling his notebook from his inside jacket pocket.

'That's what we hope to find out.'

That was two of them.

'It's not easy to get rid of a body, is it? From what Alex said it sounded as if there was a lot of blood. And from Dublin city centre?' She raised her eyebrows.

Neither of the guards reacted. The female guard reached inside her jacket for her own notebook and a pen.

'Can you tell us how long you've known Alex Walsh?'

'We went to school together – well, different schools, but we were in the same year. We met all the time at Model UN stuff, and debates.'

'And more recently?'

'We've been friends on Facebook for ages, but I only bumped into him again when I came to Dublin earlier this year. I was in uni in London. I came back to Ireland last year to finish my undergrad online – the Covid situation had got really scary. I lived down in Wexford in my parents' old house. I knew Alex had got a place in Dublin, but I only moved up here in May and then we met up again. I'd started working for Riverview. They're sponsoring my MSc so I don't get out much between working and study, I'm not really in touch with anyone else outside work—'

The male guard cut in: 'And how do you know Detective Chief Inspector Mike Wesley?'

'He's my sister's partner. They have a daughter, Daisy.'

The female guard leaned forward slightly. Brioni had felt her watching her closely while the other one asked questions.

'Tell us what happened the other night.'

'At the hotel, you mean?'

They both nodded.

Brioni grimaced. 'I went into the bar to get some food—'

The male guard interrupted. 'But you said you were in Wexford?'

'Yes, but I'm up and down a lot. I live here, obviously. I took a week off to catch up with my assignments, but I decided to come up to town for coffee with a friend. I did some shopping and then when I started driving back at about 6.30, I called into the Reynolds Regency House to get something to eat. It's on the way.' She wavered for a moment, trying to decide how much detail was needed. Saying she'd gone there to spy on Laurence after hacking into his computer didn't feel like a good plan – but it was better to be as straight as possible with them. 'My friend said her husband might be at the hotel and to look out for him.'

'And was he?'

'Yes, for a bit, but he looked busy. I didn't want to interrupt.' Brioni felt a sense of unease opening in her stomach.

'Did he see you?'

Brioni shrugged, shaking her head. 'Not sure. He doesn't know me. It's his wife I know, she's a friend of Marissa's – my sister.'

'Tell us what happened from when you arrived?'

Brioni shrugged. 'I saw Alex on my way in. He looked as if he was waiting for someone. We have this thing – I'm his date buddy, I'm the one who arrives to rescue him when they go wrong.' She paused. 'He broke up with the girl he's been dating since school about six months ago. He's knocking some craic out of Tinder but he's *really* bad at making matches. We hang out at the Reynolds a lot, so when I saw him, I guessed that's what he was up to. I didn't want to cramp his style, so I left him to it and went into the bar to order some food, then I got caught up reading something on my phone. The next thing I realised it was getting late and I really needed the loo, so I decided to make a move.'

The female guard took over. 'Did you speak to your friend's husband?'

Brioni shook her head. 'Like I said, I don't know him personally. He's Laurence Howard, he owns the hotel. He was talking to this guy in a suit by then, it looked as if he was having a meeting, so I thought I'd leave it.'

'But you said hello to Alex?'

'When I came out of the loo, he was coming out of the lift.'

Brioni felt the male guard looking at her hard.

'Who saw you in the bar?'

Brioni opened her eyes wide and shrugged. 'The staff? I used my credit card for the food.'

The female guard pulled out a sheet of A4 paper, folded down the centre so it would fit in her inside pocket. She passed it to Brioni.

'Can you tell us if you recognise any of these women?'

The printout was a panel of passport-sized photographs, twelve of them in four rows.

Brioni scanned it. Nina was in the middle of the second row.

'This one looks familiar.' She screwed up her face. 'She's got long brown hair?'

Their faces were impassive. The female guard raised an eyebrow.

'Have you seen her recently?'

Brioni took a moment to look as if she was thinking.

'I'm pretty sure she was in the bar at the Reynolds. She came in for a few minutes to talk to my friend's husband – she gave out shite to him. I couldn't hear what she said but she was pretty cross. Then she left.'

'Do you know her name?'

'No idea, sorry.' Brioni shrugged. 'Who is she?'

The female guard's face was impassive. 'We can't tell you who any of the women in the pictures are. But you're sure you've seen the woman in the second row, and you last saw her talking to your friend's husband – Laurence Howard – in the Reynolds Regency House?'

'Yes, I think so. She's very striking. I think I would have remembered if I'd seen her anywhere else. She must be on the hotel CCTV?'

Brioni looked at the two guards, seeing a glimmer of reaction in the eyes of the female guard, but they weren't giving anything away.

Chapter 47

CRESSIDA WAS SITTING in front of the fire in the living room when Laurence finally came home. She was watching the embers dying, legs crossed, her foot tapping. It was almost midnight. She threw on another log.

Emily-Jane had gone to bed. The guards' visit had upset her and it had taken Cressida a long time to calm her after they left. They'd sat on the sofa and Cressida had hugged her, reassuring her that their lives weren't at risk, that the attack on Ferryman wasn't personal.

But even as she'd said it, she'd begun to wonder herself.

Was someone trying to destroy Laurence, or was this some complex scheme he'd come up with for some nefarious reason she wasn't seeing? It wouldn't be the first time he'd 'sailed close to the wind', as he called it. He'd always seen business strategy as some sort of Olympic sport, one you had to excel at, and not just beat but crush your opponents. He was the one who'd built the Howard Group into an international chain, getting the company into a position that meant when his brother Pierce originally came up with the idea for Ferryman, it had the capacity to invest.

There was a reason he was so successful – he was utterly driven, and his mission in life wasn't to make more friends.

The crunch of tyres on the drive alerted Cressida to his arrival. She reached for her glass of wine, and took a slow, controlled sip. It was going to be really hard to talk to him calmly; she could feel her temper building, but losing it would weaken her. She knew what he was like – he exploited every tiny crack in an argument, and this was one she wanted to have the upper hand in.

He better have some answers for her this time.

As the front door closed and she heard his feet on the wooden boards of the hall, she called out, 'I'm in here!'

He stuck his head around the living room door.

'I thought you'd be in bed.'

At the sound of his voice, rage spontaneously flared inside, licking and spitting like the flames in the fireplace. But she needed to keep calm. She wanted him to feel he could open up to her. Staying where she was on the sofa, she looked over her shoulder at him, pausing to make sure she kept her voice level.

'Em's gone up. She was exhausted. The guards were here.'

He'd been about to withdraw his head, but as he caught the end of the sentence, he paled. Cressida turned to her glass of wine and took another sip. She had the bottle on the floor beside her. Her second bottle, in fact, but she was taking this glass slowly.

Behind her, she could feel he was hesitating. There was a frisson in the air, like electricity; his need to know what had been said, why the guards had called – she could imagine the questions were fighting for space in his head just like they were in hers.

Seeing that she wasn't going to say more, he came into the room. She heard the door close. He walked around to the other end of the sofa and leaned on the grand piano.

As far away as he could get and still have a conversation.

'What did they want?'

She turned to look at him. He had his hands in his trouser pockets, his jacket open. He was wearing the leather belt she'd bought him for Christmas.

There were so many things she could say, arrows she could throw, but she took a long slow breath.

'They're investigating what made Emily-Jane ill. Like the doctor said at the hospital, they think it's the same thing – a poison – that caused Kate Spicer to collapse.'

'They think or they know?'

Just like him to split hairs.

'They're the guards, Laurence, "think" is a figure of speech. They've analysed some flowers that were delivered to Kate and they believe – sorry, *know* – they were covered in a toxic substance that caused her to collapse. Some sort of venomous secretion from a toad.'

His eyes on the carpet, frowning, he rattled the change in his pocket.

'But who sent them? The flowers, I mean?'

'That is the question we're all asking. Would you sit down instead of hovering? It's very annoying.'

It took him a moment to think about it, but then he moved to the other sofa and sat down opposite her. Watching him, she paused for a second before speaking.

'They think Em was poisoned by flowers as well. Although they were actually sent to me, Em was just the one who opened them.'

She had to give him credit for his acting ability. He looked startled for a moment and opened his mouth to speak, but she cut him off.

'The flowers were from Blooming Fabulous. The order was placed from your account.'

'But I didn't send them.' He at least had the dignity to look aghast. 'How …? Did someone hack my account? Christ.'

He put his hands to his face, rubbing it and bringing his fingertips together in front of his mouth as if in prayer. Cressida shifted on the sofa, uncrossing her legs and leaning forward, deliberately trying to stay calm.

'It's not really the "who had access" thing that worries me, Laurence, it's the "who had access and wanted to kill me" thing that is the issue. The toxin is lethal. Em hardly inhaled any, and although this Spicer woman did, she was apparently found quickly, otherwise things could have been very different.'

'Her name's Kate.'

'I know. I also know you went to meet her at the 1796 to have a massage very early the same morning. But you're fine.' She fought to keep the note of sarcasm out of her voice. 'The guards checked all the oils in the massage suite, nothing nasty there.' She paused. 'What intrigues me is what on earth you were doing there at that time in the morning. She must have come in specially, which leads me to wonder if that's *all* you went in for?'

Cressida could tell from his empty face that he was thinking carefully. He really was a master at masking his emotions.

There was a long pause.

A long pause during which he focused on the glazed top of the coffee table, and the dancing light from the fire reflected there.

She leaned forward again. 'I need some answers, Laurence.'

He ran his hands across his face.

'I don't know anything about poison. I didn't send the flowers – obviously. I went in to get a massage as I had a big day.' He paused. 'I'm working on a big deal with SpeakEasy Telecom, I told you about them.'

He'd neatly skirted the issue of Kate completely. Cressida was so tempted to ask him about the jewellery, the Chanel dress, whether it was some sort of new uniform for staff, but she knew if she revealed that, he'd wonder where she'd got her information from.

'But SpeakEasy haven't been able to get a licence in the UK because of these data protection policies Em keeps talking about.' He shrugged as she continued. 'How much did he offer you to make this happen?'

Cressida could almost see the thoughts going through Laurence's head as he weighed up how much he could tell her. Then he said it.

'Ten million dollars if I could get it past the board. Cash payment, deposited in an offshore account.'

Her eyes on her glass, Cressida kept her face blank as the number bounced around inside her head.

'And what do your fellow board members think of SpeakEasy joining the Ferryman portfolio?'

There was another long pause. Cressida watched him closely. A log shifted in the fireplace, sending a flurry of sparks up the chimney. Laurence put his hands on the coffee table, palms down, his fingers splayed, and took a deep breath. She cut in, before he could speak.

'I think you need to tell me everything.'

He nodded slowly. 'They weren't keen.'

Cressida put her glass down carefully on the coffee table.

'You didn't share with them the possibility of splitting the ten million?'

He shook his head silently.

'So …?' She rolled her hands, encouraging him on with the story. How much was he going to reveal?

269

'The reason I had the massage was because I needed to unwind. There was stuff happening. I had to set some meetings up for the next day to persuade them individually SpeakEasy were a good partner. It was very delicate.'

'And did you?' Cressida didn't know how she was keeping her temper; she wanted to pick up the wine bottle and throw it at him. She felt as if she was speaking to a child. 'Did you persuade them?'

'Yes, pretty much. But then there was this data security attack and we all got distracted.' He rubbed his face again.

'Indeed.' She paused. 'I think there are a few more elements in this story though, don't you?' He looked up at her, surprised, as she continued. 'The hacking seems to be very coincidental to a deal of this size happening. How do you know it's not SpeakEasy who have orchestrated the attack? If they were prepared to pay ten million to work with you, wouldn't it be much easier to find a way to compromise the company that would devalue it so much they could just buy you out?' She tapped the base of her glass on her knee. 'But that doesn't explain the flowers, does it? I can understand someone who wants to attack you personally sending flowers to me – the whole world knows I'm your wife. But why the manager of the spas? What *possible* reason could someone have had to risk sending flowers to her, too – a random member of staff? I mean, doesn't sending two bouquets double their chances of getting caught?' Cressida injected just the right amount of incredulity into her statement. 'It rather raises the question of what the connection could be between me and Kate Spicer?'

Laurence shrugged, as if he was at a loss. It was too much for Cressida and she suddenly snapped, her voice louder than she intended.

'Oh, for fuck's sake, Laurence, I know you were having an

affair with her. And not only do I know, but Nina Rodríguez, your other bit of skirt knew, too, didn't she? Who else knew, Laurence? Who else? What other dirty little secrets are you hiding?' Her voice had risen as she spoke, all regard for keeping this conversation calm and civilised, gone.

He looked directly at her. She had to give him full marks for keeping his face devoid of emotion under pressure. His voice was clear, raised slightly but still calm.

'Nina's not my bit of skirt. She doesn't mean anything.'

'But Kate Spicer does? How long has that been going on for? How long? Because someone else knows about it. And where the hell is Nina, by the way? She's your data whizz-kid. Why isn't she in the office, trying to find this leak?'

Laurence suddenly stood up. 'I don't know, all right? I don't know what the fuck's going on. I'm sure it's not Ackroyd. I know it's not, he's on my side, we've got strategies in play that will make us all a lot of money.' He sounded to Cressida as if he was trying to convince himself.

He went to the fireplace, leaning both hands on the mantelpiece, his back to her. His voice was low when he spoke.

'You and Em are my world, you know that.' He turned around to face her. 'I'd never do anything to endanger you.'

'It's a bit late for that, Laurence, you already have. Someone has tried to kill me and …' Cressida couldn't bear to say her daughter's name. 'To *kill* me, Laurence. Hear that word. I think you're putting too much trust in this Ackroyd character. There are some very questionable business practices in that country. It's not the same as here.'

'He's solid, I keep telling you. He's here next week, you can meet him, decide for yourself.'

'Perfect. Invite him to dinner. Let's see exactly what he's like. Bring him here so there's no danger your conversation will be overheard and we'll find out exactly what's going on, will we?'

'Mum, can you two keep it down? I was trying to sleep.'

Cressida almost jumped physically. She hadn't heard Emily-Jane's feet on the stairs. Laurence spun towards the door, crossing the distance between the fireplace and Emily-Jane in a couple of strides.

'Darling, I'm so sorry. We're just both a bit stressed. How are you feeling?'

He tried to put his arms around her but she pushed him away.

'I'm grand, Dad. Someone tried to kill Mum with some poisonous flowers but everything's just grand.'

She turned and slammed the door behind her.

Chapter 48

'YOU'VE A VISITOR.' The nurse smiled conspiratorially as she came into Kate's room and checked her blood pressure, deftly wrapping the cuff around her upper arm. She had an impish look in her eye. 'A man. He's waiting outside.'

Kate grinned, shaking her head. 'It's not what you think, Megan, I can assure you.'

Megan was only in her twenties, and since Kate had regained consciousness she had kept her regaled with the dramas of her love life. There were moments when Kate had felt the need to take notes.

'Who is it, did he say?' Kate smoothed her hair, mussed up from the pillow, hope bubbling inside her.

Had Laurence come back at last? She had a vague memory of him sitting beside her when she'd first been brought in, but she'd been so ill, she was starting to wonder if that was some sort of hallucination. He'd texted a few times to see how she was. Well, perhaps not a few times. Perhaps twice.

She knew it was hard for him to get away, that work was busy, but ... but ... Kate chided herself. They had an arrangement. A complicated arrangement. And whatever promises he'd made, Laurence needed to be careful.

He was so like his brother Pierce in so many ways. Outwardly, at least. When she looked at him sitting in her living room, his face lit by the fire, or in his office in the evening, the lights dimmed, he could almost be Pierce. It was their personalities that were so different. Laurence was the businessman, hard to the core. Pierce had been the ideas man, creative like she was, disorganised but with a mind that moved at warp speed when it homed in on something. They were two halves of the same coin in many ways, but Pierce's definition of success had been different. Laurence was the one always pushing, always wanting to achieve. His favourite quote was Richard Branson's 'If your dreams don't scare you they aren't big enough.'

Kate's dreams had been big once, but then she'd fallen in love. And love meant compromise. She sighed to herself and, conscious of Megan standing at the end of the bed, tried to keep the smile on her face as tears pricked at her eyes. Now when she thought of the happy times, they were all stolen moments. Beautiful moments, that had made beautiful memories, but stolen nonetheless.

Megan checked her watch and, jotting down the last of her notes, was clicking the top of her pen when the door opened, interrupting Kate's thoughts. She pulled herself up in the bed, hoping she didn't look too terrible. But as Megan took a step backwards and she got a clear view of the door, she realised it wasn't Laurence at all.

'Philip? What are you doing here? Don't you have a holiday empire to run?'

Philip French grinned at her. 'Came to see how you were doing. I was going to bring flowers but …' He cocked an eyebrow at her and instead produced a huge box of chocolates from behind his back.

'She really doesn't want any more flowers.' Megan looked at him meaningfully. 'Right, I'll be back shortly. Don't overdo it, you're still weak. No dancing.'

Kate threw her a withering look. 'I doubt …'

As she spoke, Philip began an elaborate sashay across the room and, pulling out the chair beside the bed, pirouetted around it before sitting down. He looked at Megan innocently.

'No dancing, strictly. Sitting, only sitting. See – chair, sitting.'

Megan pulled open the door, shaking her head at his tomfoolery. 'I'll leave you to it.'

As the door closed, Kate grinned. 'Pierce always said you were an absolute idiot. I don't know how Laurence put you on the board.'

Philip grinned for a moment, then turned more serious.

'Total fool. One of us has to be. How are you feeling? Have the cops any leads?'

'You make it sound like a TV drama. They haven't told me if they have any leads, as you put it. But I guess they've lots of things to check.'

'Cressida got some, too. Some of those flowers. Same delivery.'

Kate felt her colour drain. 'Nobody told me that. Is she OK?'

Philip grimaced. 'She didn't open them, apparently. Emily-Jane did. She was in here, too. She didn't get as big a dose as you, though. She's fine. And it helped that they'd been able to screen you first. They knew how to treat her.'

Kate closed her eyes for a moment in disbelief. 'How's Laurence?'

'Hasn't he been in?'

Kate shook her head, opening her mouth to speak, but Philip held up his hands.

'I know, Kate, I've known for years. You don't have to pretend with me. I was in school with both of the Howards, remember. Pierce was my best pal.'

Kate looked over his shoulder, avoiding his gaze. She didn't think she had the emotional strength to start explaining now. He couldn't know everything, surely?

Obviously unaware of her swirling thoughts, Philip paused for a moment before answering, his face suddenly serious.

'That's what I've come to talk to you about. A whole load of stuff has been happening at Ferryman while you've been sick. And it's not good stuff. Laurence is in trouble.'

Chapter 49

LAURENCE HEARD HIS phone ringing from the depths of a dreamless sleep. He'd taken some tablets – he wasn't even sure what – but he knew full well that with so many thoughts swirling around in his head, he'd be awake all night unless he took something.

He reached for the phone on the bedside locker, at the same time realising with a shiver, like a cold gust of wind, that he was in the spare room.

It stopped ringing, but he hardly noticed as the events of the last twenty-four hours came thundering into his mind.

Holy fucking God, what a night.

First Red McQuaid calmly saying he'd removed a woman's body from a suite in the Reynolds and a clean-up team had been sent in to get rid of the blood. He hadn't even flinched. The body had been removed to the Dublin Mountains where unfortunately ('*unfortunately*') someone's dog had found it. His voice had been matter-of-fact and his expression hadn't even changed, as if he was giving a report on the efficiency of a new laundry service or how much champagne they had used this month.

As if moving bodies was completely normal.

Perhaps it was in his world.

Laurence had felt his temperature drop about ten degrees and had worked so hard not to react that he'd ground his teeth.

'*But it's an expensive business, you need the right people ...*' McQuaid had nodded sagely at that point, as if he was agreeing with himself.

Money – it always came back to money.

And then, the minute he'd walked in the front door, as if dropping 10k to a career criminal wasn't enough for one night, Cressida had started on him. He couldn't tell her the truth about Kate; it was just too complicated, would hurt too many people.

His phone in his hand, Laurence pulled the duvet up over his shoulder, wishing Cressida had thrown his pyjamas at him across the hall last night, rather than the T-shirt he was presently wearing. His eye roamed over the duck egg blue walls, to a huge seascape that hung on the wall beside the door. It was more of a stormscape, greys crashing across the canvas, figurative seagulls caught in gale. Had he seen that painting before? He didn't think so. He took a breath in between his teeth. He hadn't even realised this room was blue, in all honesty. Perhaps he didn't spend enough time at home.

How the fuck did Cressida know about Kate anyway? *And* Nina? He thought he'd been very discreet there. There was a possibility, he supposed, that someone had seen him leave Kate's apartment, but he'd been very careful with Nina. He rubbed his eyes, wincing slightly at the memory of their first night together after the staff summer party. He should never have gone with it, but she was gorgeous and she'd practically undressed him in the lift.

Had one of the staff blabbed? The CCTV was very clear in every corridor; had someone seen them talking, or heading into the lift together? And who would tell his wife, instead of coming to him first? It didn't take a genius to work out that he'd pay very well to keep that one quiet.

It just didn't make any sense.

Cressida had been spitting hot coals last night, had thrown his suit and a clean shirt across the landing, telling him he'd better get used to the spare room.

Jesus, if she knew Nina was dead in a ditch, or more accurately, on a slab in the state pathologist's office, he'd be sleeping in the garden, assuming she hadn't brained him with a bottle first.

As she'd poured herself another glass of wine last night, he'd thought for a moment that she was seriously thinking about it.

But McQuaid had assured him – sitting there in the middle of the cocktail bar as if he was having a perfectly normal conversation about his staff – that all signs of Nina's identity had been removed. And her body had been washed in bleach to remove any DNA. Laurence's stomach turned again. He'd bleached himself at the thought of that, had felt his colour draining as he'd got a much too clear mental picture of what needed to be done to erase someone's identity.

So many questions had crowded his mind. What the hell had she been doing in a suite in the first place? And she'd been in bed, naked, when she'd been found. What wasn't Tony Strachan telling him? It just all seemed insane. He knew she was fiery, and she'd been mad as hell when she'd walked into the bar, but …

And who the fuck was this kid with the floppy hair they kept talking about? He'd seen some blurry stills, but the lad had been wearing glasses and a scarf and his face wasn't clear on the video. Tony was sure, though, that he'd been the one who had called reception to say there had been an accident with the champagne.

Some bloody accident. Keeping the staff quiet had cost a fortune, quite apart from the whole removal issue. Strachan had done the right thing – probably. Laurence still wasn't totally sure about him going solo on sorting it out and calling in McQuaid. But holy feck.

The kid had been waiting for Nina in the hall and they'd gone up in the lift together. She'd been all over him on the way up. And then the girl from room service had called to the door with the champagne order, taking it inside. She'd come out a few minutes later, but there'd been some mix-up in hospitality, and a second bottle had been on its way up when reception got the call about 'the accident' and then the kid had vanished. They'd tracked him on CCTV, talking to some woman with brown hair in the atrium, and car park security had them on CCTV again in the basement parking area, but there was mud all over her number plates, so they only had a partial. It was registered in Dublin.

Marvellous.

How many black Citroën C5s were there with a Dublin reg? Thousands?

Laurence became aware that his phone had started ringing again, prodding him insistently. Who the fuck was that calling at six on a Sunday morning?

He looked at the caller ID. It was Ethan, the data analysis team leader.

'Howard.'

'Sorry to wake you. We've got a problem. Nemesis have published the data from one hundred key Ferryman accounts and flagged it to the media.'

Perhaps it was shock, but the words he was hearing didn't quite join up into sentences in Laurence's head. He pulled himself up on the pillow.

'What? Say that again.'

'Purchasing data going back six months, the account holder ID, a partial card number, the customer's delivery details and their passwords have been published on the Dark Web. All the news desks have been sent a link.'

It took a moment to sink in.

'Only a partial card number?'

'So far. But it's the first eight numbers, so they obviously have the full sequence. If anyone triangulates the email address with the password on another site it will be easy to get the last four. People aren't very careful with their passwords.'

'But, doesn't everyone have a secondary confirmation thing to stop unauthorised access?'

'Some sites have it, but not all. Basically there's a lot of information out there, and this is only the start. These guys aren't messing.'

The words 'purchasing history' suddenly arrived in Laurence's brain. Holy fucking God. He had a very good idea what level of heat that information might throw up.

'Who? Whose accounts?'

'We're still going through them. There's a few media people, sports people, the Taoiseach, your personal account and the rest of the board. Honestly, it's only the tip of the iceberg, but a very conspicuous tip.'

'Shit. *Shit.*'

Laurence put his hand to his forehead and tried to massage away the pain that had arrived there like compressed air trapped by a valve. *They'd think it was him.* The guys on the board would think he'd leaked the data, the very purchasing history that he'd discussed with them before all this had blown up – he'd suggested they needed to pass the SpeakEasy motion, or resign from the board.

But his own purchasing history.

Fuck. Cressida would see Kate's birthday present – the jewellery. The dress for Pierce's anniversary mass. He pressed his fingertips to his forehead. His heart was pounding in his chest.

Taking a deep breath, he hauled himself up in the bed, trying to isolate the different issues from each other and focus on what to do next. The word *shitshow* was never closer to the truth.

'Can we say the purchase history is fake? That they don't have all the info they're pretending to have?'

There was a pause at the other end. Ethan didn't sound too sure as he replied.

'You could do a press release, I suppose. The media will have started checking, though. Some people will deny it's real, probably say it's been added to discredit them.' He paused. 'There's some quite colourful stuff here.'

That was damn right. Laurence hadn't believed his eyes he'd looked through the information on Nina's USB stick. *What the hell was going on?*

Then it hit him. Maybe Cressida was right – maybe this *was* Ackroyd's strategy. Destroying Ferryman would save SpeakEasy ten million dollars hard cash and land Ackroyd a company with billions of users at a knockdown price. He'd have to rebuild customer confidence to start trading again, but the public had short memories.

Then another thought skidded into his mind.

Nina had said someone was following her.

She was the weak link here. She knew about their deal, she understood the Ferryman systems better than anyone, and she liked a nice life. Had the million he'd transferred to her account not been enough for her? Had she double-crossed Ferryman and, knowing the type of money involved, tried to do some sort of deal with SpeakEasy? He knew he'd mentioned her name to Ackroyd. And Ackroyd could find her easily enough.

Holy fucking God, had Ackroyd arranged to have Nina killed, but first sent those flowers to Cressida and Kate as some sort of message – a warning?

Laurence closed his eyes. If all this *was* a message, it was coming through loud and clear.

But Ackroyd was playing a dangerous game.

And he, Laurence Howard, had Red McQuaid in his corner. Laurence felt despair turning to rage.

'Mr Howard, are you still there?' Ethan's voice came through the phone, making him start.

'Yes, yes. Just give me a minute.'

Laurence could feel his mind cranking up, looking at all the options, running over the possibilities.

McQuaid was a man known for his fondness for the nicer things in life as well. He'd made it clear that for the right fee he could make all sorts of things go away. And he owed Laurence now. He'd been paid to get Nina out of the hotel cleanly, but she'd been found. He'd shaken off any suggestion that his team might be at fault, but when it came down to it, that was the case.

Would Red McQuaid be big enough to handle Dirk Ackroyd? Did it matter? McQuaid could very clearly demonstrate that Laurence wasn't putting up with any nonsense ... and if he became a casualty? Perhaps that killed two birds, so to speak. Laurence knew for certain that the McQuaids looked after their own. If Ackroyd went after McQuaid, there'd be no stopping the rest of the McQuaid brothers.

Laurence tapped the corner of his phone on his teeth. Perhaps it was time to have a full and frank conversation with the CEO of SpeakEasy, and inviting him to the dinner Cressida had suggested would be the perfect opportunity.

'Ethan? Yes, I'm still here. I'm on my way into the office. Get a press release drafted saying that elements of the data published are fake, designed to make headlines. We think they're scaremongering and have very limited information. I'll be with you in half an hour.'

Chapter 50

EARLY MORNING AUTUMN sunshine was flowing into Brioni's apartment as she brought her coffee into the living room. She yawned; she'd had a lot of problems sleeping last night, finally giving up and heading for the shower at six. Turning over in her head the events that had unfolded during her two evenings in the cocktail bar had kept her awake all night. That, and trying to figure out the series of events that had led to Nina's body winding up in a forest in the mountains. Thoughts had run through her head like rapids, gathering pace as the night had gone on.

Now, sitting at the circular table at the end of the living room in her sweatpants and college sweatshirt, the sun on her face, she'd switched the TV to a radio station, raising the volume with the remote control as she opened the lid of her laptop, only half concentrating.

Until she caught the word 'Ferryman', and her brain skidded to a halt, her whole body freezing.

'*Events at Ferryman are escalating with the publication ...*'

As if one dead employee wasn't enough.

Brioni reached over to check her phone to see if Cressida had texted. Nothing yet, but perhaps she hadn't heard the news.

Brioni was quite sure Laurence had.

When the guards had left last night, they'd seemed to be satisfied with her description of seeing Nina and Laurence, and meeting Alex at the Reynolds Regency House.

Brioni glanced at her phone again – it was just past 7 a.m. Was it too early to ring Cressida? By the sounds of things, she would be waking up to a press pack outside her front door again. Brioni rubbed the tattoo on the inside of her wrist. She was sure Cressida would call as soon as she could.

Focusing on the radio, Brioni took a sip of her coffee. It had cooled while she'd been listening but she hardly noticed.

'*We're waiting for a statement from Ferryman, but early indications are that some of the information regarding customers' purchasing history may have been fabricated to grab press attention.*'

Before the reporter could say more, Brioni's phone began to ring. Banging the cup down, she snatched it off the table. But it was Alex, not Cressida.

'Hey, Bri, you OK?'

'I should be asking you that.'

Alex let out a loud sigh at the other end. He was outside somewhere – she could hear traffic in the background. At least he wasn't locked up in a garda station.

'I'm grand. I'm heading back to Kevin Street, the guards have got some more questions. I think they want to go over my statement now they've got your side of things. But did you hear the news?'

'Have they identified the body? Is it Nina?'

'I don't think they know for sure yet. But they've arrested that gangster guy Red McQuaid – well, one of his team, anyway. Switch it on and you'll see it.'

Brioni reached for the remote. 'I'm just listening to the bit about the hackers releasing all that data. Here, let me put the TV on.'

Brioni aimed the remote at the TV and flipped stations, turning the sound down so she could hear Alex at the same time. The RTE news channel was on to the next story and the screen was filled with garda cars. She turned the sound up a fraction.

'Caught on CCTV close to the Reynolds Regency House hotel, Diarmuid Duggan is a well-known member of McQuaid's staff. Seen in the early hours heading out of the city, his distinctive BMW jeep was seen again on the N11 heading into the Dublin Mountains. Bad Dog, as Duggan is known locally, has served a previous six-year sentence for grievous bodily harm and possessing a firearm. He was implicated in the shooting of Kevin O'Keefe, one of McQuaid's rivals, earlier this year.'

'Are you watching?'

Alex's voice made Brioni jump – she'd almost forgotten he was at the other end of the phone as she watched a heavy-set man in a dark grey T-shirt being escorted to a garda car, his hands in handcuffs.

'Yep – how did they find him so soon?'

'His fingerprints were on the body according to the *Irish World* – they always seem to get the scoop on anything criminal.'

'How can you leave fingerprints on a body?'

'On her skin. They said the whole body was cleaned, but he must have picked her up after that or something.' Brioni felt her stomach turn the coffee over as Alex continued. 'They found her up past Johnnie Fox's pub, she was half-buried but they must have planned to go back and do a better job. This guy's dog found her. It's the second time he's found a body, according to the papers.'

'Jaysus.'

'They've got to be able to identify her, now they have a body and we've given them her name. I just hope they can find her family. She must have people who love her.'

Brioni let out a sigh. Maybe Nina had thought Laurence loved her, and look how that had turned out.

'The two that came here last night had this sheet of photographs and asked me to point her out.'

'That's good.' She heard a siren in the background as he continued. 'They should find her on the CCTV from the bar.'

'Let's hope that hasn't been erased as well. Mike said there had been a big cover-up job. Oh jeepers, something else is happening. Just a sec.'

Her eye drawn to the TV news, Brioni watched as the man she'd seen talking to Laurence in the bar – the manager of the Reynolds Regency House – was escorted out of a glazed door and guided into the rear of a police car.

At the other end of the line, Alex said, 'I'm watching, too, just got it on my phone. I think the shit's about to hit the fan.'

Chapter 51

STANDING BESIDE THE pool, Cressida felt a strange sense of calm. Perhaps it was because it was so warm in here, the sound of the water gently swishing on the tiled walls almost therapeutic. She'd thought Laurence was mad installing a wave machine – well, utterly mad for building this whole room, really – but now it was one of the few parts of the house where she could truly shut off from the world outside. At moments like this she wondered why she didn't use it more often.

The press had started gathering outside the gates shortly after seven, her phone and the buzzer on the gate going continually. She'd rolled over in bed and hidden under the duvet for a few minutes while she worked out what she needed to do today, and if she could do it from inside the house. Thank God their main living space was at the back of the house, out of sight of the road.

Finally getting up, she'd decided that coffee and a swim were what she needed to start the day. She couldn't face fighting her way through the flashbulbs to go to the gym, but some time on her own and some peace and quiet would help her sort out her head.

Now standing with her toes over the edge of the tiles, her hair in a ponytail, she looked at the blue water, star-like lights glistening up at her from its depths, listening to its gentle movement. Just to be doubly sure of some privacy, she'd activated the electric blinds on all the windows around the pool and now she felt as if she was in a warm, safe bubble.

She dived in, feeling the water wrapping her in its caress, opening her eyes underwater as the power of her dive took her almost to the middle of the pool. Feeling her lungs straining, she broke the surface and, twisting, powered to the end with a deft backstroke. Above her the ceiling was painted like an Italian cathedral, clouds and cherubs in one corner bleeding into a midnight sky lit with stars. It was an impossibly expensive folly, a room of pure excess, but something Laurence had dreamed of since he was a child. The cars, the fancy dinners … all paled into comparison beside it. This room was the true symbol of his success.

Cressida turned on to her stomach and, kicking off the end wall, swam back, focusing on nothing except the moment, the feel of the water on her skin, the lighting in the room, the reflections playing around her. Three more lengths and she felt her mind was clear enough to start focusing on Laurence, and how she was going to make him pay for the mess he'd brought down on her and their daughter.

Someone had tried to kill her, and had almost killed Emily-Jane in the process, and for that Cressida could never forgive him.

As she cut through the water Cressida could feel the adrenaline building, the endorphins released with the exercise beginning to hit her bloodstream. And ideas began to form.

The more she'd thought about it last night, the surer she'd been that Dirk Ackroyd and SpeakEasy had to be behind everything that was going on. Someone was closing in on Laurence and Ferryman. Didn't they say the reasons for murder were usually greed, lust or jealousy? Cressida was starting to think that Dirk Ackroyd was scoring high for greed and jealousy. He wanted a part of Ferryman, and he wanted the big payout that it would bring him.

And it looked as if he was prepared to do anything to get it.

With each stroke, ideas began to coalesce in Cressida's head. Laurence had said Ackroyd was in Dublin this week. She'd already suggested he come to dinner; now she needed to make that happen. It was perfectly natural for them to invite him. Perhaps after a few glasses of wine they could get a clearer idea of his intentions, and see what he might let slip. Especially if he was in a private house well away from the media – perhaps he'd show his hand.

Reaching the end of the pool, Cressida flipped over and started a new length. If she could get him to say something that would show the world that this hacking thing was something to do with SpeakEasy, that Ferryman was a victim of a takeover attempt, then perhaps the company could recover and the share price would go back up.

From what Laurence had told her of him, and her own research, Ackroyd was the arrogant type who might be inclined to brag. She just needed him to say something that would make Laurence finally see sense and step away from this deal. Bringing SpeakEasy into the Ferryman portfolio would be catastrophic for consumer confidence.

If Ferryman's stock plummeted, the divorce settlement she was going after would be significantly reduced, and she had to think of Emily-Jane's future. She had as much of a reason to protect Ferryman as Laurence did.

The key would be to get everything Dirk Ackroyd said recorded. And hidden cameras would always be better than trying to voice record on a phone where anything could go wrong. Cressida needed something reliable, something professionally recorded, that would be admissible in court.

She reached the end of the pool again and, putting her hands flat on the tiles, pulled herself out, reaching for her towel. She rubbed her face and hair and wrapped it around her shoulders, pausing for a moment to work out what she needed to do.

Could she ask Brioni to help? She'd helped so much already, but Cressida felt they'd become friends over the past few days. There certainly wasn't anyone else she could discuss it with. What was that phrase about adversity bringing people together? Cressida felt sure Brioni wanted to know the answers to all of this as much as she did at this stage.

Thinking about dinner, an idea landed in Cressida's head. Perhaps Brioni could pretend to be part of the staff? She was smart and could watch everyone unobserved, and having her here would give Cressida a bit of moral support – which, right now, she definitely needed. With so much going on she didn't know if she'd feel safe with this Ackroyd guy in the house.

Cressida rubbed her arms with the towel. Brioni would probably be able to recommend someone who could wire up some cameras, too. They'd didn't have much time and she needed someone very discreet.

Padding over to the table where she'd left a glass of water, Cressida took a quick sip, glancing at her phone screen as she did so. Brioni had tried to call her. Picking up another towel, she wrapped it around her middle and sat down on the edge of the lounger. From this side of the pool she had a clear view of the internal doors, so there was no danger of Emily-Jane wandering in and overhearing a sensitive conversation, like Cressida had the other night.

Brioni picked up as soon as Cressida hit the *call* button.

'Have you been watching the TV news?'

'No, I've been having a swim. I can't face that yet. Has something else happened? They haven't arrested Laurence?'

'Not that I know of. They've released more information about the woman's body.'

'Like what?'

Cressida felt the dark shadow of worry suddenly chill her. She pulled the towel closer around her shoulders. As soon as Nina was identified, the press would know she worked for Ferryman, and this whole situation would escalate. The media would go nuts. It was bad enough that the Reynolds Regency House was being linked to her death.

'There was a garda press conference about half an hour ago. They obviously need help identifying her. But listen – they said she was five foot six and had dark hair, and she had a tattoo, a spider in a web, on the inside of her thigh.'

Cressida wasn't seeing the significance of this at all. Her head still full of plans for Ackroyd, she rubbed her face.

'So ... does it mean something? A spider's a bit weird, isn't it?'

'I googled it and apparently in Latin American gang tattoos, it's a symbol that represents a life of crime.'

'Good God. So Nina perhaps wasn't the high-flying tech executive we thought she was, at all?'

'Well, she might have been that, too. But more importantly, Alex is 100 per cent sure Nina didn't have any tattoos. Definitely not on the inside of her thigh, anyway.'

Cressida wasn't too sure she wanted the full details of how he knew that, but before she could say anything, Brioni continued.

'Alex is sure the body isn't Nina's.'

Chapter 52

I T TOOK A moment for Cressida to register what Brioni was saying.

'But how can it *not* be Nina?' She leaned forward on the lounger. Despite the towels wrapped around her and the warmth of the pool room, she felt chilled. She could hear a coffee machine gurgling in the background as Brioni answered.

'That's the bit I don't understand either. Unless there were two women dressed like Nina in the hotel that night, and they somehow switched places between the bar and the lift, I've no idea. But Alex is sure the woman he was with definitely didn't have a tattoo. He's at the garda station now.'

'But I don't understand …'

Cressida heard Brioni hesitate. 'The press are saying the guards are talking to one of the McQuaid gang about disposing of the body, and they've brought in the Reynolds hotel manager. It has to be the same body. It just isn't who we thought it was.'

Cressida ran her hand over her face again. She knew someone else who she was pretty sure had got a look at the inside of Nina's thigh, and who would definitely know if she had a tattoo like that. Had Alex just missed it in the heat of the moment? A thought shot into Cressida's head: maybe Nina's criminal background had been the reason Laurence had employed her in the first place. Dora had mentioned that she'd worked for a lot of technology companies before Ferryman, all short-term. Had she been blackmailing her way around cyberspace? Had her projects been personal ones?

Cressida realised that Brioni was still waiting for her to say something.

'I've no idea what's going on but listen, I need to talk to you about something else I need help with. I know you've got dragged into all of this, though, so if it's a no, just say. Can I call you back shortly? I'm just out of the pool.'

'No problem, and of course I'll help, whatever it is. I want to get to the bottom of this as much as you do. I'm going to call Mike in London now and see if he can find anything out about what's happening.'

'Thank you, Bri. Honestly I don't know how I'd be coping with all of this without you.'

Cressida ended the call and looked at her phone screen, hardly registering a text from Laurence.

Gone to the office, back later.

She almost rolled her eyes.

The body had to be Nina. Alex must be mistaken.

As Cressida stood up she heard the door from the hallway open.

'Mum, are you in there? There are about a hundred photographers outside the gate. What's going on?'

Emily-Jane came in, wrapped up in her soft fleece dressing gown, its deep purple making her face look even paler. She had the belt tied tightly and her hands thrust in the pockets.

Cressida stood up and, putting her phone down for a moment, pulled on her robe.

'I know, love. I'm sorry, I didn't want to wake you to tell you. I've let the guards know. There's not a lot they can do just yet. Let me get dressed and I'll call your father and find out what's happened now.'

'There might be something on the news.'

Cressida sighed. 'I really don't think we need to find out via the TV. It's all wild speculation in the media. They make half of it up. Promise me you won't put on the TV or radio? And try and stay off social media. They'll be trying to see what we're doing, and will add everything up together and come up with their own nonsensical theory.'

Emily-Jane looked at her. Her lip was trembling, and something inside Cressida snapped. Laurence had done this. All of it. And there was no way she was taking any more.

Crossing to Emily-Jane, Cressida slipped her arm around her shoulders and cradled her head against her chest.

'Don't worry, my darling, it will all blow over. Why don't you read a book? Or watch a movie? I'm sure *The Great Gatsby* is on Netflix.'

Emily-Jane pulled away, her smile weak,

'Mum, I've seen it at least three times. But yes, I'll keep off my phone. I'll just text Chloe and Georgia to tell them I'm switching it off. Do you think the guards can move the cameramen? They make me so edgy. I keep thinking they're going to try and put something through the front door.'

'They'll have to climb the gates first –' Cressida ushered Emily-Jane out of the pool room ahead of her – 'and that'll give the guards a reason to arrest them.'

*

Fifteen minutes later, her hair still wet, Cressida had thrown on a flame-red tracksuit and moved the sofas in the breakfast room around so Emily-Jane could curl up and watch TV at the back of the house. She'd closed all the curtains at the front, which didn't help with the lack of light from the overcast October sky, but they had electricity for a reason. And the smart system Laurence had installed meant that she didn't even have to go into each room to do it, risking a long lens catching her in action.

'Here's your hot chocolate. I've got some croissants in the oven. They'll only be ten minutes.'

'Thanks, Mum.' Emily-Jane looked up at her. 'Tell me what Dad says?'

'Will do, love, now just relax there. I won't be a minute. I'm going to call him from the study on the landline. With all this hacking trouble I don't trust the mobile.'

Upstairs, Cressida called Laurence's mobile. It took a moment to connect, a moment in which she looked out of the upstairs window over the sea to Dalkey Island. It was a blustery day, the waves white-tipped, lapping at the sharp rocks, dark where they met the water. A moment later the call went straight to his voicemail.

Unbelievable.

But if the press were here, they were probably outside the office, too, and perhaps he'd turned his mobile off. Cressida tried his direct office line. It rang out. Perhaps he was in a meeting.

Cressida redialled, calling Dora's mobile phone. It might be Sunday, but with everything happening, Cressida was sure Laurence's secretary was on full alert.

Dora must have recognised their home number on the caller ID. She picked up immediately.

'Cressida, is that you? Is everything all right?' The normally cool Dora sounded unusually flustered.

'I'm fine, Dora, knee-deep in journalists but the gates are solid. Are you all right? What's happening? I've been trying to get hold of Laurence.'

'Just a moment.' There was a pause, and Cressida heard a door open and close. The outer door to Dora's office? Was she checking that no one was listening? 'Are you still there?'

'Yes, yes of course.' Cressida heard a sigh as Dora sat down in her chair. 'I came in to the office when I saw the news. I really don't know what to make of it. The guards are here talking to Laurence. They were here when I arrived – from the cybersecurity unit about this hacking thing. It's just so terrible. How could they publish all that information? There really is evil in this world.' She paused for breath, but before Cressida could say anything, she continued. 'Poor Laurence looked so pale when I came in, and so did Ethan from downstairs. I took them all coffee but they both looked as if they'd been up all night so I ordered everyone in some breakfast, too, just croissants and some sandwiches, they looked as if they needed it.'

Cressida opened her eyes wide, biting her tongue. She really wanted to know what they were talking about, not what they were eating. Dora kept going, like a ship that had finally got its sails up and had caught the wind.

'I've been so worried, Cressida. It's so stressful for Laurence and the shares are just tumbling this morning. The board want to call an emergency meeting at lunchtime, even though it's Sunday, but I don't know if he'll be able to get away. Another lot of guards have just arrived.' She lowered her voice a notch. 'I thought they must be more of the same, but as I was closing the door I heard them say they were here about a murder. A murder! Well, I almost collapsed right there and then.'

'Who were they talking about, Dora? What's happened?'

Cressida started to pace Laurence's study, her eyes on the royal blue carpet as she listened hard, trying to pick up any sounds in the background.

'Well, this is it. I'm really not sure. What I do know is that Nina Rodríguez from the data team – the one you were asking about, actually – has gone missing. I mean, what a time to disappear when you're the one who works in the cybersecurity end of things. She's supposed to be the best of them in there—'

Cressida interrupted her. 'Who said she's gone missing?'

'Ethan's been trying to get hold of her for a few days. He eventually sent one of the team around to her apartment and the landlord said she'd terminated the lease, but all her things were there. When the building manager went in it looked as if she was planning to go back, she was half packed as if she was in the middle of moving out.' Cressida could almost hear Dora shaking her head. 'There was milk in the fridge and mugs on the draining board.'

Cressida opened her mouth to reply but didn't get a chance.

'They've reported her missing. HR don't have any next of kin on file and nobody seems to know who her friends are.'

Cressida finally managed to get a word in.

'Are the guards there talking to Laurence about her? Do they think something's happened to her?'

'I think they must be. Who else could they be here about?'

Chapter 53

I N LAURENCE HOWARD'S office the atmosphere was a lot tenser than he would have liked. He looked across his desk at the two detectives standing immediately in front of him, and let out a sigh. The other two were in his peripheral vision, but if he started to worry about them, he knew he'd look twitchy. Right now he needed to focus on one problem at a time.

'I can't believe it. Why didn't Tony inform me?' He paused, shaking his head again. He knew he was repeating himself but that's what people in shock did, wasn't it? And he needed to give his brain time to catch up. 'I was literally *at* the hotel the other night and he *introduced* me to Red McQuaid and neither of them said a word. I can't believe it. Tony's been nothing but reliable in all the time he's worked for us.'

'Tell me when you first found out Nina Rodríguez was missing.' The lead officer's face didn't change as he spoke.

In his forties, he was wearing a dark sports jacket and slacks, his shoes polished to a mirrored shine. His shirt was starched and his tie a perfect match with the earthy colours of his jacket. Unlike his previous visitors, this guy didn't have a hair out of place. Laurence had been so absorbed in discussing the hackers when this second lot of guards had arrived, he had no idea what the guy's name was. All he'd heard was the word *murder* and he'd suddenly found himself frozen, holding his breath as he fought to keep his face deadpan.

Laurence ran his hand across his mouth. The morning sun was streaming in the window behind him now, warming the back of his neck, making the men in front of him squint slightly. Or perhaps that was their natural expression when they were talking to a suspect. Laurence wasn't entirely sure, but one thing he was under no illusion about was that these guys were a lot more acerbic than the first lot who had arrived. Laurence scowled, as if he was thinking hard.

'Ethan told me. There was so much happening here, Ethan was keeping me posted all day Friday on his progress – or lack of, rather – on trying to find out how the hackers had got in. I didn't get down to the data floor until really late Friday night. His team has been working around the clock. I expected Nina to be there, but they hadn't seen her.' He paused. 'We knew it was strange, she's very ambitious and very, very, clever. This security fiasco is exactly the type of thing she'd be mad keen to get involved with. She's an expert on cyberattacks – I mean the detail of them. Our disaster gives her the potential to really shine. Ethan had been trying to get hold of her, but she wasn't answering her phone. He thought she must have been sick.' He rubbed his hand over his face. 'None of it makes any sense, frankly.'

'Murder rarely does.'

The detective looked at him hard. Laurence felt almost as if he was trying to see inside him. He just wished he'd sit down. He was standing in front of the desk with his feet apart, clearly trying to intimidate him. In fact, none of them had sat down. They were all standing around as if they might need to make a fast getaway at any moment, the youngest guy leaning against the opposite wall, no tie, his leather jacket unzipped. He was blond, vaguely reminded Laurence of Daniel Craig. Which didn't help at all.

The detective standing in front of him crossed his arms and scowled, the fabric of the sports jacket straining across his shoulders.

'So Nina Rodríguez worked on the team that is dealing with this hacking?'

'Yes, as I told you, and your colleagues.'

'And when she disappeared you didn't think that was in any way strange, and that perhaps the two incidents could be connected?'

'Like I told you, I only found out she hadn't turned up for work on Friday night. I didn't even know she was missing. I haven't had time to think about it.'

Laurence paused, frowning. His heart rate had increased the moment they'd walked into the room, and it wasn't showing any signs of slowing.

'It's Sunday today.' The detective looked at him pointedly.

'I know. Look, I've had a lot on my mind. I'm not personally responsible for every employee. If they don't want to come into work then I can't make them.' Laurence stopped and took a breath, suddenly feeling he was on shaky ground. He shook his head slowly. 'It could definitely be linked to the cyberattack. I mean ... I don't know. Hacking's normally remote, isn't it, a bunch of nerds in an office. They aren't usually the types to kill people?' His voice trailed off.

'And what type of people kill, do you think?' Leather Jacket spoke now from the far wall. Laurence felt his stomach turn over at the sarcastic tone in the younger detective's voice.

'I've no idea, honestly. It's not my area of expertise. Perhaps it *was* the hackers. Perhaps they knew she'd have a better chance of stopping them than anyone else.' Laurence sighed and rubbed his face with his hands. 'Are you sure the body is Nina? I mean, it could be anyone – aren't women always turning up dead in the Dublin Mountains?'

He cringed as he said it. Leather Jacket raised his eyebrows.

'It could be anyone indeed, that's why we're here. We've secured DNA from a hairbrush in Nina Rodríguez's apartment and we are fast-tracking those results. So we should all be better informed very soon.'

Laurence nodded slowly. 'The thing is, these hackers … I'm on the verge of doing a deal with an American company called SpeakEasy. I'm starting to wonder if they could be behind all this. If our stock falls, like it has done, we become vulnerable to a hostile takeover. They want a foothold in the comms market in Europe, and we're a gateway.'

'So tell me more about that.' Sports Jacket uncrossed his arms and stuck his hands in his trouser pockets, the movement revealing a shoulder holster.

Laurence felt his mouth go dry.

Chapter 54

WHEN SHE'D EXPLAINED her idea to Brioni on the phone, Cressida had felt a surge of relief at her reaction. She'd been only too happy to help, had immediately suggested a company who could wire up a covert video system. And she didn't think Cressida and Emily-Jane being on their own with Ackroyd in the house, even with Laurence present, was a good idea, any more than Cressida did. Too much had happened that seemed to route back to SpeakEasy's interest in Ferryman.

Brioni had said the audiovisual guys would be fast, but Cressida had only just put Emily-Jane's breakfast plates in the dishwasher when she heard the gate buzzer and her phone vibrated with a text. Looking at the CCTV trained on the road, she pipped open the gate and the garage doors, pushing the intercom to tell them to drive straight in. Their van had a green and gold logo, with Serpent Security emblazoned on the side – the press would think that they were getting their security systems checked out. No doubt, it would be front page news tomorrow, but perhaps that was a good thing. It might show the public that the Howards felt just as threatened by recent events as everyone else.

Crossing the hall, Cressida opened the internal door into the garage as they drove in. Keeping back so there was no danger of anyone getting a photograph of her, she buzzed the huge double doors closed. The garage was like an aircraft hangar. It had been designed to store Laurence's boat when it was out of the water in the winter, as well as four cars, but now he didn't have time to sail; the boat was in Spain and the garage was empty, only his vintage MG parked at the back gathering dust.

'Thanks for coming so fast, and on a Sunday, too.'

The two men who climbed out of the van were both young, and from their toned arms, Cressida guessed they worked out. Around the same age, perhaps mid-twenties, they wore matching navy polo shirts and navy workmen's trousers, their heavy brown belts obviously designed to carry tools. One was dark, the other ginger. He had a silver hoop earring in one ear.

'Why don't we go through the service door and I can show you what needs doing.'

Stepping into the garage, Cressida pulled the hall door closed behind her, and led the way to the back of the garage, their boots ringing on the concrete floor.

'This is the access for cleaning the pool.' She unlocked the door and pushed it open. 'You can get to the changing rooms and the showers through that door, and this one takes you to the pump room. Come through here and I'll show you where I need the cameras.'

Cressida glanced down at their heavy work boots, hesitating for a moment as she pushed open another door at the far side of the pump room.

Right now, boot marks were the least of her problems.

The changing rooms and pump room were at the opposite end of the pool to the bar, but as always the smell of chlorine was strong.

'Very nice. The office said you needed a covert system – cameras and sound in two rooms?' The dark one looked up towards the bar area at the top of the pool as he spoke.

'Yes please. In here principally, and in the dining room. I know the sound will be tricky with the water and the high ceiling, but I think that end will be the key area to cover.' She gestured towards the bar. 'And the dining room will be easier.'

The younger one ran his hand over his ginger hair, cropped short, as he scanned the room, the overhead lights reflecting off the water in the pool creating patterns as the water moved.

'Everything invisible?'

'Yes please.'

'No problem, we've got cameras that look like smoke alarms, clocks, all sorts. We'll find something that will work in each location.'

'Do you think it'll take long?'

The dark one answered: 'We'll be as quick as we can. We'll use your Wi-Fi to connect everything. There's always a possibility with covert surveillance that someone might get wise to it and try to block the signal, but it's very unlikely. Have you got somewhere where we can put the equipment?'

Cressida bit her lip for a moment. She hadn't thought about where the recording part of this might go.

'Oh, the robe room. The door's up here.'

Walking up the side of the pool, past the loungers, she pointed to a door discreetly tucked into the corner of the tiled wall to her left.

'There's a towel and robe room behind that door that backs on to the laundry room in the kitchen. You can go straight through to the back of the kitchen from here if you need to. The house all sort of links up – the dining room is accessible from the other side of the kitchen, too, through the servery door. It's all quite close together.'

'Sounds good, let's have a look.'

'We'll go through the robe and laundry rooms so you can get your bearings.'

As Cressida pushed open the kitchen door, Emily-Jane's head shot up over the back of the sofa like a meerkat on watch, her eyebrows raised in question. Following Cressida inside, the two men grinned at her.

'This is my daughter, Emily-Jane, but she'll pop upstairs in a few minutes, out of your way.'

Cressida looked meaningfully at Emily-Jane who, blushing, slid down on the sofa.

Crossing the kitchen and pushing open the servery door, Cressida took the two workmen into the dining room on the far side of the house. They hardly ever used this room these days – it was really a bit of a waste of space – but it was the perfect room to entertain a visiting American in, with its huge antique mahogany dining table in the middle, and gilt-framed oil paintings of ships at sea lining the walls.

'You'd need a map in this place.' The ginger one grinned as he followed her back into the kitchen. 'Can we …?' He indicated the open door to the laundry room.

'Be my guest.'

The dark one crossed the bright white tiles and stuck his head into the robe room.

'This is very handy. I think this will work as our recording base.'

'Can I get you both a coffee before you start?'

The dark one smiled appreciatively. 'No, you're grand, just ignore us. We've got a bit to do so we'll get straight on. You want it done today?'

'Please, if you can. And if you can show me how to make sure it's all working …'

'No problem. Leave us to it. We'll just get our tools.'

'What's happening?'

Emily-Jane's head popped up again as soon as Cressida came into the kitchen, closing the door firmly behind her. She went and leaned over the back of the sofa. She didn't want the engineers overhearing her conversation.

'Nothing much. I just want to make sure the security is up to scratch given what's going on. And your father's gone and invited this American he's doing business with over for dinner on Tuesday, so I wanted to get it all done before he gets here. We don't want to look like a building site if there are guests coming.'

Emily-Jane looked at her, frowning, processing what she'd said.

'The guy from SpeakEasy is really coming here?'

'Tuesday evening. You might need to make yourself scarce, unless you want to join us?'

Emily-Jane scowled. 'Honestly, I'd rather stick pins in my eyes. I've told Dad what I think of SpeakEasy. He never listens, does he?' She paused. 'What are you having for dinner?'

Cressida sighed; she knew Emily-Jane wasn't feeling well, but she wasn't up to histrionics right now.

'I'm getting caterers in, so I'm not sure yet, I need to find out if this guy is vegan or anything. Assuming he isn't, beef, I think.'

Emily-Jane screwed up her nose. 'I'll stay upstairs. Can I order in?'

Cressida nodded just as the two workmen reappeared behind her and returned to their van via the kitchen door. Emily-Jane watched them, waiting for the door to close behind them before she spoke in a stage whisper.

'You could have warned me you had two hot dudes coming to fix things. I'd have got dressed. Chloe and Georgia will *not* believe this.'

Cressida threw her a warning look. 'Don't say anything to anybody, Em, I don't want the press getting hold of this. And lovely as Chloe and Georgia are, they could let something slip. It's very important. We've enough trouble as it is.'

Emily-Jane sighed. 'That's for sure. How long are they here for?'

'A few hours at least, I'd guess.'

'I'll go up and have a rest and come back down later.'

'I think that would be an excellent idea. I'll bring you up some lunch.'

Chapter 55

Upstairs in her bedroom, Emily-Jane moved her iPad over and flopped onto her bed for a few minutes, her eyes closed. The croissants and cocoa had given her a boost of energy but she could feel her heart beating hard after the trip up the stairs. The doctors had said she'd feel fatigued for a while, but how long was a while? She just wanted to get back to normal, to go and hang out with Chloe and Georgia, to return to school.

After a few minutes she opened her eyes.

There was something she needed to do while her mum was busy downstairs keeping an eye on the camera installation hunks. Emily-Jane sighed. If she was feeling better she'd have been able to chat to them, but right now she really didn't have the energy. Which was worse than awful, because they were both gorgeous. She'd been about to send a sneaky picture to Clo and Georgi when her mum had come into the kitchen.

Just as well she hadn't.

Her mum was right about people knowing too much. Someone in school had given that journalist her phone number, and although she'd blocked him now, she'd been terrified when he'd started messaging her.

Christ, what had Dad done to bring all of this down on them?

He thought he was so smart, but it had been Uncle Pierce who was the real innovator in the family. Emily-Jane could still remember him coming over to the house; he'd been the best uncle, never forgot her birthday. He'd bought her Bea Bear.

Her dad had kept everything going and he'd built Ferryman based on Pierce's model, but it hadn't been his idea. And now the prospect of growth had turned him stupid. Pierce would never have even entertained SpeakEasy. Ever since her dad had started talking about them, Emily-Jane had been questioning him about their ethics.

Life wasn't just about making money.

Money was an enabler, she was under no illusions there, but not at any cost. Ben and Jerry had the right idea. They'd built a sustainable business and paid their people properly. Whenever she'd tried to talk to her dad about the minimum wage he'd wave her away. She'd ended up doing a ton of googling to find out what people earned at Ferryman, and it didn't make good reading unless you were in head office.

Emily-Jane turned over and, powering up the iPad, she opened her email, firing off a message to Danny Boy. Her mum would be tied up downstairs for a bit, but she knew she didn't have a lot of time.

While she waited for the email to land, Emily-Jane reached for her phone and found Spotify, connecting to her speakers so the room filled with sound. The theme tune to *Big Little Lies*. Perfect for her current mood.

Rolling slowly off the bed, she went into the bathroom, picking up her hairbrush and pulling it through her hair. She looked pale, dark rings around her eyes. She was a wreck.

Almost dying really wasn't good for your skin.

Staring hard at herself, Emily-Jane pulled a face. She felt as if she'd aged in the past few days. Suddenly a whole load of things in her life had become real, very real, as if everything had switched from a soft filter to high definition. She closed her eyes and, leaning on the sink, rested her forehead against the mirror over it. For a moment she felt as if she didn't have the energy for this.

But it wasn't about her now, and she'd come this far.

Opening her eyes and standing straight, Emily-Jane dropped her hairbrush into the sink and reached for her make-up bag. Concealer first, and then she'd need a *lot* of foundation.

Deftly she worked the colour on to her cheeks and started on her eyes. Smoky but natural. Lip gloss last.

Taking a last look in the mirror, she pulled her hair up into a high ponytail. The next track was playing on her phone now and she swayed to the beat. Katie Perry's 'Firework'. It was almost last century, but she loved it.

On the bed, Emily-Jane woke up her iPad and checked her email. Nothing new. She clicked back over the old emails. Danny Boy had wondered where she was, had wanted to chat several times in the last few days. When she'd finally been able to use her phone, she'd told him she had the flu.

Emily-Jane bit her lip. If he wasn't around now, she'd have to make him a video.

He'd like that. Engagement was crucial to get what she needed. And with everything happening, she was going to have to speed things up.

Logging in to Spotify on her iPad, she chose a different track and reached for her phone, turning on the camera and switching to selfie mode.

'Curtain close.' She waited for a moment as her bedroom curtains swished shut. 'Lamps on.'

The fact that the house was listening to her all the time creeped her out, but the smart system definitely had its uses when she was low on energy.

Emily-Jane had a good look at the image captured on the screen. If she was recording, she needed to stage her video to make it look spontaneous. Turning around, she pulled the cushions on her bed into a pile, sitting Bea Bear down next to her. Hopping off the bed, she unwrapped herself from her dressing down and reached over to turn on the pink fairy lights that hung around the bed.

Conscious of the time, she slipped onto the duvet, sitting cross-legged, and switched the phone to selfie again. Lifting it up, she fluffed up her hair and slipped the ribbon strap of her camisole off her shoulder. After being so quiet for so long, she needed to give Danny Boy something to think about.

Chapter 56

IT WAS STARTING to rain as Laurence pulled his jacket around himself and trotted from the car park to St Vincent's private hospital. He glanced at his watch again. It was after four. He'd been with the police almost all day. First in the office, and then he'd gone down to the station to give his statement. Not that he could answer half of their questions. They'd been very interested in Nina – obviously – but also in who could have ordered the flowers for Kate and Cressida.

As Sports Jacket had said, it was as if the women in his life were being picked off. Literally. Who on earth would want to do that? Laurence still couldn't believe that Emily-Jane and Kate had got involved in all of this. He knew that he'd upset a lot of people in business – you had to, to get what you wanted. It was dog eat dog out there, and there was no room to be nice when there was money and market share at stake.

But who would hate him enough, personally, to do that?

And more importantly, how did they know about the inside track of his personal life? That was the bit that was making him feel really sick. Had someone been following him?

Laurence pushed open the swing doors to the hospital and walked purposefully down the broad corridor towards the lift. It felt more like a hotel lobby than a hospital, cream sofas on either side separated by trees in tubs. It was relatively quiet, the air filled with Sunday afternoon calm, a few people sitting having coffee.

Outside the lift Laurence hit the *call* button and looked expectantly at the arrow above it, lit to show it ascending. He didn't have much time, knew he had to get back to Cressida – and Emily-Jane – to see how she was. Pursing his lips, he let out a sharp breath of annoyance. A week ago everything had been on track to him landing ten million dollars in an offshore account and adding an extra facet to the Ferryman offering that would extend its reach even further.

And then all this. What the hell had he done to deserve it? Emily-Jane was always going on about karma, about how good energy brought good things, and how life was all about balance. He didn't believe it himself; success was about being one step ahead, not about balance. It was about being faster and sharper and using all your skills to get where you wanted to go.

Had he used all his skills? He glanced up to see the lift had got to the third floor. Or had he gone one step too far? Perhaps Emily-Jane had been right when he'd first mentioned SpeakEasy. Her mouth had fallen open and she'd looked at him in horror. He'd no idea how she even knew who they were, but then she spent a lot of time on Reddit, so perhaps she'd read a few things, and just like her mother, had wanted to know everything.

It was the only explanation he could think of. She'd been going through an activism phase, so part of him was sure she had been overreacting.

Now he wasn't so sure.

But Dirk had been nothing but helpful whenever he'd met him, or they'd subsequently zoomed, as keen for this deal as he was. As the cops had said today, someone had murdered Nina and it was more than likely that same somebody had also sent those flowers. He couldn't say he'd noticed the tattoo they'd mentioned, but he wasn't about to tell them that.

Laurence shivered and looked behind him. He'd suddenly got the feeling that he was being watched, as if a dark shadow had passed over his soul. He rubbed his face. Was he getting paranoid now?

The lift pinged, interrupting his train of thought. The doors slid open and he stepped inside with relief, scanning the sofas and entrance corridor as the doors slowly closed again. He couldn't see anyone he recognised, but that didn't mean anything.

Upstairs, Kate looked pale, but she was awake, and the moment he pushed the door to her room open, her face lit up.

'Hey, gorgeous, how are you doing?'

Closing the door gently behind him, he went to sit in the chair positioned beside the bed, reaching out for her hand as it rested on the sheet.

'Much better now. Still pretty shook, I'm so weak, but definitely much better. The doctors are pleased.'

She raised her head slightly to speak to him, but the effort appeared to wear her out and she fell back onto the pillow.

'That's brilliant news.' He sighed. 'I was with the cops this morning. They still don't know who sent the flowers.'

Kate sighed and squeezed his hand.

He wasn't about to tell her about Nina or the flowers being sent to Cressida; he needed her to get better and worry wouldn't help.

'It's so weird. I was so sure they were from you. It has to be some sort of accident, something that got on to the flowers when they were imported. It sounds as if a whole batch was affected.' She paused. 'Did the guards ever find a card?'

He shook his head, realising that the doctors or the guards must have said something about there being more than one bouquet. Did Kate know who they'd been sent to? He really wasn't ready to get into a discussion on that – it would mean bringing her up to date on everything.

'They examined the whole of your office, but nada.'

'I don't know. I just want to get home to Mitzi and get my strength up so I can go back to work. But I saw the news. What on earth is happening with this data thing?'

'It's nothing to worry about. Hackers who think they can hold us to ransom. Half of it has been blown up by the press, but we have it under control.' He sat down on the edge of her bed, hoping he sounded convincing. He needed to change the subject. 'You can go part-time, you know, just a few hours. Full-time is going to be too much. Get an assistant in to do the paperwork.'

She patted his hand. 'I know, lovely, but you know me, I need to be busy.' She paused. 'Laurence, I'm worried – the company—'

He held his hand up to stop her. Ever since he'd known her she'd been full of energy and ideas. Nothing could stop her. Pierce had always laughed at the way she looked at everything from every angle. And now here she was, lying pale in a hospital bed.

'We'll talk when you're fully better. Not before. I don't want you to waste energy on worrying, I want you to focus on recovery.'

Laurence was about to say more, but his phone rang. Kate lifted her hand to indicate he should take it.

It was the guards. Sports Jacket, to be more precise.

What on earth did he want now?

Chapter 57

'THANKS SO MUCH, and thanks for being so fast.'

Cressida led the two Serpent Security technicians across the hall and to their van in the garage. She watched as they loaded their toolboxes into the rear of the van. Slamming the doors closed, they climbed in and waved as she hit the button to open the huge double garage doors. Hanging back, still conscious of the possibility of the press loitering about outside the gates, she watched as they reversed outside, swinging the compact vehicle around on the gravel. She hit the door closure button before they got to the gate sensor and the external gates opened. There was no point in taking risks.

The two boys had managed to get all the cameras installed without leaving any traces of their work, and they'd set it all up to route to a laptop that was currently concealed underneath a pile of towels in the robe room. Cressida had had a good look and you couldn't see the cameras at all. They were little fisheye things cunningly disguised as smoke alarms above the bar in the pool room, and in the ceiling in the dining room. As the guys had shown her, they gave an almost 360° view. They were really quite remarkable.

What was even more remarkable was that Emily-Jane hadn't come down while they'd been fitting them, and Laurence hadn't suddenly appeared and blundered into the middle of everything. So Cressida was the only person in the house who knew exactly what had been installed.

And that was precisely how she wanted to keep it.

Locking the internal door to the garage behind her, Cressida walked across the hall to see what was happening outside, to make sure no one had tried to sneak in while the gates had been open for the few seconds it had taken the van to exit. Taking a quick look out of the peephole in the front door, she could see there were still a few cameramen hanging about, but hopefully as it grew dark, and with a bit of luck, rained, they'd move on.

Cressida turned, hesitating at the bottom of the stairs. She was desperate to call Brioni and give her an update, but she really needed to check on Emily-Jane first. Skipping up the stairs, she pushed Emily-Jane's door open a crack. She was curled up on the bed asleep, her dressing gown pulled over her. Cressida crept in and pulled one of her furry fleece throws off the end of the bed, tucking it around her.

Emily-Jane must have been listening to music or chatting to her friends – she'd left her iPad and her phone on top of the duvet beside her. They woke up as Cressida picked them up to put on her bedside table, the screens lighting the darkened room momentarily. Emily-Jane stirred, and Cressida put them down quickly. She wanted Emily-Jane to sleep as much as possible; being so ill had utterly worn her out, evidenced by the dark circles under her eyes. Creeping out again, Cressida closed Emily-Jane's door as quietly as she could and almost ran downstairs to the kitchen.

Her phone was on the counter. As she called Brioni's number, Cressida grabbed a mug and, resting the phone on her shoulder, popped a coffee pod into the machine. Brioni must have been sitting beside her own phone – she picked up before Cressida had even hit the *start* button on the coffee machine.

It only took her a moment to bring Brioni up to date.

'They were brilliant, and so tidy. They've installed the cameras and a laptop so we can see everything. It'll be recorded here and backed up at their control centre. We just need to make sure Laurence brings Ackroyd to the bar in the pool for a drink before dinner. That shouldn't be a problem if I suggest they go through to look at the view. I can delay the food long enough for them to have a drink or two.'

'When is he arriving?'

'I'm still waiting for Laurence to tell me, but he's landing late tomorrow I think. They've got meetings, so I suggested dinner on Tuesday evening might work best. He's only here till Thursday, apparently.'

'That sounds perfect. I can come over on Tuesday afternoon? I think pretending to be waiting staff is a good idea – people never notice who is serving them. I'll dress as a waitress – white shirt, black trousers? I can wear one of my wigs.'

'That would be great. I've told the caterers I have my own staff organised. They're delivering the food early afternoon. You'll just need to do the drinks and serve up.'

'How about I see if Alex can come? He'd make a great barman.'

The coffee machine gurgled and Cressida picked up her coffee and took a sip, drinking it black. She felt as if she'd been living on her nerves while the cameras were being fitted, dreading having to explain what was going on if Laurence appeared, and right now she needed the caffeine hit.

'That wouldn't be a bad idea. If Alex is here, he can sort things out in the kitchen and you and I can make sure Mr SpeakEasy stays in camera shot. I don't want him wandering around the house and us missing something crucial about what's going on.'

'Sounds good. How's Emily-Jane doing?'

Cressida sighed. 'She's definitely better, but she's just so cross about Laurence's deal with SpeakEasy. It's not often she gets that upset about things he does. I'm worried she might set herself back.'

'I'm sure she'll be grand. Her reaction's understandable when you look at their track record. And the timing of this cyberattack is very suspicious.'

'Something's going on. And someone's got it in for Laurence. If it's not Dirk Ackroyd, I'm worried it could be one of the other board members.'

'If it is Ackroyd, let's hope with enough drink on board he'll let something slip.'

'God, I hope so, I can't go on much longer like this …'

Chapter 58

'Brioni? can you hear me?' DCI Mike Wesley sounded as if he was striding down a corridor, footsteps echoing as his shoes squeaked on what Brioni knew was a highly polished floor in the corridors of New Scotland Yard. 'I've only got a minute, we've a suspect in custody and the clock's ticking.'

'What's up?'

Sitting at the table in her living room, her laptop open, it was already dark outside, the evening drawing in. Brioni picked up the remote and turned the TV news down.

'This body the guards have got – Interpol got a hit on that tattoo.'

'How …?' She didn't finish the sentence. It wasn't even really a sentence, more a string of questions. *How did he know? How were Interpol involved?* Conscious of the stress in his tone, she shut up and let him continue.

'Long story, but the victim was staying in London. She flew from here to Dublin early on Thursday. She's from LA originally – the guys here have been keeping an eye on her. We know who she is and, more importantly, who paid for her ticket to London. She's been staying in The Shard as a guest of SpeakEasy Telecoms, apparently. We've intel that suggests she's a contract killer.'

For once Brioni didn't know what to say. What on earth was she doing in Dublin, and how had she got into the hotel room? More to the point, *who* had hired her? And who was she supposed to kill? *And who had killed her?* The questions whirled around Brioni's head as if they were inside a washing machine, getting more and more tangled with each rotation. *Who had Alex even slept with?*

'Obviously you don't know any of this. It's been passed to Dublin. But you need to be careful, Bri. I don't know what's going on over there, but it's serious and it's not some love triangle that's got out of hand.' She heard a door open. 'I'd guess the guys there will put Laurence under surveillance, in case he's next. I've got to go but I'll call you if I hear anything else.'

Brioni hung up, her head pounding.

The dead woman was a contract killer?

Mike had said she was from Los Angeles; could she be Latina? Was this woman actually Nina? Had she been paid by SpeakEasy all along? Brioni had assumed the woman who'd come in to speak to Laurence that night in the bar was Nina; she'd certainly looked like her photo on LinkedIn, but now she came to think about it, had he actually said her name? Just because she was an attractive woman with long dark hair and a South American accent, that didn't mean she *was* Nina. Perhaps the woman who had accosted Alex wasn't Nina at all?

But the tattoo. The body had a tattoo, and Alex had been sure the woman he had slept with didn't have one. Brioni tapped the side of her phone on her chin. Alex might have thought he'd have noticed it, but Brioni was quite sure he wasn't thinking about tattoos while he was in bed with her. Perhaps he was wrong?

Running her fingers into her hair, she pulled at the roots as she tried to work it out. Perhaps they had it all wrong, but if the dead woman wasn't Nina, where was she? Mike had said the tattoo belonged to a contract killer they'd tracked from London. Had she killed Nina and taken her place?

And if *that* had happened, who had killed *her*?

Brioni had no idea. The only person who could positively identify the woman who had come into the bar in the Reynolds Regency House was Laurence Howard, and Brioni was quite sure the guards would be asking him that exact question.

She sighed. Tuesday was going to be very interesting. She was desperate to find out how this Dirk Ackroyd fitted into the picture. From all her googling, Brioni had discovered that he had some fairly unsavoury associates. Had been a friend of Jeffrey Epstein's. That spoke for itself. She'd also found a photo of him at some party with Richie Murphy, one of the Ferryman board members on her list. Had that been how Laurence had got involved with him in the first place?

Brioni looked at her phone. Should she tell Cressida? Would knowing Ackroyd's company had funded this woman's trip to London help? Or would it just frighten her even more? The guards knew his company was involved – if there was a real threat, she was sure they'd tell Cressida.

But what the hell was Laurence Howard playing at, that he was mixing with the type of people who hired contract killers? It sounded like something right out of the movies.

Chapter 59

'MUM, DO I have to go to school this week?'

Cressida swung around to find Emily-Jane standing in her pyjamas, bleary-eyed, at the kitchen door. Her heart broke for a moment. Emily-Jane looked so young and vulnerable standing there, rubbing her eyes like she had when she was little. Putting the mug she was holding under the nozzle of the coffee machine, Cressida smiled.

'Of course not, love. You need to be 100 per cent better before you go anywhere.'

'Good.' Emily-Jane rubbed her face again. 'I do feel miles better, but I'd just like a quiet day.'

'A quiet few days wouldn't go amiss.'

Emily-Jane started at Laurence's voice coming from the sofa on the other side of the kitchen.

'Aren't you going to work today?'

Pushing her sleep-mussed hair out of her face, she scowled across the room at him.

He sat up and swung around to look at her over the back of the sofa.

'That's nice. I take a morning off to spend with my girls and that's the reaction I get.'

Cressida let out an internal sigh at Emily-Jane's scowl and mentally counted to three to stop herself biting back at him.

His girls.

Her husband really knew how to charm his teenage daughter. She pressed the button on the machine, the kitchen immediately filled with the rich smell of coffee. She was going to need plenty of caffeine to get her through the next few days. As if she'd heard her, Emily-Jane continued.

'Are you like *actually* taking the morning off, Dad? In the middle of this data security breach thing. I mean … timing?'

Clicking her tongue to get her daughter's attention, Cressida opened her eyes wide, signalling for Emily-Jane to hush, but she could see from the look on her face that she very obviously wasn't about to stop.

Beside Cressida, the oven pinged. A distraction, *thank God.* She couldn't deal with being the peacemaker and trying to defuse in-house tension this morning; she had too much on her mind.

'There's the croissants. Now, who'd like one?'

Emily-Jane squinted at her. 'Croissants again?'

'Yes, young lady, that's enough of your cheek, sick or not. Sit down if you want one.' Cressida opened the oven and slipped them from the tray onto a waiting plate. 'I've got hot chocolate ready for you, I even used your special mug. I was just about to bring it up.'

Emily-Jane pulled out a stool at the counter and picked up her mug. Sitting down, she wrapped her hands around its undulating hand-thrown surface, the white glaze like water rising against the terracotta clay. She took a sip and blew on it.

'I want to do that pottery course again in the summer, and make some more mugs. Drinking from it really feels as if you're connecting to the planet.'

Cressida half-smiled. 'We'll see, earth child. Mind, it's hot.'

Emily-Jane threw her an 'I know' look and, setting it down for a minute, put her chin on her hands. Cressida looked at her, concerned.

'You sure you're feeling better?'

'Yes, just tired. I couldn't get to sleep last night.'

'That's because you conked out for a nap yesterday afternoon.'

Behind them, Laurence stood up. He was wearing jeans with a navy tweed jacket, his shirt open at the neck. Emily-Jane turned and looked at him, frowning.

'Like you're really not going into the office at all?'

He came across the kitchen and grabbed another stool beside the marble island.

'Not till later. I've got to call into the garda station again on the way in, they've got more questions. I might be there for a while from what they were saying.'

Emily-Jane scowled. 'So you aren't *actually* taking the morning off to be with us. What's happening? Have they found out who sent the flowers?'

'Not yet, chicken. As soon as I know anything I'll tell you.'

Emily-Jane didn't look as if she believed him. Pulling back the sleeve of her dressing gown, she reached for a croissant and took a bite, speaking with her mouth full.

'What's happening with the hacking?'

'Ethan and his team are still working on it. He still can't find any indications of an infiltration. The security systems are all working fine. He's starting to think it could have been someone on the inside.'

Really?' Emily-Jane's eyebrows shot up. Cressida leaned over and put Laurence's coffee down on the marble worktop in front of him as she continued. 'Who on earth could have done that? Who would have that level of access?'

Laurence cleared his throat and reached for the mug.

'We had a woman working for us who has disappeared rather mysteriously. Ethan's starting to think she may have let someone else in to scrape the servers. The guards are looking at it.'

'What would make her do that, though, and compromise the whole company?'

Glancing at Emily-Jane, Laurence shrugged. 'We think she may have been coerced, or was being blackmailed in some way. It's completely out of character. And everyone's very worried something might have happened to her. The guards are looking for her. But anyway, Ethan has all the systems secured now, we hope, which means there's no danger of anything else being compromised.'

Emily-Jane took a sip of her hot chocolate.

'It sounds as if this Nemesis crew got everything the first time. They don't need to go back in. The press are hopping.'

Cressida glanced from her daughter to Laurence. He put a spoon into his coffee and stirred it thoughtfully, not looking up. Emily-Jane opened her mouth to speak again but Cressida cut across her, trying to change the subject.

'What time is Ackroyd landing?'

'This afternoon. He wants to get settled in to his hotel this evening. I think he's got some people to see, and then we've a meeting in the morning.'

'I've got dinner organised for eight o'clock tomorrow. Just two staff to help do drinks and serve. The food's coming earlier.'

Emily-Jane looked in disbelief at her parents, her face suddenly flushed. Cressida could almost feel the heat of her daughter's temper rising.

'You're mad getting involved with him, I keep telling you. And now you're inviting him to the *house*? *Seriously*?'

Laurence answered her as if she was about seven.

'Ferryman is doing a huge deal with SpeakEasy. You don't have to be here, you can stay upstairs.'

Emily-Jane glanced at Cressida as she shook her head slowly.

'But SpeakEasy, Dad? And have you checked him out? You know he was one of Trump's inner circle?'

Cressida opened her mouth to cut in again. She could feel they were heading for a row of the magnitude of the first one they'd had when SpeakEasy had been mentioned. But Laurence got there before her, his voice hard.

'It's a big company, Em, a big deal. I'm doing business with the company, not him personally. Politics don't come into it. Honestly, I don't know where you get these ideas. You sound like your Uncle Pierce with your high ideals.'

'But, Dad, if someone is morally reprehensible as an individual, don't you think that calls into question their business practices? There was a good reason the British turned down the SpeakEasy licence, and they'll do business with *anyone* if they pay enough.'

His eyes on his mug, Laurence shook his head.

'I know what I'm doing, darling.'

'You don't, Dad, you really don't.' Emily-Jane put her hot chocolate down with a crack and swung off the stool. 'You'll see. You just wait. You'll see.'

Cressida jumped as the door slammed behind her.

Chapter 60

SITTING IN HIS jeep, Laurence glanced out of the front windscreen at the clouds scudding across the moon. Leaving Cressida and Emily-Jane, still in a huff, this morning, he'd gone straight into town, ending up spending much longer in a garda interview room than he'd intended. And then, when he'd finally got to the office, it had been besieged by the press.

He'd definitely had better days.

Now parked only a few minutes from home beside a pocket of woodland locked between the road and the sea, he watched as seagulls circled the jagged rocks that plunged into the waves to his right, their cries setting his teeth on edge.

The burner phone he'd bought lay on the seat next to him, fully charged. The message that had been left with this number had supposedly come from the Reynolds Regency House switchboard, and related to casino opening times. It was some sort of code Tony Strachan used, apparently.

Now he just had to wait.

Laurence drummed his fingers impatiently on the steering wheel. Strachan had been questioned for most of the day yesterday, and had been a guest of the state last night, the charge of accessory to murder hanging over him. His lawyer seemed to be remarkably unconcerned by the seriousness of the situation, or perhaps just confident that the McQuaids had everything under control. He'd been 'recommended', according to Strachan. And Laurence was pretty sure that he could guess by whom.

He glanced at the clock on the dash. It was already nearing seven and Dirk Ackroyd would be landing soon. Thank God, his plane was delayed. Laurence wasn't scheduled to see him until tomorrow, but after his conversation with Detective Sports Jacket this morning, the less time he spent with the CEO of SpeakEasy, the better.

Laurence rubbed his hand over his face. He didn't know what the fuck was going on, but the detective had been very clear that a company linked to SpeakEasy had paid this Camila whatever-her-name-was's plane fare from London to Dublin. On Thursday. For a moment in the interview room, Laurence had thought he was going to be physically sick.

Something had caused Nina to vanish and left this other woman, Camila … García – her name jumped into his head – dead in the Dublin Mountains. Had she killed Nina and left her in a skip somewhere, or hidden in a service corridor of the Reynolds Regency House? Ever since Sports Jacket had told him, Laurence had jumped every time his phone rang, expecting it to be someone telling him they'd found Nina's body hidden in a store cupboard, or at the back of one of the walk-in freezers.

Perhaps he watched too much Netflix.

Strachan had been arrested before Laurence had had a chance to ask him about what could have happened. And as Sports Jacket had pointed out, the security tapes from that night didn't show anything – anything at all.

But the fact remained that Nina was still missing. And Dirk Ackroyd was on his way to Dublin.

Suddenly the phone began to ring, its tone loud and unfamiliar. Laurence grabbed it off the seat.

'Hello?'

'Good evening, Laurence. How was your day?' Red McQuaid's voice was calm, as if this sort of thing was routine in his world. *It probably was.*

Despite McQuaid's unworried tone, Laurence could feel his heart rate increasing, his palms beginning to sweat. This phone wasn't connected to him, but he didn't know how long it took the guards to triangulate the location of a call being made to another phone.

His mind hopping, Laurence tried to calm himself. The one thing he knew about Red McQuaid was that, for all his years as head of one of Dublin's most notorious crime families, he'd never been arrested. McQuaid wouldn't compromise himself.

Christ, he wasn't good at this.

Laurence tried to keep his voice level as he spoke.

'Did the cops tell you who the woman was?'

'I've had a long and interesting chat with our friends in the gardaí, but I don't know anything about a woman?'

McQuaid injected just the right amount of puzzled into his tone that for a split second Laurence thought he was being serious. Laurence took a deep breath and spoke slowly, making sure he got all the facts in, in the shortest possible time.

When he'd finished, he could almost hear McQuaid shrugging.

'And how does any of that concern me?'

'The CEO of SpeakEasy is flying into Dublin this afternoon. He's coming to dinner at my house in Dalkey tomorrow night. I don't know what the fuck is going on, but someone's been trying to attack me. I need protection tomorrow evening and I'm hoping you can help me with that. I want to find out what the hell is going on, but I don't trust him.'

'It'll be expensive.'

'Not a problem.'

'I wasted seven hours with the guards yesterday. Seven hours of my life I'll never get back. I don't need any more grief from this source. Tell me what's happening tomorrow night.'

'Dinner at my house at eight. My wife's got caterers coming in. It's just me, Dirk Ackroyd and my wife. My daughter doesn't want to get involved but she'll be in the house.'

'That's Emily-Jane? Sensible girl.'

How did he know Em's name?

Before Laurence could formulate the thought fully, McQuaid continued.

'Expect two extra barmen at six. They'll need to suss the place. This guy isn't going to travel without protection, we need to make sure we're ready for anything. Whatever shit he's got planned, it stops now. Get rid of this phone. You don't need to contact me again.'

Laurence opened his mouth to reply, but McQuaid had already hung up.

He looked at the phone in his hand for a moment. Would Ackroyd come to Dublin with protection?

Christ almighty.

Perhaps he travelled with a driver who doubled as a bodyguard? He hadn't mentioned bringing anyone else to dinner with him, but perhaps Laurence was supposed to know that?

This was all getting too fucking unreal for words.

About to get out of the car, Laurence glanced in his rear-view mirror to check if the road was clear behind him, the hairs suddenly standing up on the back of his neck. The light from the street lamps was weak here, the driveways opening on to the road in deep shadow. Straining his eyes, he looked closely for movement. He kept getting the feeling he was being watched. It had happened first in the car park below the office, then in the hospital as he was waiting for the lift. And now it was happening again. He looked hard into the mirror. The road was empty, the houses on both sides tucked away behind high walls.

Even though he couldn't see anyone, the feeling didn't go away. Perhaps he was just getting paranoid. He'd never believed in the sixth sense, or the horoscopes Cressida read out from the paper every Sunday; it was all nonsense about Cressida being a typical Leo and him a typical Aquarius. Although the way Emily-Jane behaved sometimes, you'd guess she was pure Taurus. When she got an idea into her head, she just charged at it.

He checked the mirror again.

He was being ridiculous.

He swung the car door open and got out into the dusk, the wind swirling around him, bitterly cold, making his eyes smart and the tips of his ears sting.

Pulling his coat around him, he kept his head down as he strode across the pavement and into the park, his eyes adjusting as he left the lights of the road behind him. Following the concrete path that bisected it, he swung off to the right, down a track into the trees and heavy scrub. It was pitch dark here, but he was very familiar with the narrow path that led along the clifftop to a point where, if the undergrowth had been cut back, you'd be able to see around the headland out to Killiney Beach. Shielded from view by the trees, Laurence knew it was totally secluded. He'd come here to fish when he was at school, knew the craggy rocks and the tiny paths, only passable by small boys and goats, like the back of his hand. A few years ago a girl had been murdered here, her body thrown over the cliff to look like suicide. She'd only been found because she'd been spotted from the sea.

Holly and brambles clawing at his coat, Laurence threaded his way along the path, conscious that the soles of his street shoes had little purchase on the wet grass and mud. A moment later he reached a gap in the gorse, the sound of the waves swirling below suddenly clearer. Taking a step forward, he glanced around and pulled the phone from his pocket, quickly dismantling it.

Seeing he had something in his hand, the crowd of seagulls began to circle, screaming, calling their friends. His fingers frozen by the cold air, he fumbled as he pulled out the battery and SIM card, hurling them into the sea. The SIM, a tiny piece of white and red plastic, was caught by the wind and lodged on a rock. Would anyone see it? It was so small ... Hastily, Laurence hurled the rest of the phone into the churning waters below.

He'd just have to trust McQuaid now.

Chapter 61

B Y MID-MORNING THE next day, Cressida had everything in place. She'd spent Monday afternoon at the clinic going through her patient files. She'd been in touch with her team on the phone, but it looked as if she was going to need to take even more time off and she wanted to get everything straight. She'd felt a sense of relief when she'd got home last night; at least the clinic was one thing she didn't have to worry about.

She'd slept fitfully. Laurence had come home in a foul temper, having spent half the day in the garda station, and had gone straight up to his office, only reappearing to make himself a toasted sandwich. Eventually she'd heard the door of the spare room close.

Now the food for this evening had been delivered and she was standing in her bedroom, the doors to her wardrobe wide open while she worked out what to wear. She needed to look smart and confident, but not as if she was trying too hard. She riffled through the rails, her hand settling on a crimson jersey wrap dress she'd bought to speak at a conference in Limerick. It was flattering and comfortable, and she could dress it up with heels and some chunky jewellery to make it look more evening. There would be a lot going on tonight, and the last thing she wanted to worry about was too much cleavage or shoes that pinched.

She pulled the dress out of the wardrobe and held it up against her. It was definitely an improvement on the pink sweatshirt and jeans she was wearing. Over her shoulder in the reflection, she saw the bedroom door open.

Emily-Jane. No longer in her pyjamas but in a black velour leisure suit, the designer's logo picked out in diamante. Her hair was freshly washed, a sure sign that she was on the mend. Cressida smiled at her in the mirror and opened her mouth to speak but Emily-Jane got there first, her face creased in a frown.

'I cannot believe you're letting that man come to the house, Mother. I mean, with everything going on at Ferryman as well, and the press all over the place.'

'I know, Em. But we need to do this for your father. It'll be fine.' Deliberately misunderstanding Emily-Jane's real concerns, Cressida continued as if serving dinner was her biggest problem. 'I've booked some specialist staff to help with the food so we don't have to worry about that. And your father has a couple of barmen coming apparently, so there'll be more staff than guests. God knows why he doesn't trust that the people I've hired can mix a gin and tonic, but honestly, I didn't have the energy to argue.'

'Well, don't think I'll be having dinner with him. I mean ... Trump? Children in cages? It makes my skin crawl.'

Emily-Jane sat down heavily on the edge of Cressida's bed and started examining her nails.

'Emily-Jane, you've never met him. He could be a perfectly nice man the media connected with ... with that administration. You know what they're like – it's not as if we haven't fallen foul of them, too.'

Scowling, Emily-Jane looked up and pouted at Cressida. Putting the dress over her arm, she turned around properly.

'There's no need for you even to say hello to him. Your father needs to talk to him, so they'll probably have drinks in the bar, and then we'll go through to the dining room.' Cressida paused. 'He'll come straight into the garage and all the curtains will be closed, so there won't be anything for the press to get a photo of.' Cressida knew she sounded more like she was trying to reassure herself than Emily-Jane as she continued. 'The staff will be in the kitchen. If you need anything, just come down and ask. You can easily stay out of his way.'

'They're going to be in the bar? What if I want a swim?'

'Have it earlier. I thought you'd be happy in your room, you spend enough time up there. There will be loads of food. I'll get some dropped up to you and then you won't need to come down for anything.'

'I'm not five, Mother, bribing me with ice cream isn't going to work.'

'I'm not bribing you, Em. We just have to trust your father and let this happen. We don't have to like this guy, just give him and your dad time to talk privately. Now, what do you think of this dress?'

Cressida held it up in front of her. Emily-Jane scowled and stood up, sticking her hands in the pockets of her jogging pants.

'It's a bit middle-aged, Mum, but I'd definitely go with that. Safer than your normal going-out stuff. Don't say I didn't warn you.'

Turning, Emily-Jane marched out of the room, but before Cressida could call after her, her phone pipped with a text.

Brioni was at the gate.

*

Cressida hung back from the internal door as Brioni pulled her little black Citroën into the garage, letting the huge doors close behind her before she stepped forward. Maybe she was getting paranoid about telephoto lenses but it was better to be safe. Brioni grinned as she got out of the car and looked around the garage.

'This is bigger than my apartment.'

Cressida grimaced. 'Come inside so I can walk you through my plan. I'm so glad to see you.' She smiled. 'And good hair.'

Brioni grinned at her, smoothing the sleek tresses of her dark wig.

'I just hope Laurence doesn't recognise me.'

'I don't think he's that observant right now. He's got a lot on his mind. Is Alex on his way?'

'Yep, he's getting the DART later. I'll give him a lift home.'

'Perfect. Come inside, let me show you where everything is.'

Grabbing her backpack from the passenger seat, Brioni closed her car door and followed Cressida into the hall, her soft-soled boots silent on the polished wooden floors.

'Wow, this is a beautiful house.'

Cressida looked at her, smiling. The hall always had this effect on guests; its sheer size, double height and gallery had been her idea. She needed light, and here in the centre of the house, the glazed roof provided it.

'Thank you. It was Laurence's parents' house, a tribute to the 1980s when we moved in. We gutted it and redesigned the layout a bit, the original hall was so dark. The kitchen's through there, it's my favourite room, it looks right out over the island.' Cressida indicated the open door opposite them.

'Mum?' Emily-Jane's voice came from above. They both looked up. Emily-Jane was leaning over the banisters at the top of the stairs. 'What time are they coming again?'

'It's just one guy, and your dad said he'd be driving so his chauffeur can take the night off.' Cressida said it more to Brioni than to Emily-Jane. 'He should be here about eight. How many times have I told you?' She paused, conscious that the nerves fluttering in her stomach were making her snappy. She softened her tone. 'Do you want to come down and say a quick hello? This is Brioni, she'll be looking after the food for this evening. If you need anything, just ask her.'

Emily-Jane pulled a face and her head disappeared over the banister.

Cressida sighed, catching Brioni's eye. 'That was Emily-Jane, as you probably gathered. She's seventeen.' It was explanation enough.

In the kitchen, Cressida pushed the door closed behind them as Brioni unzipped her parka and slipped it off, putting her backpack on one of the kitchen stools. Cressida could see the silver corner of her laptop poking out.

'Emily-Jane's really cross about this SpeakEasy thing. I do hope she's not going to turn up in the middle of dinner and start cross-examining Dirk Ackroyd.'

'I'm sure she won't, but I'll keep an eye out just in case. Is she feeling better?'

'Yes, thank God. Kate Spicer only got out of hospital last night apparently. Em was very lucky.' Cressida paused. 'Let me show you where everything is. We can talk properly in the pool room. All the insulation means it's soundproofed and photographers can't get around to the back of the house.'

She indicated a monitor screen built into a panel beside the kitchen door.

'You can see the whole drive from here, so you'll know if any of them reappear. It's a smart system, so as well as this panel, everything's connected to our phones.' She lowered her voice, her eyes shining. 'Wait till you see what your camera guys have done.'

Brioni went to take her laptop out of her backpack.

'Is a smart system secure?'

Cressida rolled her eyes. 'Laurence is all about gadgets. He wanted to be able to open the gates if he needs to and check the security cameras if we're away. He's got the heating on it, and the curtains, so he can adjust everything if we get delayed, or the weather changes. It's a bit over the top if you ask me.'

'It can be hacked, too, you know. I think I'd see if you can ask your security company to bypass it until this Ferryman thing is sorted out.'

Cressida looked from the security panel to Brioni, her face pained.

'Dear God, you're right. I'll tell Laurence tonight.' She took a breath, trying to focus on what they needed to do now; she really didn't have space in her head for worrying about anything else. 'Look, that's the door to the dining room.' Cressida pointed across the kitchen. 'We designed it so you can come in and out discreetly through here.'

Brioni opened it and looked inside.

'Gorgeous room – it's like a club or something.'

Smiling, Cressida turned around and pointed to the laundry room door.

'And this way is now the nerve centre.' Inside the laundry room, Cressida carefully closed the door behind them. 'From here, you have access to the back door through there.' She pointed to a glazed door between a coat rack and a huge American freezer. 'And through this door is the robe room.'

Brioni grinned. 'That sounds extremely grand.'

'It's actually just a glorified airing room. We hang all the pool robes and keep the towels in here.' Cressida pushed open another door. 'It connects with the pool room as well. You can see there's plenty of space. The security guys have everything connected to a laptop – it's behind here.'

She went over to a shelving unit full of neatly stacked fluffy white towels and pulled out a pile. They'd been cleverly folded to conceal an open laptop.

'Neat. Is it recording now?'

'Not yet. I'm going to text their control centre when I want it switched on. They'll check it's all working.'

'Excellent. You don't want to go to all this trouble and then have a glitch with the recording. Does Laurence suspect Dirk Ackroyd of being involved in the cyberattack and Nina's disappearance?'

Cressida shrugged. 'I really don't know. I think he's looking at the bigger picture, the profits from a deal. I mean ...' She sighed. 'I'd guess the guards must have told him about the body, and Nina's still missing, apparently. I keep telling myself it's perhaps because he doesn't want to worry me, but actually I think he knows more about all of this than he's letting on.' She paused. 'At least if I don't know, I can't be called as a witness in court.'

'If it comes to that. Which hopefully it won't.' Brioni paused. 'So now, assuming we're right, let's see what this Ackroyd guy has to say. These types of men can't resist being top dog. He's probably feeling very pleased with himself that Ferryman is falling into his hands, and this is the perfect opportunity for him to show Laurence he's behind everything. Once he doesn't think anyone else is listening, he might even say something about the hacking.' She paused again. 'And you never know, Laurence might drop something about his relationship with Nina that will give you extra ammunition in the divorce court.'

Chapter 62

BRIONI HAD HAD a bad feeling about how this dinner was going to pan out ever since Cressida had suggested the plan to her, and it was only getting worse. She'd wanted to be involved – the thought of Cressida and Emily-Jane on their own in the house with only Laurence as support didn't bear thinking about – and Cressida was right, Dirk Ackroyd might say something that would explain everything, but personally, Brioni didn't even want to breathe the same air as him. Particularly not now that she knew he was directly connected to a contract killer – but she didn't want to tell Cressida any of that. Cressida needed to be cool and confident tonight, not terrified.

She glanced over at Alex, who was standing at the marble island in Cressida's kitchen, polishing glasses. He was wearing a black waistcoat buttoned up over a crisp white shirt, a bowtie at his neck. She was glad he was here; she'd been worried about how he was coping with everything that had happened over the last few days. Perhaps tonight they'd find out what was really going on from Ackroyd, and it would offer some sort of resolution for him.

The 'barmen' had arrived earlier, and looked decidedly unlike bar staff. Laurence had told Cressida that they would double as security in case they had any more problems with the press, but that wasn't making Brioni feel any better. Both over six feet tall and blocky, they looked more like bouncers in their black suits, their shaved heads only adding to the impression. And once they'd seen Alex had the champagne under control, they'd gone off to inspect the pool room and get their bearings in the house. They were outside now. They must have walked the full perimeter, the security lights in the garden flicking on as they crossed the deck outside the kitchen window.

This Dirk guy was dangerous, and these two being here just confirmed to Brioni that Laurence knew that. The guards who were investigating the multiple cases linked to Ferryman must have warned him, but he hadn't called off the dinner. Instead he'd brought in a couple of bodyguards. Was he putting Cressida and Emily-Jane in more danger?

Brioni glanced at her watch: 7.55. Only five minutes to go until Laurence arrived with Ackroyd.

*

In the pool room, Cressida moved the ice bucket an inch to the right and took another look at the bar, glancing up again at the camera. She'd texted the CCTV company to make sure they could still see the images properly now that the sun had gone down. They'd assured her that the cameras were state-of-the-art and only needed a fraction of the light of normal security cameras. So that was one less thing to worry about, at least.

This end of the pool was raised slightly, a set of steps leading down from the bar area to the edge of the water. Moving all the loungers to the inside wall, she'd opened the blinds to the sea on the opposite side and lowered the lighting. Now there was a wonderful night-time view of Dalkey Sound, lights twinkling on the horizon, giving Laurence another reason to bring Ackroyd in here before dinner. She could almost hear him spouting about the history of the island and the secret passage from the ruined monastery to the mainland.

Cressida drew in a shaky breath and checked her phone again. Laurence had texted twenty minutes ago to say they were coming directly from the office. Almost on cue, her phone pipped with another text.

At the gates.

This was it.

Hurrying out to the kitchen, her heels clicking on the tiles, she found Brioni looking at the security monitor, watching the gates slowly open. The main course was in the oven, the scents of pork and cider filling the kitchen. Cressida had decided against beef – it was so easy to ruin if they were engrossed in conversation and got to the table late. Brioni looked over her shoulder as she heard the internal door.

Cressida steadied herself, one hand on the island.

'They're here. Alex, can you go through to the pool and be ready at the bar?' She indicated the way she'd just come. 'As soon as the drinks are poured, slip back in here?'

'No problem, I'm a dab hand with a cocktail.'

Brioni suddenly paled. 'Is that a good idea? What happens if Laurence saw the tapes in the Reynolds before they were altered and recognises him?'

Alex's eyebrows shot up. Cressida paused, processing what she'd said.

'It'll be fine. There's no way he's going to expect Alex to turn up in his house, and if he does recognise him, perhaps it'll give him enough of a fright to tell the guards what's really going on. Alex is totally safe here with us. I won't take my eye off him, I promise.'

Brioni nodded slowly. 'You're right. I don't know why I'm so nervous.'

Cressida smiled at her reassuringly. 'Where have those two bar staff gone?'

'They went out through the garage, I think they were doing another tour of the perimeter.'

Cressida raised her eyes to the ceiling and went to open the door, slipping into the cavernous hallway just as the front door opened.

Chapter 63

I N THE KITCHEN, Brioni caught the door to the hall before it closed, glancing nervously at Alex. She put her foot in the crack so she could hear and see what was happening at the front door. Laurence was supposed to have come in through the garage, but obviously he'd decided a grand entrance through the front door was a better idea. Brioni just hoped Ackroyd had kept his head down to avoid any lingering press cameras.

'Here we are, do come in. This is my wife, Cressida.'

Brioni watched as the door swung open and Laurence stood back to show his guest into the hallway.

Dirk Ackroyd looked vaguely like his profile picture on the SpeakEasy website. Overweight and jowly, he was heavily tanned, his hair swept over a bald pate. There was no question in Brioni's mind that someone with excellent Photoshop skills had had a go at the photo. Either that, or Ackroyd had gained a considerable amount of weight. And years. At least that meant that any photographers who were still outside wouldn't recognise him.

As Laurence stepped into the hall, one of the security guys came in behind him, checking outside the front door before he gently closed it. Turning to stand with his back against it, his hands behind him, feet spread apart, he appeared to be contemplating the stairs, his face blank. Cressida stepped forward, her hand outstretched to their guest. Brioni tried to focus on Ackroyd instead of the security guy looming behind him, who was evidently not going to be serving any drinks this evening.

'Welcome to our home, I hope your flight was good yesterday.'

Brioni couldn't see her face from behind, but it sounded as if Cressida was smiling.

'Thank you, great to be here at last. It's years since I was in Ireland.'

Instead of shaking Cressida's hand, Ackroyd held out his coat to her, obviously expecting her to take it. Before Cressida could react, Brioni materialised beside her and took it from him, taking a step back to stand beside the hall table. She could feel Ackroyd looking her up and down as Cressida addressed him.

'I do hope your hotel is comfortable.'

'Great, thank you. Really something. The hospitality is always awesome in your little country, isn't it?' Finally looking at Cressida, he took her in with a glance around the impressive hallway. 'Great place you have here.'

Obviously aware of the increasing tension, Laurence stepped forward quickly.

'Come inside, we've got the bar well stocked and a few minutes to relax before we eat. We have a great view of the island.'

'Do come this way.'

Leaving Laurence standing in the hall, Cressida guided Ackroyd towards the pool room, catching Brioni's eye as she did so.

Behind her, Laurence began to follow them but a distinct

chirping sound stopped him in his tracks. Oblivious to Brioni, he paled and reached inside his jacket. Brioni turned to go into the kitchen, but a muttered 'Jesus Christ' made her hesitate. Her hand on the door, she looked over her shoulder to see Laurence staring at his phone, his face confused.

He turned away from her, searching for a number. She stayed where she was, praying he didn't turn around. From the other end of the corridor Brioni could hear Ackroyd's voice. They must have left the pool room door open, thinking Laurence was following them.

As if he'd just registered the bouncer guy stationed at the front door, Laurence glanced at him as he put the phone to his ear.

'It's Laurence Howard. Yes. Look, Nina Rodríguez has just texted me. She sent me a selfie, she's standing beside a pool in some resort – looks like the Caribbean.' He paused. 'Yes, I know, I'll forward it now. But listen – she's beside a table with a bunch of flowers on it. They look like the same ones that were sent to Kate and Cressida.' He paused again. 'Yes, it's only short. She just said "Missing you."'

Brioni felt her eyes widen as she listened. Nina had sent him a photo of *the* flowers, not just any photo. This was a grade A power play – she was making it very clear that she had got away with attempted murder. She was some player – how had she managed to get out of the country? Everyone was hunting for her in freezing Dublin and she was living it up in the sunshine. And Brioni would bet it was somewhere that didn't have an extradition agreement with Ireland.

'Yes, yes. Look, I can't talk now, Dirk Ackroyd has just arrived for dinner, I have to go. I'll call you later.'

Laurence clicked off the phone and straightened for a moment, his back still to Brioni. She glanced at the security guard, but his face was impassive. Perhaps he was used to not listening to sensitive conversations. Pushing the kitchen door open, she slipped inside.

Chapter 64

IN THE POOL room, Cressida had no idea what was keeping Laurence. She was just extremely grateful that Alex was standing behind the bar, making conversation about the merits of Irish whiskey over Scotch.

Keeping several feet back from him, Cressida sipped a glass of white wine and pretended to listen, her stomach churning. Ackroyd had pulled up a stool at the bar and had his elbows on it, watching closely as Alex produced bottle after bottle of Laurence's vintage collection, holding them up to the light to show him the colour. He had laid out a row of crystal tumblers in front of the American, and was about to start pouring when Laurence appeared at the door.

'Sorry about that, always something happening the minute you take an evening off.'

Ackroyd looked at Laurence over his shoulder. 'Nothing to worry about, I hope.'

'Nothing at all, nothing at all. I see our man is showing you my collection. You really have to try …'

Laurence faltered for a moment as he looked at Alex, his face puzzled. Seeing his frown, Cressida said brightly, 'Can you take over here, darling? I'm just going to check on things in the kitchen. Why don't Alex and I leave you to it?'

'Of course. No need to hurry back. We've got some things to discuss. I can pour.'

Hardly glancing at Cressida, Laurence pushed up a flap concealed in the bar counter, looking at Alex hard as he paused to let him out. Nodding politely, Alex slipped around Laurence.

Catching his eye, Cressida indicated that Alex should follow her out to the hall. He'd arrived at the bar through the robe room, but she didn't want him going back that way.

When they were both safely on the other side of it, Cressida let the hall door fall shut behind them and leaned on it for a moment, closing her eyes and catching her breath.

'Do you think he recognised me?' Alex had stopped just ahead of her, his face pale.

Cressida raised her eyebrows. 'If he did, it means he saw those security tapes that mysteriously disappeared. Or, at the very least, some stills from them.' She pursed her lips. She didn't want to dwell on that fact right now. She had too much to do. 'Come on, let's get moving.'

Pulling herself together, she followed Alex to the kitchen, glancing at the man still standing with his back to the front door, the jacket of his black tuxedo straining over his chest. He studiously avoided her eye, looking up into the roof space above the mezzanine as if he was interested in the night sky.

God only knew what Laurence was thinking, hiring security staff. What was he worried about?

In the kitchen, Brioni had already laid the plates out on the counter ready for warming. She glanced up as she heard the door.

'The starter's on the table. Are they talking?'

Brioni indicated the door to the laundry room with a jerk of her head, her sleek brown wig catching the overhead lights.

'I hope so.' Cressida turned to Alex, who had started opening the wine. 'Are you OK, Alex? Sit down and have a glass of that. I think we're all going to need it before this evening's out.' She turned to Brioni. 'He did a double take when he saw Alex.'

'Laurence, you mean?'

Cressida nodded. 'I think he might have recognised him, but I bet he hasn't worked out where from. Will you be OK in here on your own for a bit, Alex? Just yell if you need us, we'll only be inside. I'll leave this door open.'

Cressida indicated the laundry room.

A few moments later, Cressida and Brioni were inside the robe room. Earlier in the afternoon, Cressida had brought a free-standing clothes rail down from upstairs and positioned it at right angles across the room, hanging extra fluffy white robes on it, so if anyone did happen to glance in through either door – from the pool room or the laundry room – they would see the rail and not the two of them standing behind it.

Brioni slid the first few robes over and squeezed in under the rail. Cressida followed, turning to adjust the garments and ensure there were no gaps between them.

'I'm starting to think Emily-Jane might be right about that Ackroyd character, he's really ...' Keeping her voice to a whisper, Cressida wrinkled her face, looking for the word that was evading her.

'Nauseating?' Brioni said, and Cressida nodded.

Moving the pile of towels that had been positioned in front of it, Brioni pulled out the laptop from the shelf. As soon as she touched the trackpad, the screen came to life. Cressida sighed with relief. The cameras that had been installed were working just as well as they had when they'd been fitted. They had a clear view of the whole pool room from the bar counter outwards.

Ackroyd was sitting at the bar, a glass in his hand. Picking up the earbuds plugged into the laptop, Brioni handed one to her and they leaned in close to the screen. Sharing the sound feed wasn't ideal, but as Cressida glanced over at her, Brioni nodded to indicate that she could hear.

'So what's happening with this data security breach now, Laurence?' Ackroyd's voice rang out loud and clear, amplified by the water. 'Have you plugged the leak?'

There was a pause before Laurence answered. He was still behind the bar, just out of camera shot. They heard the tinkling of ice.

'I was hoping you could tell me about that, Dirk.'

Cressida could feel her heart rate increasing as she glanced at Brioni. Laurence sounded tense; he'd put great emphasis on Ackroyd's first name, had said it as if he was spitting it out.

'I want this deal to go ahead with no shit on anyone's shoes, Howard. We've got the whole of Europe to play for, that's potentially billions. I want Ferryman squeaky clean by the time we announce the deal.' They watched as Ackroyd took a slow sip of his whiskey. 'There seems to have been a lot going on in this city recently.' He took another sip. 'Tell me who Kate Spicer is. I need to know where the skeletons are. We don't want any dirty laundry being aired that could lead to questions about your judgement, do we?'

Cressida caught Brioni's look of surprise out of the corner of her eye, but kept her eyes fully focused on the screen.

How would Laurence answer this one?

Ackroyd continued without taking a breath. 'Where I'm from, we keep our dicks in our pants in public. What goes on behind closed doors is your business, but—'

'What the hell are you talking about?' Laurence cut him off before he could finish.

'I know things, Laurence. My people tell me things. I know your wife and this Kate Spicer both received flowers that contained a toxic substance, which makes me wonder what your relationship is with this *Ms* Spicer.'

Cressida reached out for Brioni's arm, gripping it, her eyes locked on the screen. She hadn't expected Kate Spicer to come up in the conversation. She found herself holding her breath as she waited for his reply.

It took a long time coming.

'Well?' Ackroyd barked, slamming his glass down.

'Kate Spicer,' Laurence replied slowly, drawing the words out, 'is a very good friend of mine. She was very close to my brother, and on his deathbed, he made me swear I'd look after her.'

'Look after her how, exactly?'

Laurence paused and Cressida could almost feel his anger cracking across the bar. He'd never liked being questioned about his actions.

'We were on the cusp of launching Ferryman when Pierce was killed. It was a difficult time.'

Cressida released her grip on Brioni's arm and made an open-handed gesture. *Why couldn't he just admit it?* As if reading her mind, Brioni slowly shook her head.

'You expect me to believe you aren't involved with her?' Ackroyd wasn't letting it go. 'Someone had good reason to think you were.'

'Yeah, well, I'm starting to think that someone might have been Nina Rodríguez, who I'm also starting to think is a very dangerous lady and just a little crazy.'

'That's been taken care of.' Ackroyd's tone was final.

'Really? Funny you should say that, I think that's exactly what a woman called Camila García thought she was doing – taking care of business. When you say I need to be squeaky clean, I think my board are going to need to know SpeakEasy are squeaky clean, too. I think they're going to be very interested to find out what García did in your organisation.'

'Who?'

'I believe she's from Los Angeles. She was a guest of SpeakEasy at the Shangri-La hotel in The Shard in London, and was flown here to Dublin by your company. What was she doing in the UK, Ackroyd? Delivering your message to selected government representatives? Trying to sway them in your direction, maybe? She was being watched by the security services, apparently. Are they going to find she gave them the slip before she came to Ireland, so she could do another job for you?'

'What sort of job are you talking about?' Ackroyd's voice was guarded.

'An assassination, perhaps. She was a contract killer, I believe?' Laurence made it sound offhand. 'The thing is, she wasn't very good. Nina Rodríguez, the woman she was supposed to be killing, appears to be in full health and enjoying the sunshine in … I'll have to look at the picture she sent to remind me where she said she was – and Camila García is in the Irish state morgue. On a slab.'

Cressida realised she was holding her breath as they watched Ackroyd shrug.

'Nothing to do with me.'

'Just like the cyberattack on the Ferryman customer database was nothing to do with you, Dirk? Just like you had nothing to do with paying Nina to hack my systems. Did you think you'd clean up after yourself by having her killed?'

Cressida could feel her heart beating even harder. She leaned one hand on the towel shelf. Every muscle in her body was tense.

'You're making it up.' Ackroyd leaned forward and hissed at Laurence. 'You can't prove anything – you're a fantasist.'

As he spoke there was a loud splash behind him. Ackroyd spun around in his seat.

Cressida felt herself almost lift off the floor. She glanced at Brioni. 'What on earth …?'

On the screen they could see a dark shape under the water, heading down the pool. Someone had dived in at the opposite end while they'd all been focused on the conversation unfolding in the bar.

'Who is it?' Brioni couldn't keep the disbelief out of her voice. *Who else could be here?*

A moment later, Emily-Jane's head appeared out of the water. She rested her arms on the edge of the pool closest to them for a few seconds and then levered herself out of the water with practised ease. Her hair was tied up in a high ponytail and she was wearing a 1950s-style red polka-dot bikini.

Cressida began to move towards the door. Brioni grabbed her wrist, holding her back, as inside the pool room, Dirk Ackroyd jumped off his stool. He looked at Emily-Jane, aghast, as she stood up, his mouth hanging open.

'Hello, Danny Boy, how are you today?' Her tone was hard-edged. 'I wore this especially, I know how much you like me wet—'

Laurence's voice cut across hers. 'Emily-Jane, what the hell are you doing here? You know we're entertaining.'

Cressida watched as Emily-Jane reached for the end of her ponytail and nonchalantly squeezed the water out of it. It was as if she was giving Ackroyd a show.

What the hell?

'So are you going to tell my dad what sort of a lecherous paedophile sleaze you are, Danny Boy, or will I? The papers are going to have some fun with this, aren't they? All those recordings. All those photos of Mr Wonka. I've emailed them to everyone this evening, with the details of your parties as well. I went for the *New York Times*, the *Irish Times*, and CNN, just to be sure. What did you tell me, Danny Boy? Never trust people? You were so right.'

Chapter 65

I N THE LAUNDRY room, Cressida's face was slowly draining of colour, her mouth open. Brioni could see from her eyes that something was clicking into place in her head.

'Oh my God. The text.' Her voice was barely a whisper. 'Em had a text from someone called Danny Boy. I can't remember what it said exactly, but it was weird.'

'From Ackroyd?'

'It must have been. Do you think he's been grooming Em?' Cressida's hand shot to her mouth and she looked as if she was about to throw up. 'I need to go to her …'

Brioni held her back, keeping her voice low.

'Hold on, she's all right for the moment, and Laurence is out there. It sounds as if she knows what she's doing. Let's see what Ackroyd says.'

As Brioni spoke, there was movement on the screen and they saw Laurence come out from behind the bar, his jaw taut, fists clenched. His voice was dangerously low when he spoke.

'What the hell's going on here? Get a robe on, Emily-Jane. What is she talking about, Ackroyd?' His voice began to rise but Emily-Jane didn't move. 'Get a damned robe on, Emily-Jane. Now!'

Emily-Jane looked archly at Ackroyd. 'I think you'd better tell him. Or will I show him the messages? I've sent them all to the police as well, by the way.'

'Robe, Emily-Jane!' Laurence was shouting now.

Deliberately swinging her hips, Emily-Jane sauntered towards the door of the robe room. Neither Ackroyd nor Laurence noticed that it had opened marginally before she got there, an arm with a tattoo at the wrist shooting out to pull her inside.

'Shush.' Before she could speak, Brioni closed the door, wrapping a white robe around Emily-Jane's shoulders. 'We need you to be really quiet.'

'What the hell are you doing?'

Masking her surprise with temper, Emily-Jane scowled at Brioni just as she caught movement out of the side of her eye. Leaning forward, she swooshed back the robes on the rail.

'Mum?'

Brioni could feel her heart rate accelerating; what was Laurence Howard going to do now? She knew a few people who would deck Ackroyd at this point and probably push him into the pool for good measure.

'Shush, keep your voice down.' Brioni's whisper was loud but it did the trick.

Emily-Jane looked from Cressida to the laptop screen, her voice low when she spoke again. 'What the hell's going on?'

Cressida glared back at her. 'I could ask you the same thing, young lady.'

Before Emily-Jane could answer there was an ear-splitting explosion on the other side of the door, the sound amplified by the water, bouncing off the tiled walls. All three of them reacted immediately, instinctively sinking to their knees. Cressida reached for Emily-Jane, who scrambled through the gap below the robes hanging on the rail.

Brioni glanced at Cressida. Her eyes were wild as she crouched beside Emily-Jane, her arm around her shoulders. Brioni tried to look at the laptop screen above her head, but it was impossible to see what was going on from this angle.

Brioni had disconnected her earpiece when she'd gone to let Emily-Jane in. She inched forward, easing open the door and put her eye to the crack.

At the other end of the pool, down beside the changing rooms, Brioni could see the dark shape of a woman standing with her feet braced apart. The light was dim, but she looked as if she was dressed from head to toe in tight-fitting black. Brioni couldn't see her face clearly from this distance, but she could see that she was holding a revolver, two-handed, aiming it at the top of the pool.

'Sounds as if you have a lot to tell us, Mr Ackroyd.'

The woman's voice reached Brioni across the water and she froze.

She had a very distinctive accent.

Brioni turned away from the door and hissed at Cressida, 'It's Nina. She's got a gun. That was a shot! Call the guards.'

Cressida opened her mouth to speak but Brioni didn't catch what she said. She had already turned back to the crack in the door, her eyes and ears trained on the figure at the other end.

Suddenly the door halfway down the pool that led to the hallway flew open. The guy who had been guarding the front door barrelled through, holding a weapon double-handed, waving it around trying to cover both ends of the pool at the same time. He'd obviously never been in the military, or had any idea what a stealth approach was. Another shot rang out and he fell backwards, rolling to the ground, clutching his shoulder.

Brioni had to give it to Nina – she was a great shot.

Her voice rang out again from the other end of the pool.

'So, Mr Ackroyd, have you told Laurence how much you paid me to compromise Ferryman? Was it as much as you were paying him to blackmail the board into voting to allow a partnership? I do hope so. Or I might be rather annoyed.'

'Who the hell are you? Put that gun down, you stupid bitch.' Ackroyd's Texan accent seemed to have got stronger now he was under real pressure.

'I do not think I am a stupid bitch, Dirk. Camila García was the stupid bitch. Trying to break into my room and kill me, dressed as a maid? She must have thought I was an easy target.'

Ackroyd seemed to be paralysed beside his stool, his glass still in his hand. From this angle he looked to Brioni even more overweight than when he'd arrived at the front door. Brioni was pretty sure he wouldn't be running anywhere any time soon. His voice was shaking as he shouted back, trying to hide his fear with bravado.

'What are you talking about? Why are you here? Do you want money?'

'More money, do you mean? No, Dirk, I am not greedy. Five million is enough for me, plus the very juicy data I discovered. I still have that up my sleeve. It is quite amazing who uses Ferryman.'

'So why are you here?'

Brioni watched through the crack in the door as Nina shook her head, her ponytail swishing. It was almost as if she was laughing.

She had complete control of the situation.

Or thought she had.

How long would it take for the guards to get here?

Nina continued, interrupting Brioni's thoughts.

'Why am I here? I would have thought that was obvious. It is payback time. I do not like people who double-cross me, Dirk. Laurence is just weak, I have what I needed from him.'

'They'll get you, Nina, the police are watching.' Brioni could hear the anger in Laurence's voice.

'I doubt it, Laurence, this room is soundproofed, remember? The oaf outside did not even hear me coming, and he is going to be unconscious for a few hours. Oh … and I changed the entry settings on the gates. These smart systems are impenetrable unless you know how to break them. The guards will have to climb over the wall and knock down the front door. I think we have a few more minutes.' She paused. 'Now, Dirk, just to make sure we fully understand where we are, I know Emily-Jane has enough dirt on you to put you through a very long trial, but you know something, you have some very fancy lawyers, and I am not going to risk you missing out on what you deserve. She is a very clever young lady, Laurence, you should be proud of her.'

'Put the gun down, Nina. Let's talk about this.'

'Talk about what? You leading me on and cheating on your wife? Or do you want to talk about your business associate jerking off while grooming your daughter?'

As Nina adjusted her stance there was a crash somewhere towards the front of the house. Brioni jumped physically.

'I think that was my cue.' The sound of another shot reverberated around the pool, and for a moment Brioni felt as if everything had frozen. Then Nina's voice rang out across the water. 'Remember my name, Laurence. Whenever you get close to crossing that line again, remember my name.'

Brioni watched as Nina turned and ran straight at the glazed windows at the end of the pool room, hitting them with her outstretched arms, pushing open what had to be a fire door. Brioni expected the security lights to flood the garden, but they remained off as she vanished into the darkness.

Brioni yanked open the door, the heat of the pool and the smell of chlorine hitting her like a wave. To her right, the security guard lay motionless on the ground; to her left, Laurence was standing over the apparently lifeless form of Dirk Ackroyd, looking at him as if he'd just crawled out of a swamp.

Laurence glanced at her, his face alabaster.

'You'd better look after that guy, and call an ambulance. I think this piece of shit can wait.'

As he spoke, the door from the hallway burst open and two armed guards appeared, weapons drawn. Laurence looked across at them calmly.

'I hope you've got someone on the quay. She went that way. I'd guess she's a boat waiting.'

Chapter 66

By the time Brioni got to Alex in the kitchen, Emily-Jane had already found him. Wrapped up in a white bathrobe, her long hair matted from her swim, she was sitting on the sofa beside him discussing, from what Brioni could gather, whether she should do law at Trinity or UCD. His face pale, bowtie loose, he looked up sharply as Brioni came in. If she was honest, Brioni didn't think he was absorbing all of what Emily-Jane was saying. It did seem to be rather an incongruous moment to launch into university discussions, given the circumstances, but then Emily-Jane was turning out to be quite a surprising young woman.

The house, outside the kitchen at least, had filled with men in uniform, several in white forensic overalls. The pool room had been taped off and a couple of very serious-looking detectives had taken over the front room. Cressida was leaning on the kitchen island, her arms folded, a rapidly disappearing glass of red wine in one hand. She turned to Brioni.

'Have they got everything?'

'I've copied everything we recorded and the garda technical guys are going to process it. It looks as if Nina came in this afternoon – the camera caught her walking across the end of the pool to push open that fire door. She must have hacked the smart system and shut down the alarm.'

Cressida nodded slowly. 'Ready for her escape.'

'She certainly planned all this. I think Laurence was right about her having a power boat, or maybe a jet ski waiting. She vanished pretty quickly.'

Cressida nodded again, her eyes fixed on her glass. 'Laurence is in the front room talking to the guards. I think they're going to have their work cut out trying to find her.' Cressida paused, lowering her voice. 'She said he slept with her, didn't she? I did hear her correctly.'

Brioni moved over to lean beside her on the edge of the counter, keeping her own voice low.

'Yes. She said he'd led her on – sounded as if he'd made her promises he couldn't keep. She didn't sound very impressed.'

Cressida looked at her sideways. 'And then there's Kate Spicer. What did he say? They're very good friends?' Cressida paused, her tone laced with sarcasm. 'What's that supposed to mean? My God. He's up to his neck in it, isn't he? Hearing that conversation with Nina at the start of all of this made me think it was just another woman, but it's so much worse. Now I don't know what to feel.'

'You've got what you need for the divorce court, anyway. But I think you need to talk to him. See what the truth is. He owes you that, at least.'

Cressida took a sip of her wine. 'I'm not sure he knows what the word means. Let's just hope he tells me before the press do. They're going to have some fun with this – Ackroyd dead, two security guards seriously injured.'

Brioni grimaced. 'I hope the big one's OK, he lost a lot of blood.'

'You were brilliant. I don't think I could have waited that long with him.'

'Sorry about your towels, they're ruined.'

Cressida shrugged. 'They can be replaced.'

'Mother? Can I go upstairs and get dressed yet? Have they finished all that fingerprint stuff in the hall?' Emily-Jane swung her legs off the sofa, obviously ready to move.

Cressida put her glass of wine down decisively. 'I'll go and check. What did the detective say when you finished talking to him?'

'He said they'd be as quick as they could. I should have asked him to get me some clothes when he went up for my iPad.' She pouted.

'I'm sure they won't be long.' Cressida turned to Brioni. 'I'm going to talk to Laurence now, get the truth out of him about everything – the women, this deal, the hacking, everything. He could end up in a prison cell and I can't have this burning in my mind, not knowing.'

Chapter 67

'ARE YOU SURE you'll be all right?'

Brioni drew up outside Alex's apartment complex and put on her hazard lights.

It was hard to read his expression in the darkness as he looked across the car at her and rubbed his face. He'd been pretty quiet since the guards had told them that they could go earlier, had hardly said anything on the drive from Dalkey into the city. He opened his mouth to answer her and then stopped himself, as if he was rethinking his approach. He tried again.

'Where do you think she is now?'

'Who? Nina?'

He glanced across at her. Brioni pursed her lips, thinking, and then wriggled to get more comfortable in her seat. She checked her rear-view mirror before answering.

Despite being a main arterial road, it was late and the traffic was quiet now, the glow from scattered street lights reflecting off puddles on the pavements. There were cars parked on both sides of the road, but she couldn't see any movement as she peered into the shadows. Nina had a habit of turning up unexpectedly; Brioni wasn't taking any risks.

'I think she planned tonight very carefully. She went straight out that door – she knew it was there and she knew the path outside took her to the jetty. I think she either went down the coast and into one of the ports south of Dalkey, like Bray or Greystones, or straight into town, up the Liffey. My money's on her heading south. If I was her, I'd have left a car somewhere and I'd be heading for a ferry port now.'

'Not an airport?'

'Maybe, but that's what you'd expect, and let's face it, Nina specialises in the unexpected.'

'But surely they'd stop her? The ferry people, I mean.'

'If she changes her appearance and uses a false passport, she might get through. But she's been hiding out for the last few days, so maybe she's got somewhere she can lie low, and then leave the country at her leisure when the excitement has died down.'

Alex looked thoughtfully out of the windscreen at the raindrops coursing down it.

'She had everything planned, didn't she? Well, almost. You know the guards were outside the whole time – one of them told me they were watching Laurence, and the balloon went up when those two security guys turned up. They recognised them as McQuaid's men.' He glanced across the car at her. 'They thought the two stooges had come to intimidate Laurence or threaten Ackroyd or something. That's how they got there so fast when the first shot went off.' He paused, taking off his glasses for a moment to polish the lenses. 'They literally climbed the gate and came in through the patio doors. Between the gunshot and these two guys in black appearing at the kitchen window, I thought we were all going to get shot. I couldn't believe it could happen to me twice in a week.'

Brioni leaned over and squeezed his arm. She couldn't resist a smile.

'Perhaps you've got nine lives.'

He opened his eyes wide in disbelief. 'You couldn't make it up, could you? And you know how the "hackers" –' he did the rabbit ears thing with his fingers – 'called themselves Nemesis? Nemesis was the goddess of divine retribution and revenge – the *goddess*. I don't know why I didn't realise sooner. It was only when Emily-Jane was telling me what went on with Nina in the pool that the penny dropped.' He paused. 'Well, more rolled down a mountain, actually. She had to have had this planned for a long time, had the whole Nemesis thing set up ready to go. When she thought Laurence had put a contract on her it pushed her over the edge. *She* was the one who released the data on the Dark Web and notified the press. We should have realised it was a woman from the start.'

'She'd sent the flowers before then, though. To Kate and Cressida, I mean.'

'Perhaps that was supposed to frighten him, to show him she really meant business.'

'Or perhaps it was just jealousy. She couldn't have Laurence so she didn't want anyone else to. Perhaps she thought she'd found her soulmate.' Brioni pulled a face. 'I think the way Cressida feels now, Nina would be welcome to him. They certainly have a lot in common when it comes to ruthlessness.' She hesitated, looking at him sideways. 'You were getting on very well with Emily-Jane.'

'We're going to act for her, if she needs representation. Well, my dad is. Apparently she's been compiling photographs and information on a whole load of men who were involved in some model agency scam in the States – that's how she tracked down Ackroyd to begin with. It sounds as if it could blow up. I texted my dad earlier, explained a bit. He's still mad, but at least I'm not Public Enemy Number 1 any more.'

Brioni let out a breath. 'I think Ackroyd claimed that title way ahead of you.'

He grimaced. 'Dad did criminal law before he went into corporate, he wants all the details when he gets back. Emily-Jane says Laurence will fund any lawsuits – he can't not, really, given all that material she sent to the media. He's got the money, and the world's going to be waiting to see what he does next.' Alex glanced across at her. 'Emily-Jane wants to do an internship next summer. I think my dad will help there, too. She's *very* sharp.'

'Like her father.'

'I'm not so sure about that. Laurence Howard thinks he's clever, but you know it's a bit like Bismarck's war on two fronts – really not a good plan.'

Brioni turned in her seat. 'Alex, what are you talking about?'

'Women. Too many at once. You can't play women off each other. It never works. That's where Laurence Howard went wrong.'

Brioni grinned. 'I think you're right there. Still, Emily-Jane got her brains from somewhere. Perhaps they're from Cressida, she's pretty sharp, too.'

Alex nodded slowly and Brioni realised he'd moved on in his mind again. He ran his hand into his fringe.

'Do you think Nina will come back? After me, I mean. I'm the only one who can positively identify that she was in the suite before Camila García was killed.'

Brioni thought about it for a few seconds.

'Honestly, if she thought you were a threat, I think she'd have done something about it then. She knew you were in the shower even if Camila didn't. Half the country will be looking for her now, so she's not going to turn up on your doorstep. She'd be sure to be caught.'

Alex let out a ragged sigh. 'You say that, but she must have been hiding in the house most of the afternoon. She's like bloody Houdini.'

Brioni twirled her earring thoughtfully. She'd been thinking a lot about how long Nina might have been in the house, was pretty sure she must have let herself in to recce it before tonight.

'She must have disabled the security by getting into Laurence's smart system, and then hid in the changing rooms. I hate to point it out, but you were in and out of the pool area all afternoon. If she'd recognised you, and she wanted to, she could have picked you off fairly easily. Just like she did that other security guard. I think she only goes after the bad guys.'

Alex stared out of the front windscreen of the car, his eyes fixed on a point somewhere in the distance as he digested this news. Brioni glanced across at him again.

'I think you're fine, really. She's got bigger fish to fry, as they say.'

He frowned. 'How do you think she knew? About tonight, I mean?'

Brioni screwed up her nose. She'd given this a fair bit of thought, too, and there seemed to be one very obvious way.

'I think she's been listening in to conversations in the house through the smart system. Everything in that house is listening, from the curtains to the lights. I'd say she's been recording everything since she hooked up with Laurence in the first place. I reckon she's done this before, too.'

'Done what? Hacked a load of data?'

Brioni nodded. 'I did some digging and all the companies she's worked for before have been leaders in tech, but she's left them after just a few months.'

'Leaving a trail of destruction and broken hearts behind her?'

Brioni couldn't help grinning. 'I think so. Her apartment is in a pretty swanky area, too. I reckon she was working towards the big one – Ferryman. Now she's got millions in some offshore account – and you can be sure it's been moved from wherever Laurence sent it, or converted into bitcoin or something.'

Alex grimaced. 'I think Ackroyd met his match. He sounds like a right sleaze.'

'I'm with you. I'm impressed with Emily-Jane, though. She's a very determined kid. She didn't like what SpeakEasy were all about, and when her dad wouldn't listen, she set about finding a way to show him. I doubt she expected to find out the sort of dirt she did, but she played Ackroyd at his own game.'

'How do you think Emily-Jane hooked up with him? I wanted to ask her earlier, but it didn't seem the moment. I guessed it was something to do with that model agency thing.'

Brioni put her elbow on the car window ledge.

'She said something about seeing a news article that connected him with Epstein. She must have put two and two together and recognised that was his vulnerability, then hunted him down online. She guessed he'd need more stimulation of the kind he got at those Epstein parties, but he needed to be very careful with everyone watching Epstein's associates.' She paused, tapping the top of the steering wheel as she thought. 'Emily-Jane said she found a photo of him online and it went from there.' She frowned. 'He was obviously bribing Laurence so he could get his hooks into Ferryman, and then found out Nina was the one with access to the data, so he bribed her, too – she said something about him paying her just before she shot him. In his world, money talks and there's nothing like having all your bases covered.'

'Doesn't talk loud enough, obviously.'

'He would probably have been fine if he hadn't tried to double-cross her.' Brioni made a hissing sound. 'Nina isn't someone you mess with. Camila García must have got some shock when Nina turned on her.'

'She wasn't the only one.' Alex looked decidedly glum. 'The press will be all over this tomorrow. I think I'm going to work from home.'

'That seems like a very sensible plan. The guards will probably want to talk to us again. And I'll be talking to Cressida tomorrow, I'm sure. I'll let you know if there are any developments.'

'So you think I'm OK to go home? There's no chance of Nina coming after me?'

Brioni smiled across at him. 'Lock the doors and don't let anyone in under any circumstances. Except me, obviously. But I think she's gone now. She had her chance, several times, and she didn't take it. You must have impressed her.' Brioni couldn't resist teasing him.

He threw her a withering look and put his hand on the car door.

'Text me?'

'Of course. Now don't look so worried.' As Brioni pulled him into a proper hug, he buried his face in her neck. The spark she'd felt when he'd dropped in on her in Wexford was definitely still there, despite his subdued mood. 'You'll be fine. I'm going to go down to Wexford as soon as I'm done with the guards. Why don't you come down and stay for a few days?'

Chapter 68

*I*F SHE'D TURNED *her phone off first, instead of realising he hadn't hung up and listening in, perhaps nobody would have died.*

As Cressida sat in front of the dying embers of the fire, her head in her hands, the thought went around her head again.

It was well after midnight and Laurence, as she'd predicted, had ended up going down to the police station to give his statement. But he was back now and sitting opposite her in the living room, swishing a brandy around his glass. She looked up at him, looked properly at him for what felt like the first time in ages.

Sitting forward on the sofa, his navy suit creased, the trouser legs spattered with what she suspected was blood, he looked exhausted, the lines under his eyes deep, his face pale. He was just as attractive as he'd been when she'd married him, worn out and stressed-looking, but she was all out on sympathy. He deserved everything that was coming his way. All she wanted now, was the truth.

His eyes fixed on his glass, its intricately cut sides caught the glow of the fire, sending prisms of light bouncing off the walls. He cleared his throat, obviously choosing his words carefully.

'That inspector said you had surveillance cameras installed to watch my meeting with Ackroyd. Was that Emily-Jane's idea?'

Cressida drew in a breath. 'No. It was mine. For various reasons.' She fought to keep the accusatory tone out of her voice. This wasn't the time for a row. Not yet, anyway. She wanted to hear what he had to say first. 'Thank God absolutely everything's on the recording. There's no room for any doubt about who shot who.' Cressida paused, pursing her lips. 'So tell me about Nina.'

He shook his head, his eyes filling with tears.

'I didn't realise she was totally insane. I knew she wanted the money, she has very expensive tastes. But this … I didn't expect any of this.'

'I don't think any of us did.'

Laurence shook his head again. 'And he was … Ackroyd … Did Em tell you what was going on?'

'Laurence, do you honestly think I'd have let anything like that continue if I'd known? No, I had no idea. I've no idea *what* she was thinking.'

'If it ends up in court, his lawyers will probably call it entrapment.'

'She thought she was protecting the company. Protecting us.' Cressida shrugged. 'She went after him because you wouldn't listen to her. I'm sure the press will be all over this – more girls might come forward, but it seems Em's got quite a dossier on Ackroyd and his associates.'

Cressida picked up her glass and looked at it. There was a hairline crack down the side.

When had that happened?

She didn't have the energy to get up and get another one; she took a sip of her wine. It was the perfect temperature, full-bodied and rich. Looking at the glass again, she noticed a tiny chip in the rim. She twirled it around so the chip was away from her mouth, and looked across at Laurence.

'So are you going to tell me? About you and Nina?'

He looked at his own glass again, as if it held all the answers. Then he looked directly at her.

'Honestly, it was just a thing. I had a bit much to drink at the summer party, but I think she must have spiked my brandy. It's all very hazy. It really didn't mean anything.'

'The first time? Then what?'

'You've seen her. She just kept turning up, at the office, in the 1796. She'd text me to meet her there after work for a quick drink. I couldn't get away from her.'

For a moment Cressida almost believed him.

But then she remembered the other one.

'And Kate Spicer. Tell me about her. Ackroyd said he "knew" about her.' She made a rabbit ears gesture with her fingers and sat back in the chair, watching him. 'What did he know exactly?'

Laurence shook his head. 'He didn't know anything, he put two and two together and made five.' He shrugged. 'There's nothing to tell.'

Cressida could feel her temper rising, like a flame taking hold.

'I think I should be the judge of that, don't you? You said you and Kate were *very* good friends.'

'We are, we—'

Cressida interrupted him, 'Good enough friends that someone – Nina, apparently – risked sending her those flowers. The same ones that were sent to me. That feels like a very personal attack, Laurence – on you, on the women in your life.' She almost spat it out.

He took a sip of his brandy and put the glass down on the table in front of him, rubbing his hand over his face. He obviously wasn't going to answer, so she continued.

'So, what's the story? Why would you be personally affected if something happened to Kate Spicer? Why would Nina have targeted her, of all the thousand plus people who work for you?'

Laurence looked at her and sighed. 'I swore I'd never tell, but—'

'People have died, Laurence. I think whatever promise you've made has rather been superseded, don't you?'

He closed his eyes for a moment. 'Jesus.'

'I don't think he's going to help you now. Nina could have shot Emily-Jane, do you realise that? That bullet could have ricocheted anywhere.'

'I know. You think I don't know? Tonight wasn't about Kate. It was about Nina getting even with me, with Ackroyd. He sent that woman to Dublin to kill her. She'd done her job, she wasn't useful to him any more and she was a potentially dangerous leak.'

Cressida looked at him. Was he avoiding her question? She raised her eyebrows and looked at him meaningfully.

'So how *exactly* does Kate fit into all this?'

He sighed, his voice low. 'I promised Pierce I'd look after her.'

'Pierce? What on earth has your brother got to do with this?' Cressida looked at him in disbelief.

'My *twin* brother. My *deceased* twin brother.' He said it forcefully, as if he was reliving the loss all over again. 'He and Kate were … She was his … They were very good friends. Just before he died, he made me promise to look after her. I'd had my suspicions, but he told me then, she loved him, and he loved her …'

'What? I don't believe you, Laurence. Pierce would never … What do you mean exactly by *good* friends?'

379

He stood up abruptly and went to lean on the mantelpiece, his back to her, his drink forgotten.

'I know you were close, but you didn't know him that well. She was his mistress.'

Cressida felt a chasm open up inside her as the room began to spin. She closed her eyes tightly, willing it to stop.

How was she only finding this out now?

'While he was married to Sinéad?'

'Exactly. It would have been too complicated for him and Sinéad to separate. Almost all their friends were friends they knew as a couple, people who had no idea he had another woman in his life. And it wasn't my business to have an opinion, to be honest.'

Cressida didn't know what to say. 'I still don't understand. How could he live a completely double life and none of us realise?'

Laurence shrugged. 'He dated Kate years ago, but he had to keep it quiet. She wasn't exactly marriage material – she wanted to study beauty, you can just imagine the old man's reaction. And her parents …' He shook his head. 'Anyway, they split up. He'd been on and off with Sinéad for years, they seemed to have row after row, like that huge one the night we met. But I guess he never got Kate out of his system.'

'The night we met?' Cressida put her hand to her head as her mind shot back to a house party in Killiney. 'I didn't know he was dating Sinéad then. Was he seeing this Kate when he married her?'

Cressida couldn't keep the shock out of her voice. She'd known Pierce before she'd known Laurence, but she hadn't known any of this.

'I don't know.' He threw up his hands and turned around to look at her. 'Does it matter now? I didn't keep notes on his women – there were quite a few.'

Cressida looked at him in disbelief. This was a side of Pierce she'd never known. She'd thought … She shook her head.

This evening just kept on giving.

Perhaps sensing her incredulity, he continued. 'Kate never asked him to leave Sinéad. I don't know why, maybe they were happy as things were?' He paused again. 'But Kate was devastated when he died. I'm glad he told me. Mistresses are secret, aren't they? They don't get told when someone they love dies. They can't go to a funeral and grieve because their love was secret, too. It made her loss worse somehow.'

'Clearly she had you to talk to.' Cressida's voice was steely.

Laurence looked up sharply. 'There's never been anything between us. She's like the sister I never had. She understands the business, Pierce gave her … She just gets it, she was there at the start—'

'And I don't?'

'Of course you do, but you've been busy building your own company. Look, I promised to keep his secret, to take care of her, to make sure she was comfortable. I guess Nina saw our connection and made it into something it wasn't.'

'Are the guards sure it was Nina who sent the flowers? I mean, there's not another woman out there, someone else you've got some sort of private arrangement with?'

'They don't know for sure. But Nina sent me a photo this evening, of her beside a pool, and there are some of those big orange flowers in the picture.'

'Parrot flowers?'

He nodded. 'The detective I spoke to reckons the display beside her is identical to the bouquets you were both sent. The details were never released to the press, so there's only one way she can know what they looked like.'

'Because she sent them.' Cressida felt anger bubbling inside her. 'Why try and kill us, for God's sake? What had we done to her?'

As she said it, Cressida began to realise why Nina had sent them. It wasn't what she'd done, or what Kate Spicer had done – it was what Laurence had done that was the problem here. Nina might have been playing all sorts of high-powered tech games, but sending the flowers was an act of pure vengeance against the women in his life. Perhaps for her, their relationship was more than a fling. Cressida turned away to look at the fireplace, not trusting what messages her face might be sending out. His actions had put them all in danger.

As if he hadn't heard her, Laurence continued. 'The detective is sure she was sending some sort of coded message with that photograph.'

'That she sent the flowers, or that she was enjoying life beside a pool?'

Laurence sighed audibly, his patience obviously running thin.

'Both. Obviously she wanted us to think she'd left the country.'

'Brioni said she was clever.' Cressida said it half to herself.

'Who's Brioni?'

'The girl who was helping me here this evening. She's a cybersecurity expert. She helped me with the cameras. It was her friend Alex who ended up in bed with Nina at the Reynolds before that woman got shot. She picked him up in the lobby.'

'What? How do you know?'

'It's a long story. Brioni was keeping an eye on Nina that evening, so she was in the Reynolds, too. She didn't realise Nina had hit on her friend until afterwards.' Cressida paused. 'I think Nina knew damn well she was being followed, and that the woman tailing her wasn't looking for the number of her hairdresser.' Cressida's tone dripped sarcasm. 'She thought you'd organised to have her killed. That's why she picked up the first man she saw – to prove to you and to herself she didn't need you.'

'What happened then? I mean, after the lift?' Laurence said it guardedly, as if he didn't already know.

Cressida let out an impatient breath. 'Maybe you can tell me, Laurence. Camila wound up naked and dead, so I'd guess Nina changed into her clothes and left the premises. We may never know because the security tapes have mysteriously vanished.'

He nodded slowly, as if things were falling into place. As Cressida suspected, he very obviously knew a lot more about that night than he was letting on to the police.

'You seem very well informed.'

He put his hands in his pockets and moved slightly, blocking the remaining heat from the fire. Cressida shivered.

'I know lots of things. Really, you have no idea.'

'That guy she picked up had a lucky escape. She's like a black widow.'

'Nina or Camila?'

Laurence rolled his eyes. 'Both. Christ, if Ackroyd hadn't tried to have her killed, Nina might not have hacked the database, or shot him. He deserved everything he got.'

Cressida leaned forward on the sofa and picked up her wineglass. Crack or no crack, right now she needed it. Right now, she wanted to drink her way into oblivion and wake up in the morning with everything sorted out, with her life as it had been. She stopped with her glass in mid-air. Did she really want that? Her life before this evening had been a lie. She was married to a man who thought it was perfectly OK to sleep with his staff, to keep secrets, to blackmail his friends.

She put her glass on the table.

'So what happens now?'

Before he could answer, Laurence's phone rang, the sound cutting through the silence.

But it wasn't the guards this time. It was Kate Spicer.

Two weeks later

BRIONI'S MOUTH DROPPED open, the latte in front of her forgotten.

'So what happened then?'

Cressida sighed, playing with the handle of her coffee cup, looking at the froth of bubbles pop under the sprinkling of chocolate powder. It was mid-afternoon and the cafe was just as quiet as it had been the last time they'd been here, which meant that both of them had to keep their voices down so the staff couldn't hear their conversation.

They'd recognised Cressida the minute she'd walked in, despite the thick cashmere scarf pulled half-up over her face and her dark glasses. Two weeks in Italy had given her a bit of a tan, but hadn't changed the fact that she'd been plastered across the newspapers for days.

Cressida leaned forward, so Brioni could hear her. The moment Laurence's phone had rung was seared on her memory like a brand.

'I just keep thinking, if I'd put the phone down right at the start of all of this, if I hadn't listened—'

Brioni tucked a lock of hair behind her ear and cut Cressida off decisively.

'None of this is your fault, Cress, it's Laurence's – all of it. And he deserves everything he gets.'

Cressida sighed and shook her head.

'Tell me, Cress, or I'm going to die of anticipation. I know what the papers said, but what *actually* happened?'

Cressida looked back at her, and leaned closer in to the table. After being besieged by the press, Cressida had decided to take Emily-Jane to their villa in Italy until things calmed down, and she hadn't wanted to update Brioni on the phone in case anyone was listening in. This was the first chance they'd had to meet in person.

Cressida took a deep breath. 'It turns out the whole Ferryman concept was Kate Spicer's idea. She developed it with Pierce. He brought Laurence in, Laurence brought his friends from school to the table, and then they had an incredible concept *and* they had capital.'

'And that was why Laurence kept her a secret all this time? Because it was her idea?'

'Well, that and the fact she and Pierce were inseparable. It turns out she owns a significant percentage of Ferryman. Pierce gave her stock when they first started, as a thank you, I suppose. He was never as hard-nosed as Laurence, and he knew they would have had nothing without Kate. She was happy to stay in the background while they were an item. But the thing is, when he died, he left his portion of the company to her – well, the half that wasn't Sinéad's. I assumed Laurence had it, but honestly I never really thought about it. Sinéad didn't care, she doesn't understand business. She's got millions in the bank and that's all she's worried about.' Cressida took a sip of her coffee. 'Kate's been investing in start-ups, helping small businesses get off the ground for years as an angel investor – she has a whole team working for her, apparently. She never needed to get involved in running Ferryman. She had the money and she's not ambitious for herself, she just likes helping people. She could have given up her own job years ago, but she loves it, apparently. I can relate to that.' She paused. 'She called me in Italy and explained everything.'

'So what did she say on the phone that night? To Laurence, I mean.'

'Well, first she said she'd got out of hospital the night before, and she was really mad Laurence didn't know. He'd been so caught up, basically he'd forgotten to check on her. She was feeling very neglected.' Cressida pursed her lips. 'I know *that* feeling.'

Brioni rolled her hands. 'And …?'

Cressida raised her eyebrows. 'Remember that conversation you overheard where Nina said she'd got a load of dirt on the other members of the board? Well, it turns out the board members Laurence had tried to blackmail got together. He'd been gambling on them not wanting their secrets to get out, but they've known one another for years.' She scowled. 'He just doesn't understand loyalty and friendship, I suppose. I'd guess they probably knew worse things about one another than anything he'd discovered. I mean, everyone has secrets, don't they? Anyway, when they realised what was going on, they decided to orchestrate a management buyout.' Cressida's face twitched; there was a sort of poetry to this that she was still enjoying. 'The thing is that one of them, Philip French, was Pierce's best friend in school. He knew Laurence, too, obviously, but they never really got on as well as him and Pierce. And it turns out Philip knew all about

Kate. He guessed she'd have some stock, so after Laurence tried to blackmail them into voting to allow the SpeakEasy hook-up, he went to see her in hospital. They realised that, with their combined holding, they could oust Laurence without needing to bring the rest of the management in at all.'

'Holy cow. The papers didn't say anything like that.'

'No … they agreed to announce it as his retirement, after everything that happened with Ackroyd and Emily-Jane. But actually they booted him out.'

'And he didn't try to fight it? To challenge Kate for her stock?'

Cressida shook her head. 'He might have wanted to, but she has proof Ferryman was her idea. She has all her notes, whole email chains discussing it.' Cressida took a sip of her coffee. 'The board were worried Laurence might try and publish everything he'd found out about them anyway, but they agreed to say it was all fabricated. No one had access to the database to disprove their story, if they all stuck together.'

Cressida was suddenly back in the living room, looking at the colour drain from Laurence's face, watching him stagger, the phone clamped to his ear. As he'd sat on the sofa, she'd caught a snatch of Kate's voice, her words set hard in Cressida's memory.

'This was Pierce's company, he always said you were too greedy. Not everything in this world is about money. Integrity, Laurence – that's a concept you clearly don't understand.'

'I can't believe he was really going to blackmail his friends to land this deal. After they'd taken the risk to invest in Ferryman right at the start.'

Brioni's words brought Cressida back to the cafe.

'I know. I told him to leave, to get out of the house.'

'And what did he say to that?'

'He still didn't get it. I mean, how could I ever trust him on anything ever again? As if Nina wasn't bad enough, he'd lied about Kate, and he'd been prepared to ruin the men who built Ferryman with him.' Cressida took another sip of her coffee. 'He's moved into the 1796. He's got twenty-four-hour room service and he's five minutes from the office, so he's not exactly suffering. He might have been chucked out of Ferryman, but the Howard Group is still his company.'

There was a pause, as Brioni took it all in.

'How's Emily-Jane taking it?'

Cressida sighed. 'She's fine. There's a lot of Pierce in Emily-Jane – she's a creative like him, but she's very grounded.' She could see a puzzled look pass across Brioni's face. She'd said too much. She continued on quickly. 'It must be the Howard genes. Anyway, Emily-Jane thinks Laurence is a thieving idiot, so she's good with the whole thing. She thinks he and Nina were cut from the same cloth.' Cressida could almost see Brioni's mind ticking. She tried to draw it in a different direction. 'Any updates on Nina? Has Marissa's partner heard anything?'

Brioni shook her head. 'Not a peep. Everyone's looking for her, though, apparently.'

Cressida took a sip of her coffee. 'I don't think any of us know who Nina really is, or what she's capable of. I don't think I ever knew who Laurence was either, in all honesty.' She paused, putting her cup down carefully, avoiding Brioni's eye as she cleared her throat. 'It seems everyone has secrets.'

THE END

Acknowledgements

Every book is a collaborative effort – the ideas behind each story are often sparked by a conversation or a comment, a 'lightbulb' moment that connects with something already in my head. I string the words together, but without my brilliant agent Simon Trewin who gets to hear all those ideas first (and often adds to them), my superb editor Sarah Hodgson, with her invaluable and incredibly experienced eye, and the ever-patient Steve O'Gorman, my copy editor who *literally* spots all the repetitions, this book would not be the one you've just read. (A few excess *literally*s needed attention in this text, along with shaking heads and the pursing of lips, ahem.)

I cannot thank the team who pull everything together on the promotion side enough for their hard work – from everyone at Atlantic Books to Gill Hess in Ireland, to the fabulous book bloggers and reviewers who are so vital in the process, and so wonderfully supportive. There are *lots* of books published every single day and making any one stand out is a challenge all of its own. The book community, from librarians to booksellers, make such a huge difference by bringing each book to new readers – thank you!

With this book, my online writing group Writers Ink were hugely helpful when I needed classical inspiration for the name of the hacking group. They came up with lots of ideas, with Francis Fahy suggesting Nemesis, which was perfect in every way.

I strive for accuracy in all areas of fiction, and call on many experts when I'm researching. Bestselling author and former Police Commander Graham Bartlett is my go-to for UK police procedure, and a brilliant resource for writers. Huge thanks, too, to Professor Jim Fraser for his help with forensics – his book *Murder Under the Microscope* is superb. Often it takes hours of research to inform one line, and sometimes that line never even makes it into the book, but without it, the story wouldn't work. Rex Fox O'Loughlin gets to hear the stories as they develop in every book, and is my invaluable support in all things mathematical, scientific and technical, plus a font of facts and fascinating general knowledge that often work their way in and can change the path of a plot.

My biggest thank you goes to you, my reader, for sticking with the story so far. If this is your first Sam Blake, I hope you want to dip into more – I've written both a police procedural series, kicking off with *Little Bones*, where we meet kick-boxing champion garda Cat Connolly, and standalones *Keep Your Eyes on Me* and *The Dark Room*. If you liked Brioni, you'll find more of her story in the digital prequel *High Pressure*, a standalone story, but one which links the series books and the standalones. In all my books, my characters inhabit the same world, one that you will recognise the more you read. I hope that you enjoy spotting the references to other books and recognise the occasional recurring character.

For random insights into my writing life, cats, art and more, do follow me on social @SamBlakeBooks, I'd love to say hello.

There's lots of information on the inspiration behind each book at my website www.samblakebooks.com. I'd love you to join my mailing list to keep up to date with book news – I also have lots of fun thriller giveaways and book-related competitions.

Read on for an exclusive early extract
from Sam Blake's chilling new thriller

THE
MYSTERY
OF
FOUR

The tall bluish purple flowering aconite, also known as Jupiter's helm, monkshood, wolfsbane, devil's helmet or queen of poisons, comes from a group of over 250 species of flowering plants belonging to the Ranunculaceae family .

Highly poisonous, growing to an elegant metre in height, Aconitum is native to Europe where it is extensively cultivated. Often used by florists, Aconitum's deep blue hue and flower-clustered stems makes it a particularly appealing perennial for ornamental gardens. Flowering from May to October, it has won many awards, such as the Royal Horticultural Society's Award of Garden Merit. The roots and tubers are traditionally used to treat muscle-bone illness, paralysis due to stroke and other ailments.

There is a narrow margin of safety between a therapeutic and a deadly dose.

Prologue

ALMOST MIDNIGHT. The garden is ink-black, as though it's been washed with a brush, details of marble statues and sweeping steps picked out by the weak moonlight.

Below, a bronze fountain cast in the likeness of Apollo splashes water into the lake, disturbing the stillness of the hour. Accompanied by the distant scream of a fox, the hoot of an owl, the night sounds meld into backdrop for what is to come.

"The stars move still, time runs, the clock will strike."

Skirting the high granite wall, careful footsteps crunch on the gravel to the end of the path where towering gates stand open, wrought-iron flourishes picked out with golden ivy leaves, visible even in the darkness.

Now cutting across the neatly mown grass in front of the glasshouses, and through another set of matching gates.

Beyond, a series of round rose beds and square ponds are linked like gems in a necklace along the formal Rose Walk, leading to the wishing well and the yew maze. On either side, crowded flower beds wait for the morning sunshine, their scent heavy, trapped between high walls covered in more roses, their stems entwined, thick with thorns.

A black shape slips into the foliage unseen, green eyes watching. *Almost there. This will be the last trip.*

It's been a long journey, the planning detailed, but there's been a lot of time for that. Now, the last act will be easy.

The water in the ponds is deathly still, the fragrance of roses and buddleia heavy in the night air.

Just before the last set of gates, tucked into the corner, is the Poison Garden. Fenced in to keep the unsuspecting public safe, the brass sign is dull without the sun to light it. Stepping onto the bone-dry earth, trowel ready, the tall purple-flowered stems are hard to see, buried deep in the shrubbery. But it is the roots that are the most potent, dried and ground to a lethal powder.

Watching her suffering as she slowly succumbs will be poetry indeed.

Glancing up, windows mirror-like in the darkness, the house is quiet now. As if it's waiting.

Waiting to see what happens.

Because it's all about to happen.

"The time is come."

THURSDAY

Chapter 1

'I'M SORRY, JUST run that past me again?' Tess Morgan turned up the speaker on her phone and ran her hands into her bubbly chestnut curls, narrowing her eyes, as if it would help her better understand the man who had just called.

And possibly ruined her life.

Wherever he was, she could hear traffic, the pip of a pedestrian crossing. He had a strong Northern Irish accent, but that didn't mean anything.

'I wanted to talk to you about Eoin Doyle. We've received some information about the disappearance of Fidelma Hoey. I believe Doyle works for you?'

'And you are again?'

'Jerry Lynch, *Daily News*.'

The *Daily News* was an Irish national tabloid – as her best friend Genevieve's eternally elegant mother Clarissa put it so aptly, a rag she wouldn't clean her shoes on. Getting a call from them was never going to be good. Tess cleared her throat.

'Eoin doesn't work for me, I don't really know him at all. I mean I know *of* him, but only what I've heard.'

'I had information that he was involved in the restoration of Kilfenora House. You *do* own Kilfenora House?'

'Yes, yes I do.' Tess paused for a moment, thinking hard. 'It's possible he was working for one of the contractors – maybe? I'd have to check. I didn't employ him personally.'

'I did wonder about that, given that you live alone.'

Tess wasn't sure if she was more surprised by his tone or the fact he was implying knowledge of her domestic arrangements. Either way it was creepy.

'I'm sorry?'

'Eoin Doyle has been connected to the disappearance of several women over the past ten years. They all lived alone.'

Tess tried to catch her thoughts and process what he was saying. Eoin Doyle lived in the village, had done all his life. He had a conviction for assaulting his ex-wife, she knew about that, and there had been rumours about the guards being interested in his activities around the times various women had disappeared in Wicklow. According to local gossip, Doyle maintained that he'd just been in the wrong place at the wrong time – albeit on more than one occasion.

Enough times for him to be taken in for questioning, but not enough to land him in court.

Although that *could* have had less to do with his innocence and more to do with the fact that the missing women's bodies had never been found. The Gardai kept denying that a serial killer might be at work, but it was in all the papers that they'd launched a single investigation into what had been dubbed the 'Radio Snatcher' disappearances, and were drawing links between them.

But what the hell had this got to do with Kilfenora?

'I'm sorry . . . Jerry, is it? I'm still not clear how this relates to me.'

'We've had a tip-off that there might be an area of interest to the Gardai on the edge of the Kilfenora estate.'

Tess looked blindly out of her office window, barely focusing on the tiny front garden and its riot of summer colour. Across the lane Clarissa's black cat Merlin sulked around the wide stable yard entrance, keeping to the shade of the granite walls. Tess squinted, trying to make sense of what Lynch was saying. *What was an area of interest?*

'You're going to have to spell it out for me, I'm still not following.'

'A body, Ms Morgan. We've had a tip-off that one of the women Eoin Doyle is thought to have been involved with has been buried in a place called Fury Hill. I believe that's on your property.'

For once, Tess was lost for words.

Chapter 2

*H*OW COULD THERE *be a body on Kilfenora land?*

Pulling her cheery bright red front door closed behind her, not feeling in the slightest bit bright or cheery, Tess headed down the tiled path that bisected the front garden of the Butler's Lodge. There was a welcome breeze today, albeit slight, the scent of lavender strong as she pulled open the wrought-iron gate, the sounds of excited children drifting up from the direction of the wishing well.

They had eight days to go before the official opening weekend, when the newly restored Tudor manor with its now tamed gardens would be officially thrown open to the public, and the past two and a half years of sweat, occasional tears and many sleepless nights would finally come to fruition.

Unless, of course, the entire place was covered in crime scene tape and the drive blocked by news camera vans.

Tess felt herself wincing at the thought. The apparently inexplicable disappearances of several women from their homes was one of the biggest ongoing news stories in the country. The last one had been eight years ago, but every year since, their stories had been revisited by the press. And the local gossips in The Cross Keys.

Walking across the dusty lane that divided her cottage from the back entrance to Kilfenora House, Tess felt as if she had brain freeze. Lynch's words were caught in a loop in her head, a loop that was getting tighter and tighter the more she thought about it, and was starting to hurt.

How on earth could this be happening now?

Ever since she'd bought what was left of Kilfenora House and moved in to renovate it, the part of her mind that was constantly on media alert had been looking for press angles and photo opportunities. The opening weekend – with the vintage car rally, a craft and farmers' market, and the stage production of *Doctor Faustus* that they were putting on in the ballroom – was carefully engineered to hit as much of the speciality press as possible, as well as catch national coverage.

But a body on her land? The thought of a killer who targeted single women being anywhere near her property – even eight years ago – filled her with dread, personally and professionally. Kilfenora House was set in a huge estate, and despite the alarm system, it had occurred to Tess more than once that it would take the guards at least twenty minutes to get here from the nearest station if she hit the panic button. Twenty minutes during which anything could happen.

Tess could feel her heart rate increase at the thought. And if that wasn't enough, if the press got hold of this news, now, the week before the opening, she'd be besieged for all the wrong reasons.

As her bank manager was constantly reminding her, there was a lot riding on this weekend being a success. More than a lot, in fact. Pretty much every last penny. As well as friendships and the livelihoods of half the village.

None of them could afford for this weekend to be a flop.

The press was crucial in the mix, but this really wasn't the sort of coverage she'd had in mind at all. She needed people to come to Kilfenora to spend money and see the house in all its refurbished glory, to bring their children and their grannies to see the gardens; not to take selfies at a crime scene – assuming they weren't frightened into staying away in the first place.

And more to the point, why had a reporter called her and not the Gardai themselves?

Tess was still only half concentrating as she reached the shade of the broad stone arch that spanned the entrance to the cobbled stable yard.

It was even hotter today than it had been earlier in the week. The tiny part of her mind not panicking about bodies was thankful that at least they had the weather on their side. Although, as of twenty minutes ago, and Lynch's phone call, the weather suddenly seemed a lot less significant.

Glancing at her clipboard but barely seeing today's checklist, Tess mentally took a deep breath, fighting the growing black hole of fear that was manifesting somewhere deep in her stomach. *She needed more information.* Then she could worry about it properly – or, more precisely, try and look for a solution.

She could be totally overreacting.

Genevieve, still her best friend after all these years, had been saying since their first day in senior school that she overthought things. And Tess knew she was exhausted, to say nothing of the fact that she hadn't been feeling at all well recently. She needed to be sensible; now was *not* the time to panic. Although parking the maelstrom of dread making her already queasy stomach roll, was a lot easier said than done.

As soon as she'd ended the call with Lynch, Tess had phoned the local Garda station to find out what the real story was, only to be met with bafflement. Which did give her some hope that it was all a big mistake, a tabloid journalist making a story out of nothing. But as she'd ended the call to the guards, another thought had hit her and made her feel worse, if that was possible.

Could this 'tip-off' be something to do with the creep who had trolled her on Twitter and Instagram for so long? Part of her had been waiting for something to happen – maybe this was it?

The trolling had started soon after the first newspaper report that she'd bought the house, and had gone on for almost two years. Vitriol about her, and how Kilfenora would become a penance, how she'd regret returning to Ireland. She'd laughed at it at first, but it had gradually got more frightening: about how she'd get her comeuppance; how she'd pay for 'it', whatever 'it' was.

She'd ended up ignoring her mentions, but the whole point of using social media as a way to build the Kilfenora name was engagement. Then, six months ago, when the TV restoration show had launched, it had become even worse, taking a step up from being abusive and menacing, to plain terrifying. Every time she blocked one account, another appeared in its place.

Twitter was predictably useless and the guards couldn't do anything because the tweets were worded so carefully. Which made the whole thing worse – whoever it was, was clearly intelligent. It had been Gen who had finally persuaded her to come off social media completely, finding her a media student to take over scheduling, showing followers that the accounts were all managed externally. Just to be on the safe side, Gen had made the village Facebook private at the same time.

And it had all stopped. Just like that. Overnight.

Which proved that it was personal.

Had whoever it was found a new way to attack her now, by tipping off a journalist with some sort of crazy story that could end up ruining her?